LJ

"All this time I've been restraining myself because I thought you were a respectable lady. All this time when you only wanted this."

He swooped in then and devoured her mouth, ravishing her softness, making no allowance for her smaller size, her femininity. She moaned, whether in pain or desire, she could not tell.

"You should have told me that this is what you wanted." He raised his head to gasp. "I would've obliged you."

She seemed incapable of coherent thought, let alone speech.

"You only had to say the word and I could have taken you on my desk in the library, in the carriage with John Coachman up front, or even here in the garden. God knows I could have tumbled you at any time. Or can't you admit that you want to bed a man whose face looks like mine?"

She tried to shake her head, but it fell helplessly. His hand dropped to her hips and jerked them into his own.

"This is what you crave. What you traveled all the way to London for," he whispered against her mouth.

D1021793

JUL 3 1 2013

Raves for Elizabeth Hoyt's Prince Trilogy

The Raven Prince

"Hoyt expertly spices this stunning debut novel with a sharp sense of wit and then sweetens her lusciously dark, lushly sensual historical romance with a generous sprinkling of fairy-tale charm." —*Chicago Tribune*

"Hoyt's superb debut historical romance will dazzle readers with its brilliant blend of exquisitely nuanced characters, splendidly sensual love story, and elegant writing expertly laced with a dash of tart wit." —*Booklist*

"I didn't want it to end!"
—Julia Quinn, *New York Times* bestselling author

The Leopard Prince

"Not to be missed...a delight from start to finish. The story is so well written, the characters so engaging, that one would have to call Elizabeth Hoyt the new master of the historical romance genre." —HistoricalRomanceWriters.com

"4½ Stars! TOP PICK! An unforgettable love story that ignites the pages not only with heated love scenes but also with a mystery that holds your attention and your heart with searing emotions and dark desire." —*RT Book Reviews*

The Serpent Prince

"4½ Stars! TOP PICK! Fantastic...magically blends fairy tale, reality, and romance in a delicious, sensual feast."
—*RT Book Reviews*

"Exquisite romance...mesmerizing storytelling...incredibly vivid lead characters, earthy writing, and an intense love story."
—*Publishers Weekly*

Praise for
The Legend of The Four Soldiers Series

To Taste Temptation

"Hoyt...is firmly in control of her craft with engaging characters, gripping plot, and clever dialogue."
—*Publishers Weekly*

"4½ Stars! Hoyt's new series...begins with destruction and ends with glorious love. She begins each chapter with a snippet of a legend that beautifully dovetails with the plot and creates a distinct love story that will thrill readers."
—*RT Book Reviews*

To Seduce a Sinner

"4½ Stars! TOP PICK! Hoyt's magical fairy-tale romances have won the hearts of readers who adore sizzling sensuality perfectly merged with poignancy. Her latest showcases her talent for creating remarkable characters and cherished stories that make us believe in the miracle of love."
—*RT Book Reviews*

"Hoyt expertly sifts a generous measure of danger into the latest intriguing addition to her Four Soldiers, Georgian-era series. Her ability to fuse wicked wittiness with sinfully sensual romance is stunning."
—*Booklist*

To Beguile a Beast

"Hoyt works her own brand of literary magic…in the exquisitely romantic, superbly sensual third addition to her extraordinary Georgian-set Legend of the Four Soldiers series."
—*Booklist*

"4½ Stars! TOP PICK! A magical love story that reads like a mystical fable and a very real and highly passionate romance. Hoyt has found a unique niche that highlights both her storytelling abilities and her considerable talents for depth of character and emotion."
—*RT Book Reviews*

To Desire a Devil

"Rich with dangerous intrigue, suffused with desire, and spiked with wit, *To Desire a Devil* is nothing less than brilliant."
—*Booklist* (starred review)

"4½ Stars! TOP PICK! The kind of powerfully emotional, sensual romance, tinged with fairy tale, that readers have come to expect from this gifted storyteller."
—*RT Book Reviews*

Acclaim for The Maiden Lane Series

Notorious Pleasures

"Emotionally stunning…The sinfully sensual chemistry Hoyt creates between her shrewd, acid-tongued heroine and her scandalous sexy hero is pure romance."
—*Booklist*

"Fans of historical detail will love [*Notorious Pleasures*]… the mysterious happenings provide excitement and suspense."
—*Publishers Weekly*

Wicked Intentions

"4½ Stars! TOP PICK! A magnificently rendered story that not only enchants but enthralls."   —*RT Book Reviews*

"Hoyt brings steamy sensuality to the slums of early eighteenth-century London...earthy, richly detailed characterizations and deft historical touches."

—*Publishers Weekly*

ELIZABETH HOYT

THE RAVEN PRINCE

SAN DIEGO PUBLIC LIBRARY
LA JOLLA BRANCH

3 1336 00170 4916

GRAND CENTRAL
PUBLISHING

NEW YORK   BOSTON

This book is a work of fiction. Names, characters, places, and incidents are the product of the author's imagination or are used fictitiously. Any resemblance to actual events, locales, or persons, living or dead, is coincidental.

Copyright © 2007 by Nancy M. Finney
Excerpt from *Thief of Shadows* copyright © 2011 by Nancy M. Finney
All rights reserved. In accordance with the U.S. Copyright Act of 1976, the scanning, uploading, and electronic sharing of any part of this book without the permission of the publisher is unlawful piracy and theft of the author's intellectual property. If you would like to use material from the book (other than for review purposes), prior written permission must be obtained by contacting the publisher at permissions@hbgusa.com. Thank you for your support of the author's rights.

Grand Central Publishing
Hachette Book Group
237 Park Avenue
New York, NY 10017
www.HachetteBookGroup.com

Grand Central Publishing is a division of Hachette Book Group, Inc.
The Grand Central Publishing name and logo is a trademark of Hachette Book Group, Inc.

The publisher is not responsible for websites (or their content) that are not owned by the publisher.

Printed in the United States of America

First printing: April 2007
Reissued: August 2010
First limited edition printing: April 2012

10 9 8 7 6 5 4 3 2 1

ATTENTION CORPORATIONS AND ORGANIZATIONS:
Most HACHETTE BOOK GROUP books are available at quantity discounts with bulk purchase for educational, business, or sales promotional use. For information, please call or write:

Special Markets Department, Hachette Book Group
237 Park Avenue, New York, NY 10017
Telephone: 1-800-222-6747 Fax: 1-800-477-5925

*For my husband, FRED, my own wild blueberry pie—
sweet, tart, and always comforting.*

Acknowledgments

Thank you to my agent,
SUSANNAH TAYLOR, for her good humor
and staunch support; to my editor,
DEVI PILLAI, for her wonderful enthusiasm
and excellent taste; and to my critique partner,
JADE LEE, who plied me with chocolates at
crucial moments and persistently repeated,
"Believe!"

Chapter One

Once upon a time, in a land far away, there lived an impoverished duke and his three daughters. . . .
—from *The Raven Prince*

LITTLE BATTLEFORD, ENGLAND
MARCH, 1760

The combination of a horse galloping far too fast, a muddy lane with a curve, and a lady pedestrian is never a good one. Even in the best of circumstances, the odds of a positive outcome are depressingly low. But add a dog— a very big dog—and, Anna Wren reflected, disaster becomes inescapable.

The horse in question made a sudden sideways jump at the sight of Anna in its path. The mastiff, jogging beside the horse, responded by running under its nose, which, in turn, made the horse rear. Saucer-sized hooves flailed the air. And inevitably, the enormous rider on the horse's back came unseated. The man went down at her feet like a hawk shot from the sky, if less gracefully. His long limbs sprawled as he fell, he lost his crop and tricorn, and he landed with a spectacular splash in a mud puddle. A wall of filthy water sprang up to drench her.

Everyone, including the dog, paused.

Idiot, Anna thought, but that was not what she said. Respectable widows of a certain age—one and thirty in two months—do not hurl epithets, however apt, at gentlemen. No, indeed.

"I do hope you are not damaged by your fall," she said instead. "May I assist you to rise?" She smiled through gritted teeth at the sodden man.

He did not return her pleasantry. "What the hell were you doing in the middle of the road, you silly woman?"

The man heaved himself out of the mud puddle to loom over her in that irritating way gentlemen had of trying to look important when they'd just been foolish. The dirty water beading on his pale, pockmarked face made him an awful sight. Black eyelashes clumped together lushly around obsidian eyes, but that hardly offset the large nose and chin and the thin, bloodless lips.

"I am so sorry." Anna's smile did not falter. "I was walking home. Naturally, had I known you would be needing the entire width of the throughway—"

But apparently his question had been rhetorical. The man stomped away, dismissing her and her explanation. He ignored his hat and crop to stalk the horse, cursing it in a low, oddly soothing monotone.

The dog sat down to watch the show.

The horse, a bony bay, had peculiar light patches on its coat that gave it an unfortunate piebald appearance. It rolled its eyes at the man and sidled a few steps away.

"That's right. Dance around like a virgin at the first squeeze of a tit, you revolting lump of maggot-eaten hide," the man crooned to the animal. "When I get hold of you, you misbegotten result of a diseased camel humping a sway-backed ass, I'll wring your cretinous neck, I will."

The horse swiveled its mismatched ears to better hear the caressing baritone voice and took an uncertain step forward. Anna sympathized with the animal. The ugly man's voice was like a feather run along the sole of her foot: irritating and tantalizing at the same time. She wondered if he sounded like that when he made love to a woman. One would hope he changed the words.

The man got close enough to the bemused horse to catch its bridle. He stood for a minute, murmuring obscenities; then he mounted the animal in one lithe movement. His muscular thighs, indecently revealed in wet buckskins, tightened about the horse's barrel as he turned its nose.

He inclined his bare head at Anna. "Madam, good day." And without a backward glance, he cantered off down the lane, the dog racing beside him. In a moment, he was out of sight. In another, the sound of hoofbeats had died.

Anna looked down.

Her basket lay in the puddle, its contents—her morning shopping—spilled in the road. She must've dropped it when she dodged the oncoming horse. Now, a half-dozen eggs oozed yellow yolks into the muddy water, and a single herring eyed her balefully as if blaming her for its undignified landing. She picked up the fish and brushed it off. It, at least, could be saved. Her gray dress, however, drooped pitifully, although the actual color wasn't much different from the mud that caked it. She plucked at the skirts to separate them from her legs before sighing and dropping them. She scanned the road in both directions. The bare branches of the trees overhead rattled in the wind. The little lane stood deserted.

Anna took a breath and said the forbidden word out loud in front of God and her eternal soul: "Bastard!" She held her breath, waiting for a thunderbolt or, more likely, a twinge of guilt to hit her. Neither happened, which ought to have made her uneasy. After all, ladies do not curse gentlemen, no matter what the provocation.

And she was, above all things, a respectable lady, wasn't she?

By the time she limped up the front walk to her cottage, Anna's skirts were dried into a stiff mess. In summer, the exuberant flowers that filled the tiny front garden made it cheerful, but at this time of year, the garden was mostly mud. Before she could reach it, the door opened. A small woman with dove-gray ringlets bobbing at her temples peered around the jamb.

"Oh, there you are." The woman waved a gravy-smeared wooden spoon, inadvertently flinging drops on her cheek. "Fanny and I have been making mutton stew, and I do think her sauce is improved. Why, you can hardly see the lumps." She leaned forward to whisper, "But we are still working on dumpling making. I'm afraid they have a rather unusual texture."

Anna smiled wearily at her mother-in-law. "I'm sure the stew will be wonderful." She stepped inside the cramped hall and put the basket down.

The other woman beamed, but then her nose wrinkled as Anna moved past her. "Dear, there's a peculiar odor coming from . . ." She trailed off and stared at the top of Anna's head. "Why are you wearing wet leaves in your hat?"

Anna grimaced and reached up to feel. "I'm afraid I had a slight mishap on the high road."

"A mishap?" Mother Wren dropped the spoon in her agitation. "Are you hurt? Why, your gown looks as if you've wallowed in a pigsty."

"I'm quite all right; just a bit damp."

"Well, we must get you into dry clothes at once, dear. And your hair—Fanny!" Mother Wren interrupted herself to call in the general direction of the kitchen. "We'll have to wash it. Your hair, I mean. Here, let me help you up the stairs. Fanny!"

A girl, all elbows, reddened hands, and topped by a mass of carroty hair, sidled into the hall. "Wot?"

Mother Wren paused on the stairs behind Anna and leaned over the rail. "How many times have I told you to say, 'Yes, ma'am'? You'll never become a maid in a big house if you don't speak properly."

Fanny stood blinking up at the two women. Her mouth was slightly ajar.

Mother Wren sighed. "Go put a pot of water on to heat. Miss Anna will be washing her hair."

The girl scurried into the kitchen, then popped her head back out. "Yes, mum."

The top of the steep stairs opened onto a miniscule landing. To the left was the elder woman's room; to the right, Anna's. She entered her small room and went straight to the mirror hanging over the dresser.

"I don't know what the town is coming to," her mother-in-law panted behind her. "Were you splashed by a carriage? Some of these mail-coach drivers are simply irresponsible. They think the entire road is theirs alone."

"I couldn't agree with you more," Anna replied as she peered at her reflection. A faded wreath of dried apple blossoms was draped over the edge of the mirror, a memento from her wedding. "But it was a single horseman in this case." Her hair was a rat's nest, and there were still spots of mud on her forehead.

"Even worse, these gentlemen on horses," the older woman muttered. "Why, I don't think they're able to control their animals, some of them. Terribly dangerous. They're a menace to woman and child."

"Mmm." Anna took off her shawl, bumping her shin against a chair as she moved. She glanced around the tiny room. This was where she and Peter had spent all four years of their marriage. She hung her shawl and hat on the hook where Peter's coat used to be. The chair where he once piled his heavy law books now served as her bedside table. Even his hairbrush with the few red hairs caught in its bristles had long ago been packed away.

"At least you saved the herring." Mother Wren was still fretting. "Although I don't think a dunking in mud will have improved its flavor."

"No doubt," Anna replied absently. Her eyes returned to the wreath. It was crumbling. No wonder, since she had been widowed six years. Nasty thing. It would be better in the garden rubbish pile. She tossed it aside to take down later.

"Here, dear, let me help you." Mother Wren began unhooking the dress from the bottom. "We'll have to sponge this right away. There's quite a bit of mud around the hem. Perhaps if I applied a new trim . . ." Her voice was muffled as she bent over. "Oh, that reminds me, did you sell my lace to the milliner?"

Anna pushed the dress down and stepped out of it. "Yes, she quite liked the lace. She said it was the finest she'd seen in a while."

"Well, I have been making lace for almost forty years." Mother Wren tried to look modest. She cleared her throat. "How much did she give you for it?"

Anna winced. "A shilling sixpence." She reached for a threadbare wrap.

"But I worked five months on it," Mother Wren gasped.

"I know." Anna sighed and took down her hair. "And, as I said, the milliner considered your work to be of the finest quality. It's just that lace doesn't fetch very much."

"It does once she puts it on a bonnet or a dress," Mother Wren muttered.

Anna grimaced sympathetically. She took a bathing cloth off a hook under the eaves, and the two women descended the stairs in silence.

In the kitchen, Fanny hovered over a kettle of water. Bunches of dried herbs hung from the black beams, scenting the air. The old brick fireplace took up one whole wall. Opposite was a curtain-framed window that overlooked the back garden. Lettuce marched in a frilled chartreuse row down the tiny plot, and the radishes and turnips had been ready for a week now.

Mother Wren set a chipped basin on the kitchen table. Worn smooth by many years of daily scrubbing, the table took pride of place in the middle of the room. At night they pushed it to the wall so that the little maid could unroll a pallet in front of the fire.

Fanny brought the kettle of water. Anna bent over the basin, and Mother Wren poured the water on her head. It was lukewarm.

Anna soaped her hair and took a deep breath. "I'm afraid we will have to do something about our financial situation."

"Oh, don't say there will be more economies, dear," Mother Wren moaned. "We've already given up fresh meat except for mutton on Tuesdays and Thursdays. And it's been ages since either of us has had a new gown."

Anna noticed that her mother-in-law didn't mention Fanny's upkeep. Although the girl was supposedly their maid-cum-cook, in reality she was a charitable impulse on both their parts. Fanny's only relative, her grandfather, had died when she was ten. At the time, there'd been talk in the village of sending the girl to a poorhouse, but Anna had moved to intervene, and Fanny had been with them ever since. Mother Wren had hopes of training her to work in a large household, but so far her progress was slow.

"You've been very good about the economies we've made," Anna said now as she worked the thin lather into her scalp. "But the investments Peter left us aren't doing as well as they used to. Our income has decreased steadily since he passed away."

"It's such a shame he left us so little to live on," Mother Wren said.

Anna sighed. "He didn't mean to leave such a small sum. He was a young man when the fever took him. I'm sure had he lived, he would've built up the savings substantially."

In fact, Peter had improved their finances since his own father's death shortly before their marriage. The older man had been a solicitor, but several ill-advised investments had landed him deeply in debt. After the wedding, Peter had sold the house he had grown up in to pay off the debts and moved his new bride and widowed mother into the much-smaller cottage. He had been working as a solicitor when he'd become ill and died within the fortnight.

Leaving Anna to manage the little household on her own. "Rinse, please."

A stream of chilly water poured over her nape and head. She felt to make sure no soap remained, then squeezed the excess water from her hair. She wrapped a cloth around her head and glanced up. "I think I should find a position."

"Oh, dear, surely not that." Mother Wren plopped down on a kitchen chair. "Ladies don't work."

Anna felt her mouth twitch. "Would you prefer I remain a lady and let us both starve?"

Mother Wren hesitated. She appeared to actually debate the question.

"Don't answer that," Anna said. "It won't come to starvation anyway. However, we do need to find a way to bring some income into the household."

"Perhaps if I were to produce more lace. Or, or I could give up meat entirely," her mother-in-law said a little wildly.

"I don't want you to have to do that. Besides, Father made sure I had a good education."

Mother Wren brightened. "Your father was the best vicar Little Battleford ever had, God rest his soul. He *did* let everyone know his views on the education of children."

"Mmm." Anna took the cloth off her head and began combing out her wet hair. "He made sure I learned to read and write and do figures. I even have a little Latin and Greek. I thought I'd look tomorrow for a position as a governess or companion."

"Old Mrs. Lester is almost blind. Surely her son-in-law would hire you to read—" Mother Wren stopped.

Anna became aware at the same time of an acrid scent in the air. "Fanny!"

The little maid, who had been watching the exchange between her employers, yelped and ran to the pot of stew over the fire. Anna groaned.

Another burned supper.

FELIX HOPPLE PAUSED before the Earl of Swartingham's library door to take stock of his appearance. His wig, with two tight sausage curls on either side, was freshly powdered in a becoming lavender shade. His figure—quite svelte for a man of his years—was highlighted by a puce waistcoat edged with vining yellow leaves. And his hose had alternating green and orange stripes, handsome without being ostentatious. His toilet was perfection itself. There was really no reason for him to hesitate outside the door.

He sighed. The earl had a disconcerting tendency to growl. As estate manager of Ravenhill Abbey, Felix had heard that worrisome growl quite a bit in the last two weeks. It'd made him feel like one of those unfortunate native gentlemen one read about in travelogues who lived in the shadows of large, ominous volcanoes. The kind that might erupt at any moment. Why Lord Swartingham had chosen to take up residence at the Abbey after years of blissful absence, Felix couldn't fathom, but he had the sinking feeling that the earl intended to remain for a very, very long time.

The steward ran a hand down the front of his waistcoat. He reminded himself that although the matter he was about to bring to the earl's attention was not pleasant, it could in no way be construed as his own fault. Thus prepared, he nodded and tapped at the library door.

There was a pause and then a deep, sure voice rasped, "Come."

The library stood on the west side of the manor house, and the late-afternoon sun streamed through the large windows that took up nearly the entire outside wall. One might think this would make the library a sunny, welcoming room, but somehow the sunlight was swallowed by the cavernous space soon after it entered, leaving most of the room to the domain of the shadows. The ceiling—two stories high—was wreathed in gloom.

The earl sat behind a massive, baroque desk that would've dwarfed a smaller man. Nearby, a fire attempted to be cheerful and failed dismally. A gigantic, brindled dog sprawled before the hearth as if dead. Felix winced. The dog was a mongrel mix that included a good deal of mastiff and perhaps some wolfhound. The result was an ugly, mean-looking canine he tried hard to avoid.

He cleared his throat. "If I could have a moment, my lord?"

Lord Swartingham glanced up from the paper in his hand. "What is it now, Hopple? Come in, come in, man. Sit down while I finish this. I'll give you my attention in a minute."

Felix crossed to one of the armchairs before the mahogany desk and sank into it, keeping an eye on the dog. He used the reprieve to study his employer for an idea of his mood. The earl scowled at the page in front of him, his pockmarks making the expression especially unattractive. Of course, this was not necessarily a bad sign. The earl habitually scowled.

Lord Swartingham tossed aside the paper. He took off his half-moon reading glasses and threw his considerable weight back in his chair, making it squeak. Felix flinched in sympathy.

"Well, Hopple?"

"My lord, I have some unpleasant news that I hope you will not take too badly." He smiled tentatively.

The earl stared down his big nose without comment.

Felix tugged at his shirt cuffs. "The new secretary, Mr. Tootleham, had word of a family emergency that forced him to hand in his resignation rather quickly."

There was still no change of expression on the earl's face, although he did begin to drum his fingers on the chair arm.

Felix spoke more rapidly. "It seems Mr. Tootleham's parents in London have become bedridden by a fever and require his assistance. It is a very virulent illness with sweating and purging, qu-quite contagious."

The earl raised one black eyebrow.

"I-in fact, Mr. Tootleham's two brothers, three sisters, his elderly grandmother, an aunt, and the family cat have all caught the contagion and are utterly unable to fend for themselves." Felix stopped and looked at the earl.

Silence.

Felix wrestled valiantly to keep from babbling.

"The cat?" Lord Swartingham snarled softly.

Felix started to stutter a reply but was interrupted by a bellowed obscenity. He ducked with newly practiced ease as the earl picked up a pottery jar and flung it over Felix's head at the door. It hit with a tremendous crash and a tinkle of falling shards. The dog, apparently long used to the odd manner in which Lord Swartingham vented his spleen, merely sighed.

Lord Swartingham breathed heavily and pinned Felix with his coal-black eyes. "I trust you have found a replacement."

Felix's neckcloth felt suddenly tight. He ran a finger around the upper edge. "Er, actually, my lord, although, of course, I've searched qu-quite diligently, and indeed, all the nearby villages have been almost scoured, I haven't—" He gulped and courageously met his employer's eye. "I'm afraid I haven't found a new secretary yet."

Lord Swartingham didn't move. "I need a secretary to transcribe my manuscript for the series of lectures given by the Agrarian Society in four weeks," he enunciated awfully. "Preferably one who will stay more than two days. Find one." He snatched up another sheet of paper and went back to reading.

The audience had ended.

"Yes, my lord." Felix bounced nervously out of the chair and scurried toward the door. "I'll start looking right away, my lord."

Lord Swartingham waited until Felix had almost reached the door before rumbling, "Hopple."

On the point of escape, Felix guiltily drew back his hand from the doorknob. "My lord?"

"You have until the morning after tomorrow."

Felix stared at his employer's still-downcast head and swallowed, feeling rather like that Hercules fellow must have on first seeing the Augean stables. "Yes, my lord."

EDWARD DE RAAF, the fifth Earl of Swartingham, finished reading the report from his North Yorkshire estate and tossed it onto the pile of papers, along with his spectacles. The light from the window was fading fast and soon would be gone. He rose from his chair and went to look out. The dog got up, stretched, and padded over to stand beside him, bumping at his hand. Edward absently stroked its ears.

This was the second secretary to decamp in the dark of night in so many months. One would think he was a dragon. Every single secretary had been more mouse than man. Show a little temper, a raised voice, and they scurried away. If even one of his secretaries had half the pluck of the woman he had nearly run down yesterday . . . His lips twitched. He hadn't missed her sarcastic reply to his demand of why she was in the road. No, that madam stood her ground when he blew his fire at her. A pity his secretaries couldn't do the same.

He glowered out the dark window. And then there was this other nagging . . . disturbance. His boyhood home was not as he remembered it.

True, he was a man now. When he had last seen Ravenhill Abbey, he'd been a stripling youth mourning the loss of his family. In the intervening two decades, he had wandered from his northern estates to his London town house, but somehow, despite the time, those two places had never felt like home. He had stayed away precisely because the Abbey would never be the same as when his family had lived here. He'd expected some change. But he'd not been prepared for this dreariness. Nor the awful sense of loneliness. The very emptiness of the rooms defeated him, mocking him with the laughter and light that he remembered.

The family that he remembered.

The only reason he persisted in opening up the mansion was because he hoped to bring his new bride here—his prospective new bride, pending the successful negotiation of the marital contract. He wasn't going to repeat the mistakes of his first, short marriage and attempt to settle elsewhere. Back then, he'd tried to make his young wife happy by remaining in her native Yorkshire. It hadn't worked. In the years since his wife's untimely death, he'd come to the conclusion that she wouldn't have been happy anywhere they'd chosen to make their home.

Edward pushed away from the window and strode toward the library doors. He would start as he meant to; go on and live at the Abbey; make it a home again. It was the seat of his earldom and where he meant to replant his family tree. And when the marriage bore fruit, when the halls once again rang with children's laughter, surely then Ravenhill Abbey would feel alive again.

Chapter Two

Now, all three of the duke's daughters were equally
fair. The eldest had hair of deepest pitch that shone
with blue-black lights; the second had fiery locks
that framed a milky-white complexion; and the
youngest was golden, both of face and form, so that
she seemed bathed in sunlight. But of these three
maidens, only the youngest was blessed with her
father's kindness. Her name was Aurea. . . .
—from *The Raven Prince*

Who would have guessed that there was such a paucity of jobs for genteel ladies in Little Battleford? Anna had known that it wouldn't be easy to find a position when she left the cottage this morning, but she'd started with some hope. All she required was a family with illiterate children needing a governess or an elderly lady in want of a wool-winder. Surely this was not too much to expect?

Evidently it was.

It was midafternoon now. Her feet ached from trudging up and down muddy lanes, and she didn't have a position. Old Mrs. Lester had no love of literature. Her son-in-law was too parsimonious to hire a companion in any case. Anna called round on several other ladies, hinting that she might be open to a position, only to find they either could not afford a companion or simply did not want one.

Then she'd come to Felicity Clearwater's home.

Felicity was the third wife of Squire Clearwater, a man some thirty years older than his bride. The squire was the largest landowner in the county besides the Earl of Swartingham. As his wife, Felicity clearly considered herself the preeminent social figure in Little Battleford and rather above the humble Wren household. But Felicity had two girls of a suitable age for a governess, so Anna had called on her. She'd spent an excruciating half hour feeling her way like a cat walking on sharp pebbles. When Felicity had caught on to Anna's reason for visiting, she'd smoothed a pampered hand over her already immaculate coiffure. Then she'd sweetly enquired about Anna's musical knowledge.

The vicarage had never run to a harpsichord when Anna's family had occupied it. A fact Felicity knew very well, since she'd called there on several occasions as a girl.

Anna had taken a deep breath. "I'm afraid I don't have any musical ability, but I do have a bit of Latin and Greek."

Felicity had flicked open a fan and tittered behind it. "Oh, I do apologize," she'd said when she'd recovered. "But my girls will not be learning anything so masculine as Latin or Greek. It's rather unbecoming in a lady, don't you think?"

Anna had grit her teeth, but managed a smile. Until Felicity had suggested she try the kitchen to see if Cook needed a new scullery maid. Things had gone downhill from there.

Anna sighed now. She might very well end up a scullery maid or worse, but not at Felicity's house. Time to head home.

Rounding the corner at the ironmonger's, she just managed to avoid a collision with Mr. Felix Hopple hurrying in the other direction. She skidded to a halt inches shy of the Ravenhill steward's chest. A packet of needles, some yellow embroidery floss, and a small bag of tea for Mother Wren slid to the ground from her basket.

"Oh, do excuse me, Mrs. Wren," the little man gasped as he bent to retrieve the items. "I'm afraid I was not minding where my feet carried me."

"That's quite all right." Anna eyed the violet and crimson striped waistcoat he wore and blinked. *Good Lord.* "I hear the earl is finally in residence at Ravenhill. You must be quite busy."

The village gossips were all abuzz at the mysterious earl's reappearance in the neighborhood after so many years, and Anna was just as curious as everyone else. In fact, she was beginning to wonder about the identity of the ugly gentleman who had so nearly run her down the day before. . . .

Mr. Hopple heaved a sigh. "I'm afraid so." He pulled out a handkerchief and mopped his brow. "I am on the hunt for a new secretary for his lordship. It is not an easy search. The last man I interviewed kept blotting his paper, and I was not at all sure of his ability to spell."

"That would be a problem in a secretary," Anna murmured.

"Indeed."

"If you find no one today, do remember that there will be plenty of gentlemen at church on Sunday morning," Anna said. "Perhaps you will find someone there."

"I'm afraid that will do me no good. His lordship stated he must have a new secretary by tomorrow morning."

"So soon?" Anna stared. "That is very little time." A thought dawned.

The steward was trying without success to wipe the mud from the packet of needles.

"Mr. Hopple," she said slowly, "did the earl say he required a *male* secretary?"

"Well, no," Mr. Hopple replied absently, still involved with the packet. "The earl simply instructed me to hire another secretary, but what other—" He stopped suddenly.

Anna straightened her flat straw hat and smiled meaningfully. "As a matter of fact, I've been thinking lately about how much excess time I have. You may not be aware, but I've a very clear hand. And I do know how to spell."

"You are not suggesting . . . ?" Mr. Hopple looked stunned, rather like a gaffed halibut in a lavender wig.

"Yes, I do suggest." Anna nodded. "I think it will be just the thing. Shall I report to Ravenhill at nine or ten o'clock tomorrow?"

"Er, nine o'clock. The earl rises early. B-but really, Mrs. Wren—" Mr. Hopple stuttered.

"Yes, really, Mr. Hopple. There. It is all settled. I shall see you tomorrow at nine o'clock." Anna patted the poor man on the sleeve. He really did not look well. She turned to go but stopped when she remembered a very important point. "One more thing. What wage is the earl offering?"

"The wage?" Mr. Hopple blinked. "Well, er, the earl was paying his last secretary three pounds a month. Will that be all right?"

"Three pounds." Anna's lips moved as she silently repeated the words. It was suddenly a glorious day in Little Battleford. "That will do nicely."

"AND NO DOUBT MANY of the upper chambers will need to be aired and perhaps painted as well. Have you got that, Hopple?" Edward leapt down the last three steps in front of Ravenhill Abbey and strode toward the stables, the late-afternoon sun warm on his back. The dog, as usual, followed at his heels.

There was no reply.

"Hopple? Hopple!" He pivoted, his boots crunching on the gravel, and glanced behind him.

"A moment, my lord." The steward was just starting down the front steps. He seemed out of breath. "I'll be there . . . in . . . a . . . moment."

Edward waited, foot tapping, until Hopple caught up, then he continued around the back. Here the gravel gave way to worn cobblestone in the courtyard. "Have you got that about the upper chambers?"

"Er, the upper chambers, my lord?" the little man wheezed as he scanned the notes in his hand.

"Have the housekeeper air them," Edward repeated slowly. "Check to see if they need painting. Do try to keep up, man."

"Yes, my lord," Hopple muttered, scribbling.

"I trust you have found a secretary."

"Er, well . . ." The steward peered at his notes intently.

"I did tell you I needed one by tomorrow morn."

"Yes, indeed, my lord, and in fact I do have a-a person who I think may very well—"

Edward halted before the massive double doors to the stables. "Hopple, do you have a secretary for me or not?"

The steward looked alarmed. "Yes, my lord. I do think one could say that I have found a secretary."

"Then why not say so?" He frowned. "Is something wrong with the man?"

"N-no, my lord." Hopple smoothed his terrible purple waistcoat. "The secretary will, I think, be quite satisfactory as a, well, as a secretary." His eyes were fixed on the horse weather vane atop the stable roof.

Edward found himself inspecting the weather vane. It squeaked and revolved slowly. He tore his gaze from it and looked down. The dog sat beside him, head cocked, also staring at the weather vane.

Edward shook his head. "Good. I will be absent tomorrow morning when he arrives." They walked from the late-afternoon sunshine into the gloom of the stables. The dog trotted ahead, sniffing in corners. "So you will need to show him my manuscript and generally instruct him as to his duties." He turned. Was it his imagination or did Hopple look relieved?

"Very good, my lord," the steward said.

"I will be traveling up to London early tomorrow and shall be gone through the rest of the week. By the time I return, he should have transcribed the papers I have left."

"Indeed, my lord." The steward was definitely beaming.

Edward eyed him and snorted. "I shall be looking forward to meeting my new secretary when I return."

Hopple's smile dimmed.

RAVENHILL ABBEY WAS a rather daunting sort of place, Anna thought as she tramped up the drive to the manor the next morning. The walk from the village to the estate was almost three miles, and her calves were beginning to ache. Fortunately, the sun shone cheerily. Ancient oaks bordered the drive, a change from the open fields along the lane from Little Battleford. The trees were so old that two horsemen could ride abreast through the spaces between them.

She rounded a corner, gasped, and halted. Daffodils dotted the tender green grass beneath the trees. The branches above wore only a fuzz of new leaves, and the sunshine broke through with hardly any impediment. Each yellow daffodil shone translucent and perfect, creating a fragile fairyland.

What sort of man would stay away from this for almost two decades?

Anna remembered tales of the great smallpox epidemic that had decimated Little Battleford in the years before her parents moved into the vicarage. She knew the present earl's family had all died from the disease. Even so, wouldn't he have at least visited in the intervening years?

She shook her head and continued. Just past the daffodil field, the copse opened up and she could see Ravenhill clearly. It stood four stories high, built of gray stone in the classic style. A single central entrance on the first floor dominated the façade. From it, twin curving staircases descended to ground level. In a sea of open fields, the Abbey was an island, alone and arrogant.

Anna started on the long approach to Ravenhill Abbey, her confidence fading the closer she got. That front entrance was simply too imposing. She hesitated a moment when she neared the Abbey, then veered around the corner. Just past the corner, she saw the servants' entrance. This door, too, was tall and double, but at least she didn't have to mount granite steps to reach it. Taking a deep breath, she tugged on the big brass knob and walked directly into the huge kitchen.

A large woman with white-blond hair stood at a massive central table. She kneaded dough, her arms elbow-deep in an earthenware bowl the size of a kettle. Strands of hair came down from the bun at the top of her head and stuck to the sweat on her red cheeks. The only other people in the room were a scullery maid and a bootblack boy. All three turned to stare at her.

The fair-haired woman—surely the cook?—held up floury arms. "Aye?"

Anna raised her chin. "Good morning. I'm the earl's new secretary, Mrs. Wren. Do you know where Mr. Hopple might be?"

Without taking her eyes from Anna, the cook yelled to the bootblack boy, "You there, Danny. Go and fetch Mr.

Hopple and tell him Mrs. Wren is here in the kitchen. Be quick, now."

Danny dashed out of the kitchen, and the cook turned back to her dough.

Anna stood waiting.

The scullery maid by the massive fireplace stared, absently scratching her arm. Anna smiled at her. The girl quickly averted her eyes.

"Ain't never heard of a lady secretary before." The cook kept her eyes on her hands, swiftly working the dough. She expertly flipped the whole mass onto the table and rolled it into a ball, the muscles on her forearms flexing. "Have you met his lordship, then?"

"We've never been introduced," Anna said. "I discussed the position with Mr. Hopple, and he had no qualms about me becoming the earl's secretary." At least Mr. Hopple hadn't *voiced* any qualms, she added mentally.

The cook grunted without looking up. "That's just as well." She rapidly pinched off walnut-sized bits of dough and rolled them into balls. A pile formed. "Bertha, fetch me that tray."

The scullery maid brought over a cast-iron tray and lined up the balls on it in rows. "Gives me the chilly trembles, he does, when he shouts," she whispered.

The cook cast a jaundiced eye on the maid. "The sound of hoot owls gives you the chilly trembles. The earl's a fine gentleman. Pays us all a decent wage and gives us regular days off, he does."

Bertha bit her lower lip as she carefully positioned each ball. "He's got a terrible sharp tongue. Perhaps that's why Mr. Tootleham left so—" She seemed to realize the cook was glaring at her and abruptly shut her mouth.

Mr. Hopple's entrance broke the awkward silence. He wore an alarming violet waistcoat, embroidered all over with scarlet cherries.

"Good morning, good morning, Mrs. Wren." He darted a glance at the watching cook and scullery maid and lowered his voice. "Are you quite sure, er, about this?"

"Of course, Mr. Hopple." Anna smiled at the steward in what she hoped was a confident manner. "I am looking forward to making the acquaintance of the earl."

She heard the cook humph behind her.

"Ah." Mr. Hopple coughed. "As to that, the earl has journeyed to London on business. He often spends his time there, you know," he said in a confiding tone. "Meeting with other learned gentlemen. The earl is quite an authority on agricultural matters."

Disappointment shot through her. "Shall I wait for his return?" she asked.

"No, no. No need," Mr. Hopple said. "His lordship left some papers for you to transcribe in the library. I'll just show you there, shall I?"

Anna nodded and followed the steward out of the kitchen and up the back stairs into the main hallway. The floor was pink and black marble parquet, beautifully inlaid, although a bit hard to see in the dim light. They came to the main entrance, and she stared at the grand staircase. Good Lord, it was huge. The stairs led up to a landing the size of her kitchen and then parted into two staircases arching away into the dark upper floors. How on earth did one man rattle around in such a house, even if he did have an army of servants?

Anna became aware that Mr. Hopple was speaking to her.

"The last secretary and, of course, the one before him worked in their own study under the stairs," the little man said. "But the room there is rather bleak. Not at all fitting a lady. So I thought it best that you be set up in the library where the earl works. Unless," Mr. Hopple inquired breathlessly, "you would prefer to have a room of your own?"

The steward turned to the library and held the door for Anna. She walked inside and then stopped suddenly, forcing Mr. Hopple to step around her.

"No, no. This will do very nicely." She was amazed at how calm her voice sounded. So many books! They lined three sides of the room, marching around the fireplace and extending to the vaulted ceiling. There must be over a thousand books in this room. A rather rickety ladder on wheels stood in the corner, apparently for the sole purpose of putting the volumes within reach. Imagine owning all these books and being able to read them whenever one fancied.

Mr. Hopple led her to a corner of the cavernous room where a massive, mahogany desk stood. Opposite it, several feet away, was a smaller, rosewood desk.

"Here we are, Mrs. Wren," he said enthusiastically. "I've set out everything I think you might need: paper, quills, ink, wipers, blotting paper, and sand. This is the manuscript the earl would like copied." He indicated a four-inch stack of untidy paper. "There is a bellpull in the far corner, and I'm sure Cook would be happy to send up tea and any light refreshments you might like. Is there anything else you desire?"

"Oh, no. This is all fine." Anna clasped her hands before her and tried not to look overwhelmed.

"No? Well, do let me know if you need more paper, or anything else for that matter." Mr. Hopple smiled and shut the door behind him.

She sat at the elegant little desk and reverently ran a finger over the polished inlay. Such a pretty piece of furniture. She sighed and picked up the first page of the earl's manuscript. A bold hand, heavily slanted to the right, covered the page. Here and there, sentences were scratched out and alternative ones scrawled along the margins with many arrows pointing to where they should go.

Anna began copying. Her own handwriting flowed small and neat. She paused now and again as she tried to decipher a word. The earl's handwriting was truly atrocious. After a while, though, she began to get used to his looping Ys and dashed Rs.

At a little past noon, Anna laid aside her quill and rubbed at the ink on her fingertips. Then she rose and tentatively yanked at the bellpull in the corner. It was silent, but presumably a bell rang somewhere to summon someone to bring her a cup of tea. She glanced at the row of books near the pull. They were heavy, embossed tomes with Latin names. Curious, she drew one out. As she did so, a slim volume fell to the floor with a thud. Anna quickly bent to pick it up, glancing guiltily at the door. No one had yet responded to the bellpull.

She turned back to the book in her hands. It was bound in red morocco leather, buttery soft to the touch, and was without title. The sole embellishment was an embossed gold feather on the lower right corner of the cover. She frowned and replaced her first choice, then carefully opened the red leather book. Inside, on the flyleaf, was written in a childish hand, *Elizabeth Jane de Raaf, her book.*

"Yes, ma'am?"

Anna almost dropped the red book at the young maid's voice. She hastily replaced it on the shelf and smiled at the maid. "I wonder if I might have some tea?"

"Yes, ma'am." The maid bobbed and left without further comment.

Anna glanced again at Elizabeth's book but decided circumspection was the better part of valor and returned to her desk to await the tea.

At five o'clock, Mr. Hopple rushed back into the library. "How was your first day? Not too strenuous, I hope?" He picked up the stack of completed papers and glanced through the first several. "These look very well. The earl will be pleased to get them off to the printers." He sounded relieved.

Anna wondered if he had spent the day worrying about her abilities. She gathered her things and, with a last inspection of her desktop to make sure all was in order, bid Mr. Hopple good evening and set off home.

Mother Wren pounced the moment Anna arrived at the little cottage and bombarded her with anxious questions. Even Fanny looked at her as if working for the earl were terribly dashing.

"But I didn't even meet him," Anna protested to no avail.

The next several days passed swiftly, and the pile of transcribed pages grew steadily. Sunday was a welcome day of rest.

When Anna returned on Monday, the Abbey held an air of excitement. The earl had at last returned from London. Cook didn't even look up from the soup she stirred when Anna entered the kitchen, and Mr. Hopple wasn't there to greet her as had been his daily habit. Anna made her way to the library by herself, expecting to finally meet her employer.

Only to find the room empty.

Oh, well. Anna puffed out a breath in disappointment and set her luncheon basket down on the rosewood desk. She began her work, and time passed, marked only by the sound of her quill scratching across the page. After a while, she felt another presence and looked up. Anna gasped.

An enormous dog stood beside her desk only an arm's length away. The animal had entered without any sound.

Anna held herself very still while she tried to think. She wasn't afraid of dogs. As a child, she'd owned a sweet little terrier. But this canine was the largest she'd ever encountered. And unfortunately it was also familiar. She'd seen the same animal not a week ago, running beside the ugly man who had fallen off his horse on the high road. And if the animal was here now . . . *oh, dear.* Anna rose, but the dog took a step toward her and she thought better of escaping the library. Instead, she exhaled and slowly sat back down. She and the dog eyed each other.

She extended a hand, palm downward, for the dog to sniff. The dog followed her hand's movement with its gaze, but disdained the gesture.

"Well," Anna said softly, "if you will not move, sir, I can at least get on with my work."

She picked up her quill again, trying to ignore the huge animal beside her. After a bit, the dog sat down but still watched her. When the clock over the mantelpiece struck the noon hour, she put down her quill again and rubbed her hand. Cautiously, she stretched her arms overhead, making sure to move slowly.

"Perhaps you'd like some luncheon?" she muttered to the beast. Anna opened the small cloth-covered basket she brought every morning. She thought about ringing for some tea to go with her meal but wasn't certain the dog would let her move from the desk.

"And if someone doesn't come to check on me," she grumbled to the beast, "I shall be glued to this desk all afternoon because of you."

The basket held bread and butter, an apple, and a wedge of cheese, wrapped in a cloth. She offered a crust of the bread to the dog, but he didn't even sniff it.

"You are picky, aren't you?" She munched on the bread herself. "I suppose you're used to dining on pheasant and champagne."

The dog kept his own counsel.

Anna finished the bread and started on the apple under the beast's watchful eyes. Surely if it was dangerous, it would not be allowed to roam freely in the Abbey? She saved the cheese for last. She inhaled as she unwrapped it and savored the pungent aroma. Cheese was rather a luxury at the moment. She licked her lips.

The dog took that moment to stretch out his neck and sniff.

Anna paused with the lump of cheese halfway to her mouth. She looked first at it and then back to the dog. His eyes were liquid brown. He placed a heavy paw on her lap.

She sighed. "Some cheese, milord?" She broke off a piece and held it out.

The cheese disappeared in one gulp, leaving a trail of canine saliva in its former place on her palm. The dog's thick tail brushed the carpet. He looked at her expectantly.

Anna raised her eyebrows sternly. "You, sir, are a sham."

She fed the monster the rest of her cheese. Only then did he deign to let her fondle his ears. She was stroking his broad head and telling him what a handsome, proud fellow he was when she heard the sound of booted footsteps in the hallway. She looked up and saw the Earl of Swartingham standing in the doorway, his hot obsidian eyes upon her.

Chapter Three

*A powerful prince, a man who feared neither God nor
mortal, ruled the lands to the east of the duke. This
prince was a cruel man and a covetous one as well.
He envied the duke the bounty of his lands and the
happiness of his people. One day, the prince gathered
a force of men and swept down upon the little
dukedom, pillaging the land and its people until his
army stood outside the walls of the duke's castle.
The old duke climbed to the top of his battlements
and beheld a sea of warriors that stretched from
the stones of his castle all the way to the horizon.
How could he defeat such a powerful army? He
wept for his people and for his daughters, who
surely would be ravished and slain. But as
he stood thus in his despair, he heard a croaking
voice. "Weep not, duke. All is not yet lost. . . ."*
—from *The Raven Prince*

Edward halted in the act of entering his library. He
blinked. A woman sat at his secretary's desk.

He repressed the instinctive urge to back out a step and double-check the door. Instead he narrowed his eyes, inspecting the intruder. She was a small morsel dressed in brown, her hair hidden by a god-awful frilled cap. She held her back so straight, it didn't touch the chair. She looked like every other lady of good quality but depressed means, except that she was petting—*petting* for God's sake—his great brute of a dog. The animal's head lolled, tongue hanging out the side of his jaw like a besotted idiot, eyes half shut in ecstasy.

Edward scowled at him. "Who're you?" he asked her, more gruffly than he'd meant to.

The woman's mouth thinned primly, drawing his eyes to it. She had the most erotic mouth he'd ever seen on a woman. It was wide, the upper lip fuller than the lower, and one corner tilted. "I am Anna Wren, my lord. What is your dog's name?"

"I don't know." He stalked into the room, taking care not to move suddenly.

"But"—the woman knit her brow—"isn't it your dog?"

He glanced at the dog and was momentarily mesmerized. Her elegant fingers were stroking through the dog's fur.

"He follows me and sleeps by my bed." Edward shrugged. "But he has no name that I know of."

He stopped in front of the rosewood desk. She'd have to move past him in order to escape the room.

Anna Wren's brows lowered disapprovingly. "But he must have a name. How do you call him?"

"I don't, mostly."

The woman was plain. She had a long, thin nose, brown eyes, and brown hair—what he could see of it. Nothing about her was out of the ordinary. Except that mouth.

The tip of her tongue moistened that corner.

Edward felt his cock jump and harden; he hoped to hell she wouldn't notice and be shocked out of her maidenly mind. He was aroused by a frumpy woman he didn't even know.

The dog must've grown tired of the conversation. He slipped from beneath Anna Wren's hand and lay down with a sigh by the fireplace.

"You name him if you must." Edward shrugged again and rested the fingertips of his right hand on the desk.

The assessing stare she leveled at him stirred a memory. His eyes narrowed. "You're the woman who made my horse shy on the high road the other day."

"Yes." She gave him a look of suspicious sweetness. "I am so sorry you fell off your horse."

Impertinent. "I did not *fall* off. I was unseated."

"Indeed?"

He almost contested that one word, but she held out a sheaf of papers to him. "Would you care to see what I've transcribed today?"

"Hmm," he rumbled noncommittally.

He withdrew his spectacles from a pocket and settled them on his nose. It took a moment to concentrate on the page in his hand, but when he did, Edward recognized the handwriting of his new secretary. He'd read over the transcribed pages the night before, and while he'd approved of the neatness of the script, he'd wondered about the effeminacy of it.

He looked at little Anna Wren over his spectacles and snorted. Not *effeminate*. *Feminine*. Which explained Hopple's evasiveness.

He read a few sentences more before another thought struck him. Edward darted a sharp glance at the woman's hand and saw she wore no rings. Ha. All the men hereabouts were probably afraid to court her.

"You are unwed?"

She appeared startled. "I am a widow, my lord."

"Ah." Then she had been courted and wed, but not anymore. No male guarded her now.

Hard on the heels of that thought was a feeling of ridiculousness for having predatory thoughts about such a drab female. Except for that mouth . . . He shifted uncomfortably and brought his wandering thoughts back to the page he held. There were no blots or misspellings that he could see. Exactly what he would expect from a small, brown widow. He grimaced mentally.

Ha. A mistake. He glared at the widow over his spectacles. "This word should be *compost,* not *compose.* Can't you read my handwriting?"

Mrs. Wren took a deep breath as if fortifying her patience, which made her lavish bosom expand. "Actually, my lord, no, I can't always."

"Humph," he grunted, a little disappointed she hadn't argued. She'd probably have to take a lot of deep breaths if she were enraged.

He finished reading through the papers and threw them down on her desk, where they slid sideways. She frowned at the lopsided heap of papers and bent to retrieve one that had fluttered to the floor.

"They look well enough." He walked behind her. "I will be working here later this afternoon whilst you finish transcribing the manuscript thus far."

He reached around her to flick a piece of lint off the desk. For a moment, he could feel her body heat and smell the faint scent of roses wafting up from her warmth. He sensed her stiffen.

He straightened. "Tomorrow I'll need you to work with me on matters pertaining to the estate. I hope that is amenable to you?"

"Yes, of course, my lord."

He felt her twist around to see him, but he was already walking toward the door. "Fine. I have business to attend to before I begin my work here."

He paused by the door. "Oh, and Mrs. Wren?"

She raised her eyebrows. "Yes, my lord?"

"Do not leave the Abbey before I return." Edward strode into the hallway determined to hunt down and interrogate his steward.

IN THE LIBRARY, Anna narrowed her eyes at the earl's retreating back. What an overbearing man. He even looked arrogant from the rear, his broad shoulders straight, his head at an imperious tilt.

She considered his last words and turned a puzzled frown on the dog sprawled before the fire. "Why does he think I'd leave?"

The mastiff opened one eye but seemed to know that the question was rhetorical and closed it again. She sighed and shook her head, then drew a fresh sheet of paper from the pile. She was his secretary, after all; she'd just have to learn to put up with the high-handed earl. And, of course, keep her thoughts to herself at all times.

Three hours later, Anna had nearly finished transcribing the pages and had a crick in her shoulder for her efforts. The earl hadn't yet returned, despite his threat. She sighed and flexed her right hand, then stood. Perhaps a stroll about the room was in order. The dog looked up and rose to follow her. Idly, she trailed her fingers along a shelf of books. They were outsized tomes, geography volumes, judging by the titles on their spines. The books were certainly bigger than the red-bound one she'd looked at last week. Anna paused. She hadn't had the courage to inspect that little volume since she'd been interrupted by the maid, but now curiosity drove her to the shelf by the bellpull.

There it was, nestled beside its taller mates, just as she'd left it. The slim red book seemed to beckon her. Anna drew it out and opened it to the title page. The print was ornate and barely readable: *The Raven Prince.* There was no author given. She raised her eyebrows and flipped several pages until she came to an illustration of a giant black raven, far larger than the ordinary bird. It stood on a stone wall beside a man with a long white beard and a weary expression on his face. Anna frowned. The raven's head was tilted as if it knew something the old man didn't, and its beak was open as though it might—

"What do you have there?"

The earl's deep tones startled her so badly that Anna did drop the book this time. How had such a large man moved so silently? He crossed the carpet now, with no regard to the muddy tracks he left, and picked up the book at her feet. His expression went flat when he saw the cover. She couldn't tell what he was thinking.

Then he looked up. "I thought I'd order tea," he said prosaically. He tugged at the bellpull.

The big dog thrust his muzzle in his master's free hand. Lord Swartingham scrubbed the dog's head and turned to place the book in the drawer of his desk.

Anna cleared her throat. "I was just looking. I hope you don't mind—"

But the earl waved her to silence as a parlor maid appeared at the door. He spoke to the maid. "Bitsy, have Cook put together a tray with some bread and tea and whatever else she has about." He glanced at Anna, seemingly as an afterthought. "See if she has some cakes or biscuits, too, will you?"

He hadn't asked if Anna preferred sweets, so it was just as well that she did. The maid bobbed and hurried out of the room.

Anna pursed her lips. "I really didn't mean—"

"No matter," he interrupted. The earl was at his desk, pulling out ink and quills in a haphazard manner. "Look around if you choose. All these books should be put to some use. Although, I don't know that you'll find much of interest in them. Mostly boring histories, if I remember correctly, and probably moldy to boot."

He stopped to peruse a sheet lying on the desktop. She opened her mouth to try again but was distracted by the sight of him stroking the quill while he read. His hands were large and tanned, more so than a gentleman's hands should be. Black hairs grew on the back. The thought popped into her head that he probably had hair on his chest as well. She straightened and cleared her throat.

The earl looked up.

"Do you think 'Duke' is a good name?" she asked.

His face blanked for a second before it cleared. He glanced at the dog in consideration. "I don't think so. He would outrank me."

The arrival of three maids bearing heavily laden trays saved Anna from making a reply. They set up the tea service on a table near the window and then withdrew. The earl gestured her to the settee on one side while he took a chair on the other.

"Shall I pour?" she asked.

"Please." He nodded.

Anna served the tea. She thought she felt the earl watching her as she went through the ritual, but when she looked up, his gaze was on his cup. The quantity of the food was intimidating. There was bread and butter, three different jellies, cold sliced ham, pigeon pie, some cheese, two different puddings, small iced cakes, and dried fruit. She filled a plate for the earl with some of each, remembering how hungry a man could be after exercise; then she chose a few pieces of fruit and a cake for herself. Apparently the earl didn't need conversation during the meal. He methodically demolished the food on his plate.

Anna watched him while she nibbled at a lemon cake.

He lounged in the chair, one leg bent at the knee, the other extended half under the table. Her eyes followed the long length of his mud-splattered jackboots, up muscled thighs to trim hips, over a flat stomach to a chest that widened out to quite broad shoulders for such a lean man. Her gaze skittered to his face. His black eyes gleamed back at her.

She flushed and cleared her throat. "Your dog is so"— she glanced at the homely animal—"*unusual.* I don't believe I have ever seen one like it before. Where did you get it?"

The earl snorted. "The question should be, where did he get me?"

"I beg your pardon?"

The earl sighed and shifted in his chair. "He turned up one night about a year ago outside my estate in North Yorkshire. I found him along the road. He was emaciated, flea-bitten, and had a rope tangled about his neck and forelegs. I cut the rope off, and the damned animal followed me home." He scowled at the dog beside his chair.

It wagged its tail happily. The earl lobbed a piece of pie crust, which the dog snapped out of the air.

"Haven't been able to get rid of him since."

Anna pursed her lips to hide a smile. When she looked up, she thought the earl was staring at her mouth. Oh, dear. Did she have icing on her face? She hastily dabbed at her lips with a finger. "He must be quite loyal to you after you rescued him."

He grunted. "More like he's loyal to the kitchen scraps he gets here." The earl rose abruptly and rang for the tea things to be removed, the dog following his steps. Apparently tea was over.

The rest of the day passed companionably.

The earl wasn't a silent writer. He muttered to himself and ran his hand through his hair until strands of it became dislodged from his queue and fell around his cheeks in disarray. Sometimes he jumped up to pace the room before returning to his desk to furiously scribble. The dog seemed used to the earl's compositional style and snored by the fireplace, unperturbed.

When the hall clock chimed the five o'clock hour, Anna started to gather her basket together.

The earl frowned. "Are you leaving already?"

Anna paused. "The hour has struck five, my lord."

He looked surprised, then glanced out the darkening windows. "So it has."

He stood and waited while she finished and then escorted her to the door. Anna was very conscious of his presence beside her as she walked down the hall. Her head didn't quite come to his shoulder, reminding her again of how large a man he was.

The earl scowled when he saw the empty drive outside. "Where is your carriage?"

"I haven't one," she said rather tartly. "I walked from the village."

"Ah. Of course," he said. "Wait here. I'll have my carriage brought round."

Anna started to protest, but he ran down the steps and strode off toward the stables, leaving her with the dog for company. The animal groaned and sat down. She stroked his ears. They waited quietly, listening to the wind stirring the treetops. The dog suddenly pricked up his ears and got to his feet.

The carriage rumbled around the corner and pulled up before the front steps. The earl climbed out and held the door for Anna. Eagerly, the mastiff started down the front steps ahead of her.

Lord Swartingham frowned at the animal. "Not you."

The dog lowered its head and went to stand at his side. Anna placed her gloved hand in the earl's as he helped her into the carriage. For a moment, strong, masculine fingers tightened around hers; then she was released to sit on the red leather seat.

The earl leaned into the carriage. "You needn't bring a lunch tomorrow. You will be dining with me."

He signaled the driver before she could thank him and the carriage lurched forward. Anna craned her neck to look back. The earl still stood before the steps with the huge dog. For some reason, the sight filled her with a melancholy loneliness. Anna shook her head and faced forward again, chastising herself. The earl had no need of her pity.

EDWARD WATCHED THE carriage round the corner. He had an uneasy feeling that he shouldn't let the little widow out of his sight. Her presence beside him in the library that afternoon had been strangely soothing. He grimaced to himself. Anna Wren was not for him. She was of a different class than he, and, moreover, she was a respectable widow from the village. She wasn't a sophisticated society lady who might consider a liaison outside of wedlock.

"Come." He slapped his thigh.

The dog followed him back into the library. The room was cold and dreary again. Somehow it had felt warmer when Mrs. Wren had sat here. He strolled behind her rosewood desk and noticed a handkerchief on the floor. It was white with flowers embroidered in one corner. Violets, perhaps? Hard to tell since they were a bit lopsided. Edward lifted the cloth to his face and inhaled. It smelled of roses.

He fingered the handkerchief and walked to the darkened windows. His trip to London had gone well. Sir Richard Gerard had accepted the suit for his daughter. Gerard was only a baronet, but the family was old and sound. The mother had borne seven children, five of whom had lived to adulthood. Also, Gerard owned a small unentailed estate bordering his own in North Yorkshire. The man balked at adding this land to his eldest daughter's dowry, but Edward felt sure he would come around in time. After all, Gerard would be gaining an earl as a son-in-law. Quite a feather in his cap. As for the girl . . .

Edward's thoughts stopped, and for a horrible moment he couldn't think of her name. Then it came to him: Sylvia. Of course, Sylvia. He hadn't spent much time alone with her, but he'd made sure the match was agreeable to the girl. He'd asked her point-blank if the smallpox scars repelled her. She had said they did not. Edward balled his hand into a fist. Did she tell the truth? Others had lied about his scars and he had been fooled in the past. The girl could very well be telling him what he wished to hear and he would not find out her loathing until later. But what alternative did he have? To remain unmarried and childless the rest of his life for fear of a possible lie? That fate was untenable.

Edward stroked a finger across his cheek and felt soft linen against his skin. He still held the handkerchief. He stared at it a moment, rubbing the cloth with his thumb;

then he carefully folded the handkerchief and laid it on the desk.

He strode from the room, the dog shadowing him.

ANNA'S ARRIVAL HOME in a grand carriage caused an excitement in the Wren household. She could see Fanny's white face peering through the sitting room curtains as the coachman halted the horses outside the cottage. She waited for the footman to pull down the steps and then descended from the carriage self-consciously.

"Thank you." She smiled at the young footman. "And you, too, John Coachman. I'm sorry to put you all to such a bother."

"Twern't no bother, ma'am." The coachman touched his fingertips to the brim of his round hat. "Just glad we could see you safely home."

The footman leapt onto the back of the carriage, and with a nod to Anna, John Coachman clucked to the horses. The carriage had barely pulled away when Mother Wren and Fanny tumbled out of the cottage to bombard her with questions.

"The earl sent me home in his vehicle," Anna explained as she led the way back inside.

"My, what a kind man," her mother-in-law exclaimed.

Anna thought of the way the earl had ordered her to take the carriage. "Quite." She removed her shawl and bonnet.

"Did you meet the earl himself, then, mum?" Fanny asked.

Anna smiled at the girl and nodded.

"I've never seen an earl, mum. What was he like?"

"He's just a man like any other," Anna replied.

But she was uncertain of her own words. If the earl was like any other man, then why did she have a strange urge to goad him into arguments? None of the other men of her acquaintance made her want to challenge them.

"I heard he has terrible scars on his face from the smallpox."

"Fanny, dear," Mother Wren exclaimed, "our inner selves are more important than our outer husks."

They all contemplated this noble sentiment for a moment. Fanny puckered her brow as she worked it through.

Mother Wren cleared her throat. "I heard the pox scars ran across the upper half of his face."

Anna quashed a smile. "He does have pox scars on his face, but they aren't very noticeable, really. Besides, he has nice, thick black hair and handsome dark eyes, and his voice is very attractive, beautiful even, especially when he speaks softly. And he is quite tall, with very broad, muscular shoulders." She stopped abruptly.

Mother Wren looked at her strangely.

Anna twitched off her gloves. "Is supper ready?"

"Supper? Oh, yes, the supper should be ready." Mother Wren shooed Fanny toward the kitchen. "We have a pudding and a lovely roasted chicken Fanny got for quite a good price at Farmer Brown's. She has been practicing her bargaining skills, you know. We thought it would be a treat to celebrate your employment."

"How nice." Anna started up the stairs. "I'll freshen up."

Mother Wren laid a hand on her arm. "Are you sure you know what you are doing, my dear?" she asked in a low voice. "Sometimes ladies of a certain age get, well, *ideas* about gentlemen." She paused, then said in a rush, "He isn't of our class, you know. It would only lead to hurt."

Anna looked down at the fragile old hand on her arm; then she deliberately smiled and glanced up. "I am well aware that anything of a personal nature between Lord Swartingham and me would be improper. There's no need to worry."

The older woman searched her eyes a moment longer before patting Anna's arm. "Don't be too long, dear. We haven't burned the supper yet tonight."

Chapter Four

The duke turned and saw a huge raven perched on the wall of the castle. The bird hopped closer and cocked its head. "I will help you defeat the prince if you give me one of your daughters as my wife."

"How dare you, sirrah!" The old duke quivered in indignation. "You insult me to imply I would even think to wed one of my daughters to a dusty bird."

"Fine words, my friend," the raven cackled. "But be not so quick. In a moment, you'll lose both your daughters and your life."

The duke stared at the raven and saw that this was no ordinary bird. It wore a golden chain around its neck, and a ruby pendant in the shape of a small, perfect crown hung on the chain. He looked back to the threatening army at his gates and, seeing he had little to lose, agreed to the unholy bargain....

—from *The Raven Prince*

"Have you considered the name 'Sweetie'?" Anna asked as she spooned up some stewed apple.

She and the earl sat at one end of the immense dining

room table. From the fine layer of dust on the mahogany at the other end of the table, she guessed that this room must not be used much. Did the earl even take his supper here? Yet the dining room had been opened every day of the last week for their luncheon. In that week, she'd learned that the earl was not a conversationalist. After many days of grunts and monosyllabic replies, it'd become something of a game to provoke a response from her employer.

Lord Swartingham paused in the act of cutting a piece of steak and kidney pie. "Sweetie?"

His eyes were on her mouth, and Anna realized she'd licked her lips. "Yes. Don't you think 'Sweetie' a darling name?"

They both looked down at the dog beside the earl's chair. It was gnawing on a soup bone, sharp fangs glittering.

"I think 'Sweetie' may not be altogether suitable for his personality," Lord Swartingham said, placing the pie slice on his plate.

"Hmm. Perhaps you're right." Anna thoughtfully chewed. "Yet, you yourself haven't offered an alternative."

The earl sawed vigorously at a lump of meat. "That's because I'm content to let the animal remain nameless."

"Didn't you have any dogs as a boy?"

"I?" He stared at her as if she'd asked if he'd had two heads as a boy. "No."

"No pets at all?"

He scowled down at his pie. "Well, there was my mother's lapdog—"

"There, you see," Anna exclaimed in triumph.

"But the animal was a pug and an extremely irritable one at that."

"Even so—"

"Used to growl and snap at everyone but Mother," the earl mused, apparently to himself. "No one liked it. Once bit a footman. Father had to give the poor fellow a shilling."

"And did the pug have a name?"

"Fiddles." The earl nodded and took a bite of pie. "But Sammy called it Piddles. He also fed it Turkish delight just to see it get the candy stuck to the roof of its mouth."

Anna smiled. "Sammy was your brother?"

Lord Swartingham had raised a glass of wine to his lips, and he paused for a fraction of a second before sipping. "Yes." He placed the glass precisely beside his plate. "I'll need to check on various matters on the estate this afternoon."

Anna's smile died. Their play was apparently at an end.

He continued, "Tomorrow I'll need you to ride out with me. Hopple wants to show me some fields with a drainage problem, and I'd like you to take notes for us as we discuss possible solutions." He looked up. "You do have a riding habit, don't you?"

Anna tapped her fingers against her teacup. "As a matter of fact, I've never ridden."

"Never?" His eyebrows shot up.

"We don't have a horse."

"No, I suppose not." He frowned down at the pie on his

plate as if it were to blame for her lack of suitable attire. "Have you a gown you could use as a habit?"

Anna mentally ran through her meager wardrobe. "I could alter an old one."

"Excellent. Wear it tomorrow and I shall give you an elementary riding lesson. It shouldn't be too hard. We'll not be riding very far."

"Oh, but, my lord," Anna protested, "I don't want to put you to any trouble. I can ask one of the grooms to help me learn."

"No." He glared at her. "I will teach you to ride."

Overbearing man. She pursed her lips and refrained from a reply, sipping her tea instead.

The earl finished his pie in two more bites and pushed back his chair. "I'll see you before you leave this afternoon, Mrs. Wren." With a muttered "Come," he strode out of the room, the still-nameless dog following him.

Anna stared after the two. Was she peeved because the earl ordered her about, very much like the dog? Or touched that he insisted on teaching her to ride himself? She shrugged and finished the dregs of her tea.

Entering the library, she crossed to her desk and began writing. After a short while, she reached for a fresh sheet only to find there was none. Bother. Anna stood to ring for more paper and then remembered the stack in the earl's side drawer. She slipped behind his desk and pulled the drawer open. There on top of a pile of clean sheets lay the red leather book. Anna moved it aside and drew out a few sheets. A piece of paper drifted to the floor as she did so. She bent to pick it up and saw that it was a letter or a bill. A curious mark was engraved at the top. There appeared to be two men and a woman, but she could not make out what the diminutive figures were doing. She turned the letter this way and that in her hand, studying it.

The fire popped in the corner.

All at once, Anna understood and nearly dropped the paper. A nymph and two satyrs were engaged in an act that did not seem physically possible. She tilted her head to the side. Evidently, it *was* possible. The words *Aphrodite's Grotto* were engraved in ornate script beneath the rude illustration. The paper was a bill for two nights' stay at a house, and one could guess the type of house from the scandalous little picture at the top of the page. Who knew a bordello sent out monthly bills like a tailor?

Anna felt a sickening lurch in her stomach. Lord Swartingham must frequent this place if he had the bill in his desk. She sat down heavily and covered her mouth with a hand. Why should the discovery of his baser passions bother her so? The earl was a mature man who had lost his wife years ago. No person with any worldly knowledge at all would expect him to remain celibate the rest of his life. She smoothed the loathsome page on her lap. But the fact remained that the thought of him participating in such an activity with some beautiful woman brought a strange welling in her chest.

Anger. She felt anger. Society might not expect celibacy from the earl, but they certainly expected it of her. He, as a man, could go to houses of ill repute and romp all night with alluring, sophisticated creatures. While she, as a woman, was supposed to be chaste and not even think of dark eyes and hairy chests. It was simply not fair. Not fair at all.

She pondered the damning letter for a moment longer. Then she placed it carefully back in the desk drawer under the new paper. She made to close the drawer, but stopped, staring at the raven book. Anna's mouth thinned, and she impulsively snatched up the book. She slipped it in the center drawer of her own desk and returned to work. The rest of the afternoon dragged on. The earl never did return from the fields as promised.

Hours later, riding in the rattling carriage home, Anna tapped the back of one fingernail against the glass window and watched the fields turn into the muddy lanes of the village. The leather squabs smelled musty from the damp. She spotted a familiar street as they rounded a curve, and abruptly she stood and knocked on the carriage's roof. John Coachman called to the horses, and the carriage jerked to a stop. Anna descended and hastily thanked the coachman. She was in an area with houses that were both newer and a little more grand than her own cottage. The third house in from the lane was a redbrick with white trim. She knocked at the door.

In a moment, a maid peered out.

Anna smiled at the girl. "Hello, Meg. Is Mrs. Fairchild at home?"

"Good afternoon, Mrs. Wren." Black-haired Meg smiled cheerily. "The missus will be that glad to see you. You can wait in the sitting room while I tell her you're here."

Meg led the way into a little sitting room with bright yellow walls. A marmalade cat stretched on the rug, sunning itself in the dying light slanting through the windows. On the settee, a basket of sewing things lay, the threads trailing out untidily. Anna bent to greet the cat while she waited.

Footsteps pattered down the stairs, and Rebecca Fairchild appeared in the doorway. "For shame! It's been so long since you've visited, I'd begun to think you had abandoned me in my hour of need."

The other woman immediately contradicted her words by hurrying over and hugging Anna. Her belly made the embrace difficult, for it was round and heavy, thrusting before Rebecca like the full sails of a ship.

Anna returned her friend's hug fervently. "I'm sorry. You're right. I've been lax in coming to see you. How are you?"

"Fat. No, it's true," Rebecca talked over Anna's protest. "Even James, that dear man, has stopped offering to carry me up the stairs." She sat rather abruptly on the settee, narrowly missing the sewing basket. "Chivalry is quite dead. But you must tell me all about your employment at the Abbey."

"You've heard?" Anna took one of the chairs across from her friend.

"Have I heard? I've heard of practically nothing else." Rebecca lowered her voice dramatically. "The dark and mysterious Earl of Swartingham has employed the young Widow Wren for unknown purposes and daily closets himself with her for his own nefarious ends."

Anna winced. "I'm only transcribing papers for him."

Rebecca waved this mundane explanation away as Meg entered with a tea tray. "Don't tell me that. You realize that you're one of the few to actually meet the man? To hear the village gossips tell it, he hides himself away in his sinister mansion simply to deprive them of the opportunity to inspect him. Is he really as repulsive as the rumors say?"

"Oh, no!" Anna felt a spurt of anger. Surely they weren't saying Lord Swartingham was repulsive because of a few scars? "He's not handsome, of course, but he's not unattractive." Quite attractive to her anyway, a small voice whispered inside. Anna frowned down at her hands. When had she stopped noticing his scars and instead started focusing on the man underneath them?

"Pity." Rebecca appeared disappointed at the information that the earl wasn't a hideous ogre. "I want to hear of his dark secrets and his attempts to seduce you."

Meg quietly left.

Anna laughed. "He may have any number of dark secrets"—her voice hitched as she remembered the bill—"but he's very unlikely to try and seduce me."

"Of course he won't while you're wearing that awful cap." Rebecca gestured with the teapot at the offending article of clothing. "I don't know why you wear it. You're not that old."

"Widows are supposed to wear caps." Anna touched the muslin cap self-consciously. "Besides, I don't want him to seduce me."

"Why ever not?"

"Because—" Anna stopped.

She realized—horribly—that her mind had gone blank, and she couldn't think of a single reason why she didn't want the earl to seduce her. She popped a biscuit into her mouth and slowly chewed. Fortunately, Rebecca hadn't noticed her sudden silence and was now chattering on about hairstyles she thought would better suit her friend.

"Rebecca," Anna interrupted, "do you think all men have need of more than one woman?"

Rebecca, who had been in the act of pouring a second cup of tea, looked up at her in a far-too-sympathetic manner.

Anna felt herself flush. "I mean—"

"No, dear, I know what you mean." Rebecca slowly set the teapot down. "I can't speak for all men, but I'm fairly sure James has been faithful. And, really, if he was going to stray, I think he would do so now." She patted her tummy and reached for another biscuit.

Anna couldn't sit still any longer. She jumped up and started examining the bric-a-brac on the mantelpiece. "I'm sorry. I know James would never—"

"I'm glad you know." Rebecca snorted delicately. "You should've heard the advice Felicity Clearwater gave me on what to expect from a husband when one is with child. According to her, every husband is simply wait-ing—" Rebecca stopped suddenly.

Anna picked up a china shepherdess and touched the gilt on her bonnet. She couldn't see it very well. Her eyes were blurry.

"Now I'm the one who's sorry," Rebecca said.

Anna didn't look up. She'd always wondered if Re-becca had been aware. Now she knew. She closed her eyes.

"I think that any man who took his marriage vows so lightly," she heard Rebecca say, "has shamed himself unpardonably."

Anna set the shepherdess back on the mantel. "And the wife? Would she not be partly to blame if he went outside the marriage for satisfaction?"

"No, dear," Rebecca replied. "I don't think the wife is ever to blame."

Anna felt suddenly lighter. She tried a smile, though she feared it was a bit wobbly. "You are the best of friends, Rebecca."

"Well, of course." The other woman smiled like a self-satisfied and very pregnant cat. "And to prove it, I shall ring for Meg to bring us some cream cakes. Decadent, my dear!"

ANNA ARRIVED AT the Abbey the next morning dressed in an old blue worsted wool frock. She'd stayed up until well past midnight widening the skirt, but she hoped she could now sit a horse modestly. The earl was already pacing before the Abbey's entrance, apparently waiting for her. He wore buckskin breeches with brown jackboots that came to midthigh. These last were rather scuffed and dull, and Anna wondered, not for the first time, about his valet.

"Ah, Mrs. Wren." He eyed her skirt. "Yes, that will do nicely." Without waiting for a reply, he strode around the Abbey toward the stables.

Anna trotted to keep up.

His bay gelding was already saddled and busy baring its teeth at a stable boy. The boy held the horse's bridle at arm's length and looked wary. In contrast, a plump chestnut mare was standing placidly by the mounting block. The dog emerged from behind the stables and came bounding up to Anna. He skidded to a stop in front of her and tried belatedly to regain some of his dignity.

"I've found you out, you know," she whispered to him, and rubbed his ears in greeting.

"If you are through playing with that animal, Mrs. Wren." Lord Swartingham frowned at the dog.

Anna straightened. "I'm ready."

He indicated the mounting block, and Anna hesitantly approached it. She knew the theory of mounting a horse sidesaddle, but the reality was a bit more complicated. She could place one foot in the stirrup but had trouble pulling herself up to hook her other leg over the pommel.

"If you'll allow me?" The earl was behind her. She could feel his warm breath, smelling faintly of coffee, on her cheek as he bent over her.

She nodded, mute.

He placed his large hands around her waist and lifted her without any visible effort. Gently, he set her on the saddle and held the stirrup steady for her foot. Anna felt herself flush as she looked down at his bent head. He'd left his hat with the groom, and she could see a few strands of silver threading his queue. Was his hair soft or bristly? Her gloved hand lifted and, as if of its own accord, lightly touched his hair. She immediately snatched back her hand, but the earl seemed to have felt something. He looked up and stared into her eyes for what seemed a timeless moment. She watched as his eyelids lowered, and a faint flush seeped across his cheekbones.

Then he straightened and caught the horse's bridle. "This is a very placid mare," he said. "I think you'll have no trouble with her as long as there are no rats around."

She stared blankly down at him. "Rats?"

He nodded. "She has a fear of rats."

"I don't blame her," Anna murmured. She tentatively stroked the mare's mane, feeling the stiff hair beneath her fingers.

"Her name is Daisy," Lord Swartingham said. "Shall I lead you about the yard for a bit so you can get used to her?"

She nodded.

The earl clucked and the mare rocked forward. Anna clutched a handful of the mare's mane. Her whole body tensed at the unfamiliar sensation of moving so far off the ground. The mare shook her head.

Lord Swartingham glanced at her hands. "She can feel your fear. Isn't that right, my sweet girl?"

Anna, caught off guard by his last words, let go of the horse's mane.

"That's good. Let your body relax." His voice surrounded her, enfolding her in warmth. "She responds better to a gentle touch. She wants to be stroked and loved, don't you, my beauty?"

They walked around the stable yard, the earl's deep voice enchanting the horse. Something inside Anna seemed to heat and melt as she listened to him, as if she were enchanted, too. He gave simple instructions about how to hold the reins and sit. By the end of a half hour, she felt a good deal more confident in the saddle.

Lord Swartingham mounted his gelding and led off at a walk down the drive. The dog trotted beside them, sometimes disappearing into the high grass beside the drive only to reappear a few minutes later. When they reached the road, the earl let the bay have its head, galloping down the road a short distance and back again to work off some energy. The little mare watched the male antics without any sign that she wanted to break out of a walk. Anna lifted her face to the sun. She so missed its warmth after the long winter. She caught a flash of pale saffron beneath the hedges that lined the road.

"Look, primroses. I think those are the first this year, don't you?"

The earl glanced to where she pointed. "Those yellow flowers? I haven't seen them before."

"I've tried to grow them in my garden, but they don't like to be transplanted," she said. "I do have a few tulips, though. I've seen the lovely daffodils in the copse at the Abbey. Do you have tulips as well, my lord?"

He seemed a little startled by the question. "There may be tulips still in the gardens. I remember my mother gathering them, but I haven't seen the gardens in so long. . . ."

Anna waited, but he didn't elaborate. "Not everyone enjoys gardening, of course," she said to be polite.

"My mother loved to garden." He stared off down the lane. "She planted the daffodils you saw, and she renovated the great walled gardens behind the Abbey. When she died . . ." He grimaced. "When they all died, there were other, more important things to be seen to. And now the gardens have been neglected for so long, I should have them taken down."

"Oh, surely not!" Anna caught his lifted eyebrow and lowered her voice. "I mean to say, a good garden can always be restored."

He frowned. "To what point?"

Anna was nonplussed. "A garden always has a point."

He arched an eyebrow skeptically.

"My own mother had a lovely one when I was growing up at the vicarage," Anna said. "There were crocuses, daffodils, and tulips in the spring, followed by pinks, foxgloves, and phlox, with Johnny-jump-ups running throughout."

As she talked, Lord Swartingham watched her face intently.

"At my cottage now, I have the hollyhocks, of course, and many of the other flowers my mother grew. I wish I had more room to add some roses," she mused. "But roses are dear and take up quite a bit of space. I'm afraid I can't justify the expense when the vegetable garden comes first."

"Perhaps you could advise me on the Abbey's gardens later this spring," the earl said. He turned the bay's head and started down a smaller dirt track.

Anna concentrated on the business of turning the mare. When she looked up, she saw the flooded field. Mr. Hopple was already there, talking to a farmer in a woolen smock and straw hat. The man was having a hard time looking Mr. Hopple in the face. His eyes kept dragging lower to the amazing pink waistcoat Mr. Hopple wore. Something black was embroidered along the edges. As Anna drew nearer, she saw that the embroidery seemed to represent little black pigs.

"Good morning, Hopple, Mr. Grundle." The earl nodded to his steward and the farmer. His eyes flicked to the waistcoat. "That's a very interesting garment, Hopple. I don't know that I've seen the like before." The earl's tone was grave.

Mr. Hopple beamed and smoothed a hand down his waistcoat. "Why, thank you, my lord. I had it made at a small shop in London on my last trip."

The earl swung a long leg down from his horse. He gave the reins to Mr. Hopple and walked to Anna's horse. Gently grasping Anna's waist, he lifted her down. For the briefest moment, the tips of her breasts brushed the front of his coat and she felt his large fingers tighten. Then she was free, and he was turning to the steward and the farmer.

They spent the morning tramping through the field, examining the water problem. At one point, the earl stood knee-deep in muddy water and investigated a suspected source of the flood. Anna took notes in a small book he provided for her. She was glad she had chosen an old skirt to wear since it soon became thoroughly filthy about the hem.

"How do you intend to drain the field?" Anna asked as they rode back to the Abbey.

"We'll have to dig a trench across the north side." Lord Swartingham squinted thoughtfully. "That may be a problem because the land there runs into Clearwater's property, and for courtesy's sake, I'll have to send Hopple to ask permission. The farmer has already lost his pea crop, and if the field isn't made tillable soon, he'll miss his wheat—" He stopped and shot a wry look at her. "I'm sorry. You can't be interested in these matters."

"Indeed, I am, my lord." Anna straightened in her saddle and then hurriedly grabbed Daisy's mane when the horse sidestepped. "I've been most absorbed in your writings about land management. If I understand your theories correctly, the farmer should follow a crop of wheat with one of beans or peas and then with one of mangel-wurzels and so on. If that is the case, shouldn't this farmer plant mangel-wurzels instead of wheat?"

"In most instances, you would be right, but in this case . . ."

Anna listened to the earl's deep voice discussing vegetables and grains. Had agriculture always been this fascinating and she'd never realized it? Somehow she didn't think so.

AN HOUR LATER, Edward found himself bemusedly holding forth on various ways of draining a field during luncheon with Mrs. Wren. Of course the topic was an interesting one, but he'd never had occasion to talk to a woman about such masculine matters before. In fact, he had hardly any occasion to talk to women, at least since the death of his mother and sister. He'd flirted when young, naturally, and knew how to make light social chatter. But to exchange ideas with a woman as one did with a man was a new experience. And he liked talking with little Mrs. Wren. She listened to him with her head tilted to one side, the sun streaming in through the dining room window gently highlighting the curve of her cheek. Such utter attention was seductive.

Sometimes she smiled crookedly at what he was saying. He was fascinated by that lopsided smile. One edge of her rose-colored lips always tilted upward more than the other side. He became aware that he was staring at her mouth, hoping to see that smile again, fantasizing about what it would taste like. Edward turned his head aside and closed his eyes. His arousal was pressing against the front placket of his breeches, making them uncomfortably tight. He'd found he had this problem almost constantly of late when in the company of his new secretary.

Christ. He was a man above thirty, not a boy to moon over a woman's smile. The situation might be laughable if his cock didn't ache so much.

Edward abruptly realized that Mrs. Wren was asking him a question. "What?"

"I asked if you were all right, my lord," she said. She looked worried.

"Fine. I'm fine." He took a deep breath and wished irritably that she would call him by his given name. He longed to hear her say *Edward*. But no. It would be highly inappropriate for her to call him by his Christian name.

He gathered his scattered thoughts. "We should return to work." He stood and strode from the room, feeling as if he were fleeing fire-breathing monsters rather than one plain little widow.

WHEN THE CLOCK struck five, Anna tidied the small pile of transcripts she'd finished that afternoon and glanced at the earl. He was sitting scowling at the paper in front of him. She cleared her throat.

He looked up. "Is it time already?"

She nodded.

He rose and waited as she gathered her things. The dog followed them out the door, but then he bounded down the stairs to the drive. The animal sniffed intently at something on the ground and then rolled, happily rubbing his head and neck in whatever it was.

Lord Swartingham sighed. "I'll have one of the stable boys wash him before he enters the Abbey again."

"Mmm," Anna murmured thoughtfully. "What do you think of 'Adonis'?"

He gave her a look so full of incredulous horror that she was hard-pressed not to laugh. "No, I suppose not," she murmured.

The dog got up from his refreshment and shook himself, flipping one of his ears inside out. He trotted back to them and tried to look solemn with his ear still inside out.

"Self-control, lad." The earl righted the dog's ear.

At this Anna did chuckle. He looked at her sideways, and she thought his wide mouth twitched. The carriage trundled up then, and she entered with his assistance. The dog knew by now that he was not allowed to ride and merely watched wistfully.

Anna settled back and watched the familiar scenery roll by. As the carriage came upon the outskirts of town, she saw a wad of clothes in the roadside ditch. Curious, she leaned out the window to get a better look. The bundle moved, and a head with fine, pale-brown hair rose and turned toward the sound of the carriage.

"Stop! John Coachman, stop at once!" Anna pounded on the roof with her fist.

The carriage slowed to a halt, and she flung open the door.

"What is it, miss?"

She saw the startled face of Tom, the footman, as she ran past the back of the carriage with her skirts held in one hand. Anna reached the place where she had seen the clothes and stared down.

In the ditch lay a young woman.

Chapter Five

*The moment the duke agreed to his bargain, the raven
leapt into the air with a powerful rush of wings. At the
same time, a magical army streamed from the castle's
keep. First came ten thousand men, each armed with a
shield and sword. They were followed by ten thousand
archers carrying long, deadly bows and full quivers.
Finally, ten thousand mounted men galloped forth,
their horses gnashing their teeth and ready for battle.
The raven flew to the army's head and met the
prince's troops with a crash like thunder. Clouds
of dust covered both forces so that nothing could be
seen. Only the terrible cries of men at war were
heard. And when the dust finally cleared, not a trace
of the prince's army remained save for a few iron
horseshoes lying in the dirt. . . .*
—from *The Raven Prince*

The woman lay on her side in the ditch, both legs curled
as if seeking warmth. She clutched a dirty shawl about
pitifully thin shoulders. The dress beneath the shawl had
once been a bright pink but was now smeared with grime.

Her eyes were closed in a face that looked yellowish and unhealthy.

Anna held her skirt out of the way with one hand and used the other to steady herself against the bank as she clambered down to the stricken woman. She noticed a foul smell as she drew nearer.

"Are you hurt, ma'am?" She touched the pale face.

The woman moaned and her large eyes flew open, making Anna start. Behind her, the coachman and footman slid down the little slope with a rattle.

John Coachman made a disgusted noise in his throat. "Come away, Mrs. Wren. This here ain't for the likes of you."

Anna turned her eyes to the coachman in astonishment. He averted his face, watching the horses. She looked at Tom. He inspected the rocks at his feet.

"The lady is hurt or ill, John." She knit her brow. "We need to summon help for her."

"Aye, mum, we'll send back someone to take care of her," John said. "You should come to the carriage and go home now, Mrs. Wren."

"But I can't leave the lady here."

"She's no lady, if you understand my meaning." John spat to the side. "It ain't fit for you to bother yourself with her."

Anna looked down at the woman she'd drawn into her arms. She noticed now what she hadn't before: the unseemly show of skin at the woman's dress top and the tawdry nature of the material. She frowned in thought. Had she ever met a prostitute? She thought not. Such persons lived in a different world than poor country widows.

A world that her community explicitly forbade from ever intersecting with hers. She should do as John suggested and leave the poor woman. It was, after all, what everyone expected of her.

John Coachman was offering his hand to help her up. Anna stared at the appendage. Had her life always been this constrained, her boundaries so narrow that at times it was like walking a tightrope? Was she nothing more than her position in society?

No, she was not. Anna firmed her jaw. "Nevertheless, John, I do bother myself with this woman. Please carry her to the carriage with Tom's help. We must bring her to my cottage and send for Dr. Billings."

The two men didn't look happy with the situation, but under her determined gaze, they bore the slight woman between them to the carriage. Anna got in first and then turned around to help ease the woman onto the carriage seat. She braced the woman against herself with both arms to prevent her from falling off the seat on the way home. When the carriage stopped, she carefully laid the woman down and got out. John was still in the high driver's seat staring straight ahead with a furrowed brow.

Anna placed her hands on her hips. "John, come and help Tom get her into the cottage."

John muttered, but climbed down.

"What is it, Anna?" Mother Wren had come to the door.

"An unfortunate lady I found by the roadside." Anna watched the men maneuver the woman out of the carriage. "Bring her into the cottage, please."

Mother Wren backed out of the way as the men struggled to get the unconscious woman over the doorsill.

"Where shall we put her, ma'am?" Tom panted.

"I think in my room, up the stairs."

That earned Anna a disapproving look from John, but she ignored it. They carried the woman up the stairs.

"What is wrong with the lady?" Mother Wren asked.

"I don't know. I believe she may be ill," Anna said. "I thought it best to bring her here."

The men clomped back down the narrow stairs and outside.

"Don't forget to stop by Dr. Billings's," Anna called.

John Coachman waved a hand irritably over his shoulder to signify that he had heard. In a moment, the carriage had rattled away. By this time, Fanny was standing wide-eyed in the hallway.

"Could you put the kettle on for tea, Fanny?" Anna asked. She drew Mother Wren aside as soon as Fanny started for the kitchen. "John and Tom say this poor woman is not entirely respectable. I'll send her elsewhere if you say so." She looked anxiously at her mother-in-law.

Mother Wren raised her eyebrows. "Do you mean she's a whore?" At Anna's startled glance, she smiled and patted her hand. "It's very hard to get to my age without hearing the word at least once, dear."

"No, I suppose not," Anna replied. "Yes, John and Tom indicated that she is a whore."

Mother Wren sighed. "You know it would be best to send her away."

"Yes, undoubtedly." Anna lifted her chin.

"But"—Mother Wren threw up her hands—"if it is your wish to care for her here, I'll not stop you."

Anna blew out a breath in relief and ran upstairs to see to her patient.

A quarter of an hour later, there was a sharp knock on the door. Anna came down the stairs in time to see Mother Wren smooth her skirts and answer the door.

Dr. Billings, in a white bobbed wig, stood outside. "A good day to you, Mrs. Wren, Mrs. Wren."

"And to you, Dr. Billings," Mother Wren answered for them both.

Anna led the doctor to her room.

Dr. Billings had to duck to enter the bedroom. He was a tall, gaunt gentleman with a bit of a permanent stoop. The tip of his bony nose was always pink, even in summer. "Well, what have we here?"

"A woman I found in distress, Dr. Billings," Anna said. "Will you see if she is ill or injured?"

He cleared his throat. "If you'll leave me alone with this person, Mrs. Wren, I'll endeavor to examine her."

Clearly, John had told Dr. Billings the manner of woman they had found.

"I think I shall remain, if you do not mind, Dr. Billings," Anna said.

The doctor obviously did mind but could think of no reason to order Anna from the room. Despite his opinion of the patient, Dr. Billings was thorough but gentle in his examination. He looked down her throat and asked Anna to turn away so that he might scrutinize the sick woman's chest.

Then he straightened the covers over her and sighed. "I think we had better discuss this downstairs."

"Of course." Anna led the way from the room and down the stairs, stopping to ask Fanny to bring some tea to the sitting room. Then she indicated the only armchair for the doctor and sat across from him on the edge of the tiny settee, clasping her hands tightly in her lap. Was the woman dying?

"She's quite ill," Dr. Billings began.

Anna leaned forward. "Yes?"

The doctor avoided her eyes. "She has a fever, perhaps an infection of the lungs. She'll need some bed rest to recover."

He hesitated and then apparently saw the alarm in Anna's face. "Oh, it is nothing grave, I assure you, Mrs. Wren. She'll recover. She just needs time to heal."

"I am most relieved." Anna smiled. "I thought from your manner that the disease was fatal."

"Indeed not."

"Thank God."

Dr. Billings rubbed his finger along the side of his thin nose. "I'll send some men around immediately when I get home. She'll need to be taken to the poorhouse for care, of course."

Anna frowned. "But I thought you understood, Dr. Billings. We wish to nurse her here at the cottage."

A red stain seeped up the doctor's face. "Nonsense. It is entirely inappropriate for you and the elder Mrs. Wren to care for a woman of that sort."

She set her jaw. "I've discussed it with my mother-in-law, and we are both in agreement that we will care for the lady in our home."

Dr. Billings's face was now completely red. "It is quite out of the question."

"Doctor—"

But Dr. Billings interrupted her. "She's a prostitute!"

Anna forgot what she was about to say and closed her mouth. She stared at the doctor and saw the truth in his countenance: this was how the majority of the people in Little Battleford would react.

She took a deep breath. "We've decided to take care of the woman. Her profession doesn't change that fact."

"You must see reason, Mrs. Wren," the doctor grumbled. "It's impossible for you to care for that creature."

"Her condition is not contagious, is it?"

"No, no, probably not anymore," he admitted.

"Well, then, there is no reason we can't care for her." Anna smiled grimly.

Fanny chose that moment to bring in the tea. Anna poured for the doctor and herself, trying to remain as serene as possible. She wasn't used to having arguments with gentlemen, and she found it was most hard to remain resolute and not apologize. It was a rather unsettling feeling, knowing the doctor disagreed with her course, that in fact he disapproved of her. At the same time, she couldn't repress a clandestine thrill. How exhilarating to speak her mind frankly, uncaring of a man's opinion! Really, she ought to feel ashamed at the thought, but she couldn't bring herself to regret it. No, not at all.

They drank the tea in a charged silence, the good doctor having apparently decided he wasn't going to change her mind. After finishing his cup, Dr. Billings fished a small brown bottle out of his bag and gave it to Anna with instructions on how to administer the medication. Then the doctor crammed his hat on his head and wound a lavender muffler around his neck several times.

He halted by the front door as Anna was showing him out. "If you change your mind, Mrs. Wren, please call on me. I'll find an appropriate place for the young woman."

"Thank you," she murmured. She closed the door after the doctor and leaned against it, her shoulders slumping.

Mother Wren entered the hall and studied Anna. "What does she have, my dear?"

"A fever and infection of the lungs." Anna looked at her wearily. "Perhaps it would be better if you and Fanny stayed with friends until this is over."

Mother Wren raised her brows. "Who would look after her during the day while you are at Ravenhill?"

Anna stared, suddenly stricken. "I'd forgotten that."

Mother Wren shook her head. "Is it really necessary to stir up this amount of trouble, my dear?"

"I'm sorry." Anna looked down and noticed a grass stain on her skirts. It wouldn't come out—grass stains never did. "I don't mean to drag you into my mess."

"Then why not take the doctor's help? It's so much easier to simply do what people expect of you, Anna."

"It may be easier, but it isn't necessarily the right way, Mother. Surely you can see that?" She looked at her mother-in-law pleadingly, trying to find the words to explain. Her actions had made complete sense when she'd been staring at the woman's sickly face in the ditch. Now, with Mother Wren waiting so patiently, it was harder to articulate her logic. "I've always done what was expected, haven't I? Whether or not it was the right thing to do."

The older woman frowned. "But you've never done anything wrong—"

"But that's not the point, is it?" Anna bit her lip and found to her horror that she was close to tears. "If I've never stepped outside the role that's been assigned to me since birth, I've never tested myself. I've been too afraid of others' opinions, I think. I've been a coward. If that woman needs me, why not help her—for her . . . and for me?"

"All I know is that this way will lead to quite a lot of grief for you." Mother Wren shook her head again and sighed.

Anna led the way into the kitchen, and the two women prepared a thin beef tea. Anna carried it and the little brown bottle of medicine up the stairs to her room. Quietly, she cracked the door open and peeked in. The woman stirred feebly and tried to raise herself.

Anna put down her burden and crossed the room to her. "Don't try to move."

At the sound of Anna's voice, the woman's eyes flew open and she looked around wildly. "W-w-who are—?"

"My name is Anna Wren. You're in my home."

Anna hurried to bring the beef tea over to the woman. She put her arm around her patient, gently helping her to sit up. The woman sipped the warm broth and swallowed with difficulty. After she had drunk half the cup, her eyes began to close again. Anna lowered her back to the bed and gathered up the cup and spoon.

The woman caught her with a shaking hand as she turned away. "My sister," she whispered.

Anna knit her brow. "Do you wish me to notify your sister?"

The woman nodded.

"Wait," Anna said. "Let me get a bit of paper and pencil so I may write down her address." She hurried to her small dresser and tugged out the bottom drawer. Underneath a stack of old linens was a walnut writing case that had belonged to Peter. Anna took it out and settled on the bedside chair with the writing case on her lap. "Where shall I address a letter to your sister?"

The woman gasped out her sister's name and place of residence, which was in London, while Anna noted the address with a pencil on a scrap of paper. Then the woman lay back, exhausted, on the pillow.

Anna hesitantly touched her hand. "Can you tell me your name?"

"Pearl," she whispered without opening her eyes.

Anna carried the writing case from the room, shutting the door gently behind her. She ran down the stairs and went into the sitting room to compose a letter to Pearl's sister, a Miss Coral Smythe.

Peter's writing case was a flat rectangular box. The writer could place it on his or her lap and use it as a portable desk. On top was a hinged half lid that opened to reveal a smaller box for quills, a bottle of ink that fit next to it, and papers and other miscellaneous things used for correspondence. Anna hesitated. The writing case was a handsome thing, but she'd not touched it since Peter's death. While Peter lived, it had been his private possession. She felt almost a trespasser using it, especially as they had not been close toward the end of his life. She shook her head and opened the case.

Anna wrote carefully, but it still took several drafts to compose a letter. Finally, she had a missive she was satisfied with, and she put it aside to take to the Little Battleford Coach Inn tomorrow. She was putting the quill box back into the walnut writing case when she realized that something was jammed in the back. The quill box would not fit in. She opened the half lid all the way and shook out the shallow case. Then she felt with her hand at the back. There was something round and cool there. Anna gave a tug and the object came loose. When she withdrew her hand, a little gold locket nestled in her palm. The lid was prettily chased with curlicues, and on the back was a pin so a lady could wear it as a brooch. Anna pressed the thin wafer of gold at the seam. The locket popped apart.

It was empty.

Anna snapped the two halves back together. She rubbed her thumb thoughtfully over the engraving. The locket was not hers. In fact, she had never seen it before. She had a sudden urge to fling it across the room. How dare he? Even after his death, to torment her in this way? Hadn't she put up with enough when he lived? And now she found this little wretched thing lying in wait all these years later.

Anna raised her arm, the locket clenched in her fist. Tears blurred her vision.

Then she took a breath. Peter had been in his grave over six years. She was alive, and he had long ago turned to dust. She inhaled again and unfolded her fingers. The locket gleamed in her palm innocently.

Carefully, Anna placed it in her pocket.

THE NEXT DAY was Sunday.

The Little Battleford church was a small building of gray stone with a leaning steeple. Built sometime in the Middle Ages, it was terribly drafty and cold in the winter months. Anna had spent many a Sunday hoping the homily would end before the hot brick brought from home lost its heat and her toes froze completely.

There was a sudden hush when the Wren women entered the church. Several swiftly averted eyes confirmed Anna's suspicion that she was the topic of discussion, but Anna greeted her neighbors without any indication that she knew she was the center of attention. Rebecca waved from a front pew. She sat beside her husband, James, a big blond man with a rather stout middle. Mother Wren and Anna scrunched in beside them on the bench.

"You certainly have been leading an exciting life lately," Rebecca whispered.

"Really?" Anna busied herself with her gloves and bible.

"Mmm-hmm," Rebecca murmured. "I had no idea you were considering the world's oldest profession."

That got Anna's attention. "What?"

"They haven't actually accused you of it yet, but some are coming close." Rebecca smiled at the lady behind them who had leaned forward.

The woman drew back sharply and sniffed.

Her friend continued, "The town gossips haven't had this much fun since the miller's wife had her baby ten months after he died."

The vicar entered and the congregation quieted as the service began. Predictably, the homily was on the sins of Jezebel, although poor Vicar Jones did not look like he enjoyed delivering it. Anna had only to glance at the ramrod-straight back of Mrs. Jones sitting in the front pew to guess who had decided on the subject matter. At last the service came to a dreary close, and they stood to exit the church.

"Don't know why they left her palms and feet," James said as the congregation began rising.

Rebecca looked up at her husband with fond exasperation. "What are you blathering about, darling?"

"Jezebel," James muttered. "Dogs didn't eat her palms and the soles of her feet. Why? Hounds not usually that particular about their victuals, in my experience."

Rebecca rolled her eyes and patted her husband's arm. "Don't worry about it, darling. Perhaps they had different dogs back then."

James didn't look very satisfied with this explanation, but he responded to his wife's gentle nudge toward the door. Anna was touched to note that Mother Wren and Rebecca arranged themselves on either side of her with James guarding her rear.

As it turned out, however, she did not need such a loyal barricade. For while she received several censorious looks and one cut direct, not all the ladies of Little Battleford were disapproving. In fact, many of the younger ladies were so envious of Anna's new position as secretary to Lord Swartingham that it seemed to transcend her problematic championship of a prostitute in their eyes.

Anna was almost through the gauntlet of villagers outside the church and was beginning to relax when she heard an overly sweet voice at her shoulder. "Mrs. Wren, I do want you to know how very brave I think you are."

Felicity Clearwater carelessly held her small cape in one hand, the better to show off her fashionable frock. Orange and blue nosegays tumbled over a background of primrose yellow. The skirt parted in front to reveal a blue brocade underskirt, and the whole concoction draped over wide panniers.

For a moment, Anna thought wistfully of how nice it would be to wear a gown as fine as Felicity's; then Mother Wren bridled beside her. "Anna had not a thought for herself when she brought that poor woman home."

Felicity's eyes widened. "Oh, obviously. Why, to endure the displeasure of the entire village, not to mention the scolding from the pulpit she just received, Anna must not have had a thought at all."

"I don't think I shall take the lessons of Jezebel too seriously," Anna said lightly. "After all, they might apply to other women in this village, too."

For some reason, this rather weak rejoinder made the other woman stiffen. "I wouldn't know anything about that." Felicity's fingers ran blindly across her hair like spiders. "Unlike you, no one could fault me for the company I keep." Smiling tightly, Felicity swept off before Anna could think of a suitable riposte.

"Cat." Rebecca's own eyes narrowed rather like a feline.

Back at the cottage, Anna spent the rest of the day darning stockings, a talent that she'd by necessity become expert at. After her own supper, she crept up to Pearl's room and found the woman much better. Anna helped her sit up and eat some porridge thinned with milk. Pearl was quite a pretty woman, if worn looking.

Pearl fidgeted with a lock of her pale hair for several minutes before finally bursting out, "Why'd you take me in, then?"

Anna was startled. "You were lying by the side of the road. I couldn't leave you there."

"You know what kind of a girl I am, don't you?"

"Well—"

"I'm a trollop." Pearl said the last word with a defiant twist to her mouth.

"We thought you might be," Anna replied.

"Well, now you know."

"But I don't see that it makes any difference."

Pearl appeared stunned. Anna took the opportunity to spoon some more gruel into her open mouth.

"Here now. You aren't one of them religious types, are you?" Pearl's eyes narrowed in suspicion.

Anna paused with the spoon in midair. "What?"

Pearl agitatedly twisted the sheet covering her knees. "One of them religious ladies that grab girls like me to re-form them. I heard that they feeds them nothing but bread and water and makes them do needlework till their fingers bleed and they repent."

Anna looked at the milky gruel in the bowl. "This isn't bread and water, is it?"

Pearl flushed. "No, ma'am, I suppose it isn't."

"We'll feed you more substantial fare when you are up to it, I assure you."

Pearl still looked uncertain, so Anna added, "You may go any time you like. I sent a letter to your sister. Perhaps she'll arrive soon."

"That's right." Pearl seemed relieved. "I remember giving you her direction."

Anna stood. "Try not to worry; just sleep well."

"Aye." Pearl's brow was still wrinkled.

Anna sighed. "Good night."

"'Night, ma'am."

Anna carried the bowl of gruel and the spoon back down the stairs and rinsed them out. It was quite dark by the time she retired to a small pallet made up in her mother-in-law's room.

She slept dreamlessly and didn't wake until Mother Wren gently shook her shoulder. "Anna. You had better get up, dear, if you're to get to Ravenhill on time."

Only then did it occur to Anna to wonder what the earl would think of her patient.

MONDAY MORNING, ANNA entered the Abbey library warily. She'd walked all the way from her cottage dreading the confrontation with Lord Swartingham, hoping against hope that he'd be more reasonable than the doctor had. However, the earl seemed just as usual—rumpled and grumpy with his hair and neckcloth askew. He greeted her by growling that he had found an error on one of the pages she had transcribed the day before. Anna breathed a grateful sigh of relief and settled down to work.

After luncheon, however, her luck ran out.

Lord Swartingham had made a short trip into town to consult with the vicar about helping to finance a renovation of the apse. His return was heralded by the front door crashing against the wall.

"MRS. WREN!"

Anna winced at the bellow and the subsequent slamming of the door. The dog by the fire lifted his head.

"Damnation! Where is the woman?"

Anna rolled her eyes. She was in the library where she always could be found. Where did he think she might be?

Heavy-booted feet stomped across the hall; then the earl's tall form darkened the doorway. "What's this I hear about an unsuitable refugee at your home, Mrs. Wren? The doctor was at great pains to tell me of your folly." He stalked over to the rosewood desk and braced his arms in front of her.

Anna lifted her chin and attempted to look down her nose at him, no small feat since he was employing his great height to tower over her. "I found an unfortunate person in need of help, my lord, and, naturally, brought her to my home so that I might nurse her back to health."

He scowled. "An unfortunate bawd, you mean. Are you insane?"

He was far more angry than she had anticipated. "Her name is Pearl."

"Oh, fine." He pushed away from her desk forcefully. "You are on intimate terms with the creature."

"I only wish to point out that she is a woman, not a creature."

"Semantics." The earl waved a dismissive hand. "Have you no care for your reputation?"

"My reputation is hardly the point."

"Hardly the point? *Hardly the point?*" He swung around violently and began pacing the carpet in front of her desk.

The dog laid back his ears and lowered his head, following his master's movements with his eyes.

"I wish you wouldn't parrot my words," Anna muttered. She could feel a flush creeping up her cheeks, and she wished she could control it. She didn't want to appear weak before him.

The earl, at the farther end of his track, seemed not to hear her reply. "Your reputation is the only point. You are supposed to be a respectable woman. A slip like this could paint you blacker than a crow."

Really! Anna straightened at her desk. "Are you questioning my reputation, Lord Swartingham?"

He stopped dead and turned an outraged face toward her. "Don't be a ninny. Of course I'm not questioning your reputation."

"Aren't you?"

"Ha! I—"

But Anna rode over him. "If I am a respectable woman, surely you can trust my good sense." She could feel her own anger rising, a great pressure inside her head threatening to escape. "As a respectable lady, I consider it my duty to help those less fortunate than I."

"Don't use sophistry with me." He pointed a finger at her from across the room. "Your position in the village will be ruined if you continue this course."

"I may come into some criticism"—she folded her arms—"but I hardly think I'll be ruined by an act of Christian charity."

The earl made an inelegant sound. "The Christians in the village will be the first to pillory you."

"I—"

"You are extremely vulnerable. A young, attractive widow—"

"Working for a single man," Anna pointed out sweetly. "Obviously, my virtue is in imminent peril."

"I didn't say that."

"No, but others have."

"That is exactly what I mean," he shouted, apparently under the impression that if he bellowed loud enough, it would make his point. "You cannot associate with this woman!"

This was simply too much. Anna's eyes narrowed. "I cannot associate with her?"

He crossed his arms on his chest. "Exactly—"

"I cannot associate with her?" she repeated over him, this time more loudly.

Lord Swartingham looked wary at her tone. As well he should.

"What of all the men who made her what she is by *associating* with her?" she asked. "No one worries about the reputation of the men who patronize whores."

"I can't believe you would speak of such things," he sputtered in outrage.

The pressure in Anna's head was gone, replaced by a rush of giddy freedom. "Well, I do speak of such things. And I know men do more than speak of them. Why, a man could visit a harlot regularly—every day of the week, even—and still be perfectly respectable. Whilst the poor girl who has engaged in the very same act as he is deemed soiled goods."

The earl seemed to have lost the power of speech. He produced a series of snorts.

Anna couldn't stop the river of words pouring from her mouth. "And I suspect it's not only the lower classes who patronize such women. I believe men and, indeed, *gentlemen* of quality frequent houses of ill repute." Anna's lips trembled uncontrollably. "Indeed, it seems hypocritical for a man to use a whore but not help one when she is in need." She stopped and blinked rapidly. She would not cry.

The snorts coalesced into a great roar. *"My God, woman!"*

"I think I shall go home now," Anna managed to say just before she ran from the room.

Oh, Lord, what had she done? She'd lost her temper with a man and argued with her employer. And in the process, no doubt, she had destroyed any chance of continuing her work as secretary to the earl.

Chapter Six

The people of the castle danced and shouted with joy.
Their enemy had been defeated, and they no longer
had anything to fear. But in the midst of their
celebration, the raven flew back and landed before
the duke. "I have done as I said and destroyed
the prince. Give me now my price."
But which daughter would be his wife? The eldest
cried that she would not waste her beauty on a nasty
bird. The second said now that the evil prince's
army was defeated, why fulfill the bargain? Only
the youngest, Aurea, agreed to uphold her father's
honor. That very night, in what was the strangest
ceremony any had witnessed, Aurea was wed to the
raven. And as soon as she was pronounced his wife,
the raven bade her climb on his back and he flew
away with his bride clinging atop him. . . .
—from *The Raven Prince*

Edward stared after Anna in baffled rage. What had just happened? When had he lost control of the conversation?

He turned and snatched two china figurines and a

snuffbox from the mantelpiece and pelted them at the wall in rapid succession. Each exploded on impact, but it didn't help. What had gotten into the woman? He had merely pointed out—firmly, to be sure—how unsuitable it was for her to harbor such a person in her own home, and somehow it had blown up in his face.

What the hell had happened?

He strode into the hall where a startled-looking footman was staring out the front door.

"Don't just stand there, man." The footman jumped and spun at Edward's growl. "Run and tell John Coachman to take the carriage after Mrs. Wren. Silly woman'll probably walk all the way back to the village just to aggravate me."

"My lord." The footman bowed and scurried away.

Edward thrust both hands into his hair and pulled hard enough that he felt the hair come undone from his queue. *Women!* Beside him, the dog whined.

Hopple peered around the corner like a mouse popping out of its hole to see if the storm was past. He cleared his throat. "Females are quite unreasonable sometimes, are they not, my lord?"

"Oh, shut up, Hopple." Edward stomped out of the hall.

THE BIRDS HAD just begun their cheerful cacophony the next morning when the knocking started on the cottage's front door. At first Anna thought the noise part of a hazy dream, but then her eyes opened blearily and the dream dissipated.

The banging, unfortunately, did not.

Anna crawled out of her pallet and found her sky-blue wrapper. Bundling it about her, she stumbled down the cold stairs barefoot, yawning so widely her jaw creaked. The caller had by this time worked himself into a frenzy. Whoever it was had very little patience. In point of fact, the only person she knew who had such a temper was . . . "Lord Swartingham!"

He had one muscular arm braced against the lintel above her head, the other one raised in preparation for another blow to the door. Hastily he lowered his fisted hand. The dog by his side stood and wagged his tail.

"Mrs. Wren." He glowered at her. "Haven't you yet dressed?"

Anna looked down at her wrinkled wrapper and bare toes. "Evidently not, my lord."

The dog pushed past the earl's legs and shoved his muzzle into her hand.

"Why not?" he asked.

"Because it's too early to do so?" The dog leaned against Anna as she petted him.

Lord Swartingham scowled at the oblivious hound. "You mug," he said.

"I beg your pardon!"

The earl turned his scowl on her. "Not you, the dog."

"Who is it, Anna?" Mother Wren stood on the stairs, peering anxiously down. Fanny hovered in the hall.

"It's the Earl of Swartingham, Mother," Anna said as if it were usual for peers to come calling before breakfast. She turned back to him and said more formally, "May I present my mother-in-law, Mrs. Wren. Mother, this is his lordship, Edward de Raaf, the Earl of Swartingham."

Mother Wren, in a frothy pink wrapper, bobbed a perilous curtsy on the stairs. "How do you do?"

"A pleasure, I'm sure, ma'am," the man at the door muttered.

"Has he broken his fast yet?" Mother Wren asked Anna.

"I don't know." Anna swiveled to Lord Swartingham, whose scarred cheeks were reddening. "Have you broken your fast yet?"

"I . . ." He seemed uncharacteristically at a loss for words. He frowned harder.

"Ask him in, Anna, do," Mother Wren prompted.

"Won't you please join us for breakfast, my lord?" Anna inquired sweetly.

The earl nodded. Still frowning, he ducked his head to clear the lintel and stepped inside the cottage.

The elder Mrs. Wren swept down the staircase, fuchsia ribbons fluttering. "I am so glad to meet you, my lord. Fanny, hurry and put the kettle on."

Fanny squealed and dashed into the kitchen. Mother Wren ushered their guest into the tiny sitting room, and Anna noticed it seemed to shrink in size as he entered it. He sat down gingerly on the only armchair while the ladies took the settee. The dog happily made a circuit of the room, poking his nose into corners until the earl growled at him to sit down.

Mother Wren smiled brightly. "Anna must have been mistaken when she said you'd sacked her."

"What?" He gripped the arms of his chair.

"She was under the impression that you would no longer have need of a secretary."

"Mother," Anna whispered.

"That is what you said, dear."

The earl's eyes were intent on Anna. "She was mistaken. She is still my secretary."

"Oh, how nice!" Mother Wren positively beamed. "She was quite upset last night when she thought she was no longer employed."

"Mother—"

The older woman leaned forward confidentially as if Anna had disappeared from the room. "Why, her eyes were quite red when she came in from the carriage. I think she may have been weeping."

"*Mother!*"

Mrs. Wren turned an innocent gaze on her daughter-in-law. "Well, they were, dear."

"Were they, indeed?" the earl murmured. His own ebony eyes gleamed.

Fortunately, Fanny saved her from making a reply by entering with the breakfast tray. Anna noted with relief that the girl had thought to make coddled eggs and to toast some bread to go with their usual porridge. She'd even found a bit of ham. Anna sent an approving nod to the little maid, who grinned back cheekily.

After the earl had partaken of a truly amazing quantity of coddled eggs—what luck that Fanny had gone to market only yesterday—he rose and thanked Mother Wren for the breakfast. Mother Wren smiled flirtatiously at him, and Anna wondered how long it would be before the whole village heard that they had entertained the Earl of Swartingham in their wrappers.

"Can you dress for riding, Mrs. Wren?" the earl asked Anna. "I have my gelding and Daisy waiting outside."

"Of course, my lord." Anna excused herself and went to her room to change.

A few minutes later, she ran back down the stairs and found the earl waiting for her in the front garden. He was contemplating the wet earth to the side of her door where blue grape hyacinth and yellow daffodils were cheerfully blooming. He looked up when she came out of the house, and for an instant, there was an expression in his eyes that made her catch her breath. She glanced down to pull on her gloves and felt her cheeks heat.

"About time," he said. "We're later than I had planned."

Anna ignored his curtness and stood by the mare, waiting for his help to mount. The earl advanced and wrapped his big hands around her waist before throwing her up into the saddle. He stood below her for a moment, the wind teasing a lock of his dark hair, and searched her face. She stared back, all thought having fled from her mind. Then he turned to his own horse and mounted.

The day was bright. Anna didn't remember hearing rain during the night, but the evidence of it lay everywhere. Puddles stood in the lane, and the trees and fences they passed still dripped. The earl walked the horses out of the village and into the countryside.

"Where are we going?" she asked.

"Mr. Durbin's sheep have begun to lamb, and I wanted to see how the ewes are doing." He cleared his throat. "I suppose I should have told you about today's outing earlier."

Anna kept her eyes straight ahead and made a noncommittal sound.

He coughed. "I might've, had you not left so precipitously yesterday afternoon."

She arched a brow but did not reply.

There was a lengthy lull broken only by the dog's eager yelp as he flushed a rabbit from the hedge along the lane.

Then the earl tried again. "I've heard some people say my temper is rather . . ." He paused, apparently searching for a word.

Anna helped him. "Savage?"

He squinted at her.

"Ferocious?"

He frowned and opened his mouth.

She was quicker. "Barbaric?"

He cut her off before she could add to her list. "Yes, well, let us simply say that it intimidates some people." He hesitated. "I wouldn't want to intimidate you, Mrs. Wren."

"You don't."

He looked at her swiftly. He didn't say anymore, but his expression lightened. In another minute, he had kicked the bay into a gallop along the muddy lane, throwing up great clumps of earth. The dog gave chase with his tongue hanging from the side of his mouth.

Anna smiled for no reason and lifted her face to the soft morning breeze.

They continued down the lane until they came to a pasture bordered by a stream. The earl leaned down to unlatch the gate, and they rode in. As they neared the far corner, Anna saw that there were five men gathered close to the stream with a number of shepherd dogs milling about.

One of the men, an older fellow with grizzled hair, looked up at their approach. "Milord! Now, here's a right mess, then."

"Durbin." The earl nodded to the farmer and dismounted. He walked over to help Anna dismount. "What's the problem?" he asked over his shoulder.

"Ewes in th' stream." Durbin spat to the side. "Silly drabs. Must've followed each other down th' bank and now can't come up it. Three of them heavy with lamb, too."

"Ah." The earl approached the stream, and Anna followed. She could see now the five ewes caught in the swollen stream. The poor animals were tangled in the debris by an eddy. The bank was almost four feet deep at that particular point and was slippery with mud.

Lord Swartingham shook his head. "There's no help for it but to use brute force."

"Just what I was thinking meself." The farmer nodded approvingly at having his own idea confirmed.

Two men, along with the earl, lay flat on the stream's bank and reached down to pull on the sheep's wool. This, with the added incentive of the shepherd dogs harrying them from behind, convinced four of the ewes to scramble up the slimy bank. They tottered off, bleating their confusion at being so ill-used. The fifth ewe, however, was out of reach of the men on the bank. She was either too trapped or too stupid to climb from the stream on her own. Prostrate on her side, she bleated forlornly in the water.

"Gor. That one's good and stuck." Farmer Durbin sighed, and wiped his sweaty brow with the hem of his smock.

"Whyn't we send old Bess down to plague her, Da?" The farmer's eldest son fondled the ears of a black and white dog.

"Nay, lad. I don't want to lose Bess in the water. 'Tis over her head there. One of us'll have to go in after the daft beast."

"I'll do it, Durbin." The earl stepped away and took off his coat. He threw it to Anna, who barely caught it before it hit the ground. His waistcoat followed, and then he was pulling his fine lawn shirt over his head. He sat on the bank to wrestle off his jackboots.

Anna tried not to stare. She didn't often see a half-naked man. Actually, she couldn't remember ever seeing a man without a shirt in public. There were indented pox scars scattered across his torso, but she was more interested in other things. Her imagination had been correct. He did indeed have hair upon his chest. Quite a bit, in fact. Black swirls stretched across his breast and funneled down to his hard stomach. The hair narrowed to a thin ribbon that crossed his flat navel and then disappeared into his breeches.

The earl stood in his stockinged feet and half climbed, half slid down the steep bank and into the water. The muddy stream swirled around his hips as he waded to the side of the frightened ewe. He bent over the animal, working at the branches holding her. His wide shoulders gleamed with sweat and streaks of muck.

A shout rose from the watching men. The ewe was free, but in her haste to escape the stream, she had shouldered the earl, who went down in a geyser of muddy water. Anna gasped and started forward. Lord Swartingham's dog raced back and forth along the bank, barking excitedly. The earl emerged from the stream like a ragged Poseidon, water running in sheets off his torso. He was grinning even though his hair was plastered to his skull, the ribbon holding it having been lost in the stream.

The dog was still barking his disapproval of the whole proceeding. Meanwhile, the farmer and his relatives staggered about, gasping with laughter and slapping their knees. They were all but rolling on the ground in their hilarity. Anna sighed. Apparently an aristocrat getting a dunking was the most amusing thing the men had ever seen. Males were very perplexing at times.

"Oy! Milord! Do you always have trouble holding your wenches?" one of the men shouted.

"Nay, lad, she just didn't like the feel of his hand on her arse." The farmer made a graphic gesture that sent the men off again.

The earl laughed, but nodded toward Anna. Thus reminded of her presence, the men stopped their jests, although they continued to snigger. The earl lifted both hands to slick the water from his face.

Anna caught her breath at the sight. With his hands at the back of his head, squeezing the water from his hair, his muscles stood out in sharp relief. The sun glinted off his flexed arms and chest, and his black underarm hair curled damply. Rivulets of grimy water, mixed with blood from the ewe, ran down his chest and arms. His low-slung breeches clung to his hips and thighs, delineating the bulge of his manhood. He looked quite pagan.

Anna shivered.

The earl waded to shore and climbed the bank with a helping hand from the farmer's sons. Anna gave herself a shake and hurried over with his clothes.

He used the fine lawn shirt as a towel and then threw on his coat over his bare chest. "Well, Durbin, I hope you will call me the next time you are unable to handle a female."

"Aye, milord." The farmer slapped Lord Swartingham on the back. "My thanks for helping us out. Don't remember when I've seen a grander splash."

That set the men off again, and it was some little while before the earl and Anna could leave. By the time they were mounted, the earl's body was shaking with cold, but he showed no sign of hurry.

"You'll catch your death of cold, my lord," Anna said. "Please ride on to the Abbey ahead of me. You can go much faster without Daisy and me to slow you down."

"I'm quite all right, Mrs. Wren," he replied through teeth clenched to keep them from chattering. "Besides, I wouldn't want to be deprived of your dulcet company for even a moment."

Anna glared at him for she knew he was being sarcastic. "You don't have to prove how manly you are by catching the ague."

"So you consider me manly, Mrs. Wren?" He grinned like a little boy. "I was beginning to think that I battled a stinking sheep for nothing."

Anna tried, but it was impossible to keep her mouth from twitching. "I didn't know landowners helped their tenants so," she said. "Surely it is unusual?"

"Oh, certainly unusual," he replied. "I suppose the majority of my peers sit in London letting their arses widen while their stewards run their estates."

"Then why do you choose to wade into muddy streams after sheep?"

The earl shrugged his damp shoulders. "My father taught me that a good landowner knows his tenants and what they are doing. Then, too, I am more involved because of my agricultural studies." He shrugged again and smiled at her rather ironically. "And I'm fond of wrestling ewes and the like."

Anna returned the smile. "Did your father wrestle ewes as well?"

There was a silence, and she feared for a moment that she'd asked too personal a question.

"No, I don't remember him getting that dirty." Lord Swartingham watched the road ahead. "But he didn't mind wading into a flooded field in spring or overseeing the harvest in fall. And he always took me with him to mind the people and the land."

"He must've been a wonderful father," she murmured. *To have raised such a wonderful son.*

"Yes. If I'm only half as good a father to my own children, I'll be content." He looked curiously at her. "You had no children from your marriage?"

Anna glanced down at her hands. They were clenched in fists over the reins. "No. We were married for four years, but it was not God's will to grace us with children."

"I'm sorry." There seemed to be honest regret in the earl's eyes.

"As am I, my lord." *Every day.*

They were silent then until Ravenhill Abbey came into sight.

WHEN ANNA REACHED home that evening, Pearl was sitting up in bed and eating soup with Fanny's help. She was still thin, but her hair had been pulled back from her temples with a bit of ribbon, and she wore one of the little maid's old dresses. Anna took over the duty and sent Fanny down to finish making the supper.

"I forgot to thank you, ma'am," Pearl said shyly.

"It's quite all right." Anna smiled. "I only hope you feel better soon."

The other woman sighed. "Oh, I just need some rest, mostly."

"Are you from around here, or were you traveling through when you became ill?" Anna proffered a bit of beef.

Pearl chewed slowly and swallowed. "No, ma'am. I was trying to get back to London where I live. A gent brought me out here in a fine carriage promising to set me up proper like."

Anna raised her brows.

"I thought he was going to put me up in a little cottage." Pearl smoothed the sheet under her fingers. "I'm getting older, you know. I can't be working too much longer."

Anna remained silent.

"But it were just a con," Pearl said. "He only wanted me for a party with some friends."

Anna cast about for something to say. "I'm sorry it wasn't a permanent position."

"Yeah. And that weren't even the worst of it. He expected me to entertain him and his two friends." Pearl's mouth twisted down.

Two friends? "You mean you were to, um, entertain three gentlemen at once?" Anna asked faintly.

Pearl pursed her lips and nodded. "Yeah. All together or one after another." She must have seen Anna's shock. "Some of them fine gentlemen likes to do it together, sort of showing off to each other. But the girl gets hurt lots of times."

Good Lord. Anna stared at Pearl, appalled.

"But it don't really matter," Pearl continued. "I walked out."

Anna could only manage a nod.

"Then I started feeling bad on the coach back. I must've dozed off, 'cause next thing I knew, my purse was gone and I was having to try to walk since the coach wouldn't let me back on without my money." Pearl shook her head. "I would've been dead for sure if you hadn't found me when you did."

Anna looked down at her palms. "May I ask you a question, Pearl?"

"Sure. Go ahead." The other woman folded her hands at her waist and nodded. "Ask me anything you want."

"Have you heard of an establishment called Aphrodite's Grotto?"

Pearl cocked her head back against the pillow and looked at Anna curiously. "I didn't think a lady like you knew about such places, ma'am."

Anna avoided Pearl's gaze. "I heard it mentioned by some gentlemen. I don't think they knew I'd overheard."

"I don't guess not," Pearl agreed. "Why, Aphrodite's Grotto is a real high-priced bawdy house. The girls who work there have it soft, that's for sure. 'Course, I've heard that some high-class ladies go there with their faces hidden by a mask to pretend to be what I am."

Anna's eyes widened. "You mean . . . ?"

"They take whatever gent that catches their fancy in the room below and spends the night with them." Pearl nodded matter-of-factly. "Or however long they want. Some even take a room and instruct the madam to send up a man of a certain description. Maybe a short, blond fellow or a tall, red-headed one."

"It sounds a bit like picking a horse." Anna wrinkled her nose.

Pearl gave the first smile Anna had seen. "That's clever, ma'am. Like picking a stud." She laughed. "I wouldn't mind being the one that does the choosing for once, instead of the gents always getting to do the deciding."

Anna smiled a little uncomfortably at this reminder of the realities of Pearl's profession. "But why would a gentleman submit to such an arrangement?"

"The gents like it because they know they're getting to spend the night with a real lady." The other woman shrugged. "If you can call her a lady."

Anna blinked and then shook herself. "I'm keeping you from your rest. I'd better go see about my own supper."

"All right, then." Pearl yawned. "Thank you again."

All through supper that evening, Anna was distracted. Pearl's comment that it would be nice to do the choosing for once kept running through her head. She poked rather absently at her meat pie. It was true, even on her level of society, that the men got to do most of the choosing. A young lady waited for a gentleman to come calling, while the gentleman was able to decide which young ladies to court. Once married, a respectable woman waited dutifully for her husband in the marriage bed. The man made the overtures of marital relations. Or not, as the case may be. At least it had been so in Anna's marriage. She'd certainly never let Peter know she might have needs of her own or that she might not be satisfied with what occurred in bed.

Later that night, as Anna got ready for sleep, she couldn't stop imagining Lord Swartingham in Aphrodite's Grotto as Pearl had described it. The earl being sighted and chosen by some daring woman of the aristocracy. The earl spending the night in a masked lady's arms. The thoughts made her chest hurt even as she fell asleep.

And then she was in Aphrodite's Grotto.

She wore a mask and searched for the earl. Men of every description, old, young, fair, and ugly, hundreds of men, filled a hall to overflowing. Frantically, she pushed through the mass, hunting for a singular pair of black, gleaming eyes, becoming more desperate the longer her search took. Finally, she saw him across the room, and she started running toward him. But as is the way with such nightmares, the faster she tried to run, the slower she went. Each step seemed to take an eternity. As she struggled, she saw another masked woman beckon to him. Without ever having seen her, he turned away and followed the other woman from the room.

Anna awoke in the dark, her heart pounding and her skin chilled. She lay absolutely still, remembering the dream and listening to her own roughened breathing.

It was some time before she realized she was weeping.

Chapter Seven

*The huge raven flew with his new wife on his back for
two days and two nights until on the third day, they
came to fields golden with ripened grain.
"Who owns these fields?" Aurea asked, looking
down from her perch.
"Your husband," the raven replied.
They came to an endless meadow filled with fat
cattle, their hides shining in the sun.
"Who owns these cattle?" Aurea asked.
"Your husband," the raven replied.
Then a vast emerald forest spread below, rolling
over hills as far as the eye could see.
"Who owns this forest?" Aurea asked.
"Your husband!" the raven cawed. . . .*
—from *The Raven Prince*

Anna walked to Ravenhill the next morning feeling tired
and low after a restless night. She paused for a moment to
admire the sea of bluebells blooming under the trees that
lined the drive. The azure dots sparkled in the sunlight,
like newly minted coins. Usually the sight of any flower

brought a lightness to her heart, but today they did not. She sighed and continued her journey until she rounded a curve and stopped short. Lord Swartingham, striding briskly in his habitual mud-spattered boots, was coming from the stables and hadn't caught sight of her yet.

He gave a terrific bellow. "DOG!"

For the first time that day, Anna smiled. Evidently the earl couldn't find the ever-present canine and was reduced to roaring its common name.

She strolled toward him. "I don't see why he should respond to that."

Lord Swartingham swung around at the sound of her voice. "I believe that I gave the job of naming the mongrel to you, Mrs. Wren."

Anna opened her eyes wide. "I did offer three different options, my lord."

"And all of them were out of the question, as you well know." He smiled evilly. "I think I've given you quite enough time to come up with a name. You shall produce one now."

She was amused by his obvious intention to put her on the spot. "Stripe?"

"Too juvenile."

"Tiberius?"

"Too imperial."

"Othello?"

"Too murderous." Lord Swartingham folded his arms across his chest. "Come, come, Mrs. Wren. A woman of your wit can do better than this."

"How about 'Jock,' then?"

"That won't do."

"Why not?" Anna retorted saucily. "I like the name Jock."

"Jock." The earl seemed to roll the name on his tongue.

"I wager the dog will come if I call him by that name."

"Ha." He stared down his nose in the superior manner of males the world over when dealing with silly females. "You are welcome to try."

"Very well, I shall." She tilted her chin. "And if he comes, you must show me around the Abbey's gardens."

Lord Swartingham raised his eyebrows. "And if he doesn't come?"

"I don't know." She hadn't thought that far ahead. "Name your prize."

He pursed his lips and contemplated the ground at his feet. "I believe it is traditional in wagers between a woman and a man for the gentleman to ask for a favor from the lady."

Anna drew in a breath and then had trouble releasing it.

The earl's black eyes glittered at her from beneath his brows. "Perhaps a kiss?"

Oh, dear. Possibly she had been precipitous. Anna let out her breath in a puff and straightened her shoulders. "Very well."

He waved a languid hand. "Proceed."

Anna cleared her throat. "Jock!"

Nothing.

"*Jock!*"

Lord Swartingham began to smirk.

Anna drew a deep breath and let loose a most unlady-like shriek. "JOCK!"

They both listened for the dog. Nothing.

The earl slowly pivoted to face her, the crunching of his boots in the gravel drive loud in the stillness. They stood only a few feet distant. He took a step, his beautiful, heavy-lidded eyes intent on her face.

Anna could feel the blood pounding in her chest. She licked her lips.

His gaze dropped to her mouth, and his nostrils flared. He took another step, and they were now only a foot apart. As if in a dream, she saw his hands rise and grip her arms, felt the pressure of his big fingers through her mantle and gown.

Anna began to tremble.

He bent his dark head toward hers, and his warm breath caressed her lips. She closed her eyes.

And heard the dog clatter into the yard.

Anna opened her eyes. Lord Swartingham was frozen. Slowly, he turned his head, still only inches from hers, to stare at the canine. The dog grinned back, tongue hanging from his mouth, panting.

"Shit," the earl breathed.

Quite, Anna thought.

He let go of her suddenly, stepped away, and turned his back. He ran both hands through his hair and shook his shoulders. She heard him take a deep breath, but his voice was still husky when he spoke. "It appears you have won the wager."

"Yes, my lord." She hoped she sounded sufficiently nonchalant, as if she was used to having gentlemen nearly kiss her in their driveways. As if she wasn't having trouble catching her breath. As if she didn't desperately wish the dog had stayed far, far away.

"I'll be pleased to show you the gardens," the earl muttered, "such as they are, after luncheon. Perhaps you can work in the library until then?"

"Won't you be coming to the library as well?" She tried to conceal her disappointment.

He still hadn't turned to face her. "I find that there are matters that need my attention around the estate."

"Of course," Anna murmured.

He finally looked at her. She noticed his eyes were still heavy lidded, and she rather fancied he glanced at her bosom. "I'll see you at luncheon."

She nodded, and the earl snapped his fingers at the dog. As he passed her, she thought she heard him mutter something to the beast. It sounded more like *idiot* than *Jock*.

JESUS GOD, WHAT was I thinking? Edward strode angrily around the Abbey.

He'd deliberately maneuvered Mrs. Wren into an untenable position. There was no way she could have denied his crude advances. As if a woman of her fine sensibilities would have welcomed a kiss from a pox-scarred man such as he. But he hadn't thought of his scars when he drew her into his arms. He hadn't thought of anything. He'd acted on pure instinct: the lust to touch that beautiful, erotic mouth. His cock had been full, achingly erect, in seconds at the mere thought. He'd nearly been unable to let go of Mrs. Wren when the dog had showed up, and then he'd been forced to turn his back to keep her from getting an eyeful. He still hadn't relaxed.

"And what were you doing, Jock?" Edward growled down at the happily oblivious mastiff. "Your timing needs work, lad, if you want to continue devouring the bounty of the Abbey's kitchen."

Jock grinned an adoring doggy grin up at him. One ear was flopped inside out, and Edward straightened it absently. "A minute earlier or a minute later—preferably later—would've been a better moment to come gamboling up."

He sighed. He couldn't let this rampant lust continue. He liked the woman, for God's sake. She was witty and unafraid of his temper. She asked questions about his agricultural studies. She rode about his fields through mud and muck without a word of complaint. She even seemed to enjoy their jaunts. And sometimes when she looked at him, her head tilted to the side and all her attention focused solely on him, there was something that seemed to turn in his chest.

He frowned and kicked a pebble on the path.

It was unfair and dishonorable to subject Mrs. Wren to his brutish advances. He shouldn't be combating thoughts of her soft breasts, wondering if she had pale pink nipples or if they were a deeper rose color. Contemplating whether her nipples would pucker up immediately when he drew his thumb across them or wait coyly for the feel of his tongue.

Hell.

He half laughed, half groaned. His cock was once again at stand and pulsing with blood at just the thought of her. His body hadn't been this out of control since he'd been a lad with a newly deepened voice.

He kicked another pebble and stopped on the path, hands on hips, to tip his head back to the sky.

It was no use. Edward rolled his head back against his shoulders, trying to ease the tension. He would have to make a trip to London soon to spend a night or even two at Aphrodite's Grotto. Perhaps after that he could be in his secretary's presence without lustful thoughts taking over his mind.

He ground the pebble he had been kicking into the mud as he pivoted and started back to the stables. He was approaching the idea of going to London as a chore. He no longer anticipated spending the night in a demi-mondaine's bed. Instead, he felt weary. Weary and yearning for a woman he could not have.

LATER THAT AFTERNOON, Anna was reading *The Raven Prince* when the banging started. She'd only gotten as far as the third page, which described a magical battle between an evil prince and an enormous raven. It was an odd little fairy tale, but it was engrossing, and it took her a minute to recognize the sound of the Abbey's front door knocker. She'd never heard it before. Most of the callers to the Abbey came by way of the servants' entrance.

She slipped the book back into her desk and picked up a quill as she listened to the sound of rapid footsteps, probably the footman, in the hall answering the door. A vague murmur of voices, one of them feminine, then a lady's heels tapped toward the library. The footman threw open the door, and Felicity Clearwater strolled in.

Anna stood. "Can I help you?"

"Oh, don't get up. I don't want to disturb your duties." Felicity flicked a hand in her direction as she inspected the rickety iron ladder in the corner. "I've just come to deliver an invitation for Lord Swartingham to my spring soiree." She stroked a gloved fingertip over an iron rail and wrinkled her nose at the rust-colored dust that came away.

"He isn't in at the moment," Anna said.

"No? Then I must entrust it with you." Felicity sauntered to the desk and produced a heavily embossed envelope from a pocket. "You will give this . . ." She was holding out the envelope, but her words trailed away as she looked at Anna.

"Yes?" Anna self-consciously brushed a hand over her hair. Did she have a smudge on her face? Something caught between her teeth? Felicity looked as if she'd solidified into marble. Surely dirt couldn't justify that much shock.

The embossed velum in Felicity's hand trembled and fell to the desk. She glanced away, and the moment was gone.

Anna blinked. Perhaps she'd imagined the look.

"Do make sure Lord Swartingham receives my invitation, won't you?" Felicity was saying. "I'm certain he won't want to miss the most important social event in the area." She aimed a brittle smile in Anna's direction and walked out the door.

Anna absently dropped her hand to her throat and felt cool metal under her palm. She wrinkled her brow as she remembered. This morning as she'd dressed, she had thought the fichu about her neck rather plain. She'd rummaged in the tiny box that held her meager stock of jewelry, but her only pin was too big. Then her fingers had touched the locket she'd found in Peter's case. This time she'd experienced only a twinge when she saw the locket. Perhaps it was losing the power to hurt her, and she'd thought, *Well, why not?* and defiantly pinned the locket at her neck.

Anna fingered the trinket at her throat. It was cold and hard under her hand, and she wished that she'd not given in to her morning impulse.

DAMN! DAMN! DAMN! Felicity stared sightlessly from her carriage as it bumped away from Ravenhill Abbey. She'd not endured eleven years of groping and poking by a man old enough to be her grandfather to have it all fall apart now.

One would think that Reginald Clearwater's quest for children had been satisfied with the four grown sons his first two wives had borne him, not to mention the six daughters. After all, Felicity's predecessor had died giving birth to his youngest male offspring. But no, Reginald was obsessed with his own potency and the task of getting children on his wife. There were times during his twice-weekly marital visits when she wondered if it were really worth all this trouble. The man had run through three wives and still didn't have any skill in the bedchamber.

Felicity snorted.

But despite its downside, she absolutely adored being the squire's wife. Clearwater Hall was the largest house in the county, excepting, of course, Ravenhill Abbey. She had a generous clothing allowance and her own carriage.

She looked forward to lovely—and very expensive—jewelry every birthday. And the local shopkeepers nearly genuflected when she called. All in all, it was a life well worth preserving.

Which brought her back to the problem of Anna Wren.

Felicity touched her hair, skimming over it, checking for strands out of place. How long had Anna known? Impossible that the locket had been an accident. Coincidences of that magnitude just did not happen, which meant the wretched woman was taunting her after all this time. The letter that Felicity'd written to Peter had been penned in the heat of lust and was quite, quite damning. She'd placed it in the locket he'd given her and handed it to him, never thinking he would keep the silly thing. And then he'd died, and she'd been on tenterhooks, waiting for Anna to come calling with the evidence. When the locket had not turned up in the first couple of years, she'd thought Peter had either sold it or buried it—along with the letter inside—before he'd died.

Men! What useless creatures they were—aside from the obvious.

Felicity drummed her fingers on the windowsill. The only reasons for Anna to show her the locket now were either revenge or blackmail. She grimaced and ran her tongue along her front teeth, feeling their edges. Dainty, smooth, and sharp. Very sharp. If little Anna Wren thought she could frighten Felicity Clearwater, she was about to find out just how very mistaken she was.

"I BELIEVE I OWE you a forfeit, Mrs. Wren," the earl announced as he stalked into the library later that afternoon.

The sun streaming in the windows highlighted silver threads in Lord Swartingham's hair. His boots were muddy again.

Anna laid down her quill and held out her hand to Jock, who had accompanied his master into the room. "I was beginning to think you'd forgotten this morning's debt, my lord."

He arched an arrogant brow. "Are you impugning my honor?"

"If I were, would you call me out?"

He made an inelegant sound. "No. You'd probably win if I did. I'm not a particularly good shot, and my sword work needs practice."

Anna raised her chin loftily. "Then perhaps you should be careful what you say to me."

One corner of Lord Swartingham's mouth curled up. "Are you coming to the garden, or do you wish to continue bandying words with me here?"

"I don't see why we cannot do both," she murmured, and gathered her wrap.

She took his arm, and they strolled out of the library. Jock trailed them, ears perked at the prospect of a ramble. The earl led her through the front door and around the corner of the Abbey past the stables. Here the cobblestones turned to mown grass. They passed a low hedge enclosing a kitchen garden to the side of the servants' entrance. Someone had already started leeks. Delicate green wisps lined a trench that would later be filled in as the plants grew. Beyond the kitchen garden was a sloped lawn at the bottom of which was a larger, walled garden. They picked their way down the slope on a gray slate walk. As they neared, Anna saw that ivy nearly obscured the old red bricks of the wall. A wooden door was hidden in the wall, overhung with brown vines.

Lord Swartingham took hold of the door's rusty iron handle and pulled. The door squeaked and opened an inch, then stopped. He muttered something and glanced at her.

She smiled encouragingly.

He wrapped both hands around the handle and braced his feet before yanking mightily. Nothing happened for a second, and then the door gave up with a groan. Jock shot through the opening into the garden. The earl stood aside and gestured her in with a wave of his hand.

She ducked her head to peer inside.

She saw a jungle. The garden appeared to be in the shape of a large rectangle. Or at least that had been its outline at one point. A brick path, barely discernible beneath debris, ran around the inside of the walls. It connected with a central walk in the shape of a cross that divided the garden into four smaller rectangles. The far wall held another door, almost hidden beneath the skeleton of a creeper. Perhaps a second garden or a series of gardens lay beyond.

"My grandmother laid out the original plans for these beds," the earl said from behind her. Somehow they'd gone through the doorway, although Anna didn't remember moving. "And my mother expanded and developed them."

"It must have been very beautiful once." She stepped over a break in the walkway where some of the bricks had heaved out of the ground. Was the tree in the corner a pear?

"Not much left of all her work, is there?" he replied. She could hear him kicking at something. "I suppose it would be best simply to have the walls torn down and the place leveled."

Anna jerked her head around to him. "Oh, no, my lord. You mustn't do that."

He frowned at her protest. "Why not?"

"There's too much here that can be saved."

The earl assessed the overgrown garden and ruined walk with clear skepticism. "I don't see even one thing worth saving."

She shot him an exasperated glance. "Why, look at the espaliered trees on the walls."

He swiveled to where she pointed.

Anna began picking her way to the wall. She stumbled over a rock hidden in the weeds and righted herself only to catch her toe again. Strong arms caught her from behind and lifted her easily. In two long strides, Lord Swartingham was by the wall.

He set her down. "Is this what you want to see?"

"Yes." Anna, breathless, peeked at him sideways.

He stared rather grimly at the espaliered tree.

"Thank you." She turned back to the pathetic tree against the wall and was immediately distracted. "I think it's an apple tree or perhaps a pear. You can see where they're planted all around the garden walls. And this one here is in bud."

The earl dutifully examined the branch indicated. He grunted.

"And really all they need is some good pruning," she chattered on. "You could make your own cider."

"I've never much liked cider."

She lowered her brows at him. "Or you could have Cook make apple jelly."

He arched an eyebrow.

She almost defended the merits of apple jelly, but then she spied a flower hiding in the weeds. "Do you think that's a violet or maybe a periwinkle?"

The flower was a couple of feet from the edge of a bed. Anna bent from the waist to get a closer look, placing one hand on the ground to steady herself.

"Or perhaps a forget-me-not, although usually they bloom in big groups." She carefully plucked the flower. "No, I'm silly. Look at the leaves."

Lord Swartingham was very still behind her.

"I think it may be a type of hyacinth." She straightened and turned to consult him.

"Oh?" The single word came out a baritone guttural.

She blinked at his voice. "Yes, and of course where there's one, there's always more."

"Of what?"

She narrowed her eyes suspiciously. "You haven't been listening to me, have you?"

He shook his head. "No."

He was watching her intently, in such a way that Anna's breath quickened. She could feel her face heat. In the quiet, the breeze playfully blew a thin lock of hair across her mouth. He reached out very slowly and brushed it away with the tips of his fingers. The calluses on his hand rasped against the sensitive skin of her lips, and she closed her eyes in yearning. He carefully tucked the lock back into her coiffure, his hand lingering at her temple.

She felt his breath caress her lips. *Oh, please.*

And then he dropped his hand.

Anna opened her eyes and met his obsidian gaze. She stretched out her own hand to protest—or perhaps touch his face, she wasn't sure, and it didn't matter anyway. He'd already whirled and paced a few steps away from her. She didn't think he had even noticed her own aborted gesture.

He turned his head so that she could see only his face in profile. "I beg your pardon."

"Why?" She tried to smile. "I—"

He made a chopping motion with the blade of his hand. "I will be traveling tomorrow to London. I fear I have some business there that can no longer wait."

Anna squeezed her hands into fists.

"You may continue admiring the garden if you wish. I need to return to my writing." He strode rapidly away, his boots grinding against the broken bricks.

Anna opened her clenched fists and felt the crushed flower slip from her fingers.

She glanced around the ruined garden. It had so many possibilities. Some weeding by the wall over there, some planting in the bed here. No garden was ever truly dead if a proper gardener knew how to nurture it. Why, it only needed a bit of care, a bit of love. . . .

A veil of tears obscured her eyes. She wiped at them irritably with a trembling hand. She'd forgotten her handkerchief inside. The tears overflowed her eyes and rolled to her chin. Bother. She'd have to use her sleeve to mop them. What sort of lady was caught without a handkerchief? A pitiful sort of one, obviously. The sort a gentleman couldn't bring himself to kiss. She scrubbed her face with the inside of her forearm, but the tears kept reappearing. As if she'd believe that nonsense about work in London! She was a mature woman. She knew where the earl meant to do his work. In that nasty brothel.

She caught her breath on a sob. He was going to London to bed another woman.

Chapter Eight

The raven flew with Aurea for another day and night,
and everything she saw in that time belonged to him.
Aurea tried to comprehend such wealth, such power,
but it was beyond understanding. Her own father had
only commanded a small portion of the people and
lands that this bird seemed to own. Finally, on the
fourth evening, she saw a great castle, made entirely
of white marble and gold. The setting sun reflecting
off it was so bright it made her eyes hurt.
"Who owns this castle?" Aurea whispered, and
a nameless dread filled her heart.
The raven turned his huge head and regarded her with
a glinting black eye. "Your husband!" he cackled. . . .
—from *The Raven Prince*

That evening, Anna trudged home alone. After she'd
pulled together her wits in the ruined garden, she'd returned to the library intending to work. She needn't have
bothered. Lord Swartingham hadn't appeared all the rest
of the afternoon, and as she was gathering her things at
the end of the day, a young footman had brought her a

small folded card. It was brief and to the point. His lordship would be leaving very early in the morning, and thus
he would not see her before he left. He sent his regrets.

Since the earl wasn't around to protest, Anna walked
home instead of taking the carriage, partly in rebellion,
partly because she needed time alone to think and compose herself. It wouldn't do to return home with her face
long and her eyes red. Not unless she wanted to be
quizzed half the night by Mother Wren.

By the time Anna reached the outskirts of town, her
feet were aching. She'd become used to the luxury of the
carriage. She trudged on and turned into her lane, and
there she stopped. A scarlet and black coach with gilt trim
stood before her door. The coachman and the two footmen lounging against the vehicle wore matching black
livery edged with scarlet piping and yards of gilt braid.
Beside the vehicle, a gang of small boys hopped about, interrogating the footmen. Anna couldn't blame them—it
looked like minor royalty had come to call on her. She sidled around the carriage and entered her cottage.

Inside, Mother Wren and Pearl were having tea in the
sitting room with a third woman whom Anna had never
seen before. The woman was quite young, barely in her
twenties. Ice-white powdered hair swept up her forehead
in a deceptively simple style, setting off strange, light
green eyes. She wore a black gown. Black usually indicated mourning, but Anna had never seen a mourning
gown quite like this one. A cascade of shining jet-black
material flowed around the sitting woman, and the over-
skirt pulled back to reveal scarlet embroidery on the petti-
coat below. The vivid stitching repeated on the low,

square neckline and triple tiers of lace falling from the half sleeves. She looked as out of place in Anna's little sitting room as a peacock in a hen yard.

Mother Wren looked up brightly at Anna's entrance. "Dear, this is Coral Smythe, Pearl's younger sister. We've just been having a dish of tea." She gestured with her cup, almost sloshing the tea into Pearl's lap in the process. "My daughter-in-law, Anna Wren."

"How do you do, Mrs. Wren?" Coral spoke in a deep, husky voice that sounded like it should be coming from a man instead of an exotic young woman.

"I'm pleased to meet you," Anna murmured as she accepted a cup of tea.

"We must be leaving soon if we're to make London before dawn," Pearl said.

"Are you recovered enough for the journey, sister?" Coral showed little emotion on her face, but she watched Pearl intently.

"Surely you will spend the night with us, Miss Smythe?" Mother Wren asked. "Then Pearl will have a fresh start in the morning."

Coral's lips curved in a meager smile. "I would not wish to inconvenience you, Mrs. Wren."

"Oh, it's not an inconvenience. It's nearly dark out, and I can't think it would be safe for two young ladies to travel right now." Mother Wren nodded toward the window, which was indeed almost black.

"Thank you." Coral inclined her head.

After they had finished the tea, Anna led Coral up to the room Pearl had been using so that the other woman could wash before supper. She brought some linens and fresh water for the basin and was turning to leave when Coral halted her.

"Mrs. Wren, I wish to thank you." Coral watched Anna with fathomless pale green eyes. Her expression did not mirror her words.

"It's nothing, Miss Smythe," Anna replied. "We could hardly have sent you off to the inn."

"Of course you could." Coral's lips twisted in a sardonic grimace. "But that is not what I speak of. I want to thank you for helping Pearl. She has told me how sick she was. Had you not brought her into your home and cared for her, she would have died."

Anna shrugged uncomfortably. "Another person would've been along in a minute and—"

"And they would have left her there," Coral interrupted. "Do not tell me anyone would do the same as you. Anyone did not."

Anna was at a loss for words. Much as she would like to protest Coral's cynical view of humanity, she knew the other woman was right.

"My sister walked the streets to put food in my mouth when we were younger," Coral continued. "We were orphaned when she was barely fifteen, and soon thereafter, she was let go from her position as an underhousemaid in a fashionable house. She could have simply let me go to the poorhouse. Without me, she might have found another respectable job, perhaps married and had a family." Coral's lips tightened. "Instead she entertained men."

Anna winced, trying to imagine such a dismal life. Such a total lack of options.

"I have tried to persuade Pearl to let me support her now." Coral turned her head away. "But you do not want to hear our history. Suffice it to say that she is the only living thing on this earth that I love."

Anna was silent.

"If there is ever anything I can do for you, Mrs. Wren"—Coral's queer eyes bored into her—"you have but to name it."

"Your thanks is enough," Anna finally said. "I was glad to help your sister."

"You do not take my offer seriously, I see. But keep it in mind. Anything within my power I will do for you. Anything at all."

Anna nodded and started out of the room. *Anything at all* . . . She paused on the threshold and turned impulsively, before she had time to reconsider. "Have you heard of an establishment called Aphrodite's Grotto?"

"Yes." Coral's expression became opaque. "Yes, and I know the proprietress, Aphrodite herself. I can get you a night or a week of nights at Aphrodite's Grotto if that is your wish."

She stepped toward Anna.

"I can get you a night with an accomplished male whore or a virginal schoolboy." Coral's eyes widened and seemed to flame. "Famous libertines or ragpickers off the street. One very special man or ten complete strangers. Dark men, red men, yellow men, men you've only dreamed of in the black of night, lonely in your bed, snug under your covers. Whatever you long for. Whatever you desire. Whatever you crave. You have only to ask me."

Anna stared at Coral like a mesmerized mouse before a particularly beautiful snake.

She started to stutter a denial, but Coral waved an indolent hand. "Sleep on it, Mrs. Wren. Sleep on it, and on the morrow give me your reply. Now, if you do not mind, I wish to be alone."

Anna found herself in the hallway outside her own door. She shook her head. Could the devil assume the guise of a woman?

Because temptation had surely been set before her.

She walked slowly down the stairs, Coral's seductive offer lodged in her brain. She tried to shake it off, but to her horror, she found that she simply couldn't. And the more she thought about Aphrodite's Grotto, the more acceptable it became.

During the night, Anna changed her mind about Coral's outrageous offer over and over again. She would wake from hazy, ominous dreams to lie debating, only to drift off again into a world where Lord Swartingham was eternally strolling away and she futilely running after. Toward morning, she gave up the pretense of sleep and lay on her back staring sightlessly at the still-dark ceiling. She clasped her hands beneath her chin like a little girl and prayed to God to let her resist this terrible proposition. A virtuous woman should have no trouble resisting, she was sure. A proper lady would never think of sneaking off to the dens of London to seduce a man who had made it abundantly clear that he was not interested in her.

When Anna opened her eyes again, it was daylight. She got up stiffly and washed her face and throat in the chilly water in the basin, then dressed and stole quietly out the door so as not to awaken her mother-in-law.

She went out to her flower garden. Unlike the earl's garden, hers was small and neat. The crocuses were mostly over now, but some late daffodils remained. She bent to deadhead a daffodil that had stopped blooming. The sight of the tulips in bud momentarily brought peace back to her soul. Then she remembered the earl would be traveling to London today. She squeezed her eyes tight to shut out the thought.

At that moment, she heard a footstep behind her. "Have you made your decision, Mrs. Wren?"

She swiveled and saw a lovely Mephistopheles with pale green eyes. Coral smiled at her.

Anna started to shake her head, but then heard herself say, "I'll accept your offer."

Coral's smile widened into a perfect, mirthless curve. "Good. You may accompany Pearl and me back to London in my carriage." She gave a low laugh. "This should prove interesting."

She reentered the cottage before Anna could think of a reply.

"WHOA, THERE," EDWARD murmured to the bay. He held its head and patiently waited as the horse stomped and mouthed the bit. The bay was often fractious in the morning, and he'd saddled the horse earlier than usual. The sky was only just beginning to brighten to the east.

"Whoa, you old bastard," he whispered. For the first time, it occurred to him that the horse he was talking to had no name. How long had he owned the bay? A half dozen years now, at least, and he'd never bothered to name him. Anna Wren would scold if she knew.

Edward winced as he finally mounted. That was exactly why he was making this trip: to drive thoughts of the widow from his mind. He'd chosen to work off some of the restlessness—both of body and of mind—by riding to London. His luggage and valet would follow behind in the carriage. But as if to mock that plan, the newly named Jock bounded up as soon as the bay clattered out of the stables. The dog raced out the door ahead of him; he had been missing the last half hour. Now his hindquarters were covered with malodorous mud.

Edward reined his horse around and sighed. He planned to visit his fiancée and her family this trip and finalize the engagement negotiations. An overlarge, smelly mongrel would not help his cause with the Gerard family.

"Stay, Jock."

The dog sat and regarded him with big, brown, only slightly bloodshot eyes. His tail swept the cobblestone behind him.

"I'm sorry, old man." Edward leaned down to ruffle the canine's ears. The nervous gelding sidled back a couple of steps, breaking the contact. "You'll have to stay here this time."

The dog cocked his head.

Edward felt a wash of unwelcome wistfulness. The dog didn't belong in his life and neither did the lady.

"Guard, Jock. Watch her for me, boy." He half smiled, half grimaced at his own whimsy. Jock was hardly a trained guard dog. And Anna Wren wasn't his to guard in any case.

Shaking the thoughts away, he wheeled the bay and cantered down the drive.

AFTER SOME CONSIDERATION, Anna told Mother Wren that she would be traveling to London with Pearl and Coral to buy material for new gowns.

"I'm so glad we can finally afford material, but are you sure?" Mother Wren responded. Her cheeks were a rose pink, and she continued in a lower voice, "They're very nice, of course, but they are, after all, courtesans."

Anna had difficulty meeting her eyes. "Coral is very grateful for the care we extended to Pearl. They're really quite close, you know."

"Yes, but—"

"And she has offered me the use of her carriage both to take me to London and to ride back again."

Mother Wren's brows knit uncertainly.

"It's a most generous offer," Anna said softly. "It'll save us the cost of a stagecoach ride, besides being more comfortable. I'll be able to buy additional fabric with the money we would've spent on the stage."

Mother Wren visibly wavered.

"Wouldn't you like a new gown?" she wheedled.

"Well, I do worry about your comfort, dear," Mother Wren finally said. "If you are happy with this arrangement, then so am I."

"Thank you." Anna kissed her on the cheek and ran up the stairs to finish packing.

The horses were already stomping outside when Anna came down again. She hurriedly said her good-byes and climbed in the carriage, where the Smythe sisters waited.

Anna waved out the window as they drove away, much to the amusement of Coral. She was about to draw her head back in when she caught sight of Felicity Clearwater standing down the street. Anna hesitated, her eyes meeting the other woman's. Then the carriage swept past, and she sat back in the seat. She bit her bottom lip. Felicity could not possibly know why she traveled to London, but seeing her still made Anna uneasy.

Across from her, Coral raised an eyebrow.

Anna grabbed the strap over her head as the carriage turned a corner, bouncing the women inside. She lifted her chin.

Coral smiled slightly and nodded.

They made a stop at Ravenhill Abbey so Anna could inform Mr. Hopple that she'd be absent from her work for a few days. The carriage waited at the end of the drive, out of sight, while she walked to the Abbey and back. It was not until she was almost returned to the carriage that she realized Jock was shadowing her.

She turned to face the dog. "Go back, Jock."

Jock sat down in the middle of the drive and regarded her calmly.

"Now, sir. Go home, Jock!" Anna pointed to the Abbey.

Jock turned his head to look in the direction of her finger, but didn't move.

"Fine, then," she huffed, feeling silly arguing with a dog. "I'll just ignore you."

Anna walked the rest of the way determinedly not paying attention to the enormous dog following her. But when she rounded the gates of the Abbey and saw the carriage, she knew she had a problem. The footman had caught sight of her and had opened the vehicle's door in anticipation of her entering it. There was a blur and a scrabble of claws on gravel as Jock dashed past her and leapt inside the carriage.

"Jock!" Anna was appalled.

From inside the carriage came a commotion that rocked it briefly from side to side; then it stood still. The footman stared in the door. She came alongside him and hesitantly peeked in as well.

Jock sat on one of the plush seats. Across from him, Pearl watched the dog, horrified. Coral, predictably, was unperturbed and smiling faintly.

Anna had forgotten how frightening Jock could be on first sight. "I'm so sorry. He's really quite harmless."

Pearl, rolling her eyes to the side to see her, looked unconvinced.

"Here, let me get him out," Anna said.

But this proved difficult. After one menacing growl from Jock, the footman made it clear that his job did not include handling dangerous animals. Anna scrambled into the carriage to try to cajole the dog out. When that did not work, she grabbed hold of the loose fur near his neck and attempted to drag him out. Jock simply set his feet and waited while she wrestled.

Coral started laughing. "It appears that your dog wants to come with us, Mrs. Wren. Leave him alone. I do not mind another passenger."

"Oh, I couldn't," Anna panted.

"Indeed you could. Do not let us argue. Come inside and protect Pearl and me from the beast."

Jock seemed content when Anna sat. Once it was established that he would not be ejected, he lay down and went to sleep. Pearl watched him tensely for a while. When he didn't move, her head began to nod. Anna rested against the fine plush carriage cushions and thought sleepily that they were even finer than Lord Swartingham's. In a little while, she, too, was asleep, weary from the lack of rest from the night before.

They stopped once in the afternoon for a late luncheon at an inn along the high road. Shouting ostlers ran out to hold the heads of the stomping horses while the women climbed down stiffly. The inn was surprisingly clean, and they enjoyed some nice boiled beef and cider. Anna made sure to bring a bit of the meat out to the carriage for Jock. Then she let him run around the yard and frighten the stable boys before they continued on their journey.

The sun had already set when the carriage drew up before a smart London row house. Anna was surprised at the luxury of the house, but then thought of Coral's carriage and realized she shouldn't be.

Coral must have noticed her gawking at the façade, because she smiled enigmatically. "All from the kindness of the marquis." She made a sweeping gesture, and her smile turned cynical. "My good friend."

Anna followed her up the front steps and into the shadowed entryway. Their footsteps echoed on gleaming white marble floors. The walls were paneled in white marble as well, leading up to a plastered ceiling with a glittering crystal chandelier. It was a very beautiful, but very empty entrance. She wondered if it reflected its current occupant or the absent owner.

Coral turned at that moment to Pearl, who was beginning to droop from the long ride. "I want you to stay here with me, sister."

"Your marquis won't like me staying here long. You know that." Pearl looked anxious.

Coral's lips twisted the slightest bit. "Let me worry about the marquis. He will understand my wishes. Besides, he is out of the country for the next two weeks." She smiled almost warmly. "Now let me show you to your rooms."

Anna's room was a pretty little chamber done in a dusky blue and white. Coral and Pearl bid her good night, and she made ready for bed. Jock sighed heavily and lay down before the fire in the grate. She brushed out her hair and talked to him. She very firmly didn't let herself think about the morrow. But as she lay down to sleep, all the thoughts she had tried to keep at bay rushed in. Was she about to commit a grave sin? Could she live with herself after tomorrow? Would she please the earl?

To her chagrin, it was this last thought that she worried over the most.

FELICITY LIT THE candelabra from her taper and set it carefully on the corner of the desk. Reginald had been particularly amorous tonight. A man of his age should have slowed down in his bed sport.

Felicity snorted to herself. The only thing that had slowed down was the time it took him to reach completion. She could've written a five-act play whilst he huffed and sweated over her. Instead, she'd pondered the reasons a provincial widow like Anna Wren might be journeying to London. The elder Mrs. Wren, when quizzed, had claimed the trip was to purchase materials for new dresses. A plausible excuse, true, but there were many other diversions an unattached lady might find in that city. So many, in fact, that Felicity thought it might be worthwhile to discover exactly what Anna did in London.

She pulled out a sheet of paper from her husband's desk and uncapped the inkwell. She inked her quill and then paused. Who among her acquaintances in London would be the best choice? Veronica was too curious. Timothy, while a racehorse between the sheets, had, unfortunately, the same mental capacity outside the bed. Then there was . . . Of course!

Felicity smiled in self-satisfaction as she traced the first letters in her missive. She wrote to a man who was not quite honest. Not quite a gentleman.

And not nice at all.

Chapter Nine

*The raven wheeled over the gleaming white castle,
and as he did so, scores of birds flew from the walls:
thrushes and titmice, sparrows and starlings, robins
and wrens. Every songbird Aurea could recognize and
many that she could not came to welcome them. The
raven landed and introduced them as his loyal
retainers and servants. But while the raven had the
power of human speech, these smaller birds did not.
That evening, the servant-birds led Aurea to a
magnificent dining room. There she saw a long table
splendidly prepared with delicacies she'd only
dreamed of. She expected the raven to dine with her,
but he did not appear, and she ate all alone.
Afterward, she was shown to a beautiful room and
found there a nightgown of gauzy silk that was
already laid out for her on the big bed. She dressed
in this and climbed into the bed, falling immediately
into a deep, dreamless sleep. . . .*
—from *The Raven Prince*

The damned wig itched like bloody hell.

Edward balanced a plate of meringues on his lap and wished he could poke a finger under his powdered wig. Or just take the cursed thing off. But wigs were de rigueur in polite society, and visiting his prospective bride and her family definitely qualified. He'd ridden all day yesterday to get to London and had arisen unfashionably early this morning, as was his wont. And then he'd had to cool his heels for several hours before it was deemed an appropriate time to go calling. Damn society and its asinine rules anyway.

Across from him, his future mother-in-law talked to the room at large. Or, rather, lectured. Lady Gerard was a handsome woman with a broad forehead and round, light blue eyes. She capably debated the current fashion in hats all by herself. Not a topic he himself would have chosen, and by the nodding of Sir Richard's head, not one of the older man's favorites either. It would seem, however, that once Lady Gerard started talking, only an act of God could stop her. Such as a bolt of lightning. Edward narrowed his eyes. Perhaps not even that.

Sylvia, his intended, sat gracefully across from him. Her eyes were as round and blue as Lady Gerard's. She had the true English coloring: a healthy peaches-and-cream complexion and thick golden hair. She reminded him not a little of his own mother.

Edward took a sip of tea and wished it was whiskey. On the little table beside Sylvia sat a vase of poppies. The flowers were bright scarlet, and they perfectly accented the yellow and orange room. They, along with the girl perched next to them in her indigo gown, made a picture worthy of a master. Had her mother posed her there? Lady Gerard's shrewd blue eyes flashed as she expounded on gauze.

Definitely posed.

Except poppies didn't bloom in March. These must have cost a pretty penny because it was impossible to tell unless one studied the blooms closely that they were made of silk and wax.

He set aside his plate. "Would you mind showing me your gardens, Miss Gerard?"

Lady Gerard, caught in a pause, gave permission with a satisfied smile.

Sylvia rose and proceeded him through the French doors into the compact town garden, her skirts swishing behind her. They strolled silently down the path, her fingers lightly resting on his sleeve. Edward tried to think of something to say, a light conversational topic, but his mind was strangely blank. One did not discuss crop rotation with a lady, nor how to drain a field or the newest techniques in composting. In fact, there was nothing at all that interested him that he could safely discuss with a young lady.

He glanced down at his feet and noticed a small yellow flower, not a daffodil or primrose. Edward stooped to finger it, wondering if Mrs. Wren had one like it in her garden.

"Do you know what this is?" he asked Miss Gerard.

Sylvia bent to examine the flower. "No, my lord." Her smooth brows knit. "Shall I ask the gardener for you?"

"No need." He straightened and dusted off his hands. "I just wondered."

They'd reached the end of the path where a little stone bench squatted against the garden wall.

Edward withdrew a large white handkerchief from his coat and laid it on the bench. He gestured with one hand. "Please."

The girl settled gracefully and folded her hands in her lap.

He clasped his hands behind his back and absently watched the little yellow flower. "Does this alliance suit you, Miss Gerard?"

"Perfectly, my lord." Sylvia didn't look at all perturbed by the bluntness of his question.

"Then will you do me the honor of becoming my wife?"

"Yes, my lord."

"Good." Edward bent to kiss the dutifully presented cheek.

His wig itched more than ever.

"THERE YOU ARE." Coral's voice broke the silence in the little library. "I am glad you found something of interest."

Anna nearly dropped the illustrated book in her hands. She whirled to find the other woman watching her with an amused look on her face.

"I'm sorry. I guess I'm still keeping country hours. When I came down to the breakfast room, they weren't ready yet. The maid said I could look in here." Anna held up the open book in her hands as evidence, and then hastily lowered it when she remembered the explicit engravings inside.

Coral glanced at the volume. "That one is very good, but you might find this one more helpful for what you plan tonight." She crossed to another shelf, took down a slim green volume, and pressed it into Anna's hands.

"Oh. Um . . . thank you." Anna knew she was turning seven shades of red. Rarely had she been so mortified in her life.

In her yellow-sprigged morning gown, Coral looked no older than sixteen. She might have been a young lady of good family about to go out calling on other girlish acquaintances. Only her eyes spoiled the illusion.

"Come. Let us break our fast together." Coral led the way into the breakfast room where Pearl already sat.

There was a full sideboard of hot dishes, but Anna found she didn't have much appetite. She settled in a chair across from Coral with a plate of toast.

After they ate, Pearl excused herself and Coral leaned back in her chair. Anna felt her shoulder blades tense.

"Now," her hostess said, "perhaps we should make some plans for this evening."

"What do you suggest?" Anna asked.

"I have several dresses you might want to look at. Any one of them can be altered to fit you. In addition, we should discuss sponges."

"I beg your pardon?" Anna blinked. How were bathing sponges going to help her?

"You may not be aware of them." Coral sipped her tea serenely. "Sponges that can be inserted into the female body to prevent a child."

Anna's mind froze on the thought. She'd never heard of such a thing. "I . . . that's probably not necessary. I was married for four years without conceiving."

"Then we will disregard them."

Anna fingered her teacup.

Coral continued, "Do you plan to attend the downstairs reception at Aphrodite's Grotto to pick out a likely male or"—she regarded Anna shrewdly—"or do you have a specific gentleman you would like to meet there?"

Anna hesitated and took a sip of tea. How far could she trust Coral? Until now, she had rather naïvely followed Coral's lead, had literally done everything the woman had suggested. But she hardly knew her, after all. Could she entrust her with what she really wanted—with, in fact, Lord Swartingham's name?

Coral seemed to understand her silence. "I am a whore," she said. "And in addition to that, I am not a nice woman. But despite these facts, my word is gold." She watched Anna intently, as if it were very important that she believe her. "Gold. I swear to you that I will not knowingly harm or betray you or anyone who you hold dear."

"Thank you."

Coral's mouth twisted. "It is I who should thank you. Not everyone would take the word of a prostitute seriously."

Anna ignored that. "Yes, as you have guessed, I'd like to meet a particular gentleman." She took a deep breath. "The Earl of Swartingham."

Coral's eyes widened infinitesimally. "Have you made an appointment to rendezvous with Lord Swartingham at Aphrodite's Grotto?"

"No. He has no knowledge of this," Anna said firmly. "Nor do I want him to."

The other woman gave a tiny, breathy laugh. "Forgive me, I am puzzled. You wish to spend the night with the earl—intimately—without him being aware of it. Do you plan to drug him?"

"Oh, no. You mistake me." Her face must be permanently stained a deep red by this point, but Anna struggled on. "I do wish to spend the night with the earl—intimately. I just don't want him to know it is me, as it were."

Coral smiled and tilted her head skeptically. "How?"

"I'm explaining this badly." Anna blew out a sigh and tried to order her thoughts. "You see, the earl has traveled to London on business. I have reason to believe that he'll visit Aphrodite's Grotto, probably tonight." She bit her lip. "Although, I'm not sure exactly when."

"That can be ascertained," Coral said. "But how do you propose that he not know you?"

"Pearl has said that many ladies and demimondaines wear a mask when they visit Aphrodite's Grotto. I thought I might wear one as well."

"Hmm."

"You don't think it will work?" Anna anxiously tapped at the side of her teacup.

"You are employed by the earl, are you not?"

"I'm his secretary."

"In that case, you must be aware there is a much higher chance of him finding you out," Coral warned.

"But if I wear a mask—"

"There is still your voice, your hair, your figure." Coral ticked off each point on the tips of her fingers. "Even your scent, if he has been near enough to you."

"You're right, of course." Anna felt close to tears.

"I am not saying it cannot be done," Coral reassured her coolly. "Just . . . You do understand the risks?"

Anna tried to think. It was difficult to concentrate this close to what she wanted. "Yes. Yes, I think so."

Coral regarded her a moment more. Then she clapped her hands once. "Good. I think we shall first work on the costume. We will need a mask that conceals most of your face. Let us consult my maid, Giselle. She is very good with a needle."

"But how do we know if Lord Swartingham will visit tonight?" Anna protested.

"I almost forgot." Coral rang for writing utensils and began composing a letter at the breakfast room table. She talked as she wrote. "I know the proprietor and part owner of Aphrodite's Grotto. She used to go by Mrs. Lavender, but now she is Aphrodite herself. A money-grubbing old witch, but she owes me a favor. A rather large one as it happens. She probably thinks I have forgotten the matter, so she will be all the more disconcerted to receive this letter." Coral lifted her lips in a feral smile. "I make it a habit to never let a debt go, so in a way, you are doing me a kindness."

She blew upon the ink to dry it, folded and sealed the letter, then rang for a footman. "The gentlemen who patronize Aphrodite's Grotto often make an appointment in advance so that they may be assured a room and a woman for the night," Coral explained. "Mrs. Lavender will inform us if that is the case with your earl."

"And if it is?" Anna asked anxiously.

"Then we will plan." Coral poured more tea for them both. "Perhaps you can take a room, and we will have Mrs. Lavender send Lord Swartingham to you." She narrowed her eyes thoughtfully. "Yes, I think that is the best idea. We will have the room lit by only a few candles so he will not be able to see you well."

"Wonderful." Anna grinned.

Coral looked briefly startled and then smiled back with the most sincere expression Anna had ever seen on her face.

The plan just might work.

APHRODITE'S GROTTO WAS a splendid sham, Anna reflected that night as she peered from the carriage window. A four-story building, all white marble columns and gold leaf, the place was apparently magnificent. It was only on second glance that one noticed the marble of the columns was painted on and that the "gold" was tarnished brass. The carriage pulled into the mews behind the building and stopped.

Coral, sitting in the shadows across from Anna, leaned forward. "Are you ready, Mrs. Wren?"

Anna took a deep breath and checked that her mask was firmly tied on. "Yes."

She stood on shaky legs and followed Coral down from the carriage. Outside, a lantern by the back door threw a feeble light into the mews. As they picked their way up the path, a tall woman with hennaed hair opened the door.

"Ah, Mrs. Lavender," Coral drawled.

"Aphrodite, if you please," the woman snapped.

Coral inclined her head ironically.

They stepped into the lit hall, and Anna saw that Aphrodite wore a violet gown fashioned to look like a classical toga. A gold mask dangled from one hand. The madam turned shrewd eyes on Anna. "And you are . . . ?"

"A friend," Coral replied before Anna could say a word.

Anna shot her a grateful glance. She was very glad that Coral had insisted she don the mask before leaving the town house. It wouldn't be wise to expose herself to the madam.

Aphrodite gave Coral a nasty look and led the way up the stairs and down the hall to pause before a door. She opened it and gestured inside. "You have the room until dawn. I will inform the earl that you wait for him when he arrives." With that, she swooshed away.

Coral's lips curved in a secret smile. "Good luck, Mrs. Wren." And then she, too, was gone.

Anna carefully closed the door behind her and took a moment to steady her breath as she looked around. The room was surprisingly tasteful. Well, considering it was in a brothel. She rubbed her arms, trying to make them warm. Velvet curtains draped the window, a banked fire glowed in a lovely white marble fireplace, and two uphol-stered chairs stood by the hearth. She flipped back the covers on the bed. The linens were clean—or at least they appeared so.

She removed her cloak and draped it over a chair. She wore a diaphanous gown underneath that she'd borrowed from Coral. Anna supposed it was meant to be a night-dress, but it was extremely impractical. The upper half consisted mostly of lace. Coral had assured her, neverthe-less, that this was the appropriate attire for a seduction. The satin mask on her face was butterfly shaped. It cov-ered her forehead and hairline and swept down over most of her cheeks. The eyeholes were oval and tilted at the corners, giving her eyes a vaguely foreign shape. Her hair flowed about her shoulders, the ends carefully curled. Lord Swartingham had never seen her with her hair down.

Everything was ready. Anna skittered to the mantel-piece and fiddled with a candle. What was she doing here? This was a silly plan that would never work. What had she been thinking? There was yet time to renege. She could leave this room and find the carriage—

The door opened.

Anna whirled and froze. A masculine shape loomed in the doorway, silhouetted by the hall light. For a fraction of a second, she felt fear and stepped back apprehensively. She couldn't even tell if it was Lord Swartingham. Then he entered, and she knew by the shape of his head, by his stride, by the movement of his arm as he took off his coat, that it was he.

The earl laid the coat on a chair and advanced toward her in his shirt, breeches, and waistcoat. Anna didn't know what to do or say. She nervously pulled her hair back from her face and tucked it behind her ear with the crook of her little finger. She couldn't see his expression in the dim candlelight any more than he could see hers.

He reached for her and took her in his arms. She relaxed at the movement and lifted her face, expecting his kiss. But he didn't kiss her lips. Instead, he bypassed her face altogether and laid his open mouth against the curve of her neck.

Anna trembled. To have waited so long for his touch and then suddenly to have his wet tongue tracing the tendon of her neck down to her shoulder was both shocking and wonderful. She gripped his upper arms. His lips ran back and forth on her collarbone, his hot breath raising goose bumps on her skin. Her nipples puckered against the rough lace on her gown.

He slowly pulled down one shoulder of the loose nightdress. The lace caught and dragged over her nipple almost painfully as her breast was exposed. His breathing grew deeper. He shifted his hand from her shoulder to slide a callused palm over her nipple. Anna caught her breath and exhaled raggedly. She'd not been touched by a man there in over six years, and then only by her husband. The heat of his palm almost burned against her cool breast. He rubbed his wide hand back and forth, taking his time to measure her with the span of his fingers. Then he caught the nipple in the crook of his forefinger and thumb and squeezed; at the same time, he bit gently down on her shoulder.

A jolt of exquisite pleasure lanced through Anna, traveling all the way to her woman's mound. Her belly tensed with excitement. She ran her fingers over his arms, pressing and rubbing, wishing desperately that she could feel his skin under the layers of clothes.

His hair was slightly damp from the mist outside, and she could smell him: sweat and brandy and his own unique male musk. She turned her face toward him, but he pulled his head away. She followed. She wanted to kiss him. But he suddenly pushed down the other shoulder of her gown, distracting her. Without her breasts to hold it up, the gown fell to her feet. She was nude before him. There was a moment when she blinked and began to feel vulnerable, but then he put his mouth to her nipple and licked.

She started. A low, hoarse sound came from her throat.

He licked her other nipple like a cat. Slow, languid strokes that rasped over her nerve endings. He made a sound almost like a purr, furthering the illusion that he was a big predator savoring the taste of her skin.

Her legs shook and she felt weak. She was surprised to find she couldn't stand. What was this feeling taking over her body? This had never happened before. Had it been so long that she could no longer remember what lovemaking was like? Her body—her emotions—felt foreign.

But he was supporting her now, even as her legs collapsed beneath her. His mouth never leaving her breast, he picked her up and laid her on the bed, and her thoughts scattered. He ran his hands down her bare sides, and taking hold of her thighs, he parted them widely. He settled his hips against her as if he had every right. His manhood lay on her feminine flesh, and he ground down in small circular motions so that her inner lips parted. She could feel him, big and thick and *there*.

The trembling spread throughout her body.

He made a sound somewhere between a growl and a purr. He seemed to relish his position and her helplessness. He continued to rock against her, and he sucked her nipple into his hot mouth. He pulled hard, and she arched up against him frantically, almost dislodging him. He did growl then as he turned to suck her other breast. At the same time, he moved his hips up fractionally to bear down on her. She arched again as a whimper escaped her lips. But this time he was ready and did not let her shift him. He ground more firmly on her sensitive flesh. He pressed her into the mattress and dominated her with his weight and strength.

She was caught, unable to move, as he relentlessly pleasured her. He didn't let up, cramming against her inexorably with his hard loins as he sucked and sucked and sucked at her wet nipples.

She shuddered, unable to control herself. Waves of pleasure flowed from her center toward the tips of her toes. Little ripples followed, and she gasped as pieces of herself seemed to fly apart. For an ecstatic moment, joy overwhelmed her anxiety. He rocked against her nonstop, but in soft, slow brushes now, as if he knew her flesh was too sensitive to handle a firmer contact. His hands flowed in long sweeps down her sides, and he feathered open-mouthed kisses against her aching breasts.

She didn't know how long she lingered in a half daze before she felt his fingers harden, and he reached between their bodies to unbutton his breeches. It was a tight squeeze, and every movement of his hand nudged the back of his knuckles into her wet woman's place. She squirmed wantonly against his hand. She wanted more from him, and she wanted it now. He rumbled a dark chuckle. Then he drew out his hard flesh and guided himself to her entrance. She could feel heat from the head as he nudged his manhood against her softness.

He was big—very big. Of course he was big. He was a big man all around. She just hadn't realized how big. Anna quivered in feminine anxiety, but he gave her no time to balk. He was pushing, pushing his large male presence into her, and she was giving way. Submitting.

She could feel the round, smooth crown of his erection pressing into the inner ring of muscles that guarded her keep. His chest vibrated with a groan. He braced himself up on stiff arms, flexed his buttocks, and drove his entire length home. She moaned at the wonder of it: to feel his masculine flesh inside her, warm and hard and *now*. Oh, goodness it was heaven. She lifted her legs and wrapped them high over his hips and was a little startled to feel the fabric of his breeches rubbing against the inner skin of her naked thighs.

Then he pulled his penis almost all the way out and shoved it back into her, and she forgot about his clothes.

He thrust into her again and again. Hard and steady. His chest and head arched up and away from her in the darkness while his hips kept in constant, mindless, pleasurable contact. She reached up to caress his face, but he gently knocked her hands aside and bent his head to nuzzle her ear. She could hear him breathing fast now as his rhythm began to break. She ran her fingers through the hair at the back of his head and tightened her thighs about him, trying to make this moment last. He groaned into her ear, and his buttocks suddenly flexed hard beneath her heels as he convulsed and poured himself into her.

She arched, wanting to receive all that he could give. If only it would never stop.

But it did, and he was done. He collapsed down, his breath and his body spent. She caught him and held him close, and then she shut her eyes to engrave this moment on her memory. She felt the rough brush of his breeches against her legs and each and every ripple of his muscles as he breathed. She listened to his unsteady breath in her ear. It was a wonderfully intimate sound, and tears pricked at her eyes.

For some reason, she felt bizarrely maudlin. The emotion startled her. This had been the most glorious experience of her life, but it had also been totally unexpected. She had thought it would be a simple physical release, but instead it had been a wonderful kind of transcendence. It made no sense to her, but she hadn't the clarity of mind to puzzle it out.

She pushed the thought aside to examine later. Right now her legs were spread wantonly wide, sprawled where they had fallen when he stopped moving. He was still in her body, pulsing now and then with the aftershocks. She closed her eyes and savored his heavy, hot weight on her. She felt the wet warmth of his seed and could smell his sweat and the pungent scent of sex. Odd how she liked the scent, and she smiled, feeling completely relaxed as she turned her head to brush her lips against his hair.

He shifted his weight and withdrew from her body. He went slowly, and she felt each of his movements as a spreading emptiness. The feeling kept growing as he rose off the bed and buttoned the front placket of his breeches. All too soon, he reached for his coat and walked to the door.

He opened it, but then paused, his head lit from behind by the light in the hall. "Meet me here again tomorrow night." The door closed quietly behind him.

And Anna realized it was the sole time he had spoken to her that night.

Chapter Ten

*In the middle of the night, when all was black, Aurea
was awakened by passionate kisses. She was drowsy
and could not see, but the touch was gentle. She
turned and her arms wrapped around the form of a
man. He stroked and petted her so exquisitely that she
didn't even notice when he drew the nightgown from
her body. Then he made love to her in a silence broken
only by her cries of ecstasy. All night he stayed,
worshipping her body with his own, and as dawn
neared, she fell asleep again, replete with passion.
But in the morning when Aurea awoke, her lover of
the night before was gone. She sat up in her great,
lonely bed and searched for any sign of him. All she
could see was a single feather from the raven, and she
wondered if her lover had merely been a dream. . . .*
—from *The Raven Prince*

Edward threw down his quill and pushed up his spectacles
to rub his eyes. Damn. The words just would not come.

Outside his London town house, in a not very fashionable
neighborhood, he could hear the sound of delivery carts

beginning to roll up and down the street. The front door banged, and a song drifted up to his window from the maid sweeping the steps. The room had lightened since he had risen from his bed, and he leaned over to blow out the candle guttering on his desk.

Sleep had eluded him the night before. He'd finally given up in the wee hours. It was strange. He'd just experienced the best sex in his lifetime and thus should have been completely exhausted. Instead, he'd spent the long night thinking about Anna Wren and the little whore he had taken to bed at Aphrodite's Grotto.

But was she a whore? That was the problem. The question had gone around and around in his head all the night long.

When he'd arrived at Aphrodite's Grotto the evening before, the madam had simply said that there was a woman already waiting for him. She hadn't indicated whether the woman was a working prostitute or a lady of the *ton,* out for an evening of illicit pleasure. He hadn't asked either. One didn't ask at Aphrodite's Grotto. That was why so many patronized the place: A man was guaranteed anonymity and a clean woman. He hadn't been curious until after he'd left.

On the one hand, she'd worn a mask like a lady eager to conceal her identity. However, sometimes the whores at Aphrodite's Grotto wore masks to give themselves an air of mystery. But then again, she'd been so tight when he'd entered her, as if she had been a very long while without a man. Perhaps that was his imagination, remembering only what he'd wanted to feel.

He groaned huskily under his breath. Thinking of her was making him hard as a rock. It was also making him feel guilty. Because that was the other thing that had kept him awake most of the night: guilt. Which was ridiculous. Everything had been fine, wonderful, even, until his mind turned to Mrs. Wren, *Anna,* again not even a quarter of an hour after he'd left Aphrodite's Grotto. The feeling the thought of her brought—a kind of melancholy, a sense of wrongness—had stayed with him all the way home. He felt as if he had betrayed her. Never mind that she had no claim on him. That she had never even shown that she reciprocated his longing. The notion that he had been unfaithful was still there, eroding his soul.

The little whore had been shaped like Anna.

Holding her, he imagined a little what it would be like to hold Anna Wren. How it would feel to caress her. And when he'd kissed her throat, he had become instantly aroused. Edward groaned into his hands. This was ridiculous. He must rid himself of these constant thoughts of his little secretary; they were unworthy of an English gentleman. This urge to corrupt an innocent must be overcome, and he would do it through sheer willpower if need be.

He jumped up from his desk, strode over to the bellpull hanging in the corner, and yanked it viciously. Then he began putting away his papers. He took off his reading glasses and stuffed them into a cubbyhole.

Five minutes later, his summons still hadn't been answered.

Edward exhaled and glared at the door. Another minute ticked by with no sign of a servant. He drummed his fingers on his desk impatiently. Goddamnit, he had a limit.

He marched to the door and bellowed into the hallway, "Davis!"

A shuffling sound, as if from a creature called forth from the stygian depths, came from the corridor. It drew nearer. Very slowly.

"It will be sundown before you get here if you don't *hurry up, Davis!*" Edward held his breath, listening.

The shuffling did not quicken.

He exhaled again and leaned on the door frame. "I'm going to dismiss you one of these days. I'm going to replace you with a trained bear. It couldn't possibly perform any worse than you. *Do you hear me, Davis?*"

Davis, his valet, materialized around the corner holding a tray with hot water. The tray trembled. The servant slowed his already-snaillike progress even more when he saw the earl.

Edward snorted. "That's right, don't exert yourself. I have all the time in the world to stand about the corridor in my nightshirt."

The other man appeared not to hear. His movements were down to a crawl now. Davis was an aged rascal with sparse hair the color of dirty snow. His back was bent in a habitual stoop. A large mole with sprouting hairs grew by the side of his mouth as if to make up for the lack of hair above the watery gray eyes.

"I know you can hear me," Edward shouted in his ear as he passed.

The valet started as if just noticing him. "Up early, are we, m'lord? So debauched we couldn't sleep, eh?"

"My sleep was dreamless."

"That so?" Davis gave a cackle that would have done credit to a buzzard. "'Tisn't good for a man your age, not sleeping well, if you don't mind me saying so."

"What are you mumbling about, you senile old coot?"

Davis set the tray down and shot a malicious glance at him. "Drains the manly vigor, it does, if you know what I mean, m'lord."

"No, I don't know what you mean, thank God." He poured the ewer of lukewarm water into a basin on his dresser and began to wet his jaw.

Davis leaned close and said in a hoarse whisper, "Tupping, m'lord." He winked, a hideous sight.

Edward eyed him irritably as he lathered.

"It's all fine for a young man," the valet continued, "but you're getting up there, m'lord. The elderly need to preserve their strength."

"You would certainly know."

Davis scowled and picked up the razor.

Edward immediately snatched it out of his hand. "I'm not such a fool as to allow you near my neck with a sharp blade." He began scraping the soap under his chin.

"'Course, some don't have to worry about saving their strength," the valet said. The blade approached the dent in Edward's chin. "Have a problem with their cock crowing, if you know what I mean."

Edward yelped as he nicked his chin. "OUT! Get out, you evil old pisspot."

Davis wheezed as he scurried to the door. Some, hearing the whistling sound, would have worried for the old man's health, but Edward wasn't fooled. It wasn't often his valet triumphed over him this early in the morning.

Davis was laughing.

THE TRYST HADN'T gone exactly as she'd expected, Anna reflected the next morning. They had made love, naturally.

And he hadn't seemed to have recognized her. That was a relief. But really, the more she thought about Lord Swartingham's lovemaking, the more uneasy she became. He'd been a good lover. A wonderful lover, actually. She had never known such physical pleasure before, so she hadn't been able to predict that. But the way he hadn't kissed her on the mouth . . .

Anna poured herself a cup of tea. Early again to breakfast, she had the room to herself.

He hadn't let her touch his face at all. It seemed impersonal somehow. Of course that was natural, wasn't it? He imagined she was a prostitute or a woman of loose morals, for goodness sake. Therefore, he'd treated her like one. Wasn't that what she had expected?

Anna beheaded a kipper and poked the tines of her fork into its side. She should have expected it, but she hadn't. The problem was that while she had been making love, he had been . . . well . . . having sex. With a nameless prostitute. It was very depressing.

She made a face at her decapitated kipper. And what in heaven's name was she supposed to do about tonight? She hadn't planned on staying in London more than two nights. She should be leaving for home today on the first coach. Instead, she sat in Coral's breakfast room mashing up an innocent kipper.

Anna was still frowning moodily when Coral strolled into the room wearing a sheer, pale-pink wrapper trimmed with swan's down feathers.

The other woman stopped and eyed her. "Did he not come to the room last night?"

"What?" It took a moment for Anna to register the question. "Oh. Yes. Yes, he came to the room." She blushed and hurriedly took a sip of tea.

Coral helped herself to some coddled eggs and toast from the sideboard and gracefully dropped into a chair across from Anna. "Was he too rough?"

"No."

"You did not enjoy it?" the other woman pressed. "He couldn't bring you to climax?"

Anna nearly choked on her tea in her embarrassment. "No! I mean, *yes*. It was quite enjoyable."

Coral unperturbedly poured herself a cup of tea. "Then why do I find you this morning morose when you should have stars in your eyes?"

"I don't know!" Anna found to her horror that she had raised her voice. What was the matter with her? Coral was right, she'd gotten her wish, spent a night with the earl, and still she was dissatisfied. What a contrary creature she was!

The other woman had arched her eyebrows at her tone.

Anna crumbled a bit of toast, unable to meet her eyes. "He wants me to go back tonight."

"Rea-lly." The other woman drew out the word. "That is interesting."

"I shouldn't go."

Coral sipped her tea.

"He might recognize me if we meet again." Anna pushed the kipper to one side of her plate. "It would be so unladylike to return a second night."

"Yes, I do see your problem," Coral murmured. "One night at a brothel is perfectly respectable, whilst two comes perilously close to being déclassé."

Anna glared.

Coral smiled whimsically at her. "Why don't we go shopping for those fabrics you told your mother-in-law you would be bringing back. It will give you time to think. You can make up your mind later this afternoon."

"What a very good idea. Thank you." Anna set her fork down. "I'd better go change."

She rose from the table and hurried out of the morning room, her spirits lifting. She only wished she could abandon her thoughts of tonight as easily as her breakfast. Despite what she'd told Coral, Anna was very much afraid that she'd already made up her mind.

She was going to return to Aphrodite's Grotto and Lord Swartingham again.

THAT NIGHT, THE earl entered the room where Anna waited without saying a word. The only sounds were the quiet shush of the door closing and the crackle of the fire. She watched him pace forward, his face in shadow. Slowly, he shrugged out of his coat, his big shoulders bunching. And then she glided to him before he could make the first move, before he could take control. She stood on tiptoe to kiss his mouth. But he deflected the movement, drawing her close to his body instead.

She was determined this time to make their dance more personal, to make him understand that she was real. To touch at least some of him. She took advantage of her position and quickly worked the buttons on his waistcoat open. It came undone and she attacked the shirt beneath.

He reached to catch her hands, but she already had the shirt partly undone. She greedily reached for her prize: his flat, masculine nipples. Her fingers stroked through his chest hair until she found them; then she swayed forward and licked his nipples as he'd done the night before to hers, feeling vaguely triumphant that she'd gained the upper hand so soon. His hands fell away from where they had risen to catch her wrists. He caressed her bottom instead.

His height was a hindrance to her—she couldn't reach all that she wanted. So she pushed him back into one of the armchairs by the fire. It was important to her that she win this battle tonight.

He sprawled there, his shirt half-open in the firelight. She knelt between his outspread legs and slid her hands into his shirt, all the way up to his shoulders; then her fingers smoothed down his arms, taking the fabric with them. She pulled the shirt off him and let it fall to the floor. That left her free to run her hands over his beautiful, muscled shoulders and arms. She moaned her delight in finally being able to feel the power and warmth of his body. She felt light-headed with anticipation.

He stirred and brought her hands to the front of his breeches. Her fingers trembled, but she brushed his hands aside when he tried to help her. She pushed the concealed buttons through their holes, feeling his erection growing all the while beneath her fingers; then she reached inside to draw him out.

He was gorgeous. Thick and large, with pulsing veins that stood out along his shaft. A swollen crest. The sight filled her with heat. She made a crooning sound in her throat and spread the placket of his breeches as far as it would go so she could look at his chest and stomach and penis. She adored the sight: the black wiry curls of his pubic hair, the thick column, standing now to his navel, and the heavy sac of his testes beneath. His naked skin gleamed, as if gilded by the firelight.

He growled and ran his fingers into the hair behind her head. He gently urged her mouth down to his penis. For a moment, she hesitated. She'd never . . . Did she dare? Then she remembered their battle. This was but one skirmish, but it was important she win them all. And besides, she was excited at simply the thought. It was this last that decided her.

Tentatively, she grasped his erection and brought it away from his belly to her lips. She looked up. His face was flushed with arousal. Her eyelids lowered, and she enveloped the crown of his penis in her mouth. His hips jerked when her tongue touched him, and she felt the triumph rise in her again. She could control a man this way. She could control *this* man. She glanced up again. He was watching her as she licked and suckled his manhood, his ebony eyes glittering in the firelight. His fingers flexed in her hair.

She let her eyelids fall as she brought her mouth down as far as she could over his length. Then she slowly pulled up, pursing her lips and sucking on the thick shaft as it withdrew from her mouth. She heard him moan, and his pelvis arched convulsively. She licked around the ridge below the head. It felt like chamois over iron and tasted of male musk, the salt of sweat, and victory. Surely after this—after tonight—things would somehow be different. She explored that area with her tongue for a while. Then she felt his hand cover hers. He guided her fingers in a slow stroke up and down.

He groaned.

She moved her hand faster as he urged her to take his penis into her mouth again with a nudge of his hips. This time when she drew back up to the head, she tasted a saline drop at the tip. She licked the slit at the top to see if there was more. He groaned again. Anna wriggled in excitement. She'd never done anything so sexually stimulating in her life. Her body was damp and slick, and her breasts seemed to throb with each groan she wrung from him.

His hips began to move rhythmically as she worked him. The sensuous, liquid sounds of her mouth on his body were explicit in the still room. Suddenly he bucked, gasping, and tried to withdraw from her mouth. She wanted to feel his finish, though, wanted to experience this intimacy together, wanted to be with him at his most vulnerable. She held on and sucked more strongly. Tangy warmth filled her mouth. She almost came herself with the knowledge that she'd brought him complete satisfaction.

He sighed and bent down to draw her into his lap. They sprawled there for a while, the fire in the grate snapping. She leaned her head on his shoulder and pulled her hair out of her eyes with a hooked little finger. After a time, he drew her gown from her breasts. Languidly, he played with her nipples, stroking and squeezing gently for many minutes.

Anna drifted, her eyes half closed.

Then he lifted her to pull the gown all the way off. He turned her around and settled her on his lap, naked and facing him. Her legs draped over the chair's arms. She was splayed before him. Vulnerable.

Was this what she wanted? She wasn't sure. But then his fingers feathered across her belly, down to where she was open to him, and she no longer cared. He played in her curls before skimming lower. She inhaled sharply, waiting—anticipating—where he would touch her next.

He stroked through her, parting her down there.

She bit her lip.

Then he brought his fingers up, wet with her juices and smeared them over her nipples. Vaguely she was aware that she should be shocked, but somehow in this place, with this man, she was beyond the mores of society. He worked her nipples, sliding and tugging as he made sure they were both thoroughly covered with her body's moisture.

She caught her breath at the animal sensation. It was so crude, what he was doing, and it excited her terribly.

He bent his head and sucked a nipple into his mouth. He had made sure to sensitize her flesh, and she moaned and arched uncontrollably at the contact. He returned to her mound and slid his long, strong middle finger into her hollow. His thumb flicked across her stiff bud, and at the same time, he moved his finger in her.

Mewling noises built in her throat. She felt moisture sliding between her thighs.

He chuckled and brought his thumb down firmly on her sensitive knot. He suckled at her other breast. The sharp sensations at two different points of her body mingled and compounded one another until she grabbed his shoulders and arched her hips involuntarily. He brought his other hand to her back and held her steady as his thumb began to rotate.

She came explosively, gasping and shaking. She tried to close her legs, but the chair held them open. She could only hump her hips mindlessly as he pleasured her. Finally, when she began to whimper, he lifted her bottom and pushed her down on his manhood.

His breathing was labored as he slowly penetrated her slick passage. He forced her down relentlessly until she'd taken all of his thick warmth and was stretched almost painfully open. Then he carefully lifted her legs, one at a time, over the chair arms and brought them to either side of him. He lifted her up onto her knees so that just the head of his erection remained, stretching her entrance. He kept her there, balanced on top of his penis while he sucked and licked at her swinging nipples.

She moaned. He was driving her out of her mind. Frantically she tried to sink down on his burning erection, but he laughed darkly and held her poised on the edge of pleasure. She tried swiveling her hips, swirling the crown in her passage.

He broke at that, pulling her down on him again and surging into her almost violently.

Oh, yes. She smiled savagely in satisfaction. She rode him, watching his face. He caressed her breasts and tilted his head against the chair. His eyes were closed, his lips drawn back from his teeth in a near snarl; the flickering firelight made a demon's mask of his features.

Then he lightly pulled on both her nipples at the same time, and her own head arched at the sensation. Her hair cascaded down her back, swinging and brushing both her legs and his. She began to come in long, drawn-out waves, her vision clouding. His hips bucked against hers. He grabbed the cheeks of her bottom to hold her down on him, his penis fully sheathed in her passage as he ground and ground and ground against her softness, his head rolling against the chair as he came.

She fell forward, panting in the aftermath, to lie against his naked shoulder as he cradled her in his arms.

His face was half turned away, and she lazily watched him as he recovered. The lines that habitually creased his forehead and bracketed his mouth were softened. His long, inky lashes lay on his cheeks, hiding his piercing eyes. She wanted to stroke his face, to feel it with her fingertips. But by this time, she knew that he would not allow it.

Had she won what she wanted? She felt tears sting the corners of her eyes. Somehow it wasn't right. The lovemaking had been even more wonderful tonight. But at the same time, as if in proportion to her physical ecstasy, she felt the gaping hole in her psyche more keenly. Something was missing.

He suddenly sighed and shifted. His flesh slid from hers. He lifted her in his arms and carried her to the bed, laying her down gently. She shivered and tugged the coverlet over her shoulders, watching him. She wanted to speak, but what could she say?

He buttoned his shirt, tucked it in his breeches, and then buttoned those as well. He ran his fingers through his hair and grabbed his coat and waistcoat, walking to the door in the loose-jointed way of a man recently satisfied. He paused by the door. "Tomorrow."

And then he was gone.

Anna lay there a minute, listening to his retreating footsteps, feeling melancholy. She was roused by bawdy laughter somewhere in the house. She got up and cleaned herself with the water and towels that sat conveniently by. Anna tossed the wet cloth down and then looked at it. The basin and linens were provided with the room to wash after a sexual encounter. It made her feel tawdry, like a whore, and wasn't she perilously close to that state? She was letting physical desire so rule her that she met a lover in a brothel.

She sighed and donned a nondescript dark dress that she had brought along, bundled in a bag with a hooded cape and boots. Once dressed, she folded the lace gown and stuffed it into the bag. Had she left anything? Glancing around the room, she saw nothing of her own. She opened the door a crack and looked up and down the hallway. All clear. She pulled up her hood, and with her face still covered by the butterfly mask, ventured forth.

Coral had instructed her yesterday to be careful in the hallways and to go in and out only by the back stairs. A carriage would be waiting outside when she was ready to leave.

Anna moved now to the back stairs that Coral had indicated and ran down the flight. She sighed with relief when she reached the door and saw the waiting carriage. Her mask had begun to rub on the bridge of her nose. She untied it. Just as she removed the mask, three young bucks reeled around the corner of the house. Anna hastened toward the carriage.

In a sudden move, one of the men slapped another on the back in a friendly gesture. But the second man was so drunk that he lost his balance and careened into Anna, knocking both of them to the ground. "A-a-awfully sorry, m'dear."

The dandy was giggling as he tried to push himself off of Anna, elbowing her in the stomach in the process. He got as far as bracing his body on his arms, but stayed there, swaying, as if too befuddled to move any farther. Anna shoved at him, trying to shift his weight. The back door to Aphrodite's Grotto opened. The light from the door fell across her face.

The buck grinned drunkenly. A gold canine glinted in his mouth. "Why, you're not too bad at all, love." He leaned down in what he obviously considered a seductive manner and breathed an ale-filled puff into her face. "What say you an' me—?"

"Get off me, sir!" Anna hit the man's chest hard and managed to knock him off balance. He fell to the side, swearing foully as he did so. She scrambled quickly in the opposite direction, out of his reach.

"Come here, you tart. I'll—"

The dandy's friend saved her from hearing the rest of the undoubtedly obscene comment. The man hauled him up by the scruff of his shirt. "Come on, chum. No need to play with the downstairs help when we've got a couple of highfliers waiting inside."

Laughing, they dragged off their protesting friend.

Anna ran to the carriage, scrambled inside, and slammed the door behind her. She was shaking from the ugly incident. An incident that could have been much uglier.

She had never been mistaken for a woman of anything other than the highest morals. She felt degraded. Tainted. She took deep breaths and firmly reminded herself that she had nothing to be upset about. She hadn't been hurt by the fall, and the rude young man's friends had hustled him away before he had insulted her or even laid hands on her. True, he had seen her face. But it was highly unlikely that she would run into him in Little Battleford. Anna felt a little better. Surely there could be no repercussions.

Two GOLD COINS flipped through the air, flashing in the light from the back door of Aphrodite's Grotto. They were caught by hands that were remarkably steady.

"That went well."

"Glad to hear it, old boy." One of the bucks smirked, looking almost as drunk as he was supposed to be. "Mind telling us what that was all about?"

"'Fraid I can't do that." The third man's lip lifted in a sneer, and his gold tooth gleamed. "It's a secret."

Chapter Eleven

*Many months passed while Aurea lived in her raven-
husband's castle. During the day, she amused herself
by reading from the hundreds of illuminated books
in the castle's library or by taking long walks in the
garden. In the evening, she feasted on delicacies
she had only dreamed of in her former life. She had
beautiful gowns to wear and priceless jewels to
decorate herself with. Sometimes the raven would
visit her, appearing suddenly in her rooms or joining
her at dinner without any notice. Aurea found that her
strange spouse had a wide and intelligent mind, and
he would engage her in fascinating conversations.
But always the big black bird would disappear
before she retired to her rooms in the evening.
And every night, in the dark, a stranger came to her
bridal bed and made exquisite love to her. . . .*
—from *The Raven Prince*

"Hail, O defender of the turnip and master of the ewe," a
deep sarcastic voice drawled the next morning. "Well
met, my fellow Agrarian."

Edward squinted through the smoke in the cavernous coffeehouse. He could just make out the speaker, lounging at a table in the right rear corner. *Defender of the turnip, eh?* Winding his way through cluttered, age-blackened tables, Edward reached the man and slapped him hard on the back.

"Iddesleigh! It's not yet five in the afternoon. Why are you awake?"

Simon, Viscount Iddesleigh, didn't rock forward under the hearty back slap—he must have been bracing himself—but he did wince. A lean, elegant man, he wore a fashionable white-powdered wig and laced-edged shirt. To many he no doubt appeared a fop. But appearances in this case were deceiving.

"I've been known to see the light of day afore noon," Iddesleigh said, "although not often." He kicked a chair out from the table. "Sit, man, and partake of that hallowed brew called coffee. The gods, had they known of it, would've had no need of nectar on Olympus."

Edward waved at a boy serving drinks and took the proffered chair. He nodded at the silent third man sharing the table. "Harry. How're you?"

Harry Pye was a land steward on an estate somewhere in the north of England. He wasn't often in London. He must be here on business. In contrast to the flamboyant viscount, Harry almost blended into the woodwork. He was a man most would hardly notice in his ordinary brown coat and waistcoat. Edward knew for a fact that he carried a wicked dagger in his boot.

Harry nodded. "My lord. It's good to see you." He didn't smile, but there was an amused gleam in his green eyes.

"God's blood, Harry, how many times have I told you to call me Edward or de Raaf?" He signaled the boy again.

"Or Ed or Eddie," Iddesleigh cut in.

"*Not* Eddie." The boy banged a mug down, and Edward took a grateful sip.

"Aye, my lord," he heard Harry murmur, but Edward didn't bother replying.

He glanced around the room. The coffee at this house was very good. That was the main reason the Agrarian Society met here. It certainly wasn't because of the architecture. The room was crowded, with a too-low ceiling. The short door lintel was known to catch the taller members a nasty crack on the crown on entering. The tables had probably never been scrubbed, and the mugs didn't bear a close inspection. And the staff was a shifty lot who could be selectively hard of hearing when they didn't feel like serving, no matter the rank of the customer. But the coffee was fresh and strong, and any man was welcome to the house as long as he had an interest in agriculture. Edward recognized several titled men sitting at tables, but there were also small landowners up for a day in London and even working stewards such as Harry. The Agrarians were known for the strange equality of their club.

"And what does bring you to our lovely, if odoriferous, capital?" Iddesleigh asked.

"Negotiating a marital alliance," Edward replied.

Harry Pye's eyes sharpened over the rim of his mug. His hand was wrapped around the cup. There was a disconcerting space where his ring finger should have been but wasn't.

"Oh, braver man than I," Iddesleigh said. "You must have been celebrating the impending nuptials when I saw you last night at the fair Aphrodite's Grotto."

"You were there?" Edward felt oddly reticent. "I didn't see you."

"No." Iddesleigh smirked. "You looked quite, ah, *relaxed* when I saw you exit that establishment. I, myself, was engaged at the time with two eager nymphs, or I would have greeted you."

"Only two?" Harry asked, deadpan.

"We were joined later by a third." Iddesleigh's icy gray eyes sparkled almost innocently. "But I hesitated to admit the fact for fear it would cause you two to doubt your manhood by comparison."

Harry snorted.

Edward grinned and caught the boy's eye. He held up a finger for another mug. "Good God. Aren't you getting a trifle long in the tooth for such athletics?"

The viscount placed a lace-draped hand on his breast. "I assure you, on the honor of my dead and moldering forefathers, that all three wenches were wearing smiles when I left them."

"Probably because of the gold they were clutching," Edward said.

"You offend me deeply," the viscount said as he smothered a yawn. "Besides, you yourself must've engaged in debauchery of one sort or another at the goddess's domain. Admit it."

"True." Edward frowned at his mug. "But I won't be for very much longer."

The viscount looked up from inspecting the silver embroidery on his coat. "Never say you intend to be a chaste bridegroom?"

"I see no other option."

Iddesleigh's eyebrows arched. "Isn't that a rather literal—not to mention archaic—interpretation of the bridal vows?"

"Perhaps. But I think it will make for a successful marriage." Edward felt his jaw clench. "I want it to work this time. I need an heir."

"I wish you luck, then, my friend," Iddesleigh said quietly. "You must have chosen your lady carefully."

"I did indeed." Edward stared into his half-empty mug. "She is from an impeccable family; it goes back further than mine. She isn't repulsed by my scars; I know because I asked her myself—something I omitted to do with my first wife. She's intelligent and quiet. She's handsome, but not beautiful. And she comes from a large family. God willing, she should be able to give me strong sons."

"A Thoroughbred dam for a Thoroughbred sire." Iddesleigh's mouth quirked. "Soon your stables will overflow with hearty, squalling progeny. I'm sure you can hardly wait to begin getting offspring on your intended."

"Who is the lady?" Harry asked.

"Sir Richard Gerard's eldest, Miss Sylvia—"

Iddesleigh made a muffled exclamation. Harry glanced at him sharply.

"Gerard. Do you know her?" Edward finished slowly.

Iddesleigh studied the lace at his wrists. "My brother, Ethan's wife was a Gerard. As I remember, the mother was something of a tartar at the wedding."

"She still is." Edward shrugged. "But I doubt I'll have much contact with her after we're married."

Harry gravely raised his cup. "Congratulations on your betrothal, my lord."

"Yes, congratulations." The viscount lifted his cup as well. "And good luck, my friend."

A COLD NOSE against her cheek woke Anna. She peeked and saw brown canine eyes only inches from her own. They stared at her urgently. Pungent doggy breath panted in her face. She groaned and turned her head to glance at the window. Dawn was just brightening the sky from a drowsy peach color to the more alert bright blue of day.

She looked back at the watching canine eyes. "Good morning, Jock."

Jock took his forepaws from the mattress beside her head and backed up a step to sit down. He was very still, ears up, shoulder bunched, eyes alert to her every move. The very epitome of a dog waiting to go out.

"Oh, all right. I'm getting up." She padded over to the basin and made an abbreviated wash before dressing.

Dog and woman crept down the back stairs.

Coral lived in a fashionable street near Mayfair, which was lined with white stone houses only a few years old. Most of these were quiet now except for an occasional maid washing the front steps or polishing a doorknob. Normally, Anna might feel uncomfortable walking about in a strange place without an escort, but she had Jock to accompany her. He leaned closer as if to protect her whenever anyone else approached. They strolled in companionable silence. Jock was busy sniffing out the intriguing smells of the city, while she was lost in her own thoughts.

During the night, she'd thought over her situation, and when Anna awoke this morning, she'd already known what she must do. She couldn't meet him tonight. She was playing with fire, and she could no longer hide the fact from herself. In her need to be with Lord Swartingham, she'd flung aside all caution. She'd recklessly hared off to London and traipsed about a bordello as if it were a Little Battleford musicale. It was a miracle he hadn't discovered her. And the incident the night before with the drunken bucks was too close. She could've been raped or hurt or both. How hypocritical of her to scold men for doing the very thing she'd done for the past two nights. She winced at the thought of what Lord Swartingham would have said had he found her out. He was a very proud man with a terrible temper.

Anna shook her head and glanced up. They were only a few houses down from Coral's residence. Either her footsteps had led her back or Jock had a homing instinct.

She patted the dog's head. "Good boy. We had better go in and start packing for home."

Jock perked up his ears at the word *home*.

At that moment, a carriage pulled up in front of Coral's house. Anna hesitated, then retraced her steps around the corner and peeked back. Who could be calling at such an unfashionable hour? A footman jumped down from the carriage and placed a wooden step under the door before opening it. A male leg advanced, but withdrew inside the carriage again. She could see the footman moving the step an inch or two to the left; then a burly man with heavy shoulders descended. He stopped a moment to say something to the footman. From the way the servant bowed his head, it looked to be a set-down.

The burly man entered the house.

Was he Coral's marquis? Anna contemplated this turn of events while Jock waited patiently by her side. From what little she knew about the marquis, it would perhaps be prudent if she didn't meet him. She didn't want to cause trouble for Coral, and she was uneasy at the thought of letting someone of quality see her at Coral's residence. Although it was extremely unlikely she would cross paths again with a marquis, the incident the night before with the drunken bucks had made her wary. She decided to enter the house from the servants' entrance and thus perhaps escape notice.

"It's a good thing I'd planned to leave today anyway," she muttered to Jock as they crossed the kitchens.

There was a great flurry of activity in the kitchen. Maids scurried and the footmen helped bring in a mountain of luggage. Anna was hardly acknowledged as she climbed the dark back stair. Just as well. She and Jock moved soundlessly down the upper hall. Anna opened the door to her room and found Pearl anxiously waiting.

"Oh, thank God you're back, Mrs. Wren," the other woman said when she saw her.

"I took Jock for a walk," Anna said. "Was that Coral's marquis I saw coming in the front?"

"Yes," Pearl said. "Coral wasn't expecting him for another week or more. He'll be angry if he finds she has guests."

"I was just going to pack and leave, so I'll be out of his way."

"Thank you, ma'am. That'll make it ever so much easier for Coral, it will."

"But what will you do, Pearl?" Anna bent to drag out her soft bag from under the bed. "Coral said she wanted you here with her. Will the marquis let you stay?"

Pearl picked at a hanging thread on her cuff. "Coral thinks she can get him to let me stay, but I don't know. He's awful mean sometimes, even if he is a lord. And the house belongs to him, you know."

Anna nodded her understanding as she carefully folded her stockings.

"I'm glad Coral has such a nice place to live, with servants and carriages and things," Pearl said slowly. "But that marquis makes me nervous."

Anna paused with a handful of clothes in her arms. "You don't think he would hurt her, do you?"

Pearl stared back somberly. "I don't know."

EDWARD PROWLED THE bordello room like a caged tiger denied a meal. The woman was late. He checked the china clock over the hearth again. Half an hour late, damn her. How dare she make him wait for her? He reached the fireplace and stared into the blaze. He'd never obsessively gone back to the same woman. Not once, not twice, but three times now.

The sex had been so good each time. She was so responsive. She had held nothing back, acting like she was as much under his spell as he was under hers. He was not naïve. He knew women who were paid for sex often faked an excitement they did not feel. But a body's natural reaction could not be faked. She had been wet, literally soaked, in her desire for him.

He groaned. The thought of her wet pussy was having a predicable effect on his cock. Where the hell was she?

Edward swore and pushed himself away from the mantelpiece to resume his pacing. He'd even begun to daydream, in the manner of a starry-eyed stripling, about what her face looked like underneath the mask. More disturbing, he had imagined that she might look like Anna.

He stopped and placed the crown of his head against the wall, hands braced on either side. His chest expanded as he breathed deeply. He had come to London to rid himself of this awful fascination for his little secretary before he married. Instead, he'd found a new obsession. But had that stopped the original fixation? Oh, no. His longing for Anna had not only grown stronger, but was also mingled with lust for the mysterious little whore. He had two obsessions now instead of one, and they were tangled together in his overwrought brain.

He pounded his head against the wall. Perhaps he was going mad. That would explain everything.

Of course, none of this mattered to his cock. Mad or sane, it was still overeager to feel the woman's tight, slippery sheath. He stopped banging his head against the wall and looked at the clock again. She was thirty-three minutes late now.

By God's balls, he wasn't going to wait another minute more.

Edward snatched his coat up and slammed out of the room. Two gray-haired gentlemen were strolling down the hall. They took one look at his face and pressed to the side as he stormed past. He ran down the grand staircase two risers at a time and stalked into the parlor where the male customers went to mingle and meet disguised ladies and whores. He scanned the gaudy room. There were several women in bright colors, each surrounded by eager men, but only one woman wore a golden mask. She was taller than the other females and stood apart, alert to the currents in the room. Her full-face mask was smooth and serene, the eyebrows symmetrical incised arcs above the almond-shaped eyeholes. Aphrodite watched over her wares with a beady eagle eye.

Edward strode directly to her. "Where is she?" he demanded.

The madam, normally an unflappable woman, jerked at his sudden question by her side. "Lord Swartingham, isn't it?"

"Yes. Where is the woman I was to meet tonight?"

"She isn't in your room, my lord?"

"No." Edward grit his teeth. "No, she isn't in the room. Would I be down here asking after her if she were up in the room?"

"We have many other willing ladies, my lord." The madam's voice sounded ingratiating. "Perhaps I can send another to your room?"

Edward leaned forward. "I don't want another. I want the woman I had last night and the night before. Who is she?"

Aphrodite's eyes shifted behind the gold mask. "Now, my lord, you know we can't reveal the identity of our lovely doves here at the Grotto. Professional integrity, you know."

Edward snorted. "I don't give a bloody damn about the professional integrity of a whorehouse. Who. Is. She?"

Aphrodite backed a step, as if alarmed. Not surprisingly, since he now loomed above her. She made a signal with her hand to someone over his shoulder.

Edward narrowed his eyes. He knew he had only a few minutes. "I want her name—now—or I will enjoy starting a riot in your parlor."

"No need for threats. There are several other wenches here who would be eager to spend the night with you." Aphrodite's voice held a smirk. "Ones who don't mind a pockmark or two."

Edward went still. He knew well enough what his face looked like. It didn't distress him anymore—he was past the age of agonized vanity—but it did repel some women. The little whore hadn't seemed to mind his scars. Of course, last night they'd made love in the chair by the firelight. Perhaps it had been the first time she'd truly seen his face. Perhaps she had been so disgusted by the sight that she hadn't bothered to show up tonight.

Goddamn her.

Edward pivoted on his heel. He grabbed a faux Chinese vase, raised it above his head, and slammed it to the floor. It shattered explosively. Conversation in the room ceased as heads turned.

Too much thought was bad for a man. What he needed was action. If he couldn't work off his energy in bed, well, this was second best.

He was seized from behind and pulled around. A fist the size of a ham hurtled at his face. Edward leaned back. The blow went whistling past his nose. He brought his own right fist in low to the man's belly. The other man *oofed* out the air in his lungs—a lovely sound—and staggered.

Three men moved in to take the other's place. They were the big bruisers kept by the house to escort trouble-makers outside. One of them got in a roundhouse to the left side of his face. Edward saw stars, but it didn't stop him returning with a pretty uppercut.

Several of the patrons cheered.

And then after that, things became muddled. Many of the spectators appeared to be sporting men who thought the odds uneven. They joined the brawl with tipsy enthusiasm. Girls frantically scrambled over settees, shrieking and upsetting furniture in their haste to get out of the way. Aphrodite stood in the middle of the room, shouting orders that no one could hear. She stopped abruptly when someone shoved her headfirst into a bowl of punch. Tables flew through the air. An enterprising demimondaine began taking bets in the hallway from the men and girls who had flooded the stairs to view the commotion. Four more bullies and at least as many men from the upstairs rooms joined the melee. Some of the guests had clearly been interrupted in their entertainment, as they wore only breeches or—in the case of one rather distinguished-looking old gent—a shirt and nothing else.

Edward was enjoying himself immensely.

Blood ran down his chin from a split lip, and he could feel one eye slowly swelling shut. A smallish villain clung to his back and hit him about the head and shoulders. In front of him, another, bigger man tried to kick his legs out from under him. Edward sidestepped the attempt and brought his own foot up to shove against the man's other leg while his weight was off balance. He went down like a colossus.

The imp on his back was becoming a nuisance. Grabbing the man by his hair, Edward swiftly rammed himself backward into a wall. He heard a *thunk* as the man's head met the solid surface. The man slid from Edward's shoulders and landed on the floor along with a good deal of the plaster from the wall.

Edward grinned and glared around through his good eye for more prey. One of the house thugs attempted to sidle out the door. He looked wildly over his shoulder when Edward's gaze settled on him, but there were none of his brethren to come to his aid.

"'Ave mercy, milord. I don't get paid enough to be beat bloody like you done with the rest of the lads." The thug held up his hands and backed away from Edward's advance. "Why, you even did Big Billy in, and I ain't never seen a man faster than him."

"Very well," Edward said. "Although, I can't see out of my right eye, which evens the odds. . . ." He looked hopefully at the cringing bully who smiled weakly and shook his head. "No? Well, then, I don't suppose you know of a place where a man can get properly drunk, do you?"

Thus, a little while later, Edward found himself at what had to be the seediest tavern in the East End of London. With him were the house thugs, including Big Billy, now nursing a swollen nose and two black eyes but no hard feelings. Big Billy had his arm around Edward's shoulders and was attempting to teach him the words to a ditty extolling the charms of a lass named Titty. The song seemed to have a lot of rather clever double entendres that Edward suspected were lost on him since he'd been standing drinks for everyone in the room for the last two hours.

"W-who was the whore you was looking for that started all this, milord?" Jackie, the thug asking, had not missed any of the rounds of drinks. He addressed the question to the air somewhere to Edward's right.

"Faithless woman," Edward muttered into his ale.

"All wenches are faithless tarts." This bit of masculine wisdom came from Big Billy.

The men present nodded somberly, although it caused one or two to lose their balance and sit down rather abruptly.

"No. S'not true," Edward said.

"What s'not true?"

"All women faithless," Edward said carefully. "I know a woman who's as p-pure as the driven snow."

"Who's that?" "Tell us, then, milord!" The men clamored to hear the name of this feminine paragon.

"Mrs. Anna Wren." He raised his glass precariously. "A toast! A toast to the most un-un-unblemished lady in England. Mrs. Anna Wren!"

The tavern erupted in boisterous cheers and toasts to the lady. And Edward wondered why all the lights went out suddenly.

HIS HEAD WAS coming apart. Edward opened his eyes, but then immediately thought better of that idea and squeezed them shut again. Carefully, he touched his temple and tried to think why the top of his head felt like it was about to explode.

He remembered Aphrodite's Grotto.

He remembered the woman not showing up.

He remembered a fight. Edward grimaced and gingerly probed with his tongue. His teeth were all intact. That was good news.

His mind strained.

He remembered meeting a jolly fellow.... Big Bob? Big Bert? No, Big Billy. He remembered—Oh, God. He remembered toasting Anna in the worst hellhole he had ever had the misfortune to drink watered-down ale in. His stomach rolled unpleasantly. Had he really bandied Anna's name about in such a place? Yes, he thought he had. And, if he recalled correctly, the whole roomful of disreputable rogues had bawdily toasted her.

He moaned.

Davis opened the door, letting it bang against the wall, and slowly shuffled into the room bearing a laden tray.

Edward moaned again. The sound of the door had nearly made his scalp separate from his skull. "Damn your eyes. Not now, Davis."

Davis continued on his snaillike course to the bed.

"I know you can hear me," he spoke slightly louder, but not too loud, for fear of setting his head off again.

"Been in our cups have we, m'lord?" Davis shouted.

"I didn't know you'd overindulged as well," Edward said from behind the hands covering his face.

Davis ignored this. "Lovely gents what brought you home last night. New friends of yours?"

Edward parted his fingers to shoot a glare at his valet.

Evidently it bounced harmlessly off the man. "Bit long in the tooth to be guzzling so much, m'lord. Might lead to gout at your age."

"I'm overwhelmed by your concern for my health." Edward looked at the tray Davis had now managed to set on the bedside table. It held a cup of tea, already cold, judging by the scum floating on top, and a bowl of milktoast. "What the hell is this? Nursery pap? Bring me some brandy to settle this head."

Davis pretended deafness with an aplomb that would have done justice to the finest stage in London. He had had many years of practice, after all.

"Here's a lovely breakfast to put vigor back into you," the valet bawled in his ear. "Milk is very strengthening for a man at your age."

"Get out! Get out! Get out!" Edward roared, and then had to hold his head again.

Davis retreated to the door, but he couldn't resist a parting shot. "Need to watch your temper, m'lord. Might go all red in the face and buggy-eyed with apoplexy. Nasty way to go, that."

He scooted through the door with amazing dexterity for a man his age. Just before the bowl of milk-toast hit.

Edward groaned and closed his eyes, his head flopping back on the pillow. He ought to get up and start packing to go home. He'd obtained a fiancée and visited the Grotto, not once, but twice. He had, in fact, done all he'd meant to do when he'd decided to travel to London. And even if he felt far worse now than he had when he'd first come, there was no point in staying in the city. The little whore wouldn't return, he would never encounter her again, and he had responsibilities of his own to see to. And that was as it should be.

There was no room in his life for a mysterious masked woman and the transitory pleasure she brought.

Chapter Twelve

The days and nights passed as if in a dream, and Aurea was content. Perhaps she was even happy. But after several months, she began to have an urge to see her father. The urge grew and grew until all her waking moments were filled with a longing for her father's face, and she became listless and sad.

One night at dinner, the raven turned the bright ebony bead of his eye upon her and said, "What causes this malaise I sense in you, my wife?"

"I long to see my father's face again, my lord," Aurea sighed. "I miss him."

"Impossible!" the raven squawked, and left the table without another word.

But Aurea, although she never made complaint, so missed her parent that she stopped eating and only picked at the delicacies set before her. She began to waste away until one day the raven could no longer stand it. He flapped into her room angrily.

"Go, then, and visit your sire, wife," he cawed. "But be very sure that you return within a fortnight, for I would pine were you to stay longer."

—from *The Raven Prince*

"Oh, my goodness!" Anna exclaimed the next day. "What have you done to your face?"

She would notice the bruises. Edward halted and glowered at her. She hadn't seen him in five days, and the first words out of her mouth were an accusation. Briefly, he tried to imagine any of his previous, *male* secretaries daring to comment on his appearance. It was impossible. In fact, he couldn't think of anyone, save his current *female* secretary, who made such impertinent comments to him. Oddly, he found her impertinence endearing.

Not that he let it show. Edward raised a brow and tried to put his secretary in her place. "I have done nothing to my face, thank you, Mrs. Wren."

It had no noticeable effect.

"You can't call that black eye and the bruises on your jaw nothing." Anna looked disapproving. "Have you put any salve on it yet?"

She sat in her usual place at the small rosewood desk in his library. She looked serene and golden in the morning light from the window, as if she hadn't moved from the desk the entire time he had been in London. It was a strangely comforting thought. Edward noted that she had a small smudge of ink on her chin.

And something was different about her appearance.

"I haven't used any salve, Mrs. Wren, because there is no reason to." He tried to walk the remaining feet to his desk without limping.

Naturally, she noticed that, too. "And your leg! Why are you limping, my lord?"

"I am not limping."

She arched her eyebrows so high, they nearly disappeared into her hairline.

Edward was forced to glare in order to emphasize the lie. He tried to think of an explanation for his injuries that wouldn't make him look a total fool. He certainly couldn't tell his little secretary that he'd been in a brawl at a brothel.

What was it about her appearance?

"Did you have an accident?" she asked before he could think of a suitable excuse.

He seized on the suggestion. "Yes, an accident." Something about her hair . . . A new style, perhaps?

His respite was brief.

"Did you fall off your horse?"

"No!" Edward strove to lower his voice and had a sudden inspiration. He could *see* her hair. "No, I didn't fall off my horse. Where is your cap?"

As a distraction, it failed abysmally.

"I've decided not to wear it any longer," she said primly. "If you didn't fall off your horse, then what did happen to you?"

The woman would have been an outstanding success with the inquisition.

"I . . ." For the life of him, he could not think of a suitable story.

Anna looked worried. "Your carriage didn't overturn, did it?"

"No."

"Were you run down by a cart in London? I hear the streets are terribly crowded."

"No. I wasn't run down by a cart either." He tried to

smile charmingly. "I like you without your cap. Your tresses shine like a field of daisies."

Anna narrowed her eyes. Perhaps he hadn't any charm. "I wasn't aware that daisies were brown. Are you sure you didn't fall off your horse?"

Edward gritted his teeth and prayed for forbearance. "I did not fall off my horse. I have *never*—"

She raised one brow.

"*Hardly* ever been unseated from my horse."

A swift expression of enlightenment came over her features. "It's all right, you know," she said in an unbearably understanding voice. "Even the best horsemen fall off their mounts sometimes. It is nothing to be ashamed of."

Edward got up from his desk, limped across to hers, and placed both hands, palms down, upon it. He leaned over until his eyes were only inches from her hazel ones. "I am not ashamed," he said very slowly. "I did not fall off my horse. I was not thrown from my horse. I wish to end this discussion. Is that amenable to you, Mrs. Wren?"

Anna swallowed visibly, drawing his eyes to her throat. "Yes. Yes, that's quite amenable to me, Lord Swartingham."

"Good." His gaze rose to her lips, wet where she had licked them in her nervousness. "I thought of you while I was gone. Did you think of me? Did you miss me?"

"I—" she started to whisper.

Hopple breezed into the room. "Welcome back, my lord. I hope your sojourn in our lovely capital was pleasant?" The steward came to a halt when he noticed Edward's stance over Anna.

Edward slowly straightened, his eyes never leaving Anna. "My stay was pleasant enough, Hopple, although I found I missed the . . . loveliness of the country."

Anna looked flustered.

Edward smiled.

Mr. Hopple started. "Lord Swartingham! Whatever happened to—?"

Anna cut him off. "Mr. Hopple, have you time to show the earl the new ditch?"

"The ditch? But—" Hopple looked from Edward to Anna.

Anna twitched her eyebrows as if a fly had landed on her forehead. "The new ditch to drain Mr. Grundle's field. You did mention it the other day."

"The . . . Oh, yes, Farmer Grundle's ditch," Hopple said. "If you will come with me, my lord, I think you'll be interested in inspecting it."

Edward's eyes were back on Anna. "I'll meet with you in half an hour, Hopple. I've something I wish to discuss with my secretary first."

"Oh, yes. Yes. Er, very well, my lord." Hopple departed, looking befuddled.

"What was it you wished to discuss with me, my lord?" she asked.

Edward cleared his throat. "Actually, there's something I want to show you. If you'll come with me?"

Anna appeared mystified but stood and took his arm. He led her out to the hall, turning to the back door instead of the front. When they stepped into the kitchen, Cook nearly dropped her morning cup of tea. Three maids were clustered by the table where Cook sat, like acolytes around their priest. All four females came to their feet.

Edward waved them back down again. No doubt he'd interrupted a morning gossip. Without explanation, he continued through the kitchen and out the back door. They crossed the wide stable yard, his boot heels ringing on the cobblestones. The morning sun shone brightly, and the stables cast a long shadow behind them. Edward rounded a corner of the building and stopped in the shade. Anna glanced around, looking puzzled.

Edward had a sudden, awful feeling of uncertainty. It was an unusual gift. Maybe she wouldn't like it or— worse—be insulted.

"This is for you." He gestured abruptly at a muddy lump of burlap.

Anna looked from him to the burlap. "What—?"

Edward stooped and threw back a corner of the bundle. Underneath lay what looked like a bunch of dead, thorny sticks.

Anna squealed.

That noise had to be a good sign in a female, didn't it? Edward frowned uncertainly. Then she smiled up at him, and he felt warmth suffuse his chest.

"Roses!" she exclaimed.

She dropped to her knees to examine one of the dormant rosebushes. He'd carefully wrapped them in damp burlap to keep the roots from drying out before departing from London. Each bush had only a few thorny branches, but the roots were long and healthy.

"Careful, they're sharp," Edward murmured to her down-bent head.

Anna counted busily. "There's two dozen here. Do you mean to put them all in your garden?"

Edward scowled at her. "They're for you. For your cottage."

Anna opened her mouth and for a moment seemed at a loss for words. "But . . . even if I could accept them all, they must have been terribly expensive."

Was she refusing his gift? "Why can't you accept them?"

"Well, for one, I couldn't fit them all in my little garden."

"How many could you fit?"

"Oh, I suppose three or four," Anna said.

"Pick out the four you want, and I'll send the rest back." Edward felt relief. At least she wasn't rejecting the roses. "Or burn them," he added as an afterthought.

"Burn them!" Anna sounded horrified. "But you can't just burn them. Don't you want them for your own garden?"

He shook his head impatiently. "I don't know how to put them in."

"I do. I'll plant them for you in thanks for the others." Anna smiled up at him, looking a little shy. "Thank you for the roses, Lord Swartingham."

Edward cleared his throat. "You're welcome, Mrs. Wren." He had a strange urge to shuffle his feet like a little boy. "I suppose I ought to see Hopple."

She simply looked at him.

"Yes . . . Ah, yes." Good God, he was stuttering like an imbecile. "I'll just go find him, then." With a muttered farewell, he strode off in search of the steward.

Who knew giving presents to secretaries could be so stressful?

ANNA ABSENTLY WATCHED Lord Swartingham walk away, her hand fisting in the muddy burlap. She knew how this man felt against her in the dark. She knew how his body moved when he made love. She knew the deep husky sounds he produced in the back of his throat when he reached his climax. She knew the most intimate things one could know about a man, but she didn't know how to reconcile that knowledge to the sight of him in the daylight. To reconcile the man who made love so sublimely to the man who brought her rosebushes from London.

Anna shook her head. Perhaps it was too hard a question. Perhaps one could never understand the difference between the passion of a man at night and the civil face he showed during the day.

She hadn't realized what it would be like to see him again after spending two unbelievable nights in his arms. Now she knew. She felt sad, as if she'd lost something that had never truly been hers. She'd gone to London with the intention of making love to him, to enjoy the physical act as a man would: unemotionally. But as it turned out, she wasn't as stoic as a man. She was a woman, and where her body went, her emotions followed willy-nilly. The act had somehow bound her to him, whether he knew it or not.

And he could never know it now. What had transpired between them in that room at Aphrodite's Grotto must remain her secret alone.

She stared blindly down at the rose stems. Perhaps the roses were a sign that things could still be healed. Anna touched a prickly rose branch. They must mean something, surely? A gentleman didn't usually give such a lovely gift—such a perfect gift—to his secretary, did he?

A thorn pricked the ball of her thumb. Absentmindedly, she sucked on the wound. Maybe there was hope after all. As long as he never, ever discovered her deception.

LATER THAT MORNING, Edward stood calf-deep in muddy water, inspecting the new drainage ditch. A lark sang in the border of Mr. Grundle's field. Probably ecstatic it was dry. Nearby, two smock-clad laborers from Grundle's farm shoveled muck to keep the ditch free of debris.

Hopple also stood in muddy water, looking particularly aggrieved. This might be in part because he had slipped and fallen in the scummy water once already. His waistcoat, formerly an egg-yolk yellow with green piping, was filthy. The water from the ditch gushed into a nearby stream as the steward explained the engineering of the project.

Edward watched the laborers, nodded at Hopple's sermon, and thought about Anna's reaction to his gift. When Anna spoke, he had a hard time keeping his eyes off her exotic mouth. How such a mouth had come to be on such a plain little woman was a great mystery, one that apparently could enthrall him for hours. That mouth could lead the Archbishop of Canterbury to sin.

"Don't you think so, my lord?" Hopple asked.

"Oh, most definitely. Most definitely."

The steward looked at him strangely.

Edward sighed. "Just continue."

Jock bounded into view with a small, unfortunate rodent in his mouth. He leaped the ditch and landed with a splash of muddy water, completing the ruin of Hopple's waistcoat. Jock presented his find to Edward. It was immediately apparent that his treasure had left this life quite some time ago.

Hopple backed hastily away, waving a handkerchief before his face and muttering irritably, "Good gracious! I thought when that dog went missing for several days we were well rid of it."

Edward absently petted Jock, the odoriferous present still in the dog's mouth. A maggot fell with a plop into the water. Hopple swallowed and continued his explanation of the wonderful drain with his handkerchief over his nose and mouth.

Of course, after coming to know Anna, Edward had no longer found her so plain. In fact, he was at a loss to explain how he had so thoroughly discounted her the first time they met. How was it that he'd initially thought her rather ordinary? Except for her mouth, of course. He'd always been aware of her mouth.

Edward sighed and kicked at some debris under the water, sending up a splash of mud. She was a lady. That he had never been wrong about even if he had misjudged her attraction at first. As a gentleman, he shouldn't even be thinking about Anna in this way. That was what whores were for, after all. Ladies simply didn't contemplate kneeling in front of a man and slowly bending their beautiful, erotic mouths down to . . .

Edward shifted uncomfortably and scowled. Now that he was officially engaged to Miss Gerard, he must stop thinking about Anna's mouth. Or any other part of her for that matter. He needed to put Anna—*Mrs. Wren*—right out of his mind in order to have a successful second marriage.

His future family depended on it.

WHAT FUNNY THINGS roses were: prickly hard on the surface, yet so fragile inside, Anna mused that evening. Roses were one of the most difficult flowers to grow, needing much more coddling and worry than any other plant; yet, once established, they might grow for years, even if abandoned.

The garden behind her cottage was only about twenty feet by thirty, but there was still room for a small shed at the back. She'd used a candle in the gathering dusk to light her way as she had rummaged about in the shed and had found an old washbasin and a couple of tin buckets. Now she carefully laid the roses in the containers and covered them with the bitterly cold water from the little garden well.

Anna stood back and regarded her work critically. It had almost seemed like Lord Swartingham had avoided her after he'd given her the roses. He hadn't shown up for luncheon, and he'd only stopped by the library once that afternoon. But of course he had plenty of work built up over the five days that he had been gone, and he was a very busy man. She pulled the muddy burlap over the top of the washbasin and buckets. She'd set the containers in the shade of the cottage so they wouldn't burn in the sun tomorrow. It might be a day or two before she could plant them, but the water would keep them vital. She nodded and went in to wash up for supper.

The Wren household dined on roasted potatoes and a bit of gammon that night. The meal was almost over when Mother Wren dropped her fork and exclaimed, "Oh, I've forgotten to tell you, dear. While you were gone, Mrs. Clearwater invited us to her spring soiree the day after next."

Anna paused with her teacup halfway to her lips. "Really? We've never been invited before."

"She knows you're friends with Lord Swartingham." Mother Wren smiled complacently. "It would be a coup for her if he attended."

"I don't have any influence over whether the earl will attend or not. You know that, Mother."

"Do you really think so?" Mother Wren tilted her head. "Lord Swartingham hasn't made any effort to join our social diversions. He accepts no invitations to tea or dinner, and he hasn't bothered to attend church on Sundays."

"I suppose he does keep to himself," Anna admitted.

"Some are saying he is too proud to be seen at the country amusements here."

"That isn't true."

"Oh, I know he is quite nice." Mother Wren poured herself a second cup of tea. "Why, he had breakfast in this very cottage with us and very gracious he was, too. But he hasn't gone out of his way to endear himself with many others in the village. It doesn't do his reputation good."

Anna frowned down at her half-eaten potato. "I hadn't realized so many saw him in that light. The tenants on his land adore him."

Mother Wren nodded. "The tenants might. But he needs to be gracious to those higher up in society as well."

"I'll try to convince him to come to the soiree." Anna straightened her shoulders. "But it might be a job. As you say, he isn't very interested in social events."

Mother Wren smiled. "In the meantime, we need to discuss what we'll wear to the soiree."

"I hadn't even thought of that." Anna frowned. "All I have is my old green silk gown. There simply isn't enough time to have the material I brought from London made into dresses."

"It is a shame," Mother Wren agreed. "But your green gown is very becoming, my dear. The lovely color brings roses to your cheeks and sets off your hair so well. Although, I suppose the neckline is sadly out of date."

"Maybe we could use some of the trimmings Mrs. Wren bought in London," Fanny said shyly. She'd been hovering nearby throughout the conversation.

"What a good idea." Mother Wren beamed at her, making the girl flush. "We had better get started tonight."

"Yes, indeed, but there is something I want to find before we begin on the dresses."

Anna pushed back her chair and crossed to the old kitchen cupboard. She knelt and opened the bottom cabinet and peered in.

"Whatever are you looking for, Anna?" Mother Wren asked from behind her.

Anna backed out of the cabinet and sneezed before triumphantly holding up a dusty little jar. "My mother's salve for bruises and abrasions."

Mother Wren looked at the jar doubtfully. "Your mother was a wonderful amateur herbalist, my dear, and I've been grateful for her salve many times in the past, but it does have an unfortunate odor. Are you sure you need it?"

Anna got up, briskly shaking out the dust in her skirts. "Oh, it's not for me. It's for the earl. He had an accident with his horse."

"An accident with his horse?" Her mother-in-law blinked. "Did he fall off?"

"Oh, no. Lord Swartingham is much too good a horseman to fall off his horse," Anna said. "I'm not sure what exactly happened. I don't think he wants to discuss it. But he has the most terrible bruises on his face."

"On his face . . ." Mother Wren trailed off thoughtfully.

"Yes, one of his eyes looks quite bruised, and his jaw is black and blue."

"So you intend to put the salve on his face?" Mother Wren covered her own nose as if in sympathy.

Anna ignored her theatrics. "It will help him heal faster."

"I'm sure you know best," Mother Wren replied, but she didn't look particularly convinced.

THE NEXT MORNING, Anna ran her quarry to ground in the stable yard. Lord Swartingham stood firing instructions at Mr. Hopple, who was noting them as best he could in a little book. Jock lay nearby, but he got up to greet Anna when he saw her. The earl noticed, stopped, and turned his black eyes on Anna. He smiled.

Mr. Hopple glanced up at the cessation of directions. "Good morning, Mrs. Wren." He looked back to Lord Swartingham. "Shall I start on these, my lord?"

"Yes, yes," the earl replied impatiently.

The steward hurried away, looking relieved.

The earl sauntered over. "Is there something you need?" He kept walking until he stood too close to her.

She could see the fine threads of silver in his hair. "Yes," she said briskly. "I need you to hold still."

His beautiful ebony eyes widened. "What?"

"I have some salve for your face." She produced the little jar from her basket and held it up.

He eyed it dubiously.

"It's my late mother's own recipe. She swore by its healing properties."

Anna took the lid off, and the earl jerked his head back at the pungent smell that rolled up. Jock attempted to put his nose in the jar.

Lord Swartingham pulled the dog down by the scruff of his neck. "Good God. It smells like horse—" He caught her narrowed eye. "Hide," he finished lamely.

"Well, that's appropriate for the stable yard, don't you think?" she replied tartly.

The earl looked worried. "It doesn't actually have horse—"

"Oh, no." Anna was shocked. "It's composed of sheep fat and herbs and some other things. I'm not sure exactly what. I'd have to look up my mother's recipe to tell you.

But there is definitely no horse—uh, nothing objectionable in it. Now hold still."

He cocked an eyebrow at her tone but obediently stood motionless. She scooped out a greasy glob with her finger, stretched on tiptoe, and began to smooth it over his cheekbone. He was very tall, and she had to crowd rather close in order to reach his face. Lord Swartingham was silent, breathing deeply as she spread the salve carefully up near his black eye. She could feel him watching her. She took another dollop and began to rub it gently on his discolored jaw. The salve was cool but became warm and slippery as his skin heated it. She felt the faint scrape of his beard under her fingers and had to fight the urge to linger. She completed the last pass and let her hand fall.

He looked down at her.

In moving closer to him in order to apply the salve, she'd crept between his spread legs. His heat surrounded her body. She started to step away. But his hands wrapped around her arms. His fingers flexed, and he seemed to gaze intently at her. Anna held her breath. Would he . . .?

He let her go.

"Thank you, Mrs. Wren." He opened his mouth as if to say something more and then shut it. "I have some work to attend to. I'll see you later this afternoon." He nodded curtly before turning away.

Jock looked at her, whined, and then followed his master.

Anna watched them stride away, then sighed and thoughtfully put the lid back on the salve jar.

Chapter Thirteen

*So Aurea went home to visit her father. She traveled
in a golden coach drawn by flying swans, and she
carried with her many beautiful things to give to
her family and friends. But when her older sisters
saw the wonderful gifts that the younger girl had
brought home, their hearts, instead of filling with
gratitude and pleasure, wallowed in jealousy and
spite. The sisters put their beautiful, cold heads
together and began to quiz Aurea about her new home
and her odd husband. And little by little, they heard
all: the richness of the palace, the avian servants, the
exotic meals, and finally—and most importantly—the
silent, nocturnal lover. Hearing the last, they grinned
behind their pale hands and set to planting the seeds
of doubt in their little sister's mind. . . .*
—from The Raven Prince

"Farther to the top." Felicity Clearwater wrinkled her
brow and stared at the ceiling in her larger sitting room.
The drawn curtains muted the afternoon sun outside. "No.
No, more to the left."

A masculine voice muttered irritably.

"That's it," she said. "There. I think you've got it." In the corner, a crack snaked across the ceiling. She'd never noticed it before. It must be new. "Did you find her?"

Chilton Lillipin, "Chilly" to his intimates, one of whom was Felicity, spat out a hair. "My darling gosling, do try to relax. You're disturbing my artistry." He bent again.

Artistry? She suppressed a snort. She closed her eyes for a bit and tried to concentrate on her lover and what he was doing, but it was no use. She opened her eyes again. She really needed to have the plasterers in to repair that crack. And the last time they'd come, Reginald had been an absolute bear, stomping about and grumbling as if the workmen were only there to bother him. Felicity sighed.

"That's it, sweetheart," Chilly said from below. "Just lie back and let a master lover bring you to heaven."

She rolled her eyes. She'd almost forgotten the *master lover*. She sighed again. There was no help for it.

Felicity began to moan.

Fifteen minutes later, Chilly stood before the sitting room mirror, carefully adjusting his wig. He studied his reflection and slid the wig marginally to the right on his shaved head. He was a handsome man, but just a bit off, in Felicity's opinion. His eyes were pure blue, but they were set just a shade too close together. His features were regular, but his chin gave up and slid into his neck just a bit too soon. And his limbs were well muscled, but his legs were a fraction too short to be in proportion to the rest of his body. Chilly's offness continued into his personality. She'd heard rumors that, although skilled in swordplay,

Chilly proved his prowess by challenging less-accomplished men to duels and then killing them.

Felicity narrowed her eyes. She wouldn't trust Chilly at her back in a dark alley, but he did have his uses. "Did you find out where she went to in London?"

"Of course." Chilly smirked at himself in the glass. His gold canine winked back at him. "The little chit ended up at a bawdy house called Aphrodite's Grotto. Not once, but twice. Can you believe?"

"Aphrodite's Grotto?"

"It's a high-flying establishment." Chilly gave a last tug to his wig and abandoned the mirror to glance at her. "Ladies of the *ton* sometimes go there in disguise to meet their paramours."

"Really?" Felicity tried not to sound intrigued.

Chilly poured a tumblerful of the squire's best smuggled brandy. "Seems a little above a country widow."

Yes, it did. How had Anna Wren paid for such a place? The establishment Chilly described was expensive. Her lover would have to be rich. He must have a good knowledge of London and the less-reputable haunts of the *ton*. And the only gentleman who fit that description in Little Battleford, the only gentleman who had traveled to London during the same time period as Anna Wren, was the Earl of Swartingham. A triumphant shiver went down Felicity's spine.

"What's this all about, then?" Chilly peered over his glass at her. "Who cares if a brown mouse has a secret life?" He sounded a bit too curious for her taste.

"Never you mind." Felicity lounged back on the chaise and stretched luxuriantly, her breasts thrusting out.

Chilly's attention was immediately diverted. "I'll tell you someday."

"Don't I at least get a reward?" Chilly pretended to pout, an unattractive sight. He strolled closer and crowded against the edge of the chaise.

He had done well. And Felicity felt on good terms with the world. Why not humor the man? She stretched out a feline hand to the buttons on Chilly's breeches.

EDWARD PULLED THE mangled cravat from his neck that night. He had to get control of his body's impulses. He scowled and tossed the crumpled neckcloth on top of a chair. His room in the Abbey was a rather dismal place, the furniture big and clumsy, the colors drab and depressed. It was a wonder the de Raafs had been able to maintain the family line at all in such a setting.

Davis, as usual, wasn't around when he might be useful. Edward wedged the heel of his boot in the bootjack and began levering. He'd come very close to not letting go of Anna in the stable yard. To kissing her, in fact. It was exactly the sort of thing he'd been trying to prevent for the last few weeks.

The first boot fell to the floor, and he started work on the second. The trip to London was supposed to have solved this problem. And now with the marriage nearly finalized . . . Well, he had to start acting the part of a soon-to-be-married man. No pondering Anna's hair and why she had put off her cap. No contemplating how close she had stood when she'd applied the salve. And especially, he would not think of her mouth and how it would feel if he opened it wide beneath his own and . . .

Damn.

The second boot came off, and Davis, with exquisite timing, banged into the room. "Goramity! What is that smell? Pee-yeew!"

The valet held a stack of freshly laundered cravats in his hands, the apparent reason for his rare, voluntary visit to his employer's rooms.

Edward sighed. "A good evening to you, too, Davis."

"Christ all Jaysus! Fell in a pigsty, did you?"

Edward began pulling off his stockings. "Are you aware that some valets actually spend their time helping their masters to dress and undress rather than making rude comments about their person?"

Davis cackled. "Ha. Should've told me you were having problems buttoning your pantyloons, m'lord. I would've helped you."

Edward scowled. "Just put away the cravats and get out."

Davis tottered to the highboy, pulled out a top drawer, and dumped the cravats in. "What's that slimy stuff on your mug?" he asked.

"Mrs. Wren kindly gave me some salve for my bruises this afternoon," Edward said with dignity.

The valet tilted toward him and inhaled with a loud snuffling sound. "That's where the stank is coming from. It smells like horseshit."

"Davis!"

"Well, it do. Haven't smelled anything near that bad since you was a lad and fell on your arse into that pigsty back of Old Peward's farm. Remember that?"

"How could I forget with you around?" Edward muttered.

"Gor! Thought we'd never get the stank out of you that time. And I had to throw away them breeches."

"Pleasant as this recollection is—"

"'Course, you never would've fallen in if you hadn't been ogling Old Peward's daughter," Davis continued.

"I was not ogling anyone. I slipped."

"Naw." Davis scratched his scalp. "Your eyes were about falling out of your head they were, gawking at her big bubbies."

Edward grit his teeth. "I *slipped* and fell."

"Almost a sign from the Lord above, that," Davis said, waxing philosophical. "Gawp at a girl's bubbies and land in pig shit."

"Oh, for God's sake. I was sitting on the railing of the pigsty and I slipped."

"Prissy Peward sure did have big dugs, that lass did." Davis sounded a little wistful.

"You weren't even there."

"But that pigsty stank had nothing on the horseshit on your face now."

"*Dav*-vis."

The valet made his way back to the door waving a liver-spotted hand in front of his face as he went. "Must be balmy to let a woman smear horsesh—"

"*Davis!*"

"All over your face."

The valet reached the door and slanted around the corner, still mumbling. Since his progress was, as usual, slow, Edward could hear his nattering for a good five minutes more. Oddly, it became louder the farther Davis moved from the door.

Edward frowned at himself in his shaving mirror. The salve did smell terrible. He reached for a basin and poured some water into it from the pitcher on his dresser. He picked up a washcloth and then hesitated. The salve was already on his face, and it had pleased Anna to put it there. He rubbed his thumb across the edge of his jaw, remembering her soft hands.

He threw down the washcloth.

He could wash off the salve when he shaved in the morning. It wouldn't hurt to leave it on tonight. He turned from the dresser and took off the remainder of his clothes, folding and placing them on a chair as he did so. There was at least one advantage to having an unusual valet: He had learned to be neat with his apparel since Davis didn't deign to pick up after him. Standing naked, Edward yawned and stretched before climbing into the ancient four-poster bed. He leaned over and blew out the bedside candle and then lay there in the dark staring at the shadowy outlines of the bed curtains. He wondered fuzzily how old they were. Certainly older than the house itself. Had they originally been this awful shade of brownish yellow?

His eyes sleepily swept the room, and he saw near the door the shape of a woman.

He blinked and suddenly she stood by his bed.

She smiled. The same smile Eve wore when she'd held the fateful apple out to Adam. The woman was gloriously nude except for a butterfly mask on her face.

He thought, *It's the whore from Aphrodite's Grotto.* And then, *I'm dreaming.*

But the thought drifted away. She slowly rubbed her hands up her midriff, drawing his eyes with them. She cupped her breasts and leaned forward so the tips were at the level of his eyes. Then she began to pinch and tease her own nipples.

His mouth went dry as he watched her nipples elongate and turn cherry red. He lifted his head to kiss her breasts, for his mouth fairly watered with the need to taste her, but she moved away with a taunting smile. The woman lifted her flowing, honey-brown hair away from her neck. Curling tentacles clung to her arms. She arched her slender back, thrusting her breasts up and forward like juicy fruit before him. He growled and felt his cock throb against his stomach at her teasing.

The woman smiled a witchy smile. She knew exactly what she was doing to him. She smoothed her hands back down her torso, past her thrusting breasts, over her downy belly, and paused. Her fingers just touched the glinting curls of her bush. He willed her to move them farther, but she teased him, lightly combing through her maiden hair. Just when he could stand it no longer, she chuckled low and spread her legs.

Edward didn't know if he still breathed. His eyes were locked on her hands and her pussy. She parted her nether lips for him. He could see the ruby skin glistening with her fluid and smell her musk lifting from her flesh. She dipped one slender finger into her cleft. Slowly, she stroked up and found her clitoris. She petted herself, her finger moving in slippery circles on the bud. Her hips began to rotate, and she let her head fall back and moaned. The sound mingled with Edward's own groan of pure lust. He was rock hard, pulsing with need.

He watched as she tilted her pelvis toward him. She slid her middle finger into her pussy and moved it out and back again, slowly, languidly, the finger shining with her moisture. Her other hand moved faster on her clitoris, torturing the fragile nubbin. Suddenly she stiffened, her head still thrown back, and moaned, low and keening. Her finger worked furiously in and out of her body.

Edward groaned again. He could see the evidence of her orgasm sliding down her silky thighs. The sight nearly sent him over the edge. The woman sighed and relaxed, her hips swiveling sensuously one last time. She drew her fingers from herself and brought them, wet and shining, to his lips. She brushed her fingers over his mouth, and he tasted her desire. Dazedly, he looked up at her and realized that the mask had fallen away from her face.

Anna smiled down at him.

Then his orgasm took him, and he woke to the almost agonizing jerking of his cock as he gained his release.

ANNA'S EYES ADJUSTED to the cool dimness the next morning as she wandered down the packed-earth aisle of Ravenhill Abbey's stables. The building was venerable. It had served the Abbey through several reconstructions and expansions. Stones the size of a man's head formed the foundation and the lower walls. Six feet from the ground, the walls became sturdy oak that led up to the exposed rafters, vaulting twenty feet overhead. Below, stalls flanked a central aisle.

The Ravenhill stables had room for fifty horses easily, although fewer than ten were currently in residence. The relative paucity of horses saddened her. This must at one time have been a thriving, active place. Now the stables were quiet—like a grizzled, slumbering giant. It smelt of hay, leather, and decades, perhaps centuries, of horse manure. The odor was warm and welcoming.

Lord Swartingham was to meet her here this morning so they could ride out to inspect more fields. Anna's makeshift riding habit trailed in the dust behind her as she walked. Every now and then, an equine head poked curiously over a stall and nickered a greeting. She spotted the earl farther ahead, deep in conversation with the head groom. He towered over the older man. Both stood in a beam of dusty sunlight at the far end of the stables. As Anna neared, she could hear that they were discussing the problem of a gelding with a chronic limp. Lord Swartingham glanced up and caught sight of her. She paused by Daisy's stall. He smiled and turned back to the head groom.

Daisy was already saddled and bridled and tied loosely in the aisle. Anna waited, softly talking to the mare. She watched Lord Swartingham lean down to listen to the head groom, his full attention on the older man. The head groom was a wiry, aged specimen. His hands were knotted now with arthritis and healed bones, broken long ago. He carried himself proudly, his head stiffly erect. The old man, like many countrymen, talked slowly and liked to discuss a problem at length. Anna noticed that the earl patiently let him have his say, neither hurrying him nor cutting off his speech, until the head groom felt that the problem has been sufficiently mulled over. Then Lord Swartingham gently clapped the man on the back and watched him walk out of the stable. The earl turned and started for her.

Without any warning, Daisy—gentle, placid Daisy—reared. Iron-shod hooves cleaved the air only inches from Anna's face. She fell back against the stall door, cowering. A hoof thumped the wood next to her shoulder.

"Anna!" She heard the earl's shout over the startled neighing of the nearby horses and Daisy's own frantic whinnying.

A rat scurried underneath the stall door, flicking its naked tail as it disappeared. Lord Swartingham caught the horse's halter and pulled the mare forcibly away. Anna heard a grunt and the slam of a stall door.

Strong arms wrapped around her. "Dear God, Anna, are you hurt?"

She couldn't answer. Fear seemed to have clogged her throat. He ran his hands over her shoulders and arms, rapidly feeling and smoothing.

"Anna." His face lowered toward hers.

She couldn't help herself; her eyes closed.

He kissed her.

His lips were hot and dry. Soft and firm. They moved across hers lightly, before he angled his head and pressed strongly. Her nostrils flared, and she smelled horses and him. She thought irrelevantly that forever after she would associate the smell of horses with Lord Swartingham.

With *Edward*.

He skimmed her lips with his tongue, so softly that at first she thought she had imagined it. But he repeated the caress, a touch like suede leather, and she opened her mouth to him. She felt his warmth invading her mouth, filling it, stroking across her tongue. He tasted of the coffee he must have drunk at breakfast.

She clenched her fingers at the back of his neck, and he opened his own mouth wider and drew her closer to lean against him. One of his hands brushed across her cheek. She threaded her hands through the hair at his nape. His queue came undone, and she reveled in the silky feel of his hair between her fingers. He ran his tongue over her bottom lip and drew it between his teeth, gently sucking on it. She heard herself moan. She trembled, her legs hardly able to hold up her weight.

A clatter from the stable yard outside brought Anna abruptly back to her surroundings. Edward raised his head to listen. One of the stable hands was berating a boy for dropping equipment.

He turned his head back to Anna and smoothed his thumb over her cheek. "Anna, I . . ."

His train of thought seemed to slip away. He shook his head. Then, as if compelled, he brushed a gentle kiss over her mouth and lingered there a moment as the kiss deepened.

But something was wrong; Anna could feel it. He was slipping away. She was losing him. She pressed closer, trying to hold on. He ran his lips across her cheekbones and lightly, softly, over her closed eyelids. She felt his breath sift through her eyelashes.

His arms dropped, and she sensed him step away from her.

She opened her eyes to see him running his hands through his hair. "I'm sorry. That was—*God,* I'm so sorry."

"No, please don't apologize." She smiled, warmth spreading through her breast as she gathered her courage. Maybe this was the time. "I wanted the kiss just as much as you. As a matter of—"

"I'm engaged."

"What?" Anna recoiled as if he had struck her.

"I'm engaged to be married." Edward grimaced as if in self-disgust or possibly pain.

She stood frozen, struggling to comprehend the simple words. A numbness seeped throughout her body, driving out the warmth as if it had never been.

"That's why I went up to London. To finalize the marital settlements." Edward paced, his hands agitatedly running through his disheveled hair. "She's the daughter of a baronet, a very old family. I think they might have come over with the Conqueror, which is more than the de Raafs can say. Her lands—" He stopped suddenly as if she'd interrupted.

She hadn't.

He met her eyes for an agonizing moment and then looked away. It was as if a cord that had stretched between them had been severed.

"I'm sorry, Mrs. Wren." He cleared his throat. "I never should have behaved so badly with you. You have my word of honor that it won't happen again."

"I-I—" She struggled to force words through her swelling throat. "I ought to return to work, my lord." Her only coherent thought was that she must maintain her composure. Anna moved to go—to flee, really—but his voice stopped her.

"Sam . . ."

"What?" All she wanted was a hole to curl up in so she could never think again. Never feel again. But something in his face kept her from leaving.

Edward stared up at the loft as if searching for something, or someone. Anna followed his gaze. There was nothing there. The old loft was nearly empty. Where once mounds of hay must have lain, now only dust motes floated. The hay for the horses was stored below in empty stalls.

But still he stared at the loft. "This was my brother's favorite place," he said finally. "Samuel, my younger brother. He was nine years old, born six years after me. It was enough of a gap that I did not pay him much attention. He was a quiet boy. He used to hide in the loft, even though it gave Mother fits; she was afraid he'd fall and kill himself. It didn't stop him. He'd spend half the day up there, playing, I don't know, with tin soldiers or tops or something. It was easy to forget he was up there, and sometimes he'd throw hay down on my head just to aggravate me." His brows drew together. "Or, I suppose, he wanted his elder brother's attention. Not that I gave it to him. I was too busy at fifteen, learning to shoot and drink and be a man, to pay attention to a child."

He walked a few paces away, still studying the loft. Anna tried to swallow down the lump in her throat. Why now? Why reveal all this pain to her now, when it couldn't matter?

He continued, "It's funny, though. When I first came back, I kept expecting to see him here in the stables. I'd walk in and look up—for his face, I guess." Edward blinked and murmured, almost to himself, "Sometimes I still do."

Anna shoved her knuckle into her mouth and bit down. She didn't want to hear this. Didn't want to feel any sympathy for this man.

"This stable was full before," he said. "My father loved horses, used to breed them. There were lots of grooms and my father's cronies hanging around out here, talking horseflesh and hunting. My mother was in the Abbey, holding parties and planning my sister's coming-out. This place was so busy. So happy. It was the best place in the world."

Edward touched the worn door of an empty stall with his fingertips. "I never thought I would leave. I never wanted to."

Anna hugged herself and bit back a sob.

"But then the smallpox came." He seemed to stare into space, and the lines in his face stood out in sharp relief. "And they died, one by one. First Sammy, then Father and Mother. Elizabeth, my sister, was the last to go. They cut off her hair because of the fever, and she cried and cried inconsolably; she thought it her best feature. Two days later, they put her into the family vault. We were lucky, I guess, if you can call it luck. Other families had to wait for spring to bury their dead. It was winter and the ground was frozen."

He drew a breath. "But I don't remember that last, only what they told me later, because by then I had it, too."

He stroked a finger over his cheekbone where the smallpox scars clustered, and Anna wondered how often he had made the gesture in the years since.

"And, of course, I survived." He looked at her with the bitterest smile she'd ever seen, as if he tasted bile on his tongue. "I alone lived. Out of all of them, I survived."

He closed his eyes.

When he opened them again, his face was smoothed into a blank, firm mask. "I'm the last of my line, the last of the de Raafs," he said. "There are no distant cousins to inherit the title and the Abbey, no waiting obscure heirs. When I die—*if* I die without a son—it all reverts to the crown."

Anna forced herself to hold his gaze, though it left her trembling.

"I must have an heir. Do you understand?" He grit his teeth and said, as if he were pulling the words, bloody and torn, from his very heart, "I must marry a woman who can bear children."

Chapter Fourteen

*Who was her lover? Aurea's sisters inquired, their
brows creased with false concern. Why had she never
seen him in the light of day? And having never seen
him, how could she be sure he was human at all?
Perhaps a monster too horrible to be exposed to
daylight shared her bed. Perhaps this monster
would get her heavy with his child, and she would
bear something too awful to imagine. The longer
Aurea listened to her sisters, the more disquieted she
became until she knew not what to think or do.
It was then that the sisters suggested a plan. . . .*
—from *The Raven Prince*

For the rest of that day, Anna simply endured. She made
herself sit at the rosewood desk in the Abbey library. She
made herself dip her quill in the ink without spilling a
drop. She made herself copy out a page of Edward's manuscript. When she finished that first page, she made herself do it again. And again. And yet again.

That was the job of a secretary, after all.

Long ago, when Peter had first proposed to her, she'd thought about children. She'd wondered whether their children would have red or brown hair, and she'd daydreamed possible names. When they'd married and moved into the tiny cottage, she'd worried if there would be enough room for a family.

She had never worried about not having children.

The second year of the marriage, Anna had begun to watch her monthly flow. The third year, she wept every month when she saw the rust-colored stain. By the fourth year of her marriage to Peter, she knew he had turned to someone else. Whether because she was inadequate as a lover or as a breeder or both, she never found out. And when Peter died . . .

When he died, she took her hopes for a child and wrapped them carefully in a box and buried that box deep, deep in her heart. So deep, she thought never to face that dream again. Except, with one sentence, Edward had exhumed the box and ripped it open. And her hopes, her dreams, her *need* to bear a child were as fresh now as they had been when she was newly wed.

Oh, dear God, to be capable of giving Edward children! What she wouldn't do, what she wouldn't give up, to be able to hold a baby. A baby made from both of their bodies and souls. Anna felt a physical ache in her chest. An ache that expanded outward until she could hardly keep herself from curling up to hold it in.

But she must maintain her composure. She was in Edward's library—indeed, Edward sat not five feet away—and she couldn't show her pain. Fiercely, she concentrated on moving her quill across the paper. Never mind that the scratches she made with the quill were illegible, never mind that the page would have to be recopied later. She would get through this afternoon.

Several ghastly hours later, Anna slowly gathered her things, moving like a very old woman. As she did so, the invitation to Felicity Clearwater's dance fell from her shawl. She stared at it a moment. A lifetime ago she'd meant to remind Edward about the soiree. It seemed inconsequential now. But Mother Wren had said it was important that Edward participate in local social events. Anna straightened her shoulders. Just this one thing, then she could go home.

"Mrs. Clearwater's soiree is tomorrow night." Her voice creaked.

"I don't intend to accept Mrs. Clearwater's invitation."

Anna refused to look at him, but Edward's voice didn't sound much better than her own.

"You're the most important aristocrat in the area, my lord," she said. "It would be gracious to attend."

"No doubt."

"It is the best way to hear the latest village gossip."

He grunted.

"Mrs. Clearwater always serves her special punch. Everyone agrees it is the best in the county," she lied.

"I don't—"

"Please, *please* go." She still didn't look at him, but she could feel his gaze on her face, as palpable as a hand.

"As you wish."

"Good." Anna jammed her hat on her head and then remembered something. She opened her center desk drawer and took out *The Raven Prince*. She carried it over to Edward's desk, laying it softly on top. "This is yours."

She turned and left the room before he could reply.

THE HALL WAS stiflingly hot, the decorations from two years ago, and the music off-key. It was Felicity Clearwater's annual spring soiree. Every year, the citizens of Little Battleford who were lucky enough to receive an invitation put on their very best clothes and drank watery punch at the Clearwater home. Felicity Clearwater stood by the door to welcome her guests. She wore a new gown, an indigo-blue muslin this year with cascading flounce down the sleeves. The underskirt sported a pattern of flying crimson birds on a light blue field, and there were crimson bows in a V outlining her bodice. Squire Clearwater, a portly gentleman in orange-clocked stockings and the full-bottomed wig of his youth, fidgeted beside her, but it was clearly understood that the event belonged to Felicity.

Anna had made it through the receiving line with only a frosty greeting from Felicity and a rather abstracted one from the squire. Relieved to have gotten that ordeal out of the way, she hovered at the side of the room. She'd unwarily accepted a glass of punch from the vicar and now had no choice but to sip it.

Mother Wren stood beside Anna and cast anxious glances at her. Anna hadn't told her what had occurred in the stables between Edward and herself. Nor did she intend to. But her mother-in-law still sensed something was wrong. Evidently, Anna wasn't very good at pretending cheer.

She took another grim sip of the punch. She wore her best gown. She and Fanny had spent some time over it, trying to make the alterations as neat as possible. The dress was a light apple green, and they had freshened it with the addition of white lace at the neckline. The lace also hid the modification of the neckline from a curve to the more fashionable square. Fanny, in a fit of artistic invention, had devised a rosette for Anna's hair from some of the lace and a bit of green ribbon. Anna hardly felt festive, but it would have hurt Fanny's feelings not to wear the rosette.

"The punch isn't bad," Mother Wren whispered.

Anna hadn't noticed. She took another sip and was pleasantly surprised. "Yes. Better than rumored."

Mother Wren fidgeted for a moment before coming up with another conversational foray. "It's too bad Rebecca couldn't attend."

"I don't see why not."

"You know she can't be seen at social occasions, dear, so close to her confinement. In my day, we didn't dare set foot out of the house once we began to show."

Anna wrinkled her nose. "It's so silly. Everyone knows she's increasing. It isn't as if it's a secret."

"It's the propriety that matters, not what everyone knows. Besides, Rebecca is so far along, I don't think she would like to stand for hours. There are never enough seats at these dances." Mother Wren looked around the room. "Do you think your earl will come?"

"He's not *my* earl, as you well know," Anna said somewhat bitterly.

Mother Wren glanced at her sharply.

Anna tried to modulate her tone. "I told him that I thought it a good idea for him to attend the soiree."

"I hope he comes before the dancing commences. I do like to see a fine, manly figure on the dance floor."

"He mayn't come at all, and then you'll have to be content with Mr. Merriweather's form on the dance floor." Anna gestured with her cup to that gentleman, standing across the room.

Both women looked at Mr. Merriweather, a skeletal gentleman with knock-knees, who was talking to a substantial matron in a peach-colored frock. As they watched, Mr. Merriweather leaned closer to make a point and absentmindedly tilted his punch cup. A thin stream of liquid trickled down the décolletage of the lady's dress.

Mother Wren shook her head sadly.

"Do you know," Anna said thoughtfully, "I'm not sure Mr. Merriweather has ever made it through a reel without losing his place."

Mother Wren sighed. Then she glanced over Anna's shoulder at the door and visibly brightened. "I don't think I'll have to make do with Mr. Merriweather after all. There's *your* earl at the door."

Anna turned to view the entrance to the dance room and raised her cup to her lips. For a moment, she forgot it there as she caught sight of Edward. He wore black knee breeches with a sapphire coat and waistcoat. His black hair, brushed in an uncharacteristically neat queue, gleamed like a bird's wing in the candlelight. He stood nearly a head taller than any other man in the room. Felicity was plainly delighted with her luck at being the first to entice the elusive earl into a social setting. She had a firm hand on his elbow and was introducing Edward to anyone within speaking distance.

Anna smiled wryly. Edward's shoulders were bunched, and his expression was grim. Even across the room, she could tell that he was holding on to his temper by a thread. He looked to be in danger of making the faux pas of walking away from his hostess. He glanced up at that moment and caught her eye.

She sucked in her breath at the contact. Impossible to read his expression.

He turned back to Felicity and said something, then began to make his way through the crowd toward Anna. She felt liquid coolness on her wrist and glanced down. Her hand was trembling so hard she was sloshing the remains of the punch on her arm. Anna clasped her other hand around the cup to steady it. For an instant, she came close to bolting, but Mother Wren was right beside her. And she'd have to face him again sometime.

Felicity must have signaled the musicians. The violins let out a shriek.

"Ah, Mrs. Wren. A pleasure to meet you again." Edward bowed over Mother Wren's hand. He didn't smile.

Her mother-in-law didn't seem to care. "Oh, my lord, I'm so glad you could attend. Anna has been dying to dance." Mother Wren lifted her eyebrows meaningfully.

Anna wished she had bolted when she'd had the chance.

The broad hint hung there in the air between them for an uncomfortably long time before Edward spoke. "If you would do me the pleasure?"

He didn't even look at her. For goodness sake, he had been the one to kiss her!

Anna pursed her lips. "I didn't know you danced, my lord."

Edward's gaze snapped around to her. "Of course I can dance. I am an earl after all."

"As if I'd forget that," she muttered.

Edward narrowed his obsidian eyes.

Ha! She certainly had his attention now.

He held out a gloved hand, and she demurely placed her own in it. Even with two layers of fabric between their palms, she could feel his body heat. For a moment, she remembered what it was like to run her fingertips down his nude back. Hot. Sweaty. Achingly good. She swallowed.

With only a nod to Mother Wren, he towed her out onto the dance floor where he proved he could indeed dance, albeit rather heavily.

"You do know the steps," Anna said as they met to promenade down the center of the dancers.

She saw him scowl out of the corner of her eye. "I wasn't born under a rock. I know how to behave in polite society."

The music ended before Anna could form an appropriate reply. She curtsied and started to tug her hand from Edward's grasp.

He pulled her hand firmly to him and tucked it in the crook of his elbow. "Don't you dare think of deserting me, Mrs. Wren. It's your fault I'm at this bloody soiree to begin with."

Must he keep touching her? She looked around for a distraction. "Perhaps you would care for some punch?"

He looked at her suspiciously. "Would I?"

"Well, maybe not," she admitted. "But it's the only thing to drink at the present, and the refreshment table is in the opposite direction from Mrs. Clearwater."

"Then let us try the punch by all means."

He walked toward the punch table, and she found that people stepped aside naturally for him. In no time at all, Anna was sipping her second glass of weak punch.

Edward had pivoted slightly to the side to answer a question from the vicar when she heard a sly voice at her elbow. "I'm surprised to see you here, Mrs. Wren. I'd heard you had taken up a new *profession*."

EDWARD TURNED SLOWLY to face the speaker, a florid man in an ill-fitting wig. He didn't look familiar. Beside him, Anna had stiffened, her face frozen.

"Have you learned any new *skills* from your recent guests?" The man's entire attention was fixed on Anna.

She opened her mouth, but for once Edward beat her to it. "I don't believe I heard you correctly."

The swine seemed to notice him for the first time. His eyes widened. Good.

The silence in their immediate vicinity began to spread outward through the room as the guests became aware that something interesting was happening.

The fellow was braver than he looked. "I said—"

"Be very, very careful what you say next." Edward could feel the muscles in his shoulders flexing.

The other man finally appeared to comprehend the danger he was in. His eyes widened, and he visibly swallowed.

Edward nodded once. "Good. Perhaps you'd care to apologize to Mrs. Wren for what you did *not* say."

"I—" The man had to stop and clear his throat. "I am most sorry if anything I said offended you, Mrs. Wren."

Anna nodded stiffly, but the man was correctly looking toward Edward to see if he had redeemed himself.

He had not.

The man swallowed again. A bead of sweat slid greasily along the edge of his wig. "I don't know what came over me. I am most abjectly sorry to have caused you any pain whatsoever, Mrs. Wren." He pulled at his neckcloth and leaned forward to add, "I really am an ass, you know."

"Yes, you are," Edward said gently.

The man's complexion turned a sickly hue.

"Well!" Anna said. "I think it is about time for the next dance. Isn't that the music beginning?"

She spoke loudly in the general direction of the musicians, and they immediately took her up on the suggestion. She snatched Edward's hand and began marching toward the dance floor. She had quite a strong grip for such a little thing. Edward shot one last, narrow-eyed glare at the swine, and then docilely permitted himself to be led away.

"Who is he?"

Anna looked up at him as they formed the set. "He didn't really hurt me, you know."

The dance began and he was forced to wait until the figures drew them together again. "Who is he, Anna?"

She looked exasperated. "John Wiltonson. He was a friend of my husband's."

Edward waited.

"He made a proposition to me after Peter's death."

"He wanted to marry you?" His brows drew together.

"An indecent proposition." Anna's eyes were averted. "He was—is—already married."

He stopped dead, causing the couple next in line to bump into them. "He assaulted you?"

"No." She pulled on his arm, but he remained steadfast. She hissed in his ear, "He wanted me to become his mistress. I refused." The dancers behind them were beginning to pile up. "My lord!"

Edward allowed himself to be pulled into the dance again, although they were no longer in time to the music. "I never want to hear someone speak so of you again."

"A fine sentiment, I'm sure," she replied tartly. "But you can hardly spend the rest of your life following me about intimidating the impertinent."

Unable to think of a reply, he simply glared. She was right. The thought tore at him. Anna was only his secretary, plain and simple. He couldn't be with her all the time. He couldn't stop any insults. He couldn't even protect her from insulting advances. Such guardianship was the prerogative of a husband only.

Anna interrupted his thoughts. "I shouldn't have danced with you again so soon. It isn't proper."

"I don't give a damn what's proper," Edward said. "Besides, you knew it was the only method to get me away from that baboon."

She smiled up at him, and something inside his chest wrenched. How was he to keep her safe?

Edward was still pondering that question two hours later. He leaned against a wall and watched Anna lead a panting gentleman in a country reel. She clearly needed a husband, but he couldn't imagine her with a man. Or rather, he couldn't imagine her with *another* man. He scowled.

Someone coughed deferentially at his elbow. A tall young man with a bob wig stood next to him. His Geneva collar identified him as Vicar Jones.

The vicar coughed again and smiled nearsightedly at him through his pince-nez. "Lord Swartingham. So good of you to attend our little local entertainment."

Edward wondered how he managed to sound like a man twice his age. The vicar couldn't be over thirty. "Vicar. I'm enjoying Mrs. Clearwater's soiree." To his surprise, he realized that he spoke the truth.

"Good, good. Mrs. Clearwater's social events are always so well planned. And her refreshments are just delicious." The vicar demonstrated by gulping enthusiastically at his punch.

Edward eyed his own punch and made a mental note to check on the vicar's stipend. Obviously the man was not used to decent food.

"I say, Mrs. Wren is certainly cutting a dashing figure on the dance floor." The vicar squinted as he watched Anna. "She looks different tonight."

Edward followed his gaze. "She isn't wearing a cap."

"Is that it?" Vicar Jones sounded vague. "You have sharper eyes than I, my lord. I wondered if she'd bought a new dress on her trip."

Edward was raising his own cup of punch to his lips when the vicar's words sunk in. He frowned and lowered the cup. "What trip?"

"Hmm?" Vicar Jones still watched the dancers, his mind obviously not on the conversation.

Edward was about to repeat the question a little more forcefully this time when Mrs. Clearwater interrupted them. "Ah, Lord Swartingham. I see you know the vicar."

Both men started as if they'd been goosed simultaneously in the arse. Edward turned a strained smile on his hostess. He noticed out of the corner of his eye that the vicar was peering around as if for escape. "Yes, I've met Vicar Jones, Mrs. Clearwater."

"Lord Swartingham has most graciously helped with the new church roof." Vicar Jones made eye contact with another guest. "I say, is that Mr. Merriweather? I must have a word with him. If you'll excuse me?" The vicar bowed and hurried away.

Edward eyed the vicar's retreating form with envy. The man must have attended the Clearwater soirees before.

"How lovely to have a moment alone with you, my lord," Mrs. Clearwater said. "I did want to discuss your trip to London."

"Oh?" Maybe if he caught the elder Mrs. Wren's eye. It wasn't done to just abandon a lady.

"Yes, indeed." Mrs. Clearwater leaned closer. "I have heard that you were seen at some most unusual places."

"Really?"

"In the company of a lady we both know."

Edward's attention swung back to Felicity Clearwater. What the devil was the woman talking about?

"Fe-*lee*-ci-ty!" A male voice, rather the worse for drink, yodeled nearby.

Mrs. Clearwater winced.

Squire Clearwater was making his way unsteadily toward them. "Felicity, m'dear, mustn't monopolize the earl. He's not interested in talk of fashions and fr-fr-fripperies." The squire dug a pointy elbow into Edward's ribs. "Eh, my lord? Hunting's the thing. A man's sport! What? What?"

Mrs. Clearwater made a sound that, in a male, might have been considered a snort.

"Actually, I don't hunt much," Edward said.

"Hounds baying, horses galloping, the smell of blood . . ." The squire was in his own world.

Across the room, Edward saw Anna put on a wrapper. Damn it. Was she leaving without bidding him good-bye?

"Excuse me."

He bowed to the squire and his wife and pushed through the mass of people. But at this hour, the soiree had become quite crowded. By the time Edward reached the door, Anna and Mrs. Wren were already outside.

"Anna!" Edward shoved past the footmen in the hall and pushed open the door. "Anna!"

She was only a few steps away. At his shout, both she and Mrs. Wren turned.

"You shouldn't walk home alone, Anna." Edward glowered, then realized his slip. "Nor you, Mrs. Wren."

Anna looked confused, but the older woman beamed. "Have you come to escort us home, Lord Swartingham?"

"Yes."

His carriage was waiting nearby. They could ride, but then the evening would be over in a matter of minutes. Besides, it was a beautiful night. He signaled the carriage to follow behind them as they walked. He offered Anna one arm and Mrs. Wren the other. Although the ladies had left the party early, the hour was late and it was dark. A full moon shone, gloriously large in the black sky, casting long shadows before them.

As they neared a crossroads, Edward heard the sudden clatter of running feet ahead of them, loud in the quiet air. Immediately he set the ladies behind him. A slight form flew around the corner. It veered toward them.

"Meg! Whatever is the matter?" Anna cried.

"Oh, ma'am!" The girl bent double, clutching her side as she tried to catch her breath. "It's Mrs. Fairchild, ma'am. She's fallen down the stairs, and I can't help her up. I think the baby's coming, too!"

Chapter Fifteen

So Aurea flew back in her magnificent golden
carriage, her sisters' plan churning in her head.
The raven greeted his returned wife almost
indifferently. Aurea ate a splendid dinner with him,
bade the raven good night, and went to her room
to wait for her sensuous visitor.
Suddenly he was there beside her, more urgent,
more demanding than he had ever been before. His
attentions left Aurea sleepy and satiated, but she stuck
stubbornly to her plan and kept herself awake even as
she heard her lover's breath settle into the evenness of
sleep. Quietly, she sat up and felt for the candle she
had earlier left on the table beside the bed. . . .
—from *The Raven Prince*

"Oh, my Lord!" Anna tried to remember when exactly Rebecca had thought the baby would come. Surely not for another month?

"Dr. Billings is at the soiree," Edward said with calm authority. "Take my carriage, girl, and fetch him quickly." He turned and shouted instructions to John Coachman as he waved the carriage forward.

"I'll go with Meg," Mother Wren said.

Edward nodded and helped her and the maid into the carriage. "Is there a midwife to find as well?" He directed the question at Anna.

"Rebecca was going to have Mrs. Stucker—"

"The midwife is attending Mrs. Lyle," her mother-in-law interrupted. "She lives four or five miles out of town. Several ladies were talking about it at the party."

"Fetch Dr. Billings to Mrs. Fairchild first, and then I'll send my carriage for Mrs. Stucker," Edward ordered.

Mother Wren and Meg nodded from inside the carriage.

Edward slammed the door shut and stepped back. "Go, John!"

The coachman shouted to the horses, and the carriage rattled away.

Edward caught Anna's hand. "Which way is Mrs. Fairchild's house?"

"It's just ahead." Anna snatched up her skirts and ran toward the house with Edward.

The front door to Rebecca's house stood ajar. All was dark except for a curtain of light that fell from the entrance onto the walkway. Edward pushed open the door and Anna followed. She looked around. They stood in the front hall with the stairs to the upper floor immediately before them. The lower part could be seen in the light from the hall, but the higher steps were in darkness. There was no sign of Rebecca.

"Could she have moved herself?" Anna gasped.

They heard a low moan from the upper stairs. Anna ran up before Edward could move. She heard him curse behind her.

Rebecca lay on a landing midway up the staircase. Anna thanked the fates that she had stopped here, instead of falling down the longer, second flight of stairs. Her friend was on her side, the great mound of her belly more prominent in that position. Her face shone white and greasy with perspiration.

Anna bit her lip. "Rebecca, can you hear me?"

"Anna." Rebecca held out her hand, and she caught it. "Thank God you are here." She gasped and her hand tightened painfully.

"What is it?" Anna asked.

"The baby." Rebecca expelled her breath. "It's coming."

"Can you rise?"

"I'm so clumsy. My ankle is hurt." There were tears in Rebecca's eyes and traces of others on her face. "The baby is too soon."

Anna's own eyes were suddenly flooded with tears. She bit the inside of her cheek as she tried to control them. Tears would not help her friend.

"Let me carry you up to your room, Mrs. Fairchild." Edward's deep voice interrupted her thoughts.

Anna glanced up. Edward stood behind her, his face grave. She stepped to the side, letting Rebecca's hand go. Edward eased his palms under the laboring woman, then squatted and positioned her in his arms before rising in one fluid movement. He was obviously careful not to jostle Rebecca's ankle, but she whimpered and squeezed her hands in the front of his coat. Edward's lips tightened. He nodded to Anna, and she went ahead of him up the stairs and down the upper hall. A single candle flickered on a bedside table in Rebecca's room. Anna hurried to take it and to light several others. Edward turned sideways to enter, and then laid her friend gently on the bed. For the first time, Anna noticed that he was very pale.

She pushed a damp lock of hair off Rebecca's forehead. "Where is James?"

Anna had to wait for the answer as another pain hit her friend. Rebecca moaned low, and her back arched off the bed. When it was over, she was panting. "He went to Drewsbury for the day on business. He said he would return tomorrow after midday." Rebecca bit her lip. "He will be so cross with me."

Edward muttered something sharp behind them and paced to the dark bedroom windows.

"Nonsense," Anna scolded softly. "None of this is your fault."

"If only I hadn't fallen down the stairs," Rebecca sobbed.

Anna was trying to comfort her when the front door slammed below. The doctor had obviously arrived. Edward excused himself to direct the man up.

Dr. Billings tried to wear an impassive face, but it was evident that he was quite worried. He bandaged Rebecca's ankle, which had swollen already and turned purple. Anna mostly sat by Rebecca's head, holding her hand and talking to her in an attempt to calm her. It wasn't easy. According to the calculations of the midwife and Rebecca, the baby was a month early. As the night progressed Rebecca's agony grew worse, and she became despondent. She was convinced she'd lose the baby. Nothing Anna said seemed to help, but she stayed by the other woman, holding her hand and stroking her hair.

A little over three hours after the doctor had arrived, Mrs. Stucker, the midwife, blew into the room. A short, rotund woman with red cheeks and black hair, now liberally sprinkled with gray, she was a welcome sight.

"Ho! This is a night for babies, it is," the midwife said. "You'll all be glad to know Mrs. Lyle has another boy baby, her fifth, would you believe it? I don't know why she even bothers to call me. I just sit in the corner and knit until it's time to catch the wee one." Mrs. Stucker took off her wrapper and a great many scarves and threw them over a chair. "Do you have some water and a bit of soap, Meg? I do like to wash me hands before I help a lady."

Dr. Billings was looking disapproving, but he made no protest at the midwife seeing his patient.

"And how are you, Mrs. Fairchild? Holding on well, despite that ankle? My, that must have been painful." The midwife laid her hand on Rebecca's tummy and looked at her face shrewdly. "The babe's eager, isn't it? Coming early just to aggravate his mother. But you're not to worry about it. Babies sometimes have minds of their own about when they want to come out."

"Will he be all right?" Rebecca licked dry lips.

"Well now, you know I can't promise anything, luv. But you're a good, strong lady, if you don't mind me saying so. I'll do my very best to help you and that baby."

Things looked brighter after that. Mrs. Stucker got Rebecca to sit up in the bed because "babies slide better downhill than up." Rebecca seemed to regain hope. She was even able to chat between pains.

Just as Anna felt as if she were going to drop from fatigue right there in the chair, Rebecca began to moan deeply. At first Anna was terribly alarmed, thinking something must be wrong. But Mrs. Stucker wasn't perturbed and stated cheerfully that the babe would soon be there. And indeed, in another half hour, during which Anna came wide awake, Rebecca's baby was born. It was a little girl, wrinkled and small but able to bawl quite loudly. The sound brought a smile to her mother's exhausted face. The baby had dark hair that stood on end like a baby chick's fluff. Her blue eyes blinked slowly, and she turned her head to Rebecca's breast when she was snuggled against it.

"Now, then, isn't that about the prettiest baby you've ever seen?" Mrs. Stucker asked. "I know you're tuckered out, Mrs. Fairchild, but perhaps you'll take a little tea or broth."

"I'll go see what I can find," Anna said, yawning.

She slowly stumbled down the stairs. When she got to the landing, she noticed a light gleaming in the downstairs sitting room. Puzzled, Anna pushed the door open and stood there a moment, staring.

Edward sprawled on Rebecca's damask settee, his long legs hanging off the end. He'd removed his neckcloth and unbuttoned his waistcoat. One arm draped over his eyes. His other arm stretched to the floor where his hand almost enveloped a half-empty glass of what looked like James's brandy. Anna stepped inside the room, and he immediately raised his arm from his eyes, belying the impression that he had been asleep.

"How is she?" His voice was raspy, his countenance ghastly. The fading bruises stood out starkly in his pale face, and the stubble on his jaw made him look dissolute.

Anna felt ashamed. She'd forgotten about Edward, had assumed he'd gone home long ago. All this time he'd been waiting downstairs to see how Rebecca fared.

"Rebecca is fine," she said brightly. "She has a baby girl."

His expression didn't change. "Alive?"

"Yes." Anna faltered. "Yes, of course. Both Rebecca and the baby are alive and well."

"Thank God." His face hadn't lost the strained look.

She began to feel uneasy. Surely he was overly concerned? He'd just met Rebecca tonight, hadn't he? "What is the matter?"

He sighed and his arm returned to cover his eyes. There was a long moment of silence—so long she thought he wasn't going to answer the question. Finally, he spoke, "My wife and babe died in childbirth."

Anna slowly sat down on a stool near the settee. She hadn't really thought about his wife before. She knew he'd been married and that his wife had died young, but not how she'd died. Had he loved her? Did he love her still?

"I'm sorry."

He lifted his hand from the brandy glass, made an impatient movement, and then let it settle on the glass again as if too weary to find another resting place for it. "I didn't tell you to elicit your pity. She died a long time ago. Ten years now."

"How old was she?"

"She'd turned twenty a fortnight before." His mouth twisted. "I was four and twenty."

Anna waited.

When he next spoke, the words were so low she had to lean forward to hear them. "She was young and healthy. It never occurred to me that bearing the child might kill her, but she miscarried in her seventh month. The baby was too small to live. They told me it would have been a boy. Then she started bleeding."

He took his arm away from his face, and Anna could see that he was staring sightlessly at some inner vision.

"They couldn't stop it. Doctors and midwives, they couldn't stop it. The maids kept running in with more and more linens," he whispered to the horror in his memory. "She just bled and bled until her very life bled away. There was so much blood in the bed, the mattress was soaked through. We had to burn it afterward."

The tears she'd withheld for Rebecca's sake ran down Anna's cheeks. To have lost someone you loved so horribly, so tragically, how awful it must have been. And he must have wanted that baby very badly. She already knew that having a family was important to him.

Anna pressed a hand to her mouth, and the movement seemed to bring Edward out of his reverie. He swore softly when he saw the tears on her face. He sat up on the settee and reached for her. Without any sign of strain, he lifted her off the stool and onto his lap and settled her there so she sat across him, her back held by his arm. He brought her head to his chest.

One big hand gently stroked her hair. "I'm sorry. I shouldn't have told you about that. It's not for a lady's ears, especially after you've been up all night worrying about your friend."

Anna allowed herself to lean against him, his masculine warmth and the petting hand wonderfully comforting. "You must have loved her very much."

The hand paused, and then resumed. "I thought I did. As it turned out, I didn't know her that well."

She tilted her head back to see his face. "How long were you married?"

"A little over a year."

"But—"

He pushed her head back to his chest. "We hadn't known each other long when we became engaged, and I suppose I never really talked to her. Her father was very eager for the match, told me that it was agreeable to the girl and I simply assumed . . ." His voice roughened. "I found out after we were married that my face repulsed her."

Anna tried to speak, but he hushed her again.

"I think she was afraid of me, too," he said wryly. "You may not have noticed, but I've something of a temper." She felt his hand touch the top of her head softly. "By the time she was pregnant with my child, I knew that something was wrong, and in her last hours she cursed him."

"Cursed who?"

"Her father. For forcing her to marry such an ugly man."

Anna shivered. What a silly little girl his wife must have been.

"Apparently her father had lied to me." Edward's voice turned as icy as winter. "He desperately desired the match and, not wanting to offend me, forbade my fiancée to tell me that my scars revolted her."

"I'm sorry, I—"

"Shh," he murmured. "It happened a long time ago, and I have learned since to live with my face and to discern those who would try to hide an aversion to it. Even if they lie, I usually know it."

But he didn't know her lies. Anna felt cold at the thought. She'd deceived him, and he'd never forgive her if he found out.

He must've mistaken her tremble for continued sadness at his tale. He whispered something into her hair and held her closer until the warmth from his body had chased her chill away. They sat quietly then for a little while, taking comfort from each other. It was beginning to grow light outside. There was a halo around the closed sitting room curtains. Anna took the opportunity to rub her nose against his rumpled shirt. He smelled like the brandy he'd drunk—very masculine.

Edward leaned back to look down at her. "What are you doing?"

"Sniffing you."

"I probably smell fetid right now."

"No." Anna shook her head. "You smell . . . nice."

He studied her upturned face for a minute. "Please forgive me. I don't want you to hope. If there were any way—"

"I know." She got to her feet. "I even understand." She walked briskly to the door. "I came down to get something for Rebecca. She must be wondering what happened to me."

"Anna . . ."

But she pretended she didn't hear and left the sitting room. Rejection from Edward was one thing. Pity she didn't have to take.

The front door banged open at that moment to admit a disheveled James Fairchild. He was like a vision from Bedlam: his blond hair stood on end, and his neckcloth was missing.

He looked wildly at Anna. "Rebecca?"

At that moment, as if in answer from on high, there came the wavering wail of a newborn baby. James Fairchild's expression changed from frantic to dumbstruck. Without waiting for Anna's answer, he bounded up the stairs, taking the risers three at a time. Anna noticed as he passed out of sight that he was wearing only one stocking on his feet.

She half smiled to herself as she turned to the kitchen.

"I BELIEVE IT's almost time to plant, my lord," Hopple said chummily.

"No doubt." Edward squinted at the bright afternoon sun.

After a night of very little sleep, he wasn't in the mood for chitchat. He and the steward were walking a field, checking to see if it would need a drainage ditch like Mr. Grundle's. It appeared the local ditch diggers had an assured living for the foreseeable future. Jock bounded along the hedges lining the fields, poking his muzzle down rabbit holes. Edward had sent a note to Anna this morning to tell her that she need not come to the Abbey today. She could use the day to rest. And he needed a respite from her presence. He had come close to kissing her again last night, despite his word of honor. He should let her go; after he was married, he could hardly retain a female secretary anyway. But then she would have no source of income, and he'd a feeling that the Wren household needed the money.

"Perhaps if we put the drainage ditch there?" Hopple pointed to a spot where Jock was currently digging and sending up a spume of mud.

Edward grunted.

"Or perhaps—" Hopple turned and nearly tripped on a clump of debris. He looked down disgustedly at his muddy boot. "It was wise of you not to include Mrs. Wren on this outing."

"She's at home," Edward said. "I told her to spend the day sleeping. You heard about Mrs. Fairchild's confinement last night?"

"The lady had a difficult time as I understand. What a miracle that both mother and child are well."

Edward snorted. "A miracle, indeed. Damned foolish for a man to leave his wife all alone, save a little maid, that close to her confinement."

"I heard the father was quite appalled this morning," Hopple offered.

"Not that it did his wife any good last night," Edward said dryly. "Be that as it may, Mrs. Wren was up all night with her friend. I thought it only reasonable that she take the day off. After all, she's worked every day excepting Sundays since she began as my secretary."

"Yes, indeed," Hopple said. "Except for the four days when you first left for London, of course."

Jock flushed a rabbit and gave chase.

Edward stopped and turned to the steward. "What?"

"Mrs. Wren didn't come to work whilst you were in

London." Hopple swallowed. "Except for the day before you came back, that is. She worked that day."

"I see," Edward said. But he didn't see.

"It was only for four days, my lord." Hopple hastened to smooth things over. "And she was all caught up on the paperwork, so she told me. It wasn't as if she let her work lie."

Edward stared thoughtfully at the mud beneath his feet. He remembered the vicar's mention of a "trip" the night before. "Where did she go?"

"Go, my lord?" Hopple looked to be stalling. "I, er, don't know if she went anywhere at all. She didn't say."

"The vicar said she had made a trip. He intimated that she'd gone to do some shopping."

"Maybe he was mistaken," Hopple said. "Why, if a lady couldn't find what she wanted in the shops in Little Battleford, she'd have to go to London to discover better. Surely Mrs. Wren didn't go that far."

Edward grunted. He went back to staring at the ground at his feet. Only now he knit his brows. Where had Anna gone? And why?

ANNA BRACED HER feet and hauled on the old garden door with all her might. Edward had given her the day to herself, but she couldn't stay that long asleep. Instead, after spending the morning resting, she thought she'd use the free time this afternoon to plant the roses. The door remained stubbornly shut for a moment, then it gave suddenly and flew open, almost throwing her on her rear. She dusted her hands and picked up her basket of gardening tools before slipping into the neglected garden. Edward had brought her here just over a week ago. In that little time, there'd been a great change within the old walls. Green shoots were poking up in the beds and between the cracks in the walkway. Some were obviously weeds, but others had a more refined air. Anna even recognized a few: the reddish tips of tulips, the unfurling rosettes of columbine leaves, and the dew-spangled palms of lady's mantle.

Each was a treasure she discovered with delight. The garden wasn't dead. It only lay dormant.

She set down her basket and went back out the garden door to bring in the remaining rosebushes Edward had given her. She'd already planted three in her own little garden. The rosebushes lay outside, still wet from the buckets of water. Each had begun to sprout tiny green buds. She looked down at them. They had brought her such hope when Edward had given them to her. Even though that hope was dead, it didn't seem fair to let the roses languish. She would plant them today, and if Edward never visited the garden again, well, she'd know they were here.

Anna dragged the first batch into the garden and let them flop down in the muddy path. She straightened and glanced around in search of a likely spot to plant them. The garden had a pattern once upon a time, but now it was almost impossible to discern what it had been. She shrugged and decided to divide the plants evenly between the four main flower beds. She picked up her shovel and began hacking through the tangled growth in the first bed.

ANNA WAS IN the garden when Edward found her that afternoon. He was irritable. He'd been searching for her some fifteen minutes, ever since Hopple had informed him that she was at the Abbey. Really, he shouldn't have sought her out at all; he'd made just that resolution this morning. But something inside him seemed constitutionally incapable of keeping away from his secretary when he knew her to be nearby. So he was frowning at his own lack of fortitude when he spotted her. Even then he paused by the garden door to admire the picture she made. She had dropped to her knees in the dirt to plant a rose. Her head was uncovered, and her hair was coming down from the knot at the nape of her neck. In the bright afternoon sunlight, the brown locks gleamed gold and auburn.

Edward felt a tightening in his chest. He rather thought it might be fear. He scowled and paced down the path. Fear was not an emotion that a strong man such as himself should feel when confronting a meek little widow, he was sure.

Anna caught sight of him. "My lord." She brushed the hair from her brow, leaving a smear of dirt behind. "I thought I would plant your roses before they died."

"So I see."

She gave him an odd look but evidently decided to make nothing of his strange mood. "I'll plant some in each bed since the garden is laid out in such symmetrical lines. Later, if you wish, we could surround them with lavender. Mrs. Fairchild has some lovely lavender plants by her back walk, and I know she would be pleased to let me take some cuttings for your gardens."

"Hmm."

Anna stopped her monologue to brush away her hair again, further smearing the dirt on her forehead. "Bother. I forgot to bring the watering can."

She frowned and started to climb to her feet, but he forestalled her. "Stay there. I can fetch the water for you."

Edward ignored her aborted protest and strode back up the path. He reached the garden door, but something made him hesitate. Forever after, he would ponder what impulse made him pause. He turned and looked back at her, still kneeling by the rosebush. She was packing the earth around it. While he watched, Anna raised her hand and with her little finger hooked back a lock of hair behind her ear.

He froze.

All sound stopped for a terrible, timeless minute, as his world shuddered and toppled around him. Three voices whispered, murmured, babbled in his ear and then coalesced into coherent language:

Hopple by the ditch: *I thought when that dog went missing for several days, we were well rid of it.*

Vicar Jones at Mrs. Clearwater's soiree: *I wondered if she'd bought a new dress on her trip.*

And Hopple again just today: *Mrs. Wren didn't come to work whilst you were in London.*

A scarlet haze obscured his vision.

When it cleared, he was almost upon Anna and knew that he had started for her even before the voices had become understandable. She was still bent beside the rosebush, unaware of the approaching storm until he stood over her and she glanced up.

He must have worn the knowledge of her deceit on his face because Anna's smile died before it had fully formed.

Chapter Sixteen

*Cautiously, Aurea lit the candle and turned to hold it
high over her lover's form. Her breath caught, her
eyes widened, and she gave a start. A very small start,
but enough of one to send a drop of hot wax spilling
over the lip of the candle and onto the shoulder of
the man who lay beside her. For it was a man—not
monster or beast—but a man with smooth, white skin;
long, strong limbs; and black, black hair. He opened
his eyes, and Aurea saw that they, too, were black.
A piercing, intelligent black that, somehow, was
familiar. On his chest glinted a pendant.
It was in the shape of a small, perfect crown
inlaid with glowing rubies. . . .*

—from *The Raven Prince*

Anna was debating whether or not she'd set the rosebush
at the right depth in the hole when a shadow fell across
her. She glanced up. Edward stood over her. Her first
thought was that he had returned too soon to have brought
the watering can.

And then she saw his expression.

His lips were drawn back in a rictus of rage, and his eyes burned like black holes in his face. In that moment, she felt an awful premonition that he'd somehow found out. In the seconds before he spoke, she tried to rally, to reassure herself that there was no possible way he could have discovered her secret.

His words killed all hope.

"You." She didn't recognize his voice, it was so low and terrible. "You were there at the whorehouse."

She'd never been good at lying. "What?"

He squeezed his eyes shut as if at a bright light. "You were there. You waited for me like a female spider, and I fell neatly into your web."

Dear Lord, this was even worse than she had imagined. He thought she'd done it for some kind of sick revenge or joke. "I didn't—"

His eyes snapped open, and she threw up a hand to ward off the hell she saw in them. "You didn't what? Didn't travel to London, didn't go to Aphrodite's Grotto?"

Her eyes widened, and she started to rise, but he was already on her. He grasped her by the shoulders and lifted her easily, effortlessly, as if she weighed no more than thistledown. He was so strong! Why had she never before realized how much stronger the male was in relation to the female? She felt like a butterfly seized by a great black bird. He swung her body against the nearby brick wall and pinned her there. He lowered his face to hers until their noses nearly touched, and he could surely see his own reflection in her wide, frightened eyes.

"You waited there, wearing nothing but a bit of lace." His words washed over her face in a hot, intimate breath.

"And when I came, you flaunted yourself, offered your-self, and I fucked you until I couldn't see straight."

Anna felt each puff of his exhalation against her own lips. She flinched at the obscenity. She wanted to deny it, to say that it did not describe the sublime sweetness they'd discovered together in London, but the words caught in her throat.

"I was actually worried that contact with the prostitute you sheltered would ruin your good name. What a fool you made me. How could you hold back your laughter when I begged your pardon for kissing you?" His hands flexed on her shoulders. "All this time I've been restrain-ing myself because I thought you were a respectable lady. All this time when you only wanted *this*."

He swooped in then and devoured her mouth with his own, ravishing her softness, making no allowances for her smaller size, for her femininity. His lips crushed hers against her teeth. She moaned, whether in pain or desire, she could not tell. He thrust his tongue into the cavern of her mouth without preamble or warning, as if he had every right.

"You should have told me that this was what you wanted." He raised his head to gasp. "I would've obliged you."

She seemed incapable of coherent thought, let alone speech.

"You had only to say the word and I could have taken you on my desk in the library, in the carriage with John Coachman up front, or even here in the garden."

She tried to form words through the fog of her confu-sion. "No, I—"

"God knows I've been hard for days—*weeks*—around you," he ground out. "I could've tumbled you at any time. Or can't you admit that you want to bed a man whose face looks like mine?"

She tried to shake her head, but it fell helplessly as he bent her back over his arm. His other hand dropped to her hips and jerked them into his own. The unyielding hardness of his erection pressed against her soft belly.

"*This* is what you crave. What you traveled all the way to London for," he whispered against her mouth.

She moaned in denial even as her hips arched into his.

He stilled her movement with an iron grip and tore his mouth away from hers. But almost as if he couldn't leave the lure of her skin, he returned. His mouth trailed across her face to catch an earlobe between his teeth.

"Why?" His question sighed into her ear. "Why, why, why? Why did you lie to me?"

She tried again to shake her head.

He punished her with a sharp nip. "Was it a jest? Did you find it amusing to lay with me one night and then play the virtuous widow the next? Or was it a perverse need? Some women find the thought of bedding a pox-scarred man stimulating."

She jerked her head violently then, despite the pain when his teeth scraped across her ear. She couldn't— *could not*—let him think that. "Please, you must know—"

He turned his head. She tried to face him, and he did the most terrifying thing yet.

He let her go.

"Edward! *Edward!* For God's sake, please listen to

me!" Strange that this was the first time she had called him by his Christian name.

He strode down the garden path. She ran after him, her eyes blinded by tears, and tripped over a loose brick.

He stopped at the sound of her fall, his back still to her. "Such tears, Anna. Can you produce them at will like the crocodile?" And then, so softly she might have imagined it, "Were there other men?"

He walked away.

She watched as he disappeared through the gate. Her chest felt tight. She thought vaguely that perhaps she'd hurt herself in the fall. But then she heard a guttural, rasping sound, and a cold little part of her brain took note of what a strange noise her crying made.

How swift, how harsh was the punishment dealt for stepping outside her staid widow's life. All the lessons and warnings, spoken and unspoken, that she'd been taught growing up had, in fact, come true. Although, she supposed her punishment wasn't that envisioned by the moralizers of Little Battleford. No, her fate was far worse than exposure and censure. Her punishment was Edward's hatred. That and the knowledge that she had never gone to London merely for the sex. All along it had been to be with him, Edward. It was the man she'd craved, not the physical act. It seemed she had been lying to herself just as much as she'd lied to him. How ironic to have finally tumbled to that realization now when all was ashes around her.

Anna didn't know how long she lay there, her old brown dress growing damp from the overturned dirt. When her sobs finally died away, the afternoon sky had become overcast. She pushed herself up with both arms to a kneeling position and from there lurched to her feet. She wavered, but caught herself, one hand holding the garden wall for support. She closed her eyes and breathed in deeply. Then she picked up the shovel.

Soon she would have to go home and tell Mother Wren that she no longer had a job. She would face a lonely bed tonight and a thousand nights after for the rest of her life.

But for now, she'd simply plant roses.

FELICITY PLACED A cloth dampened with violet water on her forehead. She'd retired to the little morning room, a place that usually brought her quite a bit of satisfaction, especially when she thought about how much it had cost to refurbish. The price of the canary-colored damask settee alone would have fed and clothed the Wren household for five years. But at the moment, her head was simply killing her.

Matters were *not* going well.

Reginald was moping about, moaning that his prize mare had miscarried. Chilly had gone back to London in a sulk because she wouldn't tell him about Anna and the earl. And that same earl had been annoyingly obtuse at the soiree. Granted, most men in her experience were slow to one degree or another, but she wouldn't have guessed Lord Swartingham was so thickheaded. The man had seemed not to know what she hinted at. How was she going to convince him to keep Anna quiet if he was too dim to realize he was being blackmailed?

Felicity winced.

Not blackmail. That sounded too gauche. Incentive. That was better. Lord Swartingham had an *incentive* to stop Anna from blathering Felicity's past peccadilloes all over the village.

The door banged open at that moment, and the younger of her two daughters, Cynthia, skipped in. She was followed by her sister, Christine, at a more sedate pace.

"M'man," Christine said. "Nanny says we must get your permission to go to the sweet shop in town. May we?"

"Pepp-er-mint sticks!" Cynthia skipped around the settee Felicity lay on. "Le-mon drops! Turk-ish delight!" Oddly, her youngest resembled Reginald in many ways.

"Please stop that, Cynthia," Felicity said. "M'man has a headache."

"I'm so sorry, M'man," Christine replied, not sounding sorry at all. "We'll leave as soon as we get your permission." She smiled coyly.

"M'man's per-mission! M'man's per-mission!" Cynthia chanted.

"Yes!" Felicity said. "Yes, you have my permission."

"Huzzah! Huzzah!" Cynthia ran from the room, her red hair streaming behind her.

The sight made her frown. Cynthia's red hair was the bane of Felicity's life.

"Thank you, M'man." Christine closed the door primly.

Felicity groaned and rang for more toilet water. If only she hadn't written that incriminating note in a fit of sentimentality. And what had Peter been thinking to save that locket? Men truly were idiots.

She pressed her fingertips over the cloth on her forehead. Perhaps Lord Swartingham really hadn't known what she was talking about. He'd seemed confused when she had said they both knew the identity of the lady he'd met at Aphrodite's Grotto. And if, in fact, he did not know her . . .

Felicity sat up, the cloth falling unheeded to the floor. If he did not know the woman's identity, then she'd been trying to blackmail the wrong person.

ANNA KNELT IN her little garden in back of the cottage the next morning. She hadn't the heart to tell Mother Wren she'd lost her employment. It had been late when she'd arrived home the night before, and this morning she hadn't wanted to talk about it. Not yet, anyway, when the subject would only bring up questions she couldn't answer. Eventually, she'd have to work up the courage to apologize to Edward. But that could wait, too, while she licked her wounds. Which was why she worked in the garden today. The mundane tasks of caring for vegetables and the smell of the freshly dug earth provided a kind of solace to her soul.

She was digging up horseradish roots to replant when she heard a shout from the front of the cottage. She frowned and lay down the shovel. Surely nothing was wrong with Rebecca's baby? She lifted her skirts to trot around the cottage. The sound of a carriage and horses receded. A clearly feminine voice shouted again as she rounded the corner.

Pearl stood on the front step, holding another woman against her. At her approach, they both turned and Anna gasped. The other woman had two black eyes, and her nose looked as if it might be broken. It took Anna a couple of seconds to recognize her.

It was Coral.

"Oh, Lord!" Anna gasped.

The front door opened.

Anna rushed to take Coral's other arm. "Fanny, hold the door for us, please."

Fanny, wide-eyed, obeyed as they awkwardly maneuvered Coral in.

"Told Pearl," Coral whispered, "not to come here." Her lips were so swollen, the words were indistinct.

"Thank goodness she didn't listen to you," Anna said.

She judged the narrow stairs to the upper floor. They'd never make it up the steps with Coral leaning so heavily on them. "Let's bring her into the sitting room."

Pearl nodded.

They gently lowered Coral to the settee. Anna sent Fanny up the stairs for a blanket. Coral's eyes had closed, and Anna wondered if she'd fainted. The other woman was breathing sonorously through her mouth, her nose too misshapen and swollen to let in air.

Anna pulled Pearl to the side. "What happened to her?"

The other woman darted an anxious glance at Coral. "It was that marquis. He came home last night falling-down drunk; only, he wasn't so drunk he couldn't do *that* to her."

"But why?"

"He didn't have a reason as I could see." Pearl's lips trembled. At Anna's shocked stare, she grimaced. "Oh, he mumbled something 'bout her seeing other men, but that was a crock. Coral thinks of bed sport as business. She wouldn't be doing it with someone else while she had a protector. He just enjoyed putting his fists into her face."

Pearl wiped away an angry tear. "If I hadn't gotten her out when he went to piss, he probably would've killed her."

Anna put an arm around her shoulder. "We must thank the Lord that you were able to save her."

"I didn't know where else to bring her, ma'am," Pearl said. "I'm sorry to bother you after how kind you were before. If we can stay a night or two, just until Coral can get back on her feet."

"You're welcome to stay however long it takes for Coral to become well again. But I fear it'll be more than a night or two." Anna looked worriedly over at her battered guest. "I must send Fanny for Dr. Billings right away."

"Oh, no." Pearl's voice rose in panic. "Don't do that!"

"But she needs to be seen to."

"It'd be better if no one knows we're here 'sides Fanny and the other Mrs. Wren," Pearl said. "He might try looking for her."

Anna slowly nodded. Coral was obviously still in danger. "But what about her wounds?"

"I can take care of them. There aren't any broken bones. I already checked, and I can straighten her nose again."

"You can fix a broken nose?" Anna looked at Pearl strangely.

The other woman tightened her lips. "I've done it before. It comes in handy in my trade."

Anna closed her eyes. "I'm sorry. I didn't mean to doubt you. What do you need?"

Under Pearl's direction, Anna quickly gathered water, rags, and bandages, as well as the jar of her mother's salve.

Pearl worked over her sister's face with her help. The little woman was matter-of-fact, even when Coral moaned and tried to knock away her hands. Anna held down the injured woman's arms so that Pearl could finish bandaging. She sighed with relief when Pearl indicated they were done. They made sure that Coral was as comfortable as possible before retiring to the kitchen for a much-needed cup of tea.

Pearl sighed as she lifted the hot tea to her lips. "Thank you. Thank you so much, ma'am. You're so good."

Anna half laughed, a funny little croak. "It's I who should thank you, if only you knew. I need to do something good right now."

EDWARD THREW DOWN his quill and paced to the library windows. He hadn't written a coherent sentence all day. The room was too quiet, too big for his peace of mind anymore. All he could think of was Anna and what she'd done to him. Why? Why choose him? Was it his title? His wealth?

God! His *scars?*

What possible reason could a respectable woman have to don a disguise and act the part of a whore? If she'd wanted a lover, couldn't she have found one in Little Battleford? Or was it that she liked playing the whore?

Edward rubbed his forehead against the cold glass of the window. He remembered everything he had done to Anna in those two nights. Every exquisite place his hand had touched, every inch of skin his mouth had tongued. He remembered doing things he would never have dreamed of performing with a lady, let alone one he knew and liked. She'd seen a side of himself that he'd made pains to hide away from the world, a private, secret side. She'd seen him at his most bestial. What had she felt when he had pressed her head toward his cock? Excitement? Fear?

Revulsion?

And there were more thoughts he could not stop. Had she met other men at Aphrodite's Grotto? Had she shared her beautiful, lush body with men she didn't even know? Had she let them kiss her wanton mouth, let them paw her breasts, let them rut on her willing, spread body? Edward pounded the window frame with his fist until the skin cracked and blood splattered. Impossible to wipe the obscene images from his mind of Anna—*his* Anna—with another man. His vision blurred. Christ. He was crying like a lad.

Jock nudged his leg and whimpered.

She'd brought him to this. He was completely undone. And yet it made no difference because he was a gentleman and she, despite her actions, was a lady. He would have to marry her, and in doing so give up all his dreams, all his hopes, of having a family. She couldn't have children. His line would die with his last breath. There would be no girls that looked like his mother, no boys that reminded him of Sammy. No one to open his heart to. No one to watch grow. Edward straightened. If that was what life held for him, so be it, but he would make damn sure Anna knew her price.

He wiped his face and jerked the bellpull savagely.

Chapter Seventeen

The man in her bed stared at Aurea and then spoke
softly. Sorrowfully. "So, my wife, you could not let
well enough alone. I will quench your curiosity, then.
I am Prince Niger, the lord of these lands and this
palace. I have been cursed to assume the form of that
foul raven by day and all my minions to become birds
as well. My tormentor made one caveat to the spell: If
I could find a lady to agree of her own will to marry
me in my raven form, then I could live as a man from
midnight to dawn's first glow. You were that lady. But
now our time together is at an end. I will spend the
remainder of my days in that hated feathered form,
and all that follow me are also so doomed. . . ."
—from *The Raven Prince*

The next morning, Felix Hopple shifted from one foot to
the other, sighed, and knocked at the cottage door again.
He twitched his freshly powdered wig straight and ran a
hand over his neckcloth. He'd never been on an errand
quite like this one before. In fact, he wasn't sure his job
really entailed it. Of course, it was impossible to say that

to Lord Swartingham. Especially when he stared at him with smoldering, black, devilish eyes.

He sighed again. His employer's temper had been even worse than usual this past week. Very few knickknacks remained intact in the library, and even the dog had taken to hiding when the earl stalked through the Abbey.

A pretty woman opened the door.

Felix blinked and stepped back a pace. Was he at the right house?

"Yes?" The woman smoothed her skirt and smiled tentatively at him.

"Er, I-I was looking for Mrs. Wren," Felix stuttered. "The *younger* Mrs. Wren. Have I the right address?"

"Oh, yes, this is the right address," she said. "I mean, this is the Wren cottage. I'm just staying here."

"Ah, I see, Miss . . . ?"

"Smythe. Pearl Smythe." The woman blushed for some reason. "Won't you come in?"

"Thank you, Miss Smythe." Felix stepped into the tiny entryway and stood awkwardly.

Miss Smythe was staring, seemingly entranced by his middle. "Coo!" she blurted. "That's the loveliest waistcoat ever."

"Why, er, why thank you, Miss Smythe." He fingered the buttons on his leaf-green waistcoat.

"Are those bumblebees?" Miss Smythe bent down to peer closer at the purple embroidery, giving him a quite inappropriate view down the front of her dress.

No true gentleman would take advantage of a lady's accidental exposure. Felix looked at the ceiling, at the top of her head, and finally down her dress. He blinked rapidly.

"Isn't that clever?" she said, straightening again. "I don't think I've ever seen anything so pretty on a gentleman before."

"What?" he wheezed. "Er, yes. Quite. Thank you again, Miss Smythe. One rarely encounters a person of such fine sentiment about fashion."

Miss Smythe appeared a little confused, but she smiled at him.

He couldn't help but notice how lovely she was. All over.

"You said you came for Mrs. Wren. Why don't you wait in there"—she waved toward a small sitting room—"and I'll go fetch Mrs. Wren from the garden."

Felix stepped into the small room. He heard the pretty woman's retreating footsteps and the close of the back door. He paced to the mantel and looked at a little china clock. He frowned and took out his pocket watch. The mantel clock was fast.

The back door opened again, and Mrs. Wren came in. "Mr. Hopple, how can I help you?"

She was intent on rubbing the garden loam from her hands and didn't meet his eyes.

"I've come on an, er, errand from the earl."

"Indeed?" Mrs. Wren still did not look up.

"Yes." He was at a loss as to how to continue. "Won't you have a seat?"

Mrs. Wren glanced at him in puzzlement and took her seat.

Felix cleared his throat. "There comes a time in every man's life when the winds of adventure blow out, and he feels a need for rest and comfort. A need to toss aside the careless ways of youth—or at least early adulthood in this case—and settle down to domestic tranquility." He paused to see if his words had registered.

"Yes, Mr. Hopple?" She appeared more confused than before.

He mentally girded his loins and labored on. "Yes, Mrs. Wren. Every man, even an earl"—here he paused significantly to emphasize the title—"even an *earl* needs a place of repose and calm. A sanctuary tended by the gentle hand of the feminine sex. A hand guided and led by the stronger masculine hand of a, er, guardian so that both may weather the storms and travails that life brings us."

Mrs. Wren stared at him in a dazed way.

Felix began to feel desperate. "Every man, every *earl,* needs a place of hymeneal comfort."

Her brow puckered. "Hymeneal?"

"Yes." He mopped his brow. "Hymeneal. Of or pertaining to marriage."

She blinked. "Mr. Hopple, why did the earl send you?"

Felix blew out his breath in a gust. "Oh, hang it all, Mrs. Wren! He wants to marry you."

She went completely white. "What?"

Felix groaned. He knew he would make a hash of this. Really, Lord Swartingham was asking too much of him. He was only a land steward, for pity's sake, not cupid with his golden bow and arrows! There was no other choice now but to muddle on.

"Edward de Raaf, the Earl of Swartingham, asks for your hand in marriage. He would like a short engagement and is considering—"

"No."

"The first of June. Wh-what did you say?"

"I said no." Mrs. Wren spoke in a staccato. "Tell him that I am sorry. Very sorry. But there is no possible way that I can marry him."

"But-but-but . . ." Felix took a deep breath to quell his stutter. "But he is an earl. I know his temper is quite foul, really, and he does spend a good deal of time in mud. Which"—he shuddered—"he actually seems to like. But his title and his considerable—one might even say *obscene*—wealth make up for that, don't you think?"

Felix ran out of breath and had to stop.

"No, I don't." She moved toward the door. "Just tell him no."

"But, Mrs. Wren! How will I face him?"

She closed the door gently behind her, and his despairing cry echoed in the empty room. Felix slumped into a chair and wished for an entire bottle of Madeira. Lord Swartingham was not going to like this.

ANNA PLUNGED A trowel into the soft earth and viciously dug up a dandelion. What could Edward have been thinking when he sent Mr. Hopple to propose to her this morning? Obviously he hadn't been overcome by love. She snorted and attacked another dandelion.

The back door to the cottage scraped open. She turned and frowned. Coral was dragging a kitchen stool into the garden.

"What are you doing outside?" Anna demanded. "Pearl and I had to half carry you up the stairs to my room this morning."

Coral sat on the stool. "Country air is supposed to heal, is it not?"

The swelling on her face had gone down somewhat, but the bruising was still evident. Pearl had packed her nostrils with lint in an attempt to heal the break. Now they flared grotesquely. Coral's left eyelid drooped lower than the right, and Anna wondered if it would rise again with time or if the disfigurement was permanent. A small, crescent-shaped scar was scabbed over under the drooping eye.

"I expect I should thank you." Coral tilted her head back against the cottage wall and closed her eyes, as if enjoying the sunlight on her damaged face.

"It is the usual thing to do," Anna said.

"Not for me. I do not like being in other people's debt."

"Then don't think of it as a debt," Anna grunted as she uprooted a weed. "Consider it a gift."

"A gift," Coral mused. "In my experience, gifts usually have to be paid for in one way or another. But perhaps with you that truly is not so. Thank you."

She sighed and shifted position. Although she had sustained no broken bones, there'd been bruises all over her body. She must still be in a great deal of pain.

"I value the regard of women more than men," Coral continued. "It is so much rarer, especially in my profession. It was a woman who did this to me."

"What?" Anna was horrified. "I thought the marquis . . . ?"

The other woman made a dismissive sound. "He was but her instrument. Mrs. Lavender told him I was entertaining other men."

"But why?"

"She wanted my position as the marquis' mistress. And we have some history between us." Coral waved a hand. "But that does not matter. I will deal with her when I am well. Why are you not working at the Abbey today? That is where you usually spend your days, is it not?"

Anna frowned. "I've decided not to go there anymore."

"You have had a falling out with your man?" Coral asked.

"How—?"

"That is who you saw in London, is it not? Edward de Raaf, the Earl of Swartingham?"

"Yes, that's who I met," she sighed. "But he's not my man."

"It has been my observation that women of your ilk—principled women—do not bed a man unless their heart is involved." Coral's mouth quirked sardonically. "They place a great deal of sentimentality on the act."

Anna took an unnecessarily long time to find the next root with the tip of her trowel. "Perhaps you are right. Perhaps I did place a great deal of sentimentality on the-the *act*. But that is neither here nor there now." She bore down on the trowel handle, and the dandelion popped out of the soil. "We argued."

Coral regarded her with narrowed eyes for a moment and then shrugged and closed her eyelids again. "He found out it was you—"

Anna looked up, startled. "How did you—?"

"And now I suppose you will meekly accept his disapproval," Coral continued without pause. "You will hide your shame behind a façade of respectable widowhood. Perhaps you could knit stockings for the poor of the village. Your good works will surely comfort you when he marries in a few years and beds another woman."

"He's asked me to marry him."

Coral opened her eyes. "Now that is interesting." She looked at the growing pile of wilted dandelions. "But you refused him."

Whack!

Anna started hacking at the dandelion pile. "He thinks me a wanton."

Whack!

"I'm barren and he needs children."

Whack!

"And he doesn't want me."

Whack! Whack! Whack!

Anna stopped and stared at the heap of broken, oozing weeds.

"Doesn't he?" Coral murmured. "And what about you? Do you, ah, *want* him?"

Anna felt heat flooding her cheeks. "I've been without a man for many years now. I can be alone again."

A smile flickered across Coral's face. "Have you ever noticed that once you have had a taste of certain sweets— raspberry trifle is my own despair—it is quite impossible not to think, not to want, not to *crave* until you have taken another bite?"

"Lord Swartingham is not a raspberry trifle."

"No, more of a dark chocolate mousse, I should think," Coral murmured.

"And," Anna continued as if she hadn't heard the interruption, "I don't need another bite, uh, *night* of him."

A vision of that second night rose up before her eyes: Edward bare-chested, his trousers undone, lounging in that chair before the fire like a Turkish pasha. His skin, his *penis,* had gleamed in the firelight.

Anna swallowed. Her mouth was watering. "I can live without Lord Swartingham," she declared very firmly.

Coral raised an eyebrow.

"I can! Besides, you weren't there." Anna suddenly felt as wilted as the dandelions. "He was horribly angry. He said terrible things to me."

"Ah," Coral said. "He is uncertain of you."

"I don't see why that should make you happy," Anna said. "And, anyway, it's much more than that. He'll never forgive me."

Coral smiled like a cat watching a sparrow hop near. "Maybe. Maybe not."

"WHAT DO YOU mean, you won't marry me?" Edward paced from the curio shelf at one end of the small sitting room to the settee at the other end, pivoted, and came back again. Not such a great feat since he could cross the entire room in three strides. "I'm an earl, goddamnit!"

Anna grimaced. She should never have let him into the cottage. Of course, she hadn't had much choice at the time, since he'd threatened to break down the door if she didn't open it.

He had looked quite capable of doing it, too.

"I won't marry you," she repeated.

"Why not? You were eager enough to fuck me."

Anna winced. "I do wish you would stop using that word."

Edward swung around and assumed a hideously sarcastic expression. "Would you prefer *swive? Tup? Dance the buttock jig?*"

She compressed her lips. Thank goodness Mother Wren

and Fanny had gone shopping this morning. Edward was making no effort to lower his voice.

"You don't want to marry me." Anna spoke slowly and enunciated each word as if talking to a hard-of-hearing village idiot.

"Whether I want to marry you or not isn't the issue, as you well know," Edward said. "The fact is, I must marry you."

"Why?" She blew out a breath. "There is no possibility of a child. As you have made abundantly clear, you know I am barren."

"I have compromised you."

"I'm the one who went to Aphrodite's Grotto in disguise. It seems to me that *I* compromised *you*." Anna thought it commendable that she did not wave her arms in the air in exasperation.

"That's ridiculous!" Edward's bellow could probably be heard back at the Abbey.

Why did men think that saying something louder made it true? "No more ridiculous than an earl who is already engaged proposing marriage to his secretary!" Her own voice was raised now.

"I'm not proposing. I'm telling you we must marry."

"No." Anna crossed her arms.

Edward stalked across the room toward her, each step deliberate and meant to be intimidating. He didn't stop until his chest was inches from her face. She craned her neck to meet his gaze; she refused to back away from him.

He leaned down until his breath brushed across her forehead intimately. "You will marry me."

He smelled of coffee. Anna dropped her eyes to his

mouth. Even in anger, it was disgustingly sensual. She retreated a step and turned her back. "I am not going to marry you."

Anna could hear him breathing heavily behind her. She peeked over her shoulder.

Edward was looking thoughtfully at her bottom.

His eyes snapped up. "You will marry me." He held up a hand when she started to speak. "But I'll quit the discussion of when for now. In the meantime, I still need a secretary. I want you at the Abbey this afternoon."

"I hardly think"—Anna had to stop to steady her voice—"I hardly think in light of our past relationship that I should continue as your secretary."

Edward's eyes narrowed. "Correct me if I am wrong, Mrs. Wren, but weren't you the one who initiated that relationship? Therefore—"

"I said I was sorry!"

He ignored her outburst. "*Therefore*, I fail to see why I should be the one to suffer the loss of a secretary merely because of your discomfort, if that is the problem."

"Yes, that's the problem!" Discomfort didn't begin to describe the agony it would be to try and carry on as before. Anna took a fortifying breath. "I can't return."

"Well, then," Edward said softly, "I fear I'll be unable to pay you your wages to date."

"That's . . ." Anna lost her power of speech in sheer horror.

The Wren household had been counting on the money that would be paid at the end of the month. So much so that they'd already accrued several small debts at the local shops. It would be bad enough, not having a job. If she couldn't have the wages she'd already earned as Edward's secretary, the results would be disastrous.

"Yes?" Edward inquired.

"That's unfair!" Anna burst out.

"Now, dear heart, whatever gave you the idea that I played fair?" He smiled silkily.

"You can't do that!"

"Yes, I can. I keep telling you that I'm an earl, but it hasn't seemed to have sunk in yet." Edward propped a fist beneath his chin. "Of course, if you come back to work, your wages will be paid in full."

Anna closed her mouth and breathed rather forcefully through her nostrils for a bit.

"Fine. I'll come back. But I want to be paid at the end of the week," she said. "*Every* week."

He laughed. "You are so untrusting."

He lunged forward and, catching her hand, kissed the back of it. Then he turned her hand over and quickly pressed his tongue into her palm. For a second, she felt the soft, wet warmth and her intimate muscles clenched. He let go and was out the door before she could protest.

At least, she was fairly certain she would have protested.

OBSTINATE, OBSTINATE WOMAN. Edward swung himself into the bay's saddle. Any other female in Little Battleford would've sold their grandmother to marry him. Hell, most of the women in England would sell their entire family, the family retainers, *and* the family pets to become his bride.

Edward snorted.

He wasn't egotistical. It had nothing to do with him

personally. It was the title he bore that had such a high market value. Well, that and the money that came with the title. But not for Anna Wren, impoverished widow of no social standing. Oh, no. For her and her only, he was good enough to bed, but not wed. What did she think he was? A cock for hire?

Edward tightened the reins as the bay shied at a blowing leaf. Well, that same sensuality that had led her to meet him in a brothel was going to be her downfall. He'd caught her staring at his mouth in midargument, and it had dawned on him: Why not use her sexuality for his own purposes? What matter *why* she had decided to seduce him—whether because of his scars or no—the more important point was that she had. She liked his mouth, did she? She would see it all day, every day, as his secretary. And he would be sure to remind her what other things she was missing until she consented to be his bride.

Edward grinned. In fact, it would be his pleasure to show her just what rewards awaited her when they wed. With her lustful nature, Anna wouldn't be able to hold out long. And then she would be his wife. The thought of Anna as his wife was strangely comforting, and a fellow could get used to such feminine lust in a wife. Oh, yes, indeed.

Smiling grimly, Edward kicked the gelding into a gallop.

Chapter Eighteen

*Aurea stared, horrified, at her husband. Then the
first rays of dawn streamed through the high palace
window and fell upon the prince, and his form began
to shrink and convulse. The broad, smooth shoulders
shriveled and diminished; his wide, elegant mouth
protruded and hardened; and the fingers of his strong
hands metamorphosed into wispy, tarnished feathers.
And as the raven appeared, the walls of the palace
shook and trembled until it dissolved and disappeared.
There was a great whirring and flapping of wings as
the raven and all his followers took to the skies.
Aurea found herself alone. She was without clothing,
food, or even water in a dry plain that stretched in all
directions as far as the eye could see. . . .*
—from *The Raven Prince*

Anna was just about at the end of her patience. She caught
herself tapping a toe and carefully stilled her foot. She
stood in the stable courtyard while Edward argued with a
groom about Daisy's saddle. Apparently there was something wrong with it. What, exactly, she did not know,
since no one deigned to tell her, a woman, the problem.

She sighed. For nearly a week she'd bitten her tongue and dutifully done Edward's bidding as his secretary. Never mind that some of his orders were clearly calculated to make her lose her self-possession. Never mind that at least once a day Edward made some remark about the perfidy of women. Never mind that every time she'd happened to glance up, her eyes had collided with Edward's staring back at her. She'd been ladylike, she'd been meek, and it was almost killing her.

Anna closed her eyes now. Patience. Patience was a virtue she must master.

"Are you falling asleep?" Edward spoke right beside her, making Anna jump and glare, a reaction he missed, as he'd already turned away. "George says the girth is too worn. We'll have to take the phaeton instead."

"I don't think—" Anna started.

But he strode to where a team was being hitched to the vehicle.

Anna gaped and then trotted after him. "My lord."

He ignored her.

"*Edward,*" she hissed

"Darling?" He stopped so suddenly, she nearly skidded into him.

"Don't. Call. Me. That." She'd said it so many times in the last week, the words had become a chant. "There isn't room on that thing for a groom or maid."

He glanced at the phaeton casually. Jock had already jumped into the high seat and was sitting alertly, ready for a ride. "Why would I want to take a groom or maid to look at fields?"

Anna pursed her lips. "You know very well."

He raised his eyebrows.

"As a chaperone." She smiled sweetly for the benefit of the stablemen.

He leaned close. "Sweetheart, I'm flattered, but even I can't seduce you whilst driving a phaeton."

Anna blushed. She knew that. "I—"

Edward seized her hand before she could say more, pulled her to the carriage, and tossed her on the seat. He went to help the grooms hitching the horses.

"Overbearing man," she muttered to Jock.

The mastiff thumped his tail and laid his massive head on her shoulder, smearing it with canine drool. After another few minutes, Edward vaulted to the seat, making the carriage shake, and caught the reins. The horses stepped out, and the phaeton started forward with a jerk. Anna grabbed the back of her seat. Jock leaned into the wind, ears and jowls flapping. The phaeton rounded a corner fast, and she jostled against Edward. For a moment, her breast pressed against the hard slab of his arm. She righted herself and took a firmer hold of the side.

The carriage veered, and Anna bumped against him again. She glared, but it had no effect. Every time she let go of the seat back, the vehicle lurched and she was forced to grab it.

"Are you doing that on purpose?"

There was no answer.

"If you are shaking me about to put me in my place," she huffed, "I do think it is rather infantile of you."

An ebony eye glanced at her through sooty lashes.

"If you want to punish me," she said, "I can understand, but surely wrecking the phaeton would inconvenience you as well."

He slowed fractionally.

Anna placed her hands in her lap.

"Why would I want to punish you?" he asked.

"You know." Really, he was the most exasperating creature when he wanted to be.

They bowled along the lane for a bit in silence. The sky began to lighten and then blush a shy crimson. Anna could see his features more clearly. They did not look confiding.

She sighed. "I *am* sorry, you know."

"Sorry you were found out?" Edward's voice was suspiciously silky.

She bit the inside of her cheek. "I'm sorry I deceived you."

"I find that hard to believe."

"Are you implying that I'm lying?" Anna grit her teeth to hold fast to her temper, trying to remember her vow about patience.

"Why, yes, my sweet, I believe I am." His teeth sounded as if they were being ground. "You seem to have an innate facility for lying."

She took a deep breath. "I understand why you would think that, but please believe that I never meant to hurt you."

Edward snorted. "Fine. Good. You were in one of the most notorious brothels in London dressed as a high-priced whore, and I happened to walk in on you. Yes, I can see that you've been misunderstood."

Anna counted to ten. Then she counted to fifty. "I was waiting for you. *Only* you."

That appeared to take the wind out of his sails for a bit. The sun had risen fully now. They rattled around a curve and frightened two hares in the middle of the road.

"Why?" he barked.

She'd lost the thread of the conversation. "What?"

"Why did you choose me after, what, six years of celibacy?"

"Nearer seven."

"But you've been widowed six."

Anna nodded without explanation.

She could feel Edward looking curiously at her. "Whatever the time period, why me? My scars—"

"It had nothing to do with your bloody scars!" she burst out. "The scars don't matter, can't you see that?"

"Then why?"

And it was her turn to be mute. The sun was very bright now, picking out every detail, leaving nothing hidden.

She tried to explain. "I believed . . . No. I *knew* we had an attraction. Then you left and I realized you were taking what you felt for me and giving it to another woman. A woman you didn't even know. And I wanted—needed—" Anna threw up her hands in frustration. "I wanted to be the one you-you *swived* with."

Edward choked. She couldn't tell if he was appalled, sickened, or simply laughing at her.

Her temper suddenly came to a boil. "You were the one who left for London. You were the one who decided to-to *tup* another woman. You were the one who turned away from me. From us. Who is the greater sinner? I will no longer—urp!"

She gulped her words as Edward pulled the horses up so abruptly that they half reared. Jock was nearly catapulted from the seat. Anna opened her lips in alarm, but before she could protest, her mouth was covered by his. He thrust his tongue into her mouth without preamble. She tasted coffee as he stroked along her tongue, opening her lips farther for his access. Blunt fingers massaged the nape of her neck. She was surrounded by the musky scent of a man in his prime. Slowly, reluctantly, his mouth left hers. His tongue tenderly licked along her bottom lip as if in regret.

Anna blinked in the bright sunlight as he lifted his head. Edward studied her dazed features and must have been satisfied by what he saw there. He grinned, flashing white teeth. He caught up the reins and set the horses cantering down the lane, manes flying. Anna grabbed the seat back once again and tried to figure out what had just happened. It was rather hard to think with the taste of him still in her mouth.

"I'm going to marry you," Edward shouted.

For the life of her, she didn't know what to say. So she said nothing.

Jock barked once and let his tongue hang out of his mouth, flying in the wind.

CORAL TILTED HER face to the sky and felt the rays of the sun slide like liquid heat down her cheeks. She sat at the back door to the Wrens' cottage, just as she had every day since she was well enough to rise from her sickbed. Around her, small green things were poking their fingers through the black earth, and nearby, a funny little bird was making quite a lot of noise. Strange how one never noticed the sun in London. The raucous cries of thousands of voices, the sooty smoke, the sewage-laden streets distracted and obscured until one no longer looked up. No longer felt the gentle touch of the sun.

"Oh, Mr. Hopple!"

Coral opened her eyes at the sound of her sister's voice but otherwise remained still. Pearl had paused just inside the gate to the back garden. She was accompanied by a bantam man wearing the gaudiest waistcoat Coral had ever seen. He seemed shy, judging by the way he repeatedly tugged at the waistcoat. That was not surprising. Many men were anxious in the company of a woman they were attracted to. At least, the nicer ones were. But Pearl was playing with her hair, twirling and tangling it in her fingers, indicating that she was ill at ease as well. And that was surprising. One of the first things a whore learned was how to maintain a confident, indeed bold, mask when in the company of the stronger sex. It was the key to their living.

Pearl took leave of her escort with a pretty titter. She opened the gate and entered the small yard. She was almost to the back door when she noticed her sister.

"Goodness me, ducks, I didn't see you sitting there." Pearl fanned her flushed face. "You gave me a proper start, you did."

"So I see," Coral said. "You are not looking for a new prospect are you? You don't have to work anymore. Besides, we will be leaving for London soon, now that I am better."

"He's not a prospect," Pearl said. "At least not the kind

you mean. He's offered me a job as a downstairs maid at the Abbey."

"Downstairs maid?"

"Yes." Pearl was blushing. "I'm trained as one, you know. I'd make a good maid again, I would."

Coral frowned. "But you need not work at all. I told you I would look after you, and I will."

Her sister pulled back her thin shoulders and thrust her chin forward. "I'm going to stay here with Mr. Felix Hopple."

Coral stared for a short moment. Pearl's stance never wavered.

"Why?" she finally asked, her voice even.

"He's asked leave to court me, and I've told him he may."

"And when he learns what you are?"

"I think he already knows." Pearl saw her question and quickly shook her head. "No, I haven't told him, but my last stay here wasn't a secret. And if he doesn't know, I'll tell him. I think he'll have me anyway."

"Even if he accepts your former life," Coral said gently, "the other villagers may not."

"Oh, I know it will be rough. I'm not a young girl with pixie dust in her eyes anymore. But he's a proper gentleman." Pearl knelt beside Coral's chair. "He treats me so kindly, and he looks at me like I might be a lady."

"And so you will stay here?"

"You could stay, too." Pearl spoke low and reached to grasp Coral's hand. "We could both start a new life here, have families like normal folk. We could have a wee cottage like this one, and you could live with me. Wouldn't that be lovely?"

Coral looked down at her hand intertwined with her older sister's. Pearl's fingers were biscuit-colored with small, light scars around the knuckles, mementos of her years of service. Her own hand was white, smooth, and unnaturally soft. She withdrew it from Pearl's clasp.

"I'm afraid I cannot stay here." Coral tried to smile but found she couldn't. "I belong in London. I'm just not comfortable any other place."

"But—"

"Hush, dear. My lot in life was drawn a long time ago." Coral stood and shook out her skirts. "Besides, all this fresh air and sunshine can't be good for my complexion. Come inside and help me pack."

"If that's what you want," Pearl said slowly.

"It is." Coral held out her hand to pull her sister to her feet. "You have told me how Mr. Hopple feels, but you never said how you feel about him."

"He makes me feel safe and warm." Pearl blushed. "And he kisses so nicely."

"A lemon curd tart," Coral murmured. "And you always were so very fond of lemon curd."

"What?"

"Never mind, dear." Coral brushed her lips across her sister's cheek. "I'm glad you have found the man for you."

"AND FURTHERMORE, THIS crackpot theory only deepens the suspicion that your senility of the brain is now in an advanced stage. My commiserations."

Anna frantically scribbled the words as Edward paced before her rosewood desk. She'd never taken dictation before and found to her dismay that it was harder than she would have thought. The fact that Edward composed his scathing letters at a breakneck pace certainly did not help.

Out of the corner of her eye, she noticed that *The Raven Prince* was back on her desk. Ever since that ride in the phaeton two days ago, she and Edward seemed to be playing a game with the book. One morning she'd found the book lying in the center of her desk. She'd returned it to him silently, but after luncheon it'd been back on her desk again. She'd put it on Edward's desk, again, and the process had been repeated. Several times. So far, she hadn't worked up the courage to ask what, exactly, the book meant to him and why he seemed to be giving it to her.

Now Edward wandered over in the midst of his dictation. "Perhaps your sad mental deterioration has a family root." He braced a fist on her desk. "I remember your uncle, the Duke of Arlington, was similarly stubborn on the issue of swine breeding. Indeed, some say his final apoplectic fit was the result of a too-heated discussion about farrowing pens. Do you find it hot in here?"

Anna had gotten as far as writing *hot* when she realized that the last question was directed at her. She glanced up in time to see him discard his coat.

"No, the room seems most temperate." Her tentative smile froze as Edward drew off his neckcloth.

"I'm overly warm," he said. He unbuttoned his waistcoat.

"What are you doing?" Anna squeaked.

"Dictating a letter?" He arched his eyebrows in a parody of innocence.

"You're disrobing!"

"No, I would be disrobing if I removed my shirt," Edward said, doing just that.

"Edward!"

"My dear?"

"Put your shirt back on this instant," Anna hissed.

"Why? Do you find my torso offensive?" Edward leaned nonchalantly against her desk.

"Yes." Anna winced at his expression. "No! Put your shirt back on."

"You're sure you're not repulsed by my scars?" He leaned closer, his fingers trailing across the marks on his upper chest.

Her eyes helplessly followed his hypnotic hand before she snapped her gaze away. A scathing reply teetered on the edge of her tongue. She was stopped by Edward's studied ease. The question was clearly important to the impossible man.

She sighed. "I don't find you repulsive at all, as well you know."

"Then touch me."

"Edward—"

"Do it," he whispered. "I need to know." He caught her hand and pulled her to stand in front of him.

Anna looked into his face, struggling between propriety and the desire to reassure him. The true problem was, of course, that she wanted to touch him. Too much.

He waited.

She raised her hand. Hesitated. Then touched. Her

palm rested, trembling, on the juncture of Edward's throat and chest, just where she could feel the implacable beat of his heart. His eyes seemed to darken impossibly to a deeper shade of black as he stared at her. Her own breast labored to fill with air as her hand glided down over firm muscle. She could feel the indentations of the pox scars, and she paused to circle one gently with her middle finger. His eyelids fell, as if weighted. She moved to another scar and traced it as well. She watched her own hand and thought about the long-ago pain these scars represented. The pain to a young boy's body and the pain to his soul. The room was quiet save for the whisper of their mutual strained breaths. She'd never explored a man's chest in such minute detail. It felt too good. Sensual. More intimate in some ways than the act of sex itself.

Her gaze flicked to his face. His lips were parted, wet where he'd run his tongue over them. Obviously he was as affected as she. The knowledge that her mere touch had that kind of power over him sparked her own arousal. Her hand encountered the black, curling hair on his chest. It was damp with perspiration. She slowly furrowed her fingers into the tangle, watching as the wisps curled around her fingertips as if to hold her. She could smell his masculine essence rising with the heat from his body.

She swayed forward, drawn by a force beyond her will. His chest hair tickled her lips. She buried her nose in his warmth. His chest moved jerkily now. She opened her mouth and exhaled. Her tongue crept forward to taste the salt on his skin. One of them, maybe both, moaned. Her hands clutched at his sides, and she could dimly feel his arms urging her closer. Her tongue continued to explore:

tickling hair, tangy sweat, the corrugation of a male nipple.

The salt of her own tears.

She found that her eyes were leaking slowly, tears dripping down her face and mingling with the moisture on Edward's body. It made no sense, but she couldn't stop the tears. Any more than she could stop her body from yearning for this man or her heart from—*loving him.*

The realization brought her up short, cleared some of the haze from her mind. She inhaled shakily, and then pushed away from Edward's embrace.

His arms tightened. "Anna—"

"Please. Let me go." Her voice sounded scratchy to her own ears.

"Damn it." But his arms opened, releasing her.

She backed swiftly away.

He scowled. "If you think I'll forget this . . ."

"No need to warn me." She laughed too shrilly, teetering on the edge of completely losing her composure. "I already know you don't forget—or forgive—anything."

"God*damn*it, you know damn—"

A knock sounded at the library door. Edward cut himself off and straightened, running his hand impatiently through his hair and dislodging his queue. "What?"

Mr. Hopple peered around the door. He blinked when he saw the earl's state of undress but stuttered into speech nevertheless. "B-begging your pardon, my lord, but John Coachman says one of the rear carriage wheels is still being repaired by the blacksmith."

Edward scowled at the steward and snatched up his shirt.

Anna took the opportunity to surreptitiously swipe at her wet cheeks.

"He assures me it will take only a day more," Mr. Hopple continued. "Two at the most."

"I haven't that amount of time, man." Edward had finished re-dressing and now swung around and began rummaging in his desk, knocking papers to the floor as he did so. "We'll take the phaeton, and the servants can follow behind when the carriage is repaired."

Anna looked up suspiciously. This was the first she'd heard of a trip. Surely, he wouldn't dare?

Mr. Hopple frowned. "*We*, my lord? I wasn't aware—"

"My secretary will accompany me to London, of course. I'll be in need of her services, if I am to finish the manuscript."

The steward's eyes widened in horror, but Edward missed the reaction. He was staring at Anna challengingly.

She drew in a quick breath, mute.

"B-but, my lord!" Mr. Hopple stuttered, apparently scandalized.

"I'll need to finish the manuscript." Edward addressed his reasons to her, his eyes burning with a black fire. "My secretary will take notes at the Agrarian's meeting. I'll have to deal with various business matters pertaining to my other estates. Yes, I do believe it is essential that my secretary travel with me," he finished in a lower, more intimate tone.

Mr. Hopple lurched into speech. "But she's a-a—well! A female. An unmarried female, pardon my candor, Mrs. Wren. It isn't at all proper for her to be traveling—"

"Quite. Quite," Edward interrupted. "We'll have a chaperone. Be sure and bring one with you tomorrow, Mrs. Wren. We leave just before daybreak. I shall expect you in the courtyard." And he stomped out of the room.

Mr. Hopple trailed after, muttering ineffectual objections.

Anna truly didn't know whether to laugh or cry. She felt a rough, wet tongue on her palm and looked down to see Jock panting by her side.

"Whatever am I to do?"

But the dog only sighed and rolled onto his back so that his paws waved in the air absurdly, which hardly answered her question.

Chapter Nineteen

Aurea wept for all that she had lost, alone there in the endless desert. But after a while, she realized that her only hope was to find her vanished husband and redeem both herself and him. So she set out to search for the Raven Prince. The first year, she hunted for him in the lands to the east. There, strange animals and stranger people lived, but no one had heard of the Raven Prince. The second year, she traveled the lands to the north. There, freezing winds ruled the people from dawn to dusk, but no one had heard of the Raven Prince. The third year, she explored the western lands. There, opulent palaces rose to the sky, but no one had heard of the Raven Prince. The fourth year, she sailed to the farthest south. There, the sun burned too close to the earth, but no one had heard of the Raven Prince. . . .
—from *The Raven Prince*

"I'm very sorry, dear." Mother Wren wrung her hands that evening as she watched Anna pack. "But you know how open carriages make my tummy do loops. Just the thought, in fact, is almost enough t-to . . ."

Anna looked up swiftly. Her mother-in-law had turned a delicate shade of green.

She pushed the older woman into a chair. "Sit down and breathe. Would you like some water?" Anna tried to open the only window in the room, but it was stuck.

Mother Wren pressed a handkerchief to her mouth and closed her eyes. "I'll be all right in a moment."

Anna poured some water from a pitcher on the dresser and pressed the glass into her hand. The older woman sipped it, and the color began to return to her cheeks.

"It's just too bad Coral left so suddenly." Mother Wren had repeated the sentiment with variations all day.

Anna flattened her mouth.

Fanny had roused them that morning after finding a note in the kitchen. In the note, Coral had simply thanked them for their care. Anna had run upstairs to look in the room where Coral had been sleeping, but it was empty and the bed already made. There she discovered another note pinned to the pillow. Coral asked that Pearl be allowed to stay a while longer, and she'd included gold coins that clinked to the floor when Anna unfolded the note.

Anna had tried to give the money to Pearl, but the other woman had shaken her head and backed away. "No, ma'am. That there money is for you and Mrs. Wren. You've been the best friends me and Coral have ever had."

"But you'll need it."

"You and Mrs. Wren need it, too. Besides, I have a position I'll be starting soon." She had blushed. "Up at the Abbey."

Anna shook her head. "I hope Coral is all right. Her

bruises had barely begun to fade. Pearl doesn't even know where she could have gone besides back to London."

Mother Wren pressed a hand to her forehead. "Had she only waited, she could've accompanied you to London."

"Maybe Pearl wouldn't mind delaying her work at the Abbey and going with me first." Anna pulled out a drawer in her dresser and hunted for a pair of stockings without any holes.

"I rather think Pearl will want to stay here." Her mother-in-law set the glass down carefully on the floor beside her chair. "She seems to have met a gentleman at the Abbey."

"Really?" Anna half turned, her hands full of stockings. "Who do you think it is? One of the footmen?"

"I don't know. The day before last, she asked me about the household and who worked there. And then she muttered something about bees."

"Does the Abbey have a beekeeper?" Anna wrinkled her brow in thought before shaking her head and folding a pair of stockings and placing them in her bag.

"Not that I know of." Mother Wren shrugged. "In any case, I'm glad Lord Swartingham has decided to take you to London. He's such a nice man. And he's interested in you, dear. Perhaps he'll be asking you an important question there."

Anna winced. "He's already asked me to marry him."

Mother Wren jumped up and let out a squeal worthy of a girl a quarter of her age.

"And I told him no," Anna finished.

"No?" Her mother-in-law looked aghast.

"No." She carefully folded a chemise and placed it in her bag.

"Damn Peter!" The other woman stamped her foot.

"Mother!"

"I'm sorry, dear, but you know as well as I do that you wouldn't have turned that lovely man down if it hadn't been for my son."

"I don't—"

"Now, there's no use making excuses for him." Mother Wren actually looked stern. "The good Lord knows I loved Peter. He was my only son, and he was such a darling little boy. But what he did to you in your marriage was just plain unforgivable. My dear husband, had he been alive at the time, would've taken a horsewhip to Peter."

Anna felt tears prick her eyes. "I didn't realize you knew."

"I didn't." Mother Wren sat down again with a thump. "Not until that last illness. He was feverish and started talking one night when I was up with him. You'd gone to bed already."

Anna looked down at her hands to hide the fact that tears were blurring her vision. "He was so upset when he found out I couldn't have babies. I'm sorry for that."

"I'm sorry, too. Sorry that you couldn't have children together."

Anna wiped her face with her palm and heard her mother-in-law's skirts rustle as she came near.

Plump, warm arms wrapped around her. "But he had you. Do you know how happy I was when Peter married you?"

"Oh, Mother . . ."

"You were—*are*—the daughter I never had," Mother Wren murmured. "You've taken care of me all these years. In many ways, I've grown closer to you than I ever was to Peter."

For some reason, this made Anna weep harder.

Mother Wren held her, rocking slightly from side to side. Anna cried great, heaving sobs that tore from her chest and made her head hurt. It was so painful to have this part of her life exposed when she'd kept it hidden away from the light so long. Peter's infidelity had been her own secret shame to bear and suffer alone. Yet, all this time, Mother Wren had known, and what was more, she did not blame her. Her words felt like an absolution.

Finally, Anna's sobs slowed and quieted, her eyes still closed. She felt so weary, her limbs heavy and listless.

The older woman helped her to lie down and smoothed the coverlet over her. "Just rest."

Mother Wren's cool, soft hand gently brushed the hair from her forehead, and she heard her murmur, "Please be happy, dear."

Anna lay dreamily and listened to the click of the other woman's heels as she went downstairs. Even with her headache, she felt at peace.

"GONE TO LONDON?" Felicity's voice rose until it nearly cracked.

Two ladies walking by the Wren cottage glanced over at her. She turned her back to them.

The elder Mrs. Wren was looking at her oddly. "Yes, just this morning with the earl. Lord Swartingham said he couldn't do without her at his club meeting. I can't think now what they are called, the Aegeans or some such. It's amazing what these society gentlemen find to amuse themselves with, isn't it?"

Felicity fixed a smile on her face as the old woman babbled on, though she wanted to scream with impatience. "Yes, but when will Anna return?"

"Oh, I shouldn't think for another day or so." Mrs. Wren's brow knit in thought. "Perhaps even a week? Surely by the fortnight."

Felicity felt her smile congeal into a grimace. Good God, was the woman senile? "Quite. Well, I have to go. Errands, you know."

She could tell by Mrs. Wren's faltering smile that her parting was less than genteel, but Felicity didn't have the time right now. She climbed into her carriage, banged on the ceiling, then groaned as the carriage pulled away. Why had Chilly been so indiscreet? And which of her servants had gossiped? When she got her hands on the traitor, she would make sure they wouldn't work again in this county. Only this morning the squire had become irate at the breakfast table. He'd demanded to know who had been sneaking from her rooms the week before. It had quite put her off her coddled eggs.

If only Chilly had climbed through the window instead of using the servant's entrance. But no, he'd insisted that the stone on the window ledge would tear his stockings. Silly, vain man. And as if Reginald's suspicions about Chilly weren't enough, he'd commented only yesterday on Cynthia's red hair. It seemed red hair hadn't appeared in the Clearwater family in living memory. If ever.

Well, of course not, you stupid man, Felicity had wanted to scream. *Her red hair doesn't come from your family.* Instead, she'd made some vague references to her grandmother's auburn locks and hastily turned the conversation to hounds, a subject that always enthralled her spouse.

Felicity ran her fingers over her own perfect coiffure. Why was the squire finally looking at his daughters now after all this time? If that letter turned up on top of his suspicions about Chilly, her standing would take a considerable fall. She shuddered. Banishment to a shoddy little farmhouse was possible. Even *divorce,* that most awful of fates, might happen to her. Inconceivable. Not to Felicity Clearwater.

She had to find Anna and get that letter.

ANNA ROLLED OVER and punched the heavy down pillow for what seemed like the hundredth time. Impossible to sleep while waiting to be swooped down on by a circling earl.

She hadn't been surprised early this morning when Fanny, her chaperone by default, had been relegated to a following carriage. That had left Anna to drive alone with Edward in the phaeton to London. She'd been sure to position Jock between them on the phaeton's seat and had been almost disappointed when Edward hadn't seemed to notice. They'd driven all day and arrived at Edward's London town house after dark. Apparently they'd woken the staff. The butler, Dreary, had opened the door in nightshirt and cap. Still, the yawning maids had lit fires and found a cold meal for them.

Then Edward had wished her a polite good night and bid the housekeeper show her to a room. Since the servant's carriage with Fanny hadn't yet appeared, Anna had the bedroom to herself. In her room was a small connecting door, and she had grave suspicions about it. The bedroom was far too grand to be simply a guest room. He couldn't have put her in the countess's suite, could he? He wouldn't dare.

She sighed. Actually, he would.

The clock on the mantel had already chimed the one o'clock hour. Surely if Edward was coming to her, he would have done so before now? Not that it would do him any good to try her doors. She'd locked both.

Steady, masculine footsteps thumped up the stairs.

She stilled like a hare overshadowed by a bird of prey. She looked at the hall door. The footsteps drew near, the tread slowing as it reached her door. They stopped.

All of her being focused on the doorknob.

There was a pause, and then the footsteps resumed. A door farther down the hall opened and shut. Anna flopped back on her pillows. Naturally, she was relieved at this turn of events. Very, very relieved. Wouldn't any proper lady be relieved to find that she *wasn't* going to be ravished by a demon earl?

She was debating how a proper lady would present herself at a demon earl's bedroom for ravishment when the lock on the connecting door snicked open. Edward sauntered in, holding a key and two glasses.

"I thought you might like to share my brandy?" He gestured with the glasses.

"I, um . . ." Anna paused to clear her throat. "I don't care for brandy."

He held the glasses up for a moment longer before lowering them. "No? Well—"

"But you are welcome to drink it here." Anna's words collided with Edward's.

He stared at her silently.

"With me, I mean." She could feel her cheeks heating.

Edward turned his back, and for a ghastly moment, Anna thought he would leave after all. But he put the glasses down on a table, faced her again, and began removing his cravat. "Actually, I didn't come for a nightcap."

Her breath caught.

He tossed the cravat on a chair and pulled his shirt off over his head. Her eyes immediately fixed on his bare chest.

He looked at her. "No comment? I think this may be a first."

He sat on the bed to pull off first his boots and then his stockings. The bed sagged with his weight. He stood and dropped his hands to the buttons on his buckskins.

She stopped breathing.

Edward smiled wickedly and slowly flicked open the buttons. He hooked his thumbs in the waistband and shucked both pants and drawers with one movement. Then he straightened, and his smile faded. "If you're going to say no, do it now." He sounded just a bit uncertain.

Anna took her time looking him over. From hooded ebony eyes to broad muscular shoulders and lean belly to thickening manhood and weighty balls to corded thighs and hairy calves and finally to large, bony feet. The light had been dim at Aphrodite's Grotto, and she wanted to save this picture of him should she never see it again. He was beautiful standing there, offering himself to her in the candle's glow. She found her throat was too thick to speak, so she simply held out her arms.

Edward closed his eyes for a second. Had he really thought she would send him away? Then he walked soundlessly to the bed. He halted beside her. Bowing his head with unexpected elegance, he raised one hand to pull the ribbon from his queue. Black silk flowed around his scarred shoulders. He climbed in the bed and crouched over her, his hair tickling the sides of her face. He lowered his head to brush soft kisses over her cheeks, her nose, and her eyes. She tried to lift her lips to his, but he evaded her. Until she grew impatient.

She needed his mouth so much. "Kiss me." She drove her fingers into his mane and drew his face down to hers.

He opened his lips over hers, taking her breath into himself, and it felt like a benediction. This was so right. She knew that now. This passion between them was the most perfect thing in the world.

She squirmed, trying to get closer to him, but his hands and knees on either side of her body weighed down the sheet covering her. She was trapped. He ravished her mouth at his pleasure. He took his time, roughly, then softly, and then roughly once more until she felt her want melt within her.

Suddenly he reared back on his knees. There was a fine sheen of sweat on his chest, and seed dewed the tip of his penis. She moaned low in her throat at the sight. He was so magnificent, so beautiful, and at this instant in time, he was all hers.

He flicked his gaze at her face, then downward as he pulled the sheet from her breasts. She wore only her shift. He drew the thin garment tight across her bosom and examined the result. She could feel her nipples stiffening against the fabric. Tight and yearning. Waiting for his touch. He leaned down, placed his wet mouth over a nipple, and sucked at it through the shift. The sensation was so sharp she bucked. He moved to the other nipple and suckled that one as well until the tips of her breasts were draped in wet, transparent fabric. He drew back and blew on first one, and then the other nipple, making her gasp and struggle.

"Stop playing. For pity's sake, touch me." She didn't recognize her own voice, it was so husky.

"As you wish."

He grasped the neckline of the shift and with one motion, tore open the flimsy material. Her bare breasts tumbled into the chilly night air. For a second, Anna was shy. She wore no concealing mask tonight. This was her real self making love to Edward. She had no pretense to hide behind; he could see her face, her emotions. Then he swooped once again and captured her nipple in his mouth. The heated sucking after the coolness of the wet fabric almost sent her over the edge. At the same time, he burrowed long fingers in her maiden hair.

She stilled, breathlessly waiting, as he delicately sought and then found what he searched for. He began an insidious circling with his thumb. Oh, God, it felt so good. He knew exactly how to touch her. She mewled, her hips instinctively following his hand. He thrust his finger deep inside her, and she shuddered in the sudden storm of her climax.

His breath whispered over her closed eyelids. "Look at me."

She turned her head to the sound of his growl, her eyes still closed in bliss.

"Anna, look at me."

She opened her eyes.

Edward loomed over her, his face flushed, his nostrils flared. "I am putting myself in you now."

She could feel his erection nudging at her wet opening. The head began squeezing in, and her eyelids dropped in reaction.

"Anna, sweet Anna, look at me," Edward crooned.

He was halfway in now, and she struggled to keep her eyes focused. He bent his head and licked the tip of her nose.

Her eyes widened.

And he drove all the way home.

She moaned and arched against him. *So right. So perfect.* He filled her as if they were both made for this. As if they were made for each other. She curved her thighs around his hips, cradling him with her pelvis, and looked into his face. His eyes were closed, his face stark with want. A strand of inky hair had plastered itself against his jaw.

He opened his eyes then and speared her with their black intensity. "I am in you, and you are holding me. There is no going back from this moment."

She cried out at his words, and the breath within her chest seemed to tremble. His hips rocked. She wrapped her arms around him and held on as the slide of his penis shoving in and out of her drove all thought from her mind. He quickened his pace and groaned. His eyes were locked with hers; as if he was trying to communicate something unutterable. She touched the side of his face with one hand.

His big body seemed to break apart. He jerked against her hard. She began coming in waves, a joy so exquisite flooded her that she couldn't contain it. She moaned her rapture. He threw back his head at the same time and bared his teeth in a shout of pleasure. Warmth flooded her womb, her heart, and her very soul.

His heavy body lay on hers, and she felt his heartbeat. Anna sighed. Then he lethargically rolled off her. She curled into a ball on her side, her limbs pleasantly achy. The last thing she felt before surrendering to oblivion was Edward's hands on her stomach, pulling her back against his warmth.

Chapter Twenty

*In the fifth year of her search, late on a rainy night,
Aurea stumbled through a grim, dark wood. She wore
thin rags that only just covered her body; her feet
were bare and blistered, and she was lost and weary.
A single crust of bread was the only food she had. In
the gloom, she spied a flickering light. A tiny shack
stood all alone in a clearing. At her knock, a toothless
crone, bent nearly double by age, appeared at the
door and beckoned her inside.*

*"Ah, dearie," the old woman croaked. "'Tis a cold,
wet night to be alone. Come share my fire, do. But I
fear I've no victuals to offer you; my table is bare. Oh,
but what I wouldn't give for something to eat!"*

*Hearing this, Aurea took pity on the crone. She
reached into her pocket and offered the old woman
her last bit of bread. . . .*

—from *The Raven Prince*

A high, womanish scream jolted Edward from sleep the
next morning. He lurched up, shocked, and stared toward
the source of the awful noise. Davis, his gray locks strag-

gling about his grizzled face, stared back in abject horror. Beside Edward, a feminine voice made a sleepy protest. Christ! He quickly threw the sheets over Anna.

"In the name of all that's holy, Davis, what's got into you now?" Edward bellowed even as he felt his face heating.

"It's not enough that you're always at them whore-houses; now you've brought home a-a . . ." The valet's mouth worked.

"Woman," Edward finished the sentence. "But not the kind you're thinking of. This is my fiancée."

The bedsheets began to heave. He placed a hand on the upper edge, trapping the occupant within.

"Fiancée! I may be old, but I'm not stoopid. That's not Miss Gerard."

The bedcovers muttered ominously.

"Fetch the maid to start the fire," Edward ordered in desperation.

"But—"

"Go now."

Too late.

Anna had worked her way to the top of the bedclothes, and her head now emerged. Her hair was delightfully tou-sled, her mouth sinfully swollen. Edward felt a part of his own anatomy swell. She and Davis regarded each other. Their eyes narrowed simultaneously.

Edward groaned and dropped his head into his hands.

"You're Lord Swartingham's valet?" Never had a naked woman caught in a compromising position sounded so prim.

"'Course I am. And you're—"

Edward shot a glare at Davis that held the promise of dismemberment, mayhem, and the apocalypse.

Davis stopped and continued more cautiously. "M'lord's uh, lady."

"Quite." She cleared her throat and withdrew one arm from the covers to push back her hair.

Edward scowled and tucked the sheets more firmly around her shoulders. He needn't have bothered. Davis was carefully studying the ceiling.

"Perhaps," Anna said, "you could bring up his lordship's tea and send the maid to tend the fire?"

Davis jumped at this novel idea. "Right away, mum."

He was actually backing out the doorway when Edward's voice stopped him. "In another hour."

The valet looked scandalized but didn't say a word, a first in Edward's experience. The door shut behind Davis. Edward leaped from the bed, strode to the door, and turned the key in the lock. He flung it across the room where it clanged against the wall. He was back in the bed before Anna had time to sit up.

"Your valet is rather unusual," she said.

"Yes." Catching the sheet, he pulled it entirely off the bed, provoking a squeal from her. She lay all warm and sleepy and naked for his delectation. He growled in approval, and his early morning erection hardened even more. What a wonderful way to wake up.

She licked her lips, a move his cock thoroughly approved of. "I-I've noticed your boots are seldom shined."

"Davis is terminally incompetent." He placed his hands on either side of her hips and began to nip his way up her legs.

"Oh!" For a moment he thought he'd succeeded in distracting her, but she rallied. "Why do you keep him, then?"

"Davis was my father's valet before me." He paid scant attention to the conversation. He could smell his own scent on Anna's body, and it satisfied him in a primal way.

"So you keep him for sentimental—Edward!"

She gasped as he buried his nose in her maiden hair and inhaled. His scent was strongest here, in her gilded curls so soft and pretty in the morning light.

"I suppose so." He spoke into her hair, making Anna squirm. "And I'm fond of the evil old reprobate. Sometimes. He's known me since childhood and treats me without an iota of respect. It's refreshing. Or at least different."

He drew a finger through her cunny. The lips parted shyly, revealing a deep-pink interior. He angled his face to see better.

"Edward!"

"Would you like to know how I hired Hopple?" He propped himself on his elbows between her legs. Holding her spread with one hand, he teased her bud with the forefinger of his other hand.

"Ohhh!"

"And you've hardly met Dreary, but he has an interesting past."

"Ed-*ward!*"

God, he loved the sound of his name on Anna's lips. He debated licking her but decided he couldn't hold out that long this early in the morning. He moved on to her breasts where he suckled at first one and then the other.

"Then there's the entire staff at the Abbey. Would you like to hear about them?" He breathed the question in her ear.

Thick eyelashes almost hid her hazel eyes. "Make love to me."

Something inside him, maybe his heart, stopped for a second. "Anna."

Her lips were soft and yielding. He was not gentle, but she didn't protest. She opened her mouth sweetly and gave and gave and gave until he couldn't stand it anymore.

He pulled back and carefully turned her to her belly. He filled his hands with her plump arse and pulled her up toward him until she was on elbows and knees. He paused to study her vulnerable sex from this angle. His chest heaved at the sight. This was his woman, and only he would ever be privileged to see her this way.

He took hold of his cock and guided it to her wet entrance. It felt so good, he thrust in more roughly than he'd intended. Paused to gasp. Then thrust again. And again. Until her slick walls gave and he'd made a home for himself in her heat. Her muscles squeezed around him.

He grit his teeth to keep from spilling too soon.

Reaching, he stroked his palm down her spine. From her neck to her arse to the place where he entered her. He circled her there, feeling her stretched tissues and his own hard flesh impaling her.

She moaned and nudged him.

He withdrew to the head of his cock. And thrust. So hard her body slithered up the bed. He withdrew and thrust again. His hips swung faster and faster, and he flung back his head and ground his teeth.

He could hear Anna's heated cries, and he reached around her hips to find that tender nub and pinch it. The walls of her vagina began contracting in waves, and he could hold out no longer. He came in jets of almost painful pleasure, pumping into her, marking her as his. She was collapsing beneath him, and he followed her down to the bed, grinding his hips into her. Shuddering in the aftershocks.

He lay a moment, panting, and then rolled off Anna before he could crush her. He rested on his back, one arm over his eyes, and tried to catch his breath.

As the sweat dried on his body, he began to think about the position he'd put her in. She was now undoubtedly compromised. He'd nearly hurt Davis merely because of the look he'd given Anna. God only knew what he would do when someone made a comment to her, as inevitably would happen.

"You need to marry me." He winced. That had been rather blunt.

Anna apparently thought so, too. Her body jerked next to his. "What?"

He scowled. Now wasn't the time to appear weak. "I've compromised you. We must marry."

"No one knows but Davis."

"And the entire household. Do you think they haven't noticed by now that I didn't sleep in my own bed?"

"Even so. Nobody knows in Little Battleford, and that's what matters." She rose from the bed and pulled a chemise from her bag.

Edward grimaced. She couldn't be that naïve. "How long do you think before the news gets back to Little Battleford? I wager it'll return before we do."

Anna threw on the chemise and bent to rummage for something else in her bag, her bottom temptingly displayed through the thin linen. Was she trying to distract him? "You're already engaged," she said, her voice firm.

"Not for long. I've an appointment with Gerard tomorrow."

"What?" That got her attention. "Edward, don't do anything that you'll regret. I'll not marry you."

"For Christ's sake, why not?" He sat up impatiently.

She perched on the bed and rolled on a stocking. He noticed it was darned near the knee, and the sight made him even more angry. She shouldn't have to wear rags. Why wouldn't she marry him so he could take proper care of her?

"Why not?" he repeated as quietly as he could.

She swallowed and began on the other stocking, carefully smoothing it over her toes. "Because I don't want you to marry out of a sense of misplaced duty."

"Correct me if I'm wrong," he said. "Wasn't I the man making love to you last night and this morning?"

"And I was the woman making love to you," Anna said. "I share just as much responsibility for the act as you."

Edward watched her, searching for the words, the argument that would convince her.

She began tying a garter. "Peter was unhappy when I didn't become pregnant."

He waited.

She sighed, not looking at him. "Eventually, he went to another woman."

Damned, stupid bastard. Edward flung back the bed-covers and paced to the window. "Were you in love with him?" The question was bitter on his tongue, but he was compelled to ask it.

"In the beginning, when we were first married." She still smoothed the tattered silk over her calves. "Not at the end."

"I see." He paid for another man's sins.

"No, I don't think you can." She picked up the remaining garter and stared at it in her hands. "When a man betrays a woman in such a way, it breaks something in her that I'm not sure can ever be repaired."

Edward stared out the window, trying to form a reply. His future happiness depended on what he said next.

"I already know you are barren." He finally turned to face her. "I'm content with you as you are. I can promise you that I'll never take a mistress, but only time will provide real proof of my faithfulness. In the end, you must trust me."

Anna stretched the garter between her fingers. "I don't know if I can."

Edward turned back to the window so she couldn't see his expression. For the first time, he realized that he might not be able to convince Anna to marry him. The thought brought him close to something very like panic.

"OH, FOR GOD'S SAKE!"

"Hush. He'll hear you," Anna hissed in Edward's ear.

They were attending Sir Lazarus Lillipin's afternoon lecture on the rotation of crops using swedes and mangel-wurzels. So far, Edward disagreed with almost every word the poor man said. And he wasn't keeping his opinion of the man or his theories to himself.

Edward glared at the speaker. "No, he won't. The man's deafer than a post."

"Then others certainly will."

Edward looked at her indignantly. "I should hope they do." He turned back to the talk.

Anna sighed. He was behaving no worse than the rest of the assemblage and better than quite a few. The audience could only be called *eclectic*. They ranged from aristocrats in silks and lace to men in muddy jackboots, smoking clay pipes. All were crowded into a rather grimy coffeehouse that Edward had assured her was perfectly respectable.

She was doubtful.

Even now, a shouting match was breaking out in the back corner between a country squire and a dandy. She hoped it would not come to fisticuffs—or swords, for that matter. Every aristocrat in the room wore a sword as a badge of his rank. Even Edward, who eschewed the affectation in the country, had belted on a sword this morning.

He'd instructed her, before setting out, to take notes of the important points of the lecture so he could compare them to his own research later. She'd made some half-hearted scribbles, but she was uncertain how useful they'd be. Most of the lecture was incomprehensible to her, and she was a bit hazy about what exactly a mangel-wurzel was.

She'd begun to suspect that the main reason for her presence was so Edward could keep her in his sight. Since this morning he'd stubbornly maintained his argument that they must be married. He seemed to be under the impression that if he simply repeated it often enough, she would eventually wear down. And he might be right—if she could just let go of her fear of trusting him.

She closed her eyes and thought what it would be like to be Edward's wife. They would ride about his estates in the mornings, then argue politics and people over supper. He'd drag her to arcane lectures like the present one. And they would share the same bed. Every night.

She sighed. Heaven.

Edward let out an explosive snort. "No, no, no! Even a lunatic knows you cannot follow rye with turnips!"

Anna opened her eyes. "If you dislike the man so very much, why attend his presentation?"

"Dislike Lillipin?" He looked genuinely surprised. "He's a fine fellow. Simply backward in his thinking is all."

A wave of applause—and catcalls—signified the end of the lecture. Edward seized her hand in a possessive grip and started shouldering toward the door.

A voice hailed them from the left. "De Raaf! Drawn back to London by the lure of mangel-wurzels?"

Edward stopped, forcing Anna to halt as well. She peered over his shoulder at an exceedingly elegant gentleman in red heels.

"Iddesleigh, I hadn't hoped to see you here." Edward shifted so she couldn't see the man's face.

Anna tried leaning to the right but was blocked by a massive shoulder.

"And how could I miss Lillipin's impassioned rhetoric on the subject of swedes?" A hand draped in lace waved gracefully in the air. "I've even left my prize roses in bud to attend. By the by, how are the roses you procured from me when last you were in the capital? I never knew you were interested in ornamentals."

"Edward purchased my roses from you?" Anna pushed around him in her eagerness.

Icy gray eyes narrowed. "Well, well, what have we here?"

Edward cleared his throat. "Iddesleigh, may I present Mrs. Anna Wren, my secretary. Mrs. Wren, this is Viscount Iddesleigh."

She dropped into a curtsy as the viscount bowed and produced a lorgnette. The gray eyes that examined her through the lenses were much sharper than the style of speech and mode of dress had led her to imagine.

"Your *secretary?*" the viscount drawled. "*Fas*-cin-ating. And, as I remember, you hauled me out of bed at six in the morning to select those roses." He slowly smiled at Edward.

Edward scowled.

Anna backtracked. "Lord Swartingham was very generous in letting me have a few of the roses he'd purchased for the Abbey garden," she fibbed. "They're doing quite well, I assure you, my lord. In fact, all of the roses have branched out, and a few are developing buds."

The viscount's icy eyes returned to hers, and a corner of his mouth twitched. "And the wren defends the raven." He swept another, even more flamboyant bow, and murmured to Edward, "I congratulate you, my friend," before sauntering away into the crowd.

Edward's hand tightened briefly on her shoulder, then he grabbed her elbow once more and tugged her toward the door. A dam of bodies blocked the entrance. Several philosophical discussions were being carried on all at once, some by the same people.

A young man paused to watch the arguments with a look of contempt on his face. He wore a ridiculously small tricorn perched atop a yellow-powdered wig with an extravagantly curled tail. Anna had never seen a macaroni, but she'd studied the cartoons depicting them in the newspapers. The young man glanced at Anna as they neared the entrance. His eyes widened and then shifted to Edward. He leaned over and was muttering to another man when they made the sidewalk. The carriage was waiting around the block on a less-crowded street. As they turned the corner, Anna glanced back.

The macaroni stared after her.

A shiver ran down her spine before she turned away.

CHILLY WATCHED THE COUNTRY widow round the corner on the arm of one of the richest men in England. *The Earl of Swartingham.* No wonder Felicity had held back the name of the widow's lover. The potential for profit was enormous. And he had a perpetual need of blunt. Quite a bit of it, in fact. The accoutrements of a fashionable London gentleman didn't come cheaply.

His eyes narrowed as he estimated how much he could demand for the first payment. Felicity had the right idea there. In her latest letter, she'd implored him to contact

Anna Wren on her behalf. As Lord Swartingham's mistress, Mrs. Wren must have loads of jewelry and other valuable gifts that she could turn to money. Obviously, Felicity planned to blackmail Mrs. Wren without letting him in on the scheme.

He sneered. Now that he knew the setup, he could cut Felicity out altogether. She'd never been properly appreciative of his bed skills anyway.

"Chilton. Come to hear my lecture?" His elder brother, Sir Lazarus Lillipin, looked nervous.

As well he should, since Chilly had originally tracked down his brother to ask for another loan. Of course, now that he knew about Anna Wren, he wouldn't need his brother's money. On the other hand, that tailor had been quite uppity in his last communication. A little extra blunt never hurt.

"Hello, Lazarus." He linked arms with his elder brother and began making his pitch.

"Edward?"

"Hmm?" Edward furiously scribbled at his desk. He'd discarded his coat and waistcoat long ago, and his shirt cuffs were ink stained.

The candles were guttering. Anna suspected that Dreary had snuck off to bed after sending in their supper on a tray. The fact that the butler hadn't bothered to lay the dining room table for the meal spoke volumes about his experience with his master after an Agrarian Club lecture. Edward had been writing rebuttals to Sir Lazarus's ever since they'd returned.

She sighed.

Standing, she strolled over to where Edward worked and began playing with the gauze scarf tucked into the neckline of her dress. "It's quite late."

"Really?" He didn't look up.

"Yes."

She propped a hip on the desk and leaned over his elbow. "I'm so fatigued."

The scarf came loose over one breast. Edward's hand stilled. His head swiveled to watch her fingers at her bosom, only inches from his face.

Her ring finger wandered to her cleavage and dipped between her breasts. "Don't you think it's time for bed?"

In. Out. In. Out . . .

Edward surged to his feet, nearly knocking her over. He caught her and tossed her high in his arms.

Anna clutched him about the neck as she tilted. "Edward!"

"Darling?" He strode out the study door.

"The servants."

"If you think, after that little display"—he took the stairs two at a time—"that I'd waste time worrying about the servants, you don't know me."

They gained the upper hall. Edward bypassed her room and stopped at his own.

"The door," he prompted.

She turned the doorknob, and Edward pushed it open with his shoulder. Inside his bedroom, she glimpsed two heavy tables covered in books and papers. More books were stacked haphazardly on chairs and the floor.

He crossed to set her by his huge bed. Without a word, he turned her and began to unhook her dress. She caught her breath, suddenly shy. This was the first time she'd initiated their play when he knew it was her. He didn't seem repelled by her boldness, however. Far from it. She was very aware of the blunt fingertips brushing her spine through the layers of clothes. The dress sagged about her shoulders, and Edward pulled it down as she stepped out of it. He slowly untied her petticoats one by one and unlaced her stays. She faced him in only her chemise and stockings. His eyes were heavy lidded and intense, his gaze serious as he rubbed one thumb over the shoulder strap of her chemise.

"Beautiful," he whispered.

He bent and brushed a kiss over her shoulder as the strap fell. She shivered, whether at his touch or the look in his eyes, she didn't know. She could no longer pretend that this was only a physical act between them, and he must sense her emotion. She felt exposed.

His lips slid along her sensitive skin and he nipped. He moved to the other shoulder and that strap fell as well. Gently, he inched the front of the chemise down, exposing her breasts. Her nipples were already tight. He spread his hands over both mounds, his palms warm and possessive. He seemed to examine the contrast between his dark hands framing her white skin. High on his cheekbones color flamed. Anna imagined her pale pink nipples peeking between his callused fingers, and her head fell back as if weighted.

He lifted her breasts and squeezed.

She pushed herself into his hands. She could feel his gaze on her face, and then he stripped the chemise from her and lifted her to the bed. She watched as he swiftly removed his clothes and he lowered himself beside her. His hand smoothed across her naked belly. She raised her arms to draw him to her, but he gently caught her wrists and placed them by her head. Then he slid down her body until his head was level with her belly. His hands were on her inner thighs, and he pressed her legs apart.

"There's something I've always wanted to do with a woman." His voice was black velvet.

What did he mean? Shocked, she resisted. Surely he didn't want to look *there?* It had been different this morning when she'd been half asleep. Now she was fully awake.

"It's not something a man can do with a whore," he said.

Oh, Lord, could she do this? Expose herself so intimately? She craned her neck to look at his face.

His gaze was implacable. He wanted this. "Let me. Please."

Blushing, she lay back, surrendering to him and his needs. She let her knees fall open, feeling almost as if she were offering a gift of love to him. He looked down as her legs widened, then widened more until he was kneeling between her outstretched thighs, her most private places exposed. She squeezed her eyes shut, unable to watch him examine her.

He didn't do anything more, and finally she couldn't bear the waiting any longer. She opened her eyes. He was staring at her body, at her woman's place, and his nostrils flared, and his mouth curled in a look so possessive it was almost frightening.

Anna felt her opening contract in reaction. Liquid seeped from within her. "I need you," she whispered.

Then he truly shocked her. He swooped down and swiped right across her wetness with his tongue.

"Oh!"

He looked up at her face and slowly licked his lips. "I want to taste and tongue and suck you until you've forgotten your name." He smiled carnally. "Until I've forgotten mine as well."

She arched and gasped at just his words, but his hands were on her hips now, holding her down. His tongue searched through the folds of her femininity, each rasp going straight to her center. He found her clitoris and licked.

And she lost her mind. A long, low moan broke from her lips, and she twisted the pillow on either side of her head with her fists. Her hips bucked. But he wasn't going to be kept from his objective. He relentlessly tongued the nub until she saw stars and shamelessly shoved her pelvis into his face.

Then he drew her clitoris between his lips and sucked gently.

"Edward!" His name keened from her as a wave of warmth flooded her body, rolling all the way to her toes.

He was up and over her, his penis invading her, before she had time to open her eyes. She shuddered and clasped him as he pounded against oversensitive flesh. And she felt the wave rising again, carrying her endlessly on its crest. Her thighs quivered helplessly open, and she ground her pelvis up against his hardness. He responded by hooking his arms beneath her knees and pushing her legs toward her shoulders. She was as open as possible, exposed and held down as he loved her. As she took all he had to give.

"God!" It burst from his lips, more a guttural than a word. His great body was shaking helplessly, and he stiffened against her.

Her vision fractured into tiny rainbows as he drove his hard flesh into her softness again and again and again. She gasped. She never wanted this moment to end, they were linked right now, in body and in soul.

Until he slumped over her, his chest heaving in enormous gasps. She ran her hands over his buttocks, her eyes still closed, trying to make the intimacy last. Oh, how she wanted this man! She wanted to hold him like this tomorrow and fifty years hence. She wanted to be by his side every morning when he woke, she wanted his to be the last voice she heard before she fell asleep at night.

Edward shifted then and rolled to his back. She felt the cool air brush her damp skin. One lean arm bundled her close to his side.

"I have something for you," he said.

She felt a weight on her chest and picked it up. It was *The Raven Prince*. She blinked back tears and stroked the red morocco cover, feeling the indentations of the embossed feather beneath her fingers. "But, Edward, this was your sister's, wasn't it?"

He nodded. "And now it is yours."

"But—"

"Hush. I want you to have it."

He kissed her so tenderly she felt her heart fill and overflow with emotion. How could she continue to deny her love for this man? "I-I think—" she began.

"Shh, sweet. We'll talk in the morning," he murmured huskily.

Anna sighed and snuggled against him, inhaling his sharp, male scent. She hadn't felt this blissfully happy in years. Maybe never.

The morning would come soon enough.

Chapter Twenty-One

*Aurea and the old woman shared the crust of bread
before the little fire. As Aurea swallowed the last bite,
the door flew open and a tall, bony fellow came in.
The wind blew the door shut behind him.
"How fair you, Mother?" he greeted the crone.
The door opened once more. This time a man with
hair standing on end like the fluff of a dandelion
entered. "A good evening to you, Mother," he said.
Next, two more men stomped in, the wind whistling behind
them. One was tall and tanned, the other plump and
ruddy cheeked. "Hello, Mother," they cried together.
All four men sat by the fire, and as they did, the
flames blew and flickered, and the dust swirled
and spun on the floor around their feet.
"And have you guessed who I am?" The old
woman grinned toothlessly at Aurea. "These are
the Four Winds, and I am their mother. . . ."*
—from *The Raven Prince*

Anna was dreaming of a black-eyed baby the next morning
when a masculine voice chuckled in her ear and woke her.

"I've never seen anyone sleep so deeply." Lips brushed from her earlobe to her jaw.

She smiled and snuggled closer, only to find that there wasn't a warm body next to hers. Confused, she opened her eyes. Edward was standing by the bed already dressed.

"Wha—?"

"I'm going to see Gerard. Hush." He placed a finger against her lips when she would have spoken. "I'll be back as soon as I can. We'll make plans when I return." He leaned down to give her a kiss that made her thoughts scatter. "Don't leave my bed."

And he was gone before she could reply. She sighed and rolled over.

The next time she woke, a maid was drawing the curtains.

The girl looked up as she stretched. "Oh, you're awake, mum. I've brought some tea and fresh buns."

Anna thanked the maid and sat to take the tray. She noticed a folded note sitting next to the teapot. "What's this?"

The maid looked over. "I don't know, mum, I'm sure. A boy delivered it to the door and said it was for the lady in the house." She curtsied and left.

Anna poured herself a cup of tea and picked up the note. It was rather grubby. On the reverse side, it had been sealed with wax, but without any mark. She used the butter knife to open it, then raised the teacup to her lips as she read the first line.

The cup clattered to the saucer.

It was a blackmail note.

Anna stared at the nasty thing. The author had seen her at Aphrodite's Grotto and knew she'd met Edward there.

In sordid terms, he threatened to tell the Gerard family. She could prevent this disaster by coming to the salon at Aphrodite's Grotto tonight at nine o'clock. She was instructed to bring one hundred pounds hidden in a muff.

Anna set aside the missive and contemplated her cooling tea and dying dreams. Just moments before, happiness had seemed so close. She'd almost grasped it in her hand, almost held its fluttering wings. Then it had darted and flown, and she was left with empty air in her palm.

A tear fell from her cheek onto the breakfast tray.

Even if she had one hundred pounds—which she didn't—what would keep the blackmailer from demanding the same sum again? And again? He might even raise the price of his silence. If she were to become the Countess of Swartingham, she would be a prime mark. And it hardly mattered that Edward was at this very moment breaking off his engagement to Miss Gerard. She would be disgraced if the rest of society were to find out about her visits to Aphrodite's Grotto.

Worse, Edward would insist on marrying her anyway, despite a scandal. She would bring shame and disaster to Edward and his name. The name that meant so very much to him. It was impossible for her to destroy him like this. There was only one thing to do. She must leave London and Edward. Now, before he returned.

She knew no other way to protect him.

"YOU WOULD REJECT my daughter for a-a . . . !" Sir Richard's face darkened to a dangerous shade of puce. He looked in imminent danger of an apoplectic fit.

"A widow from Little Battleford," Edward finished the other man's sentence before he could find a less-suitable description for Anna. "Yes, sir."

The two men faced off in Sir Richard's study.

The room reeked of stale tobacco smoke. The walls, already a muddy brown color, were made dimmer by the soot streaks that started halfway up and disappeared into the gloom near the ceiling. A single oil painting hung slightly askew over the mantel. It was a hunting scene, with white and tan hounds closing in on a hare. Moments from being torn limb from limb, the hare's flat black eyes were serene. On the desk, two cut-glass tumblers stood half full with what was undoubtedly a fine brandy.

Neither glass had been touched.

"You have played with Sylvia's good name, my lord. I'll have your head for this," Sir Richard bawled.

Edward sighed. This discussion had turned even uglier than he'd anticipated. And his wig, as always, itched. Surely the old fellow wasn't going to call him out? Iddesleigh would never let him hear the end of it were he forced to duel a stout, gout-ridden baronet.

"Miss Gerard's reputation will not suffer from this at all," Edward said as soothingly as possible. "We'll put it out that she dismissed me."

"I'll take you to court, sir, for breach of promise!"

Edward narrowed his eyes. "And lose. I've infinitely more funds and contacts than you. I will not marry your daughter." Edward let his voice soften. "Besides, court would only serve to make Miss Gerard's name the talk of London. Neither of us wants that."

"But she has lost this entire season to find a suitable husband." The pendulous flesh under Sir Richard's chin trembled.

Ah. Now the real reason for the man's temper. He was less worried about his daughter's name than the prospect of funding another season for her. For a moment, Edward felt pity for the girl with such a parent. Then he seized the opening.

"Naturally," he murmured, "I'll want to recompense you for your disappointment."

Sir Richard's little eyes creased greedily at the corners. Edward sent up a prayer of thanks to whatever gods watched over him. He'd come altogether too close to having this man as his father-in-law.

Twenty minutes later, Edward emerged into the sunlight on the Gerard's front stoop. The old man had been a keen bargainer. Like a pudgy bulldog with one end of a bone he refused to relinquish, he'd growled and tugged and shook his head furiously, but in the end they'd come to an agreement. Edward was considerably lighter in the pocket as a result, but he was free of the Gerard family. All that remained was to return to Anna and make wedding plans.

He grinned. If his luck held out, she'd still be in his bed.

Whistling, he ran down the steps to his carriage. He only paused to pull off the awful wig and toss it to the ground before entering the vehicle. He glanced out the window as the carriage pulled away. A ragpicker was trying the wig on for size. The white-powdered wig with its stiff side curls and tail contrasted strangely with the man's filthy clothes and unshaven face. The ragpicker bent, grasped the handles of his wheelbarrow, and jauntily trundled off.

By the time the carriage pulled up before his town house, Edward was humming a bawdy tune. With the Gerard engagement out of the way, he saw no reason why he shouldn't be a married man in a month. A fortnight, if he could get a special license.

He shoved his tricorn and cape at a footman and took the stairs two at a time. He still had to win an assent from Anna, but after last night, he felt sure that she'd capitulate soon.

He rounded the stairs and strode down the hall. "Anna!" He pushed open the door to his room. "Anna, I—"

He stopped short. She wasn't in the bed. "Damnation."

He strode through the connecting door into the sitting room. It, too, was empty. He heaved a sigh of exasperation. Walking back into his bedroom, he stuck his head out the door and bellowed for Dreary. Then he paced across the room. Where was the woman? The bed was made, the curtains drawn. A fire had burned out on the grate. She must've left the room some time ago. He noticed Elizabeth's red book sitting on the dresser. There was a scrap of paper on top of it.

He started for the book as Dreary entered the room.

"My lord?"

"Where's Mrs. Wren?" Edward picked up the folded paper. His name was written on the front in Anna's hand.

"Mrs. Wren? The footmen informed me that she left the house at about ten o'clock."

"Yes, but where did she go, man?" He opened the note and began to read it.

"That's just it, my lord. She didn't say where . . ." The butler's voice buzzed in the background as Edward comprehended the words written in the note.

So sorry . . . must go away . . . Yours always, Anna

"My lord?"

Gone.

"My lord?"

She'd left him.

"Are you all right, my lord?"

"She's gone," Edward whispered.

Dreary buzzed around some more, and then he must have left, because after a while, Edward found that he was alone. He sat in front of a dead fire in his bedroom, alone. But then that was what, until very recently, he'd been most used to.

Being alone.

THE COACH RATTLED and bumped over a pothole in the road.

"Ouch," Fanny exclaimed. She rubbed her elbow, which had hit the door. "Lord Swartingham's carriage sure was better sprung."

Anna murmured an assent, but she really didn't care. She supposed she should be making plans. Deciding where to go once they reached Little Battleford. Thinking about how to raise some money. But it was terribly hard to think, let alone plan right now. It was much easier to stare out the window of the coach and let it take her where it would. Across from them, the only other occupant of the coach, a spare little man with a gray wig tilted over one brow, snored. He'd been asleep when they began their trip in London and hadn't woken since, despite the jostling of the coach and the frequent stops. From the smell that emanated from him, a pungent blend of gin, vomit, and unwashed body, he wouldn't waken if trumpets announced the second coming. Not that she cared very much either way.

"Do you think we'll be in Little Battleford by night?" Fanny asked.

"I don't know."

The maid sighed and plucked at her apron.

Anna felt a brief moment of guilt. She hadn't told Fanny why they were leaving London when she'd woken her this morning. Indeed, she'd hardly spoken to the girl at all since departing Edward's town house.

Fanny cleared her throat. "Will the earl be following us, do you think?"

"No."

Silence.

Anna glanced at the maid. Her brow was puckered.

"I thought you might be marrying the earl soon?" The girl phrased the statement as a question.

"No."

Fanny's mouth trembled.

Anna said more softly, "It's hardly likely, is it? An earl and me?"

"It is if he loves you," the little maid said earnestly. "And Lord Swartingham does. Love you, I mean. Everyone says so."

"Oh, Fanny." She turned her eyes to the window as they blurred.

"Well, it is possible," the girl insisted. "And you love

the earl, so I don't see why we're going back to Little Battleford."

"It's more complicated than that. I-I would be a liability to him."

"A what?" Fanny's mouth scrunched up.

"A liability. A millstone about his neck. I can't marry him."

"I don't know why—" Fanny broke off as the carriage clattered into an inn yard.

Anna seized gratefully on the interruption. "Let's get out here and stretch our legs."

Moving past the still-sleeping third passenger, they jumped down from the coach. In the yard, ostlers ran back and forth, tending the team of horses, unloading packages from on top of the coach, and bringing more out to replace them. The driver leaned down from his perch, shouting gossip to the innkeeper. To add to the noise and confusion, a private carriage was also stopped at the inn. Several men were bent over the right near horse, examining its hoof. The animal appeared to have either thrown a shoe or come up lame.

Anna took Fanny's elbow and moved them both beneath the inn's eaves so as not to be in the way of running men and boys. Fanny stood on one foot and then the other and finally blurted, "Excuse me, mum. I have to use the necessary."

Anna nodded and the little maid scurried off. She idly watched the men tending to the lame horse.

"When exactly will the carriage be ready?" a strident voice exclaimed. "I've been waiting an hour already in this filthy inn."

Anna stiffened at the familiar tones. Oh, God, not Felicity Clearwater. Not now. She shrank back against the inn wall, but fate wasn't pulling its punches today. Felicity walked out of the inn and immediately saw her.

"Anna Wren." The other woman's mouth pinched until unbecoming lines radiated from her lips. "Finally."

Felicity marched up and seized her arm in a commanding grip. "I can't believe I've had to travel almost all the way to London just to talk to you. And I had to cool my heels at this wretched inn. Now listen carefully." Felicity shook her arm for emphasis. "I don't want to repeat myself. I know all about your little entanglement at Aphrodite's Grotto."

Anna felt her eyes widen. "I—"

"No." Felicity cut her off. "Don't try to deny it. I've a witness. And I know you met the Earl of Swartingham there. Aiming a bit high, weren't you? I never would've guessed it of a timid little mouse like you."

For a moment, the other woman almost looked curious, but she recovered and continued before Anna could get her mouth to work.

"That's neither here nor there. This is the important part." She shook Anna's arm again, this time more roughly. "I want my locket and the letter in it back, and if you ever breathe a word about Peter and me, I'll make sure every single soul in Little Battleford hears about your indiscretion. You and your mother-in-law will be driven out of town. I'll see to it personally."

Anna's eyes widened. How dare . . . ?

"I hope"—she gave a final nasty shake—"I've made myself clear." Felicity nodded as if she'd finished with some small, domestic business. Dismissing an imperti- nent maid, perhaps. Unpleasant, but necessary. Now on to more important matters. She turned to walk off.

Anna stared.

Felicity truly thought she was a *timid little mouse*, one who would crumple in a heap of fear at threats by her late husband's lover. And wasn't she? She was running from the man she loved. The man who cared for her and wanted to marry her. Running because of a filthy blackmail note. Anna felt ashamed. No wonder Felicity thought she could tread all over her!

Anna whipped out a hand and caught the other woman by the shoulder. Felicity almost went over in the inn yard muck.

"What—?"

"Oh, you have made yourself clear," Anna purred as she backed the taller woman into the wall. "But you've made one slight miscalculation: that I'd give two farthings for your threats. You see, if I don't care what you say about me, well then you have nothing to hold over me, now, do you, Mrs. Clearwater?"

"But, you—"

Anna nodded as if Felicity had said something pro- found. "That's right. But I, on the other hand, have some- thing quite substantial about you. The fact that you tupped my husband."

"I-I—"

"And if memory serves me right"—Anna touched a finger to her cheek in mock amazement—"why it was just about the time your younger daughter was conceived. The one with red hair like Peter's."

Felicity slumped against the wall and looked at her as if she'd grown a third eye right in the middle of her forehead.

"Now what do you think the squire would say about that?" Anna asked sweetly.

The other woman tried a recovery. "Now see here—"

Anna stabbed a finger in her face. "No. You see here. If you ever try to threaten me or anyone I love again, I'll tell all the inhabitants of Little Battleford that you were bedding my husband. I'll have leaflets printed up and delivered to every house, cottage, and hovel in Essex. In fact, I'll tell the whole country. You may very well have to leave England."

"You wouldn't," Felicity breathed.

"No?" Anna smiled, not at all nicely. "Try me."

"That's—"

"Blackmail. Yes. And you should know."

Felicity's face blanched.

"Oh, and one more thing. I need a ride to London. Immediately. I'm taking your carriage." Anna wheeled and started for the carriage, grabbing Fanny, who was gawking beside the inn door, as she went past.

"But how am I to return to Little Battleford?" Felicity wailed behind her.

Anna didn't bother to look back. "You are welcome to my seat on the coach."

HE SAT IN A CRACKED leather armchair in the town house library because he could not bear the memories in his bedroom.

There was one bookcase to lend the room its name. Dusty religious volumes filled the shelves, lined in rows like tombstones in a graveyard, untouched for generations. The only window was draped in blue velvet, pulled to one side by a tarnished gilt rope. He could see the phantom roofline of the next building over. Earlier, the festering red sun had silhouetted the multiple chimneys on the roof as it set. Now it was near dark outside.

The room was cold because the fire had died.

A maid had come some time back—he wasn't sure when—to rebuild the fire, but he'd ordered her out. No one had bothered him since. Now and then, he heard murmured voices outside in the hall, but he ignored them.

He didn't read.

He didn't write.

He didn't drink.

He simply sat, holding the book on his lap, and thought and stared at nothing as the night entombed him. Jock nudged his hand once or twice, but he ignored that contact as well, until the dog gave up and lay down by his side.

Was it the pox scars? Or his temper? Hadn't she enjoyed his lovemaking? Was he too enthralled with his work? Or did she simply not love him?

That only. So small and yet everything.

If his title, his wealth, his—*God!*—his *love* had not mattered to her, he had nothing. What had driven her away? It was a question he couldn't answer. A question he couldn't let go. It engulfed him, consumed him, became the only thing that counted at all. Because without her, there was nothing. His life stretched before him in gray, ghostly tones.

Alone.

He was without anyone to touch his soul as Anna had, without the completeness she had provided. He hadn't even noticed until she was gone: there was a great, gaping hole in his being without her.

Could a man live with such a void inside of him?

SOMETIME LATER, EDWARD vaguely noticed a flurry of raised voices in the hall drawing nearer. The library door opened, revealing Iddesleigh.

"Oh, this is a pretty sight." The viscount closed the door behind him. He set the single candle he carried on a table and threw his cape and hat on a chair. "A strong, intelligent man brought low by a woman."

"Simon. Go away." Edward didn't move, didn't even turn his head at the intrusion.

"I would, old boy, if I hadn't a conscience." Iddesleigh's voice echoed eerily about the room. "But I find I have. A conscience, that is. Damned inconvenient." The viscount knelt at the cold fireplace and began assembling a pile of tinder.

Edward frowned a little. "Who sent for you?"

"Your strange elderly man." Iddesleigh reached for the coal scuttle. "Davis, I think? He was concerned for Mrs. Wren. He seems to have taken a liking to her, rather like a pullet imprinting on a swan. He may have been worried about you as well, but it was hard to tell. I can't think why you keep the creature on."

Edward didn't answer.

Iddesleigh delicately stacked lumps of coal around his tinder. It was odd to see the fastidious viscount working at such a dirty job. Edward hadn't suspected he knew how to lay a fire.

Iddesleigh spoke over his shoulder, "So, what's the plan? To sit here until you freeze? A bit passive, what?"

"Simon, for the love of God, leave me be."

"No, Edward. For the love of God—and you—I'll stay." Iddesleigh struck flint and steel, but the tinder wouldn't catch.

"She's gone. What would you have me do?"

"Apologize. Buy her an emerald necklace. Or, no, in this lady's case, buy her more roses." A spark caught and began to lick at the coals. "Anything, man, but sit here."

For the first time, Edward stirred, an uncomfortable shifting of muscles still too long. "She doesn't want me."

"Now that," Iddesleigh said as he stood and took out a handkerchief, "is an out and out lie. I saw her with you, remember, at Lillipin's lecture. The lady is in love with you, although God only knows why." He wiped his hands on the handkerchief, turning it black, then contemplated the ruined square of silk for a moment before throwing it into the flames.

Edward turned his head away. "Then why did she leave me?" he muttered.

Iddesleigh shrugged. "What man knows a woman's mind? Certainly not I. You might've said something to offend, almost surely did, in fact. Or she might've taken a sudden dislike to London. Or"—he dipped his hand into his coat pocket and held out a piece of paper between two fingers—"she might've been blackmailed."

"What?" Edward jolted upright and grabbed the slip of paper. "What are you talking . . ." His voice trailed away as he read the damned note. Someone had threatened Anna. *His* Anna.

He looked up. "Where the hell did you get this?"

Iddesleigh showed his palms. "Davis again. He gave it to me in the hall. Apparently it was on the grate in your room."

"The goddamn son of a whore. Who is this man?" Edward brandished the paper before viciously screwing it into a ball and throwing it into the fire.

"I have no idea," Iddesleigh said. "But he must frequent Aphrodite's Grotto to know so much."

"Jesus!" Edward jumped from the chair and shoved his arms into his coat. "When I finish with him, he won't be able to visit a drab. I'll cut off his stones. And then I'm going after Anna. How dare she not tell me someone was threatening her?" He stilled at a sudden thought, then swung around to Iddesleigh. "Why didn't you give the note to me at once?"

The viscount shrugged again, unperturbed by his scowl. "The blackmailer won't be at the Grotto until nine." He took out a penknife and began cleaning underneath his thumbnail. "It's only half past seven now. Didn't see much point in rushing things. Perhaps we can have a bite to eat first?"

"If you weren't so useful once in a while," Edward growled, "I would have strangled you by now."

"Oh, undoubtedly." Iddesleigh put away the knife and reached for his cape. "But it would be nice to at least bring along some bread and cheese in the carriage."

Edward scowled. "You're not coming with me."

"I'm afraid I am." The viscount adjusted his tricorn to the proper angle in the mirror by the door. "And so is Harry. He's waiting in the hall."

"Why?"

"Because, my dear friend, this is one of those times when I can be useful." Iddesleigh smiled ferally. "You'll be needing seconds, won't you?"

Chapter Twenty-Two

*The old woman smiled at Aurea's startled expression.
"My sons roam the four corners of the earth.
There isn't a man or beast or bird that they
don't know. What is it you search for?"
Then Aurea told of her strange marriage to the Raven
Prince and his avian followers and her search for her
lost husband. The first three Winds shook their heads
regretfully; they had not heard of the Raven Prince.
But the West Wind, the tall bony son, hesitated.
"Sometime back, a wee shrike told me a strange
story. She said there was a castle in the clouds
where birds spoke with human voices. If you like,
I'll take you there." So Aurea climbed on the back
of the West Wind and wrapped her arms tightly
around his throat so that she might not fall off,
for the West Wind flies more swiftly than any bird. . . .*
—from *The Raven Prince*

Harry tugged at his black silk demimask. "Tell me again
why we're going masked, my lord."

Edward drummed his fingers against the carriage door, wishing they could gallop through the London streets. "There was a small misunderstanding the last time I was at the Grotto."

"A misunderstanding." Harry's voice was soft, noncommittal.

"It would be better were I not recognized."

"Really?" Iddesleigh stopped fiddling with his own mask. He sounded fascinated. "I wasn't aware Aphrodite barred anyone from her doors. What, exactly, did you do?"

"It doesn't matter." Edward waved an impatient hand. "All you need to know is that we must be discreet when we enter."

"And Harry and I are also masked because . . . ?"

"Because if this man follows me closely enough to know about my engagement to Miss Gerard, he'll also know we three are comrades."

Harry grunted in apparent assent.

"Ah. In that case, perhaps we ought to mask the dog as well." The viscount looked pointedly at Jock, sitting upright on the bench next to Harry. The dog gazed alertly out the window.

"Try to be serious," Edward growled.

"I was," Iddesleigh muttered.

Edward ignored the other man to watch out the window himself. They were in an area near the East End that was not quite disreputable, yet not entirely respectable. He caught the movement of a skirt in a doorway as they passed. A trull displaying her wares. Less-benign shapes skulked in the shadows as well. Part of the Grotto's allure was that it straddled the narrow line between the illicit and the truly dangerous. The fact that on any given night a small portion of the Grotto's patrons were robbed or worse didn't seem to diminish its attraction; to a certain sort, no doubt, it increased the appeal.

The glow of lights up ahead gave notice that they were nearing the Grotto. In another moment, the faux Greek façade came into view. White marble and an abundance of gilt lent Aphrodite's Grotto a magnificently vulgar air.

"How do you plan to find the blackmailer?" Harry asked sotto voce as they descended from the carriage.

Edward shrugged. "At nine we'll know how big the field is." He strolled to the entrance with all the arrogance of his nine generations of aristocracy behind him.

Two burly fellows in togas guarded the doors. The drapes on the man nearest were a bit too short, revealing astonishingly hairy calves.

The guard squinted suspiciously at Edward. "'Ere now. Ain't you the Earl of—"

"I'm so glad you recognized me." Edward put one hand on the man's shoulder and extended the other in a seemingly friendly shake.

The extended palm held a guinea. The guard's fist closed smoothly over the gold piece and disappeared into the folds of his toga.

The man smiled greasily. "That's all fine and good, my lord. But after last time, perhaps you wouldn't mind . . . ?" The man rubbed his fingers together suggestively.

Edward scowled. What cheek! He leaned into the other man's face until he could smell the rot of his teeth. "Perhaps I would mind."

Jock growled.

The guard backed up, hands thrust out in a calming motion. "That's good! That's good, my lord! Step right in."

Edward nodded curtly and climbed the steps.

Beside him, Iddesleigh murmured, "You really must tell me about this misunderstanding sometime."

Harry chuckled.

Edward ignored them. They were in, and he'd more important matters to consider.

"BUT WHERE DID HE GO?" Anna stood in the entrance hall to Edward's town house, interrogating Dreary. She still wore her musty traveling clothes.

"I'm sure I don't know, ma'am." The butler seemed genuinely at a loss.

She stared at him in frustration. She'd spent all day traveling, had composed and recomposed her apology to Edward, had even daydreamed about making up afterward, and now the silly man wasn't even here. It was a bit anticlimactic, to say the least.

"Doesn't anyone know where Lord Swartingham is?" She was beginning to whine.

Fanny shifted from one foot to the other beside her. "Maybe he went looking for you, mum."

Anna switched her gaze to Fanny. In doing so, a movement at the back of the hall caught her eye. Edward's valet was tiptoeing away. Sneakily.

"Mr. Davis." She snatched at her skirts and trotted after the man more briskly than was ladylike. "Mr. Davis, wait a moment."

Drat! The old man was faster than he looked. He darted around the corner and up a back staircase, feigning deafness.

Anna panted after him. "Stop!"

The valet turned at the top of the stairs. They were in a narrow hallway, evidently the servants' quarters. Davis made for a door at the end of the corridor, but Anna was faster on level ground. She put on an extra burst of speed and reached the door before the little man. She slammed her back to the closed door, her arms outstretched on either side, barring him from his sanctuary.

"Mr. Davis."

"Oh, was you wanting me, mum?" He opened rheumy eyes wide.

"Quite." She inhaled deeply, trying to catch her breath. "Where is the earl?"

"The earl?" Davis looked around as if expecting Edward to pop out of the shadows.

"Edward de Raaf, Lord Swartingham, the Earl of Swartingham?" Anna leaned closer. "Your master?"

"Don't have to be snotty." Davis actually looked wounded.

"Mr. Davis!"

"M'lord might've had an idea," the valet said carefully, "that he was needed somewheres else."

Anna tapped her foot. "Tell me right now where he is."

Davis cast his eyes up and then to the side, but there was no help in the dim hallway. He heaved a sigh. "He might've found a letter." The manservant didn't meet her eyes. "He might've gone to a nasty house. Had an awful strange name, Aphroditty or Aphro—"

But Anna was already running down the servant's stair, skidding on the turns as she rounded them. *Oh, my God. Oh, my God.*

If Edward had found the blackmail note . . .

If he'd gone to confront the blackmailer . . .

The blackmailer obviously had no sense of honor and was probably dangerous. What would he do when cornered? Surely Edward wouldn't take on such a man by himself? She whimpered. Oh, yes, he would. If anything happened to him, it would be her fault.

Anna ran flat out through the hall, shoved past Dreary, still dithering, and banged open the door.

"Mum!" Fanny started after her.

Anna did a little spin. "Fanny, stay here. If the earl returns, tell him I'll be back soon." She turned again and cupped her hands to bellow at the carriage pulling away from the town house. *"Stop!"*

The coachman yanked hard on the reins, causing the front horses to half rear. He looked around. "What is it now, mum? Don't you want to rest a bit now you're in London? Mrs. Clearwater—"

"I need you to drive me to Aphrodite's Grotto."

"But, Mrs. Clearwater—"

"Now."

The coachman sighed wearily. "Which way is it, then?"

Anna gave succinct directions, then scrambled into the carriage she'd so recently exited. She gripped the leather straps and prayed, *Oh, dear God, let me be in time.* She couldn't live with herself if Edward were hurt.

The carriage ride was hellishly interminable, but finally she alighted and ran up the long marble steps. Inside,

Aphrodite's Grotto echoed with the chatter and laughter of London's denizens of the night. Every young buck, every aging roué, every lady mincing on the fine edge of respectability seemed to be gathered at Aphrodite's. It was a quarter to nine, and the throng was boisterous, un-inhibited, and more than slightly drunk.

Anna drew her cloak tightly about her. The rooms were hot and smelled of burning wax, unwashed bodies, and al-coholic spirits. Nevertheless, she kept the wrap on, a thin barrier between herself and the crowd. Once she glanced up and noticed leering cupids on the ceiling. They were pulling back a painted veil to reveal a voluptuously pink Aphrodite surrounded by a . . . well, an orgy.

Aphrodite seemed to wink down at her with knowing eyes.

Anna hastily averted her gaze and continued her search. Her plan was simple: find the blackmailer and lure him away from the Grotto before Edward got to him. The problem was that she didn't know who the blackmailer was. In fact, she didn't even know if it was a man. Ner-vously, she kept an eye out for Edward as well. Perhaps if she could find him before the blackmailer appeared, she could convince him to just leave. Although she had a hard time imagining Edward backing away from a fight, even one he might lose.

She entered the main salon. Here couples lounged on settees, and young bucks prowled for their evening's en-tertainment. She saw at once that it would be prudent to keep moving, so she perambulated about the room. The classical theme was continued here, with various scenes of Zeus seducing young ladies. The one of Europa and the Bull was particularly graphic.

"I told you to bring a muff." A peevish voice at Anna's elbow interrupted her thoughts.

Finally.

"I'm not paying your ridiculous price." The black-mailer didn't look that frightening. He was younger than she'd expected, with a familiar, receding chin. Anna frowned. "You're the macaroni from the lecture."

The man looked irritated. "Where's my money?"

"I've already told you, I'm not paying. The earl is here, and it's in your best interest to leave now, before he finds you."

"But, the money—"

Anna stamped her foot in exasperation. "Look, you pea-brained nit, I haven't got any money with me, and you really must—"

A large furry form leapt from behind Anna. There was a shout and a horrible, low growling. The blackmailer sprawled on the floor, his body nearly obliterated by Jock. The mastiff's bared fangs were only inches from the man's eyes, and a ridge of fur bristled down the dog's back as he continued his menacing rumbling.

Belatedly, a woman screamed.

"Hold, Jock," Edward said as he advanced. "Chilton Lillipin. I should've guessed. You must have been at your elder brother's lecture yesterday."

"Damnation, Swartingham, get this beast off me! What do you care about a sl—"

Jock barked, nearly taking off the man's nose.

Edward placed a hand on the back of the dog's neck. "I do, most certainly, care about this *lady*."

Lillipin's eyes narrowed craftily. "Then you'll no doubt want satisfaction."

"Naturally."

"I'll have my seconds contact—"

"Now." Although Edward spoke softly, his voice carried over the other man's.

"Edward, no!" This was exactly what Anna had wanted to avoid.

Edward ignored her. "I have my seconds here."

Viscount Iddesleigh and a shorter man with watchful green eyes stepped forward. Their faces were intent on this masculine game.

The viscount smiled. "Pick your seconds."

Lillipin glanced around the room from his prone position. A young man, his shirt untucked, pulled his staggering companion to the front of the crowd. "We'll second you."

Oh, God! "Edward, stop this, please." Anna spoke low.

He pulled Jock off Lillipin and toward her. "Guard."

The dog obediently stood braced in front of Anna.

"But—"

Edward looked at her sternly, cutting off her words. He shed his coat. Lillipin jumped to his feet, removed his coat and waistcoat, and drew his sword. Edward unsheathed his own weapon. The two men stood in a suddenly cleared space.

This was happening too fast. It was like a nightmare she couldn't stop. The room had grown silent, faces turned avidly at the prospect of bloodshed.

The men saluted, bringing their swords up before their faces; then each bent slightly at the knee, their blades in front of them. Slimmer and shorter than Edward, the younger man's stance was consciously elegant with his left hand curved in a graceful arc behind his head. Lillipin wore a linen shirt trimmed in fountains of Belgian lace that flowed as he moved. Edward stood solidly, his un-armed hand held out behind him for balance, not grace. His black waistcoat had only a thin line of black braid along the edge, and his white shirt was unadorned.

Lillipin sneered. "En garde!" The younger man lunged. His rapier moved in a glinting flurry.

Edward blocked the attack. His sword slid and scraped against his opponent's. He stepped back two paces as Lil-lipin advanced, weapon flashing. Anna bit her lip. Surely he was on the defensive? Lillipin seemed to think so as well. His lips curved in an oily grin.

"Chilly Lilly killed two men last year," a voice crowed from the crowd behind her. Anna drew in her breath sharply. She'd heard of the bucks in London who amused themselves by challenging and killing less-skilled swords-men. Edward spent most of his time in the country. Could he even defend himself?

The men moved in a tight circle, sweat gleaming on their faces. Lillipin lunged forward, and his sword chat-tered against Edward's. Edward's right sleeve shredded. Anna moaned, but no telltale red stained the sleeve. Lil-lipin's blade darted out again, a snake striking, and bit into Edward's shoulder. Edward grunted. This time crim-son drops fell to the floor. Anna started forward, only to be halted by Jock's jaws clamped gently around her arm.

"Blood," Iddesleigh called out, echoed closely by Lillipin's seconds.

Neither duelist wavered. The swords sang and attacked. Edward's sleeve steadily bloomed a bright red. With each movement of his arm, blood sprayed over the floor, bright droplets that were immediately smeared into streaks by the combatants' feet. Weren't they supposed to stop at the first blood drawn?

Unless they fought to the death.

Anna stuffed her fist into her mouth to stifle a scream. She couldn't distract Edward now. She stood absolutely still, her eyes brimming with tears.

Suddenly, Edward lunged and lunged again. His lead foot stomped against the floor with the ferocity of his attack. Lillipin fell back and brought his sword up to defend his face. Edward's arm made a controlled circular movement; his blade flashed up and over his opponent's weapon. Lillipin squealed in pain. The sword flew from his hand, sliding with a clatter across the room. Edward stood with the tip of his weapon pressed into the soft skin at the base of Lillipin's throat.

The younger man breathed hard, his bleeding right hand cradled in his left.

"You may have won by luck, Swartingham," Lillipin panted, "but you cannot stop me from talking once I leave this—"

Edward flung down his sword and slammed his fist into the other man's face. Lillipin staggered back, arms flailed wide, and fell to the floor with a thump. He lay still.

"Actually, I can stop you," Edward muttered, and shook his right hand.

There was a long-suffering sigh from directly behind Anna. "I knew you'd resort to fisticuffs eventually." Viscount Iddesleigh stepped around her.

Edward looked affronted. "I did duel him first."

"Yes, and your form was atrocious as always."

The man with the green eyes rounded Anna's other side and silently bent to pick up Edward's sword.

"I won," Edward said pointedly.

The viscount sneered. "Sadly so."

"Would you have preferred he best me?" Edward demanded.

"No, but in a perfect world, classic form would win every time."

"This isn't a perfect world, thank God."

Anna couldn't stand it any longer. *"Idiot!"* She hit Edward's chest, but then remembered and frantically tore at his bloody sleeve.

"Darling, what—?" Edward sounded nonplussed.

"It's not enough that you had to fight that awful man," she panted, her vision half obscured by tears. "You let him hurt you. You're bleeding all over the floor." Anna got the sleeve open and felt dizzy when she saw the terrible gash marring his beautiful shoulder. "And now you're probably going to die." She sobbed as she pressed her handkerchief, pitifully inadequate, against his wound.

"Anna, sweetheart, hush." Edward tried to put his arms around her, but she batted them aside.

"And for what? What was worth dueling that horrible man over?"

"You." Edward spoke softly, and her breath caught midsob. "You are worth anything and everything to me. Even bleeding to death in a brothel."

Anna choked, unable to speak.

He brushed his hand tenderly along her cheek. "I need you. I told you that, but you didn't seem to believe me." He took a breath and his eyes glittered. "Don't ever leave me again, Anna. I won't survive the next time. I want you to marry me, but if you can't do that . . ." He swallowed.

Her eyes filled with tears anew.

"Just don't leave me," he whispered.

"Oh, Edward." She sighed as he framed her face with bloody hands and kissed her tenderly.

He husked across her lips, "I love you."

Distantly, she heard a whoop and several catcalls. The viscount cleared his throat nearly in her ear.

Edward lifted his head but kept his eyes on Anna's face. "Can't you see I'm busy, Iddesleigh?"

"Oh, indeed. The whole Grotto can see you're busy, de Raaf," the viscount said dryly.

Edward looked up and seemed to notice their audience for the first time. He scowled. "Right. I need to take Anna home and get this"—he gestured to his shoulder—"seen to." He glanced at the unconscious Lillipin, who was now drooling. "Can you take care of that?"

"I suppose I'll have to." The viscount pursed his lips in distaste. "There must be a ship sailing somewhere exotic tonight. You don't mind, do you, Harry?"

The green-eyed man grinned. "Sailoring will do this lout a world of good." He grabbed Lillipin's feet. Viscount Iddesleigh took the other end, none too gently, and together they lifted Chilly Lilly.

"Congratulations." Harry nodded at Anna.

"Yes, felicitations, de Raaf," the viscount drawled as he walked past. "I do hope I'll merit an invite to the impending nuptials?"

Edward growled.

Chuckling, the viscount sauntered out, holding half of an unconscious man. Edward immediately clamped a hand around Anna's arm and began pushing her through the mass of people. For the first time, she noticed that Aphrodite herself watched from the edge of the crowd. Anna's mouth dropped open. The madam now stood a head shorter than previously and had catlike green eyes behind her golden mask. Her hair was powdered with gold dust.

"I knew he would forgive you," Aphrodite purred as Anna threaded her way past; then she raised her voice. "Drinks on the house for everyone in celebration of love!"

The crowd roared behind them as Anna and Edward ran down the front steps into the waiting carriage. Edward thumped on the roof and collapsed on the cushions. He hadn't let go of her for a second, and now he pulled her into his lap and covered her mouth with his own, taking advantage of her parted lips to thrust his tongue in. It was several minutes before she could draw a breath.

He drew back only to deliver a series of little nips along her bottom lip. "Will you marry me?" he breathed so close to her that the air from his body whispered across her face.

More tears blurred Anna's eyes. "I love you so much, Edward," she said brokenly. "What if we never have a family?"

He cupped her face in his hands. "You are my family. If we never have children, I will be disappointed, but if I never have you, I will be devastated. I love you. I need you. Please trust me enough to be my wife."

"Yes." Edward was already nibbling a row of kisses down her neck, so it was hard for her to get the word out, but she said it again anyway, because saying it was important.

"Yes."

Epilogue

*The West Wind flew with Aurea to a castle in the
clouds surrounded by wheeling birds. As she
stepped from his back, a giant raven alighted
beside her and transformed into Prince Niger.
"You have found me, Aurea, my love!" he said.
As the Raven Prince spoke, the birds drifted down
from the sky and turned one by one into men and
women again. A great shout of exultation arose from
the Raven Prince's followers. At the same time, the
clouds dissolved from around the castle to reveal
that it sat at the summit of a great mountain.
Aurea was dazed. "But how is this possible?"
The prince smiled, and his ebony eyes glinted.
"Your love, Aurea. Your love has broken the curse. . . ."*
—from *The Raven Prince*

THREE YEARS LATER . . .

"And Aurea and the Raven Prince lived happily ever
after." Anna closed the red morocco leather book softly.
"Is he asleep?"

Edward shifted the silk screen so it would shade the toddler from the afternoon sun. "Mmm. For some time now, I think."

They both looked at the deceptively cherubic face. Their son lay on ruby-red silk cushions, piled in the center of the walled garden at the Abbey. His short limbs sprawled, as if sleep had overcome him in midmotion. Rosebud lips pursed over the two fingers in his mouth, and a gentle wind stirred his raven curls. Jock lay beside his favorite human, unconcerned by the chubby hand that clutched his ear. Around them, the garden bloomed in full glory: Flowers spilled onto the pathways in multicolored exuberance, and climbing roses nearly covered the walls. The air was filled with the scent of roses and the hum of bees.

Edward reached over and plucked the book from her hand. He set it down next to the remains of their luncheon; then he took a pink rose from the vase in the center of the picnic cloth and shifted closer to his wife.

"What are you doing?" Anna hissed, although she had a very good idea.

"Me?" Edward tried to look innocent as he trailed the rose over the tops of her exposed breasts. He didn't succeed nearly as well as his son.

"Edward!"

One petal fell down her cleavage. He knit his brows in mock alarm. "Oh, dear."

His long fingers delved between her breasts, searching for the petal but only pushing it farther down. He wasn't doing a very good job finding it, his fingertips kept brushing over Anna's nipples.

She batted at his hand halfheartedly. "Stop that. It tickles." She squeaked as he pinched a nipple between two fingers.

Edward frowned sternly. "Shh. You'll wake Samuel." Her bodice gave way. "You must be very, very quiet."

"But Mother Wren—"

"Is seeing how Fanny fares at her new post in the next county." His breath tickled her exposed breasts. "She shan't be home until supper."

He took a nipple into his mouth.

Anna's breath caught. "I think I'm breeding again."

Edward lifted his head, his black eyes glittering. "Would you mind another child so soon?"

"I'd adore one," she said, and then sighed happily.

Edward was taking the news of her second pregnancy much better than he had the first. From the moment Anna had told him of her first pregnancy, he'd been terribly grim. She'd done her best to comfort him at the time, but she had been resigned to the fact that he wouldn't truly recover until she was safely delivered of their child. And indeed, Edward had sat white-faced beside her bed the entire labor. Mrs. Stucker had taken one look at the expectant father's face and sent for brandy, which Edward had refused to touch. Five hours later, Samuel Ethan de Raaf, Viscount Herrod, was born. He was possibly the most beautiful baby in the history of the world, in his mother's opinion. Edward had drunk nearly a third of the bottle of brandy before climbing into the big bed with his wife and newborn son and wrapping his arms around both.

Now he flipped Anna's skirts up and settled between her bared thighs. "It'll be a daughter this time."

He was trailing kisses up her neck. Both of his hands covered her breasts, and his thumbs flicked her nipples.

Anna gasped. "Another boy would be nice, too, but if it is a girl, I know what I'll name her."

"What?" He was nibbling her ear, and Anna could feel his erection pressing against her.

He probably wasn't listening, but she answered him anyway. "Elizabeth Rose."

A masked avenger dressed in a harlequin's motley protects the innocents of St. Giles at night.

When a rescue mission leaves him wounded, the kind soul who comes to his rescue is the one woman he'd never have expected...

Thief of Shadows

Please turn this page
for a preview.

Chapter One

The body in the road was the absolute cap to the day. Isabel Beckinhall, Baroness Beckinhall sighed to herself. Her carriage had come to a standstill in the worst part of London—the dirty streets of St. Giles. And *why* was she in St. Giles as dark descended? Because she'd volunteered to represent the Ladies' Syndicate for the Benefit of the Home for Unfortunate Infants and Foundling Children at the final inspection of the new Home for Unfortunate Infants and Foundling Children, more fool she.

Never volunteer. Not even when pleasantly filled with warm scones and hot tea. Warm scones were obviously the work of the Devil or perhaps Lady Hero Reading, one of the two founding patronesses of the home. Lady Hero had refilled her teacup and looked at Isabel with wide gray eyes, asking prettily if Isabel would mind meeting with Mr. Winter Makepeace, the home's dour manager, to look over the new building. And Isabel had blithely agreed like some scone-filled mindless cow.

And the damned man hadn't even shown!

"Moo," Isabel muttered to herself just as the carriage door opened to admit her lady's maid, Pinkney.

"Ma'am?" Pinkney asked, her blue eyes wide and startled. Of course Pinkney's eyes were nearly always wide and startled. She was one of the most sought-after lady's maids in London, a paragon of the latest fashion, but Isabel had privately begun to wonder if her new maid wasn't a bit dim.

"Nothing," Isabel replied, waving aside her bovine utterance. "Did you find out why it's taking so long to move the dead man?"

"Oh, yes, my lady," Pinkney said. "It's because he's not dead." Her pretty dark blond brows drew together. "Well, not yet anyway. Harold the footman is having a time pulling him aside, and you wouldn't credit it, ma'am, but he's a comic actor."

It was Isabel's turn to blink. *"Harold?"*

"Oh, no, my lady!" Pinkney giggled until she caught Isabel's steady gaze. "Er . . ." The maid cleared her throat. "The not-yet-dead-man is. He's dressed as a harlequin, mask and all—"

Isabel was no longer listening. She'd opened the door and climbed from the carriage. Outside the gray day was growing grimmer still with the advent of nightfall. Fires flared to the west and she could hear the rumbling of the rioters from that direction. They were getting closer. Isabel shivered and hurried to where Harold and the other footman were bent over a figure on the ground. Pinkney was such a ninny she'd probably mistaken the costume or the man or the mask or—

But no.

Isabel drew in a sharp breath. She'd never seen the notorious Ghost of St. Giles in person, but she had no doubt that this must be he. The prone man wore black and red motley. His floppy, brimmed hat had fallen from his head and she could see that his brown hair was tied back simply. A short sword was sheathed at his side and a long sword lay by one of his broad hands. A black half mask with a ridiculously long nose covered the upper half of his face, leaving his square chin and wide mouth revealed. His lips were parted over straight white teeth, the upper lip a little bigger than the bottom, and sensuously curved in unconsciousness.

Isabel snapped her attention up to her coachman. "Is he alive?"

"He's still breathin' at least, my lady." Harold shook his head. "Don't know for how long, though."

A shout came from nearby and the sound of smashing glass.

"Put him in the carriage," Isabel said. She bent to pick up his hat.

Tom, the second footman, frowned. "But, my lady—"

"*Now.* And don't forget his sword."

Already she could see a mass of people rounding the corner down the street. The footmen glanced at each other then as one lifted the Ghost. Harold grunted under the weight, but he made no complaint.

A crowd gathered at the end of the street, and then someone gave a shout.

The rioters had spotted the carriage.

Isabel picked up her skirts and trotted after her footmen.

·

Harold gave a great heave and dumped the Ghost and his sword into the carriage. Isabel scrambled rather inelegantly inside. Pinkney was staring wide-eyed at the Ghost, who was in a heap in the corner of the carriage, but for the moment Isabel ignored him. She tossed the hat on top of the Ghost, lifted her seat, and withdrew two pistols from the hidden compartment underneath.

Pinkney squeaked in alarm.

Isabel turned and handed the pistols to the footmen at the carriage door. "Don't let anyone climb the carriage."

Harold's jaw tightened. "Yes, my lady."

He took the pistols, gave one to Tom, and mounted the carriage.

Isabel closed the carriage door and knocked on the roof. "Fast as you can, John!"

The carriage started forward with a lurch just as something hit the side.

"My lady!" Pinkney cried.

"Hush," Isabel said.

There was a lap robe on the maid's seat and Isabel pulled it over the Ghost. She sat back on her own seat, clutching the window as the carriage rocked around a corner. Something knocked against the carriage. A grimacing face appeared suddenly at the window, tongue smearing against the glass lewdly.

Pinkney screamed.

Isabel stared at the man, her heart racing, but her gaze steady as she met his eyes. They were bloodshot and filled with maddened rage. The carriage jolted and the man fell away.

One of the pistols fired.

"My lady," Pinkney whispered, her face white, "the dead man—"

"Not-quite-dead man," Isabel muttered, eyeing the robe. Hopefully anyone glancing inside would see a robe thrown carelessly in the corner, *not* the hidden Ghost of St. Giles. She braced herself as the carriage swung wildly around a corner.

"Not-quite-dead man," Pinkney obediently repeated. "Who is he?"

"The Ghost of St. Giles."

Pinkney's robin's egg blue eyes widened. "Who?"

Isabel stared at her lady's maid in exasperation. Really, the chit was something of an idiot. "The Ghost of St. Giles? The most notorious footpad in London? Goes about in a harlequin's costume, either ravishing and murdering or rescuing and defending, depending on whose stories you believe?"

If Pinkney's eyes got any bigger they might fall out of her head altogether.

"No?" Isabel waved a hand toward the window and the shouting and screaming outside and said sweetly, "The man that mob wants dead?"

Pinkney stared horrified at the robe. "But...why, my lady?"

The second pistol fired with a deafening *BOOM*! Pinkney jumped and looked wildly at the window.

Dear God, they were out of ammunition. Isabel prayed the footmen were safe—and that they could hold off the rioters without their guns. She was an aristocrat, but that meant little to a mob such as this. Just last year a viscount had been dragged from his carriage and robbed in St. Giles.

Isabel took a deep breath and felt under the robe until she found the hilt of the Ghost's sword. She drew it out and put the heavy thing across her lap. If nothing else she could hit someone over the head with it if need be. "They want him dead because this morning he cut Charming Mickey O'Connor down from the gallows."

Pinkney actually brightened at this. "Oh, Charming Mickey, the pirate! *Him* I've heard of. They say he's handsome as sin and dresses better than the king himself."

Of course her lady's maid had heard of a well-dressed pirate.

"Quite," Isabel flinched as something hit the window, cracking the glass. "They probably chased him all the way from Tyburn gallows, poor man."

"Oh." For a moment Pinkney bit her lip. Then she looked timidly at Isabel. "But, my lady, if the mob wants him and he's in our carriage . . . ah . . ."

Isabel drew on all her strength to smile firmly. Her hand tightened on the hilt of the sword across her lap. "That's why we're not going to let them know we have the Ghost, are we?"

Pinkney blinked several times as if working through this logic, and then she smiled. The child really was quite pretty. "Oh, yes, my lady."

The lady's maid sat back as if quite confident that they were all out of danger now that everything had been explained.

Isabel twitched aside the curtains to peer through the cracked glass. She wasn't nearly as sanguine. Many of the streets in St. Giles were narrow and twisting—the reason that her carriage had been traveling so slowly earlier. A mob could move much faster afoot than they. But the mob was beginning to fall away. John Coachman had found a straight stretch of road and was urging the horses into a trot.

Isabel let fall the curtain with a heartfelt sigh of relief. *Thank God.*

Half an hour later the carriage was pulling up before her neat town house.

"Bring him inside," she ordered Harold when he pulled open the doors.

He nodded wearily. "Yes, my lady."

"And Harold?" Isabel descended the carriage still clutching the sword.

"My lady?"

"Well done. To both you and Tom." Isabel nodded to Tom.

A shy grin split Harold's broad face. "Thank you, my lady."

Isabel permitted herself a small smile before she swept into her town house. Edmund, her dear late husband, had bought Fairmont House for her shortly before he'd died, and had gifted it to her on her twenty-eighth birthday. He'd known that the title and estates would go to a distant cousin and had wanted her properly settled with her own property free of the entail. Isabel had immediately redecorated on moving in four years ago. Now the entry hall was all white marble, with soaring gilded Corinthian columns along the edges emphasizing the height of the room.

"Thank you, Butterman," Isabel said as she tucked the sword under her arm and pulled off her gloves and hat, handing them to the butler. "I need a bedroom readied immediately."

Butterman, like all her servants, was impeccably trained. He didn't even blink an eye at the abrupt order—or the sword she carelessly held. "Yes, my lady. Will the blue room do?"

"Quite."

Butterman snapped his fingers and a maid went hurrying up the stairs.

Isabel turned and watched as Harry and Tom came in with the Ghost between them.

Butterman raised his eyebrow a fraction of an inch at the sight of the unconscious man, but merely said, "The blue room, Harold, if you please."

"Yes, sir," Harold panted.

"If you don't mind, my lady," Butterman murmured, "I believe Mrs. Butterman may be of assistance."

"Yes, thank you. Please send Mrs. Butterman up as quickly as possible." Isabel followed the footmen up the stairs.

The maids were still turning back the sheets on the bed in the blue room, when the footmen arrived with their burden, but at least the fire on the grate was lit.

Harold hesitated, probably because the Ghost was quite dirty and bloody, but Isabel gestured to the bed. The Ghost groaned as the footmen laid him on the spotless counterpane.

Isabel propped his sword in a corner of the room and hurried to his side. His eyes were closed. His hat had been left in the carriage, but he still wore his mask, though it was askew on his face. Carefully she lifted the thing over his head and was surprised to find underneath a thin black silk scarf covering the upper part of his face from the bridge of his strong nose to his forehead. Two eyeholes had been cut into the material to make a second, thinner mask. She examined the harlequin's mask in her hand. It was leather and stained black. High arching eyebrows and the curving grotesque nose gave the mask a satyrlike leer.

She set it on a table by the bed and looked back at the Ghost. He lay limp and heavy on the bed. Blood stained his motley leggings above his black jackboots. She bit her lip. Some of the blood looked quite fresh.

"Butterman said 'twas a man injured," Mrs. Butterman said as she bustled in the room. She went to the bed and stared at the Ghost a moment, hands on hips, before nodding decisively. "Well, nothing for it. We'll need to undress him, my lady, and find out where the blood's coming from."

"Oh, of course," Isabel said. She reached for the buttons of the Ghost's fall as Mrs. Butterman began on the doublet.

Behind her, Isabel heard a gasp. "Oh, my lady!"

"What is it, Pinkney?" Isabel frowned as she worked at a stubborn button. Blood had dried on the material, making it stiff.

"'Tisn't proper for you to be doing such work." Pinkney sounded as scandalized as if Isabel had proposed walking naked in Westminster Cathedral. "He's a *man*."

"I assure you I have seen a nude man before," Isabel said mildly as she peeled back the man's leggings. Underneath, his smallclothes were soaked in blood. Good God. Could a man lose so much and survive? She began working at the ties to his smallclothes.

"He has bruising on his shoulder and ribs and a few scrapes, but nothing to cause this much blood," Mrs. Butterman reported as she spread the doublet wide and raised the ghost's shirt to his armpits.

Isabel glanced up and for a moment froze. His chest was delineated with lean muscles, his nipples brown against his pale skin, black, curling hair spreading between. His belly was hard and ridged, his navel entirely obscured by that same black curling hair. Isabel blinked. She had seen a man—men, actually—naked, true, but Edmund had been in his sixth decade when he died and had certainly never looked like this. And the few, discreet lovers that she'd taken since Edmund's death had been aristocrats—men of leisure. They'd hardly had more muscles than she. Her eye caught on the line of hair trailing down from his navel. It disappeared into his smallclothes.

Where her hands were.

Isabel swallowed and untied the garment, a little surprised by the tremble of her fingers, and drew them down his legs. His genitals were revealed, his cock thick and long, even at rest, his bollocks heavy.

"Well," Mrs. Butterman said, "he certainly looks healthy enough *there*."

"Oh, my, yes," Pinkney breathed.

Isabel looked around irritably. She'd not realized the maid had come close enough to see the Ghost. Isabel drew a corner of the counterpane over the Ghost's loins, feeling protective of the unconscious man.

"Help me take off his boots so we can bare his legs completely," Isabel told Mrs. Butterman. "If we can't find the wound there, we'll have to turn him over."

But as they stripped his breeches further down his legs a long gash was revealed on the man's muscled right thigh. Fresh blood oozed and trickled over his leg as the sodden material was pulled away.

"There 'tis," Mrs. Butterman said. "We could send for the doctor, my lady, but I've a fair hand with the needle and thread."

Isabel nodded. She glanced again at the wound, relieved

it was not nearly as bad as she'd feared. "Fetch what you'll need, please, Mrs. Butterman, and take Pinkney with you to help. I have the feeling he won't be much pleased by a doctor."

Mrs. Butterman hurried out with Pinkney.

Isabel waited, alone in the room save for the Ghost of St. Giles. He was unconscious, but still he was a commanding presence, his big body sprawled upon the dainty bed. Isabel looked at him. He was a man in the prime of his life, strong and athletic, nearly bare to her gaze.

All except his face.

Her hand moved almost without thought. She stretched toward the black silk mask still covering the upper part of his face. Was he handsome? Ugly? Merely ordinary looking?

Her hand began to descend toward the mask.

His flashed up and caught her wrist.

His eyes opened, assessing and quite clearly brown. "Don't."

Even the most refined lady
craves an untamed man
to release her passion . . .

Please turn this page
for an excerpt from

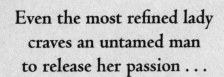

*To Taste
Temptation*

Available now.

Chapter One

❧

Now Iron Heart got his name from a very strange
thing. Although his limbs and face, and indeed all
the rest of his body, were exactly like every other
man created by God, his heart was not. It was
made from iron, and it beat on the surface of his
chest, strong, brave, and steadfast....
—from *Iron Heart*

LONDON, ENGLAND
SEPTEMBER 1764

"They say he ran away." Mrs. Conrad leaned close to
impart this bit of gossip.

Lady Emeline Gordon took a sip of tea and glanced
over the rim of the cup at the gentleman in question. He
was as out of place as a jaguar in a room full of tabby cats:
raw, vital, and not quite civilized. Definitely not a man she
would associate with cowardice. Emeline wondered what
his name was as she thanked the Lord for his appearance.

Mrs. Conrad's afternoon salon had been paralyzingly dull until *he* had sauntered in.

"He ran away from the massacre of the 28th Regiment in the colonies," Mrs. Conrad continued breathlessly, "back in fifty-eight. Shameful, isn't it?"

Emeline turned and arched an eyebrow at her hostess. She held Mrs. Conrad's gaze and saw the exact moment when the silly woman remembered. Mrs. Conrad's already pink complexion deepened to a shade of beet that really didn't become her at all.

"That is...I...I—" her hostess stammered.

This was what one got when one accepted an invitation from a lady who aspired to but didn't quite sail in the highest circles of society. It was Emeline's own fault, really. She sighed and took pity. "He's in the army, then?"

Mrs. Conrad grasped the bait gratefully. "Oh, no. Not anymore. At least I don't *believe* so."

"Ah," Emeline said, and tried to think of another subject.

The room was large and expensively decorated, with a painting on the ceiling overhead depicting Hades pursuing Persephone. The goddess looked particularly vacuous, smiling down sweetly on the assembly below. She hadn't a chance against the god of the underworld, even if he did have bright pink cheeks in this portrayal.

Emeline's current protégé, Jane Greenglove, sat on a settee nearby, conversing with young Lord Simmons, a very nice choice. Emeline nodded approvingly. Lord Simmons had an income of over eight thousand pounds a year and a lovely house near Oxford. That alliance would be very suitable, and since Jane's older sister, Eliza, had already accepted the hand of Mr. Hampton, things were falling into place quite neatly. They always did, of course, when Emeline consented to guide a young lady into society, but it was pleasing to have one's expectations fulfilled nevertheless.

Or it should be. Emeline twisted a lace ribbon at her waist before she caught herself and smoothed it out again. Actually, she was feeling a bit out of sorts, which was ridiculous. Her world was perfect. Absolutely perfect.

Emeline glanced casually at the stranger only to find his dark gaze fixed on her. His eyes crinkled ever so slightly at the corners as if he was amused by something—and that something might be her. Hastily she looked away again. Awful man. He was obviously aware that every lady in the room had noticed him.

Beside her, Mrs. Conrad had started prattling, evidently in an attempt to cover her gaffe. "He owns an importing business in the Colonies. I believe he's in London on business; that's what Mr. Conrad says, anyway. And he's as rich as Croesus, although you'd never guess it from his attire."

It was impossible not to glance at him again after this information. From midthigh up, his clothing was plain indeed—black coat and brown-and-black-patterned waistcoat. All in all, a conservative wardrobe until one came to his legs. The man was wearing some type of native leggings. They were made from an odd tan leather, quite dull, and they were gartered just below the knees with red, white, and black striped sashes. The leggings split in the front over the shoes with brightly embroidered flaps that fell to either side of his feet. And his shoes were the strangest of all, for they had no heels. He seemed to be wearing a type of slipper made of the same soft, dull leather, with beading or embroidery work running from ankle to toe. Yet even heelless, the stranger was quite tall. He had brown hair, and as far as she could tell from half-way across the room, his eyes were dark. Certainly not blue or green. They were heavy-lidded and intelligent. She suppressed a shiver. Intelligent men were so hard to manage.

His arms were crossed, one shoulder propped against the wall, and his gaze was interested. As if they were the exotic ones, not he. His nose was long, with a bump in the middle; his complexion dark, as if he'd lately come from some exotic shore. The bones of his face were raw and prominent: cheeks, nose, and chin jutting in an aggressively masculine way that was nevertheless perversely attractive. His mouth, in contrast, was wide and almost soft, with a sensuous inverted dent in the lower lip. It was the mouth of a man who liked to savor. To linger and taste. A dangerous mouth.

Emeline looked away again. "Who is he?"

Mrs. Conrad stared. "Don't you know?"

"No."

Her hostess was delighted. "Why, my dear, that's Mr. Samuel Hartley! Everyone has been talking about him, though he has only been in London a sennight or so. He's not quite acceptable, because of the . . ." Mrs. Conrad met Emeline's eyes and hastily cut short what she'd been about to say. "*Anyway.* Even with all his wealth, not everyone is happy to meet him."

Emeline stilled as the back of her neck prickled.

Mrs. Conrad continued, oblivious. "I really shouldn't have invited him, but I couldn't help myself. That form, my dear. Simply delicious! Why, if I hadn't asked him, I would never have—" Her flurry of words ended on a startled squeak, for a man had cleared his throat directly behind them.

Emeline hadn't been watching, so she hadn't seen him move, but she knew instinctively who stood so close to them. Slowly she turned her head.

Mocking coffee-brown eyes met her own. "Mrs. Conrad, I'd be grateful if you'd introduce us." His voice had a flat American accent.

Their hostess sucked in her breath at this blunt order, but curiosity won out over indignation. "Lady Emeline, may I introduce Mr. Samuel Hartley. Mr. Hartley, Lady Emeline Gordon."

Emeline sank into a curtsy, only to be presented with a large, tanned hand on rising. She stared for a moment, nonplussed. Surely the man wasn't that unsophisticated? Mrs. Conrad's breathy giggle decided the matter. Gingerly, Emeline touched just her fingertips to his.

To no avail. He embraced her hand with both of his, enveloping her fingers in hard warmth. His nostrils flared just the tiniest bit as she was forced to step forward into the handshake. Was he *scenting* her?

"How do you do?" he asked.

"Well," Emeline retorted. She tried to free her hand but could not, even though Mr. Hartley didn't seem to be gripping her tightly. "Might I have my appendage returned to me now?"

That mouth twitched again. Did he laugh at everyone or just her? "Of course, my lady."

Emeline opened her mouth to make an excuse—any excuse—to leave the dreadful man, but he was too quick for her.

"May I escort you into the garden?"

It really wasn't a question, since he'd already held out his arm, obviously expecting her consent. And what was worse, she gave it. Silently, Emeline laid her fingertips on his coat sleeve. He nodded to Mrs. Conrad and drew Emeline outside in only a matter of minutes, working very neatly for such a gauche man. Emeline squinted up at his profile suspiciously.

He turned his head and caught her look. His own eyes wrinkled at the corners, laughing down at her, although his mouth remained perfectly straight. "We're neighbors, you know."

"What do you mean?"

"I've rented the house next to yours."

Emeline found herself blinking up at him, caught off guard once again—a disagreeable sensation as rare as it was unwanted. She knew the occupants of the town house to the right of hers, but the left had been let out recently. For an entire day the week before, men had been tramping in and out of the open doors, sweating, shouting, and cursing. And they'd carried...

Her eyebrows snapped together. "The pea-green settee."

His mouth curved at one corner. "What?"

"You're the owner of that atrocious pea-green settee, aren't you?"

He bowed. "I confess it."

"With no trace of shame, either, I see." Emeline pursed her lips in disapproval. "Are there really gilt owls carved on the legs?"

"I hadn't noticed."

"*I* had."

"Then I'll not argue the point."

"Humph." She faced forward again.

"I have a favor to ask of you, ma'am." His voice rumbled somewhere above her head.

He'd led her down one of the packed gravel paths of the Conrads' town house garden. It was unimaginatively planted with roses and small, clipped hedges. Sadly, most of the roses had already bloomed, so the whole looked rather plain and forlorn.

"I'd like to hire you."

"*Hire* me?" Emeline inhaled sharply and stopped, forcing him to halt as well and face her. Did this odd man think she was a courtesan of some sort? The insult was outrageous, and in her confusion she found her gaze wandering over his frame, crossing wide shoulders, a pleasingly flat waist, and then dropping to an inappropriate portion of Mr. Hartley's anatomy, which, now that she noticed it, was rather nicely outlined by the black wool breeches he wore under his leggings. She inhaled again, nearly choking, and hastily raised her eyes. But the man either hadn't observed her indiscretion or was much more polite than his attire and manner would lead one to believe.

He continued. "I need a mentor for my sister, Rebecca. Someone to show her the parties and balls."

Emeline cocked her head as she realized that he wanted a chaperone. Well, why hadn't the silly man said so in the first place and saved her all this embarrassment? "I'm afraid that won't be possible."

"Why not?" The words were soft, but there was an edge of command behind them.

Emeline stiffened. "I take only young ladies from the highest ranks of society. I don't believe your sister can meet my standards. I'm sorry."

He watched her for a moment and then looked away.

Although his gaze was on a bench at the end of the path, Emeline doubted very much that he saw it. "Perhaps, then, I can plead another reason for you to take us on."

She stilled. "What is that?"

His eyes looked back at her, and now there was no trace of amusement in them. "I knew Reynaud."

The beating of Emeline's heart was very loud in her ears. Because, of course, Reynaud was her brother. Her brother who had been killed in the massacre of the 28th.

VISIT US ONLINE AT

WWW.HACHETTEBOOKGROUP.COM

FEATURES:

**OPENBOOK BROWSE AND
SEARCH EXCERPTS**
•
AUDIOBOOK EXCERPTS AND PODCASTS
•
AUTHOR ARTICLES AND INTERVIEWS
•
**BESTSELLER AND PUBLISHING
GROUP NEWS**
•
SIGN UP FOR E-NEWSLETTERS
•
**AUTHOR APPEARANCES AND TOUR
INFORMATION**
•
SOCIAL MEDIA FEEDS AND WIDGETS
•
DOWNLOAD FREE APPS

Bookmark Hachette Book Group
@ www.HachetteBookGroup.com